$\mathcal{A}$
WOMAN'S
WAR

A WOMAN'S WAR

S. Block

ZAFFRE

First published in Great Britain in 2019 by
ZAFFRE
80–81 Wimpole St, London W1G 9RE

A CIP catalogue record for this book is
available from the British Library.

ISBN: 978-1-78576-429-5

Also available as an ebook

3 5 7 9 10 8 6 4 2

Typeset by IDSUK (Data Connection) Ltd
Printed and bound in Great Britain by Clays Ltd, Elcograf S.p.A.

Zaffre is an imprint of Bonnier Books UK
www.bonnierbooks.co.uk

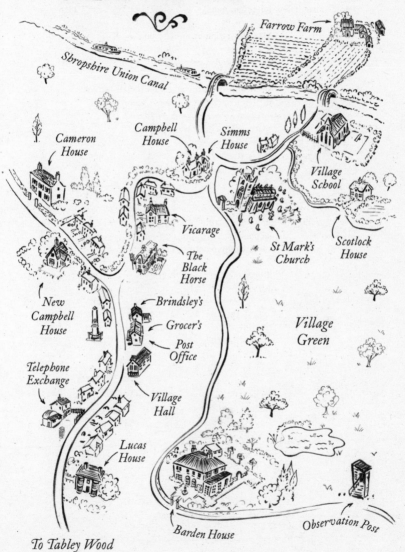

GREAT PAXFORD

Farrow Farm

Shropshire Union Canal

Cameron House

Campbell House

Simms House

Village School

Scotlock House

Vicarage

St Mark's Church

The Black Horse

New Campbell House

Brindsley's

Grocer's

Post Office

Village Green

Telephone Exchange

Village Hall

Lucas House

Barden House

Observation Post

To Tabley Wood

For Tara, with great thanks and huge respect.

Chapter 1

'LADIES, LADIES . . .' BARKED Frances Barden, silencing the massed ranks of Great Paxford's WI. It was the evening of 7 November 1940, two days after the deaths of the village GP, Will Campbell, from cancer, and of a Luftwaffe pilot who had escaped from his crashed aircraft only to be shot on local farmland. The hall was abuzz with a curious mix of sorrow for the former and intense, lurid speculation over the latter.

'Settle down, please. Thank you, thank *you*.'

The women placed their hands in their laps, fell silent, and looked at their Chair standing before them, with Pat Simms and Sarah Collingborne sitting at the small 'committee' table behind her. The rain overhead thrummed hard against the hall's roof, giving the occasion a slight undertone of menace. Frances took a deep breath, counted to five in her head to ensure she had the members' absolute attention, and began the address she had been constructing since breakfast.

'Which of us would have imagined fourteen months ago that we would find ourselves acclimatised to being at war for the second time in little over twenty years? And yet month after month we have accommodated the war within our daily lives. Rationing. Air raids. The absence of our men of fighting age. Living in a state of war has become the everyday once more. For our own sanity, we have necessarily become complacent within that state, accepting it as our new norm, behaving as if we had never lived any other way. But then something happens to puncture the complacency, remind us anew that we live in dark and dangerous times.

'I am talking, of course, of the German pilot at large in our community for three days. A deadly stranger in our midst who sent us to our locks and bolts, in case he found his way to our doorsteps. Now we know he has been found and killed we can breathe a sigh of relief, and feel immense gratitude towards the authorities for their great efforts in keeping us safe. But . . . ladies . . . the episode should serve as a reminder to every woman here that there is nothing normal about life during wartime. That everything is *ab*normal. And we should work for it to be over as soon as humanly possible.'

Neither Frances nor the women she faced had the slightest idea that the German pilot had in fact been slain by one of their own members, and would have been flabbergasted to learn that Steph Farrow had opened fire on her farm, in self-defence. The desire to believe they were looked after by benign forces of authority fed the natural assumption by everyone in Great Paxford that the pilot had been ruthlessly hunted down by the army.

'Yes, the war takes place overhead nightly,' Frances continued, 'but an episode of this nature reminds us that at any moment it can fall from the sky and land at our feet. As a consequence, we must never let our guard down. *Vigilance*, ladies, at all times, both out and about, and at home. Remind your children *daily* to stay alert and come to you with *anything* that strikes them as untoward.'

The rank and file nodded.

'We are subject to forces beyond our control. Nevertheless, we must do what is within *our* power to protect ourselves and those we love.'

On occasions such as this the membership acted as one. As Frances surveyed the gathering, she noticed many had come wearing black as a sign of respect towards Erica and her daughter, Laura, despite the fact neither were present. While Frances hadn't gone that far herself, she had unconsciously chosen to wear a more muted suit than usual. It was the same dark brown tweed she had worn upon her return to the WI after a period of mourning for her deceased husband, Peter.

On her way to the meeting, Frances had toyed with the idea of jettisoning her prepared opening remarks for a brief speech about Erica and Laura's loss. She mentioned it to her sister, Sarah. Wary of Frances's weakness for getting carried away by her own powers of oratory, Sarah had persuaded her older sister to say little about the Campbells, and allow the members to sit with their own feelings towards the family, and the loss of their beloved GP.

'Everyone knows what's happened,' Sarah had said, drawing upon the wisdom she'd developed as a vicar's wife. Her husband Adam was being held in a German prison camp, and she missed him every hour of every day, though there was nothing she could do but wait for him. 'They know what they feel about Will's death. They don't need you to express your feelings on their behalf.'

'Not even a brief word?' Frances asked, mildly disappointed to see a moment of 'profound leadership' slip from her grasp.

'Adam always placed great value on allowing people to spend time with their own thoughts at moments like this. Guidance can so often come across as needless imposition.'

Reluctantly heeding Sarah's advice, Frances looked at the women seated in solemn rows before her, and said nothing about the Campbells beyond a single sentence.

'I should now like to dedicate our rendition of "Jerusalem" to our bereaved, beloved members Erica, Laura and Kate, at this time of immense loss.'

Many women took out handkerchiefs to gently soak up wet eyes. Frances held herself in check and turned to Alison Scotlock at the piano, and nodded for her to begin.

Will Campbell had left an indelible impression on the lives of all present. The women sang their hearts out for their irreplaceable doctor. By the final line, not a single cheek was dry, the Chair's included.

Frances allowed the final, passionate refrain to drift up into the rafters and seep into the night, then nodded for everyone to sit.

'Thank you, ladies,' she said appreciatively. 'Were Erica and Laura here, they would have been extraordinarily moved. As they no doubt will be by your support at Will's funeral next week at St Mark's.'

Sarah shot an alarmed glance at Frances, suspecting she might succumb to the temptation to soliloquise about Will's death. However, her own recent bereavement enabled Frances to maintain discipline and move directly on to the Chair's report. She began by congratulating the members on their astonishing efforts with the trekker initiative.

'My dear colleagues, I struggle to see how it could have gone better, I really do. We have fed and sheltered hundreds and hundreds of people from nearby cities. There isn't a woman present who hasn't thrown herself into the operation here in the hall or up at St Mark's. We have been so successful that we have motivated three sister branches in the region to follow our lead and set up their own soup stations and shelters.'

This news brought forth a delighted round of applause. Frances raised her hands for silence once again.

'However,' she continued, 'our work only has value if we continue to offer our own programme for as long as it is needed by those who come.'

The women nodded in agreement. Except one.

'What if that's months or even years away?' called Mrs Talbot, standing in her place at the rear of the hall to ensure her point was heard by everyone.

'Then we shall commit to giving sustenance and shelter for months or years – or until our ability to do so is thoroughly exhausted. Like the men, we will give all we can to get this country through this war.'

A second round of applause. Mrs Talbot resumed her seat, glowering.

Of the women present, only Pat failed to focus on Frances's pep talk about how they would continue to tend to trekker families from nearby cities. Pat's thoughts were firmly on the previous night, when Marek had slipped into St Mark's unannounced, and had made himself known to her. In the months since his regiment had been called up, Pat had wondered and worried about him. He could have been anywhere, training for war, or already active on the continent. All she could do was wait for him to get into contact, while doubting he would with each day that passed. During those long weeks, Pat's life consisted of being simultaneously terrified for her lover and scared of her husband, Bob, whose next outburst of temper she would almost certainly trigger while being unable to predict it.

Marek's broad smile in the low light of St Mark's had been unmistakable, even beneath a flat cap pulled low over his blue eyes. When Pat's shift finished, she had hurried out into the dark churchyard and carefully picked her way behind St Mark's, where she saw a tiny orange glow from Marek's cigarette. She had run to him and they had silently embraced. Marek had kissed her and held her so tightly she'd felt momentarily, beautifully winded. Feeling Marek's body against her once again, tasting the sweet tobacco on his lips, Pat's heart had swelled in her chest. She knew they had little time together. Marek couldn't be seen by anyone from the village who might recognise him in case the sighting somehow worm its way to Bob via Great Paxford's grapevine. Life with Bob had become even more unbearable since he had found out about Pat's affair, as he sought ways to punish her for it. But with Marek's mobilisation from the region, Bob believed their relationship was categorically over. Pat was determined to maintain him in that belief. Marek had asked Pat to meet him for longer the following night, somewhere they wouldn't be seen. She had suggested they meet after the WI meeting, away from the village, by the canal. No one would see them in the blackout, under the bridge.

Pat felt as sad about Will's death as any woman in the hall, if not more so, as they had been neighbours for many years. But the prospect of seeing Marek by the canal in just a few minutes momentarily pushed her grief to one side, filling Pat with rising excitement she was unsure she could contain. Her eyes were glued to the clock above the piano. The meeting seemed to be crawling at a snail's pace from one interminable item on the agenda to the next.

When it was finally over, Pat leaned across to her temporary landlady, Joyce, and asked the older woman if she would mind walking back to the house alone as she wanted to go for a short detour to reflect on her memories of Will.

'The news has hit me for six. Will was so much more than our doctor. He was a dear friend.' She felt a little guilt using Will's death as her excuse, but in the heat of the moment it seemed the reason least open to further enquiry.

Another time Pat might well have taken herself off for fifteen or twenty minutes to reflect on what the loss of Will really meant to her. But not tonight. Tonight, Pat needed a reason to make her way back alone, via the canal. Fortune was on Pat's side. The previous chair of the WI revealed that she planned to stay behind and catch up with friends. She had no issue with Pat leaving without her.

'Haven't I made my way home by myself for many years?' Joyce said, smiling.

A steady stream of women flowed from the hall and melted into the wet night, hurrying home before they got soaked a second time. With hats pulled down and umbrellas put up it was impossible to tell one from another. Each had her eyes on the road ahead, intent on getting indoors and dry as quickly as possible.

As a consequence, no one noticed Pat's small figure hugging the shadows before turning left towards the canal instead of right towards Joyce's house, where she and Bob had been lodging since a stricken Spitfire had crashed into their home. Bob sat in the front parlour checking his watch, drawing slowly on a Woodbine, wondering where on earth she was.

Chapter 2

B<small>Y THE TIME</small> Pat reached the stone steps leading down to the canal the rain had become so intense she was almost swept down to the towpath, and her clothes were as wet on her as if she and they had just been taken out of the wash-tub. Under any other circumstances this would have left her profoundly self-conscious about her appearance. Tonight, she only cared about snatching what time she could with the man she loved to a dangerous extent. Throughout the WI meeting Pat had tried to brace herself against the possibility that Marek might not make it to their *rendezvous* for reasons he'd be unable to convey. She'd forced herself into a state of resignation about the possibility that their snatched moment around the back of St Mark's the previous night was all she would have of him for the foreseeable future. She attempted to console herself that if that were the case, it would be enough. It wouldn't be.

Pat almost turned her ankle as she hurried along the towpath but managed to grab the handrail before going over. She cautioned herself against undue haste and hurried for a further two hundred yards until she turned a corner and saw the bridge up ahead. Beneath the bridge, in its gulping black shadow, Pat saw a pinprick orange glow from a cigarette. To Pat's eyes it may as well have been a bright flare shooting up a hundred feet into the air.

He's here!

Despite the conditions, Pat broke into a run. The sound of her footsteps drew Marek out from under the bridge. Pat rushed into his arms with such force that he had to take a step back to absorb her momentum.

'I convinced myself you'd be unable to come!' she said, before kissing him.

'If I say I will come, Patricia, I will come.' He smiled.

When Bob called Pat by her full name it was an admonition, a presage to disapproval for something she had done or, more usually, had failed to do. With Marek, it was the opposite. He savoured each syllable of her name. One syllable just wasn't enough to encompass everything he felt about her.

Out of caution they stepped back under the shelter of the bridge, where they couldn't be seen even by someone who knew where to look, where Marek took off his thick trench coat and wrapped it round Pat's soaked shoulders to stop her catching a chill.

'We don't have long,' she said. 'Bob knows I'm at the WI – he'll wonder where I am if don't get home within a reasonable time.'

Marek nodded. 'We are not meeting for a few snatched moments, but to plan for later, when we will always be together.'

Pat kissed him.

'I live for that day,' she said. 'And you *must* stay alive for it. I absolutely insist.'

Though it was almost pitch black beneath the bridge, Pat could make out Marek's teeth as he laughed.

'Always wanting me to stay alive!' he laughed. 'If my CO could hear you, Patricia, he would banish you from my life for the duration of the war.'

'Then I hate your CO,' she said, and kissed him again.

'You should not. He is a good man. He gives us the very best training, which gives me the very best chance of survival.'

'Then I love your CO,' Pat said, kissing Marek once more. She needed very little excuse.

They stood beneath the bridge, and watched the rain fall in thick sheets into the canal, sending its surface dancing as each drop exploded on impact. Each felt the warmth of the other through their wet clothes.

'This is the perfect weather in which to see you,' Marek said.

'How?! It's filthy!'

'Everyone has their eyes to the floor, so I can move freely. Also, if you come to meet me in this, I *know* you love me.'

'Were you ever in any doubt?'

Marek shook his head.

'Never. I am soon to be deployed, Patricia, and I could not leave without giving you information of who to contact if you do not hear from me within one year.'

Marek took his hand from his pocket and offered Pat a folded piece of paper.

'That won't be necessary,' Pat said, 'because nothing is going to happen to you.'

'Let us be *realistic*, Patricia,' he pleaded, pressing the paper into her hand. 'It is war to the death. So. In one year, this is who to contact to find out what has happened to me. Commit these details to memory and destroy the paper.'

'Marek—'

'No. This is important. I do not want you to live your life in hope only. A living death is the worst of all things. Better to know the truth and continue with a broken heart. In time, it can mend. Take it.'

Pat reluctantly accepted the paper and held it in her hand.

'You must memorise and destroy *now*.'

Pat looked at Marek. Even in the almost-dark his eyes blazed with conviction. She took out the paper, read the address, and silently committed it to memory.

'I have it,' she said.

'You are certain?'

'I will forget many things, but I'll never forget this.'

Marek took the paper from her hand and held it up. He then lightly touched its corner with the end of his cigarette until a thin wisp of smoke emerged from it, and then a small, uncertain flame. The paper caught and Marek let it fall into the canal, burning itself into oblivion on the journey towards the water.

'Do you ever think what life will be like when this is over?' Pat asked. 'I mean . . . for us.'

'Always,' he replied. 'You shall leave Bob and we shall live in peace beside the sea. We shall take long walks along the shore. Sit in a garden in the evening, and read and talk—'

'And travel?' Pat asked, hopefully.

'When this war is over . . .' he told her, his face just a few inches from hers, 'I will spend all the seconds of my life with you. I knew this the moment we met, when I looked down at you on the ground.'

Pat's eyes had become accustomed to the dark, and she was able to pick out the features of his face she had imprinted on her mind during his absence.

'I felt the same,' she said.

'This is why we must trust one another to endure periods of silence,' Marek said. 'I am going to be doing things I cannot tell you about. Activity for the war. I will be thinking about you. You must believe it.'

'I do.'

'You must endure with Bob. Carve out a life here until I return. There is nowhere else as safe that I could put you. Surviving Bob is *your* war, Patricia.'

Pat nodded and they kissed. She knew it was time for Marek to leave.

'I will write when I return,' he said. 'Until then, do not worry.' He smiled. 'Save your tears for Nazis who cross my path.'

Pat didn't want to let him go. Nor did she want his last memory of her to be of her losing control and breaking down.

Be strong – if only until he's gone.

They kissed once more and stood holding one another for five minutes in complete silence, breathing in time, kissing intermittently. Marek finally kissed Pat for the last time, and said, 'I love you so, so much, Patricia.' He slicked back his hair, put his cap on low over his eyes, pulled his collar up around his face, looked at her for a few moments, then hurried away. Within seconds he was enveloped by the night and it was as if he was never there. For a moment Pat stood quite still, as if she had just seen a ghost.

From the very first moment they had literally bumped into one another outside the Black Horse six months earlier, Marek had demonstrated an ability to reassure Pat that everything in her life would eventually be all right. Calmness and strength radiated from him. Grace and intelligence, too. She didn't know how he did it, but his presence was entirely consoling. Standing beneath the bridge she felt more at peace than she had for weeks.

Only once Marek's footsteps had dwindled into silence did Pat feel tears prick her eyes. She let them slowly roll down her cheeks as she set out briskly for Joyce's house, allowing the rain to mingle with them as soon as they emerged. Pat could walk past anyone in the village, even Bob, and they wouldn't know she was crying her heart out. As she walked, she had only one thought, for Marek and herself.

Be strong. Fight your war. Survive. Survive.

Chapter 3

SEATED ON A hill looking down at the small village of Great Paxford, the church of St Mark's witnessed its largest attendance for a funeral for many years. In recent times, other funeral services had been respectably attended. But none had drawn the entire population of the village, in addition to many from the surrounding area. If there were empty spaces among the pews for the funeral of Will Campbell it was because large numbers of men had gone to war. Even then, on hearing the news of his death, many of those had written to Erica from barracks about how much they thought of Will. He was deeply loved and admired.

All present looked keenly at his wife Erica, now a widow at just forty-three. Her face seemed ghostly pale atop her black dress, and her small, bloodless hands gripped the gilded sides of the lectern so tightly that her daughters sat ready to dash from the front row and catch her if she collapsed. Having already eulogised her husband for several minutes, Erica found herself momentarily overwhelmed, and ground to a halt. She felt every eye upon her and closed her own to gather her thoughts. Finally, she opened her eyes, cleared her throat, and continued.

'Will always knew his limitations.' Her voice was weak from emotional exhaustion, yet strong with conviction. A voice refusing to be silenced by grief. 'Whether imposed by limitations of current medical practice, or his own knowledge and experience, Will never promised his patients more than he could deliver. He always did his utmost to offer *hope* that health would improve, but never fell into easy promises or guarantees. For Will, healthcare was a partnership between patient and doctor – he would do his very best for his patients but never left them in doubt that they had to follow his advice and not fall back on the old remedies and tonics that weren't founded on scientific principle. At the beginning of our life in Great Paxford, this made him uncompromising to some. But in time everyone came to respect Will for his determination and care. And to trust him with their lives.'

Erica looked at the familiar, strained, mournful faces seated before her, and struggled to maintain her composure. She could scarcely bring herself to look at Will's simple wooden coffin before her. She glanced down at the notes she had made to keep herself focused.

'Everyone here was a patient of Will's. But you were also his friends. That's how he thought of you – patients first, always. But also, his dear friends. If that hadn't been the case, he – we – would never have settled so completely into this village. This was where he – and we – felt at home.

For that Will was – we both are – enormously grateful to you all.'

Erica looked at her daughters, Kate and Laura, sitting in the front row. They were willing her to maintain her composure and get through what they knew would be a terrible, once-in-a-lifetime ordeal. They had every confidence she could do it. Tears drenched Laura's face. Yet having already buried a husband at only nineteen years of age, Kate had experience of managing raw emotion in public, and held back her own tears to spill later, in private.

Laura pressed a handkerchief to her eyes. She had become gripped by a terror that she might forget what her father looked like, that all her memories of him would fade and all she would be left with were stilted photographs that failed to capture Will's warmth and spirit and made him look dead, but with his eyes open. Burying her face in the handkerchief, Laura brought forth an image of her father, and began the process of burning it into her mind forever.

The image she conjured up was of Will during his last weeks, on one of their 'walks' around the village where Laura pushed him up and down the lanes so he could enjoy the glowing autumnal sunlight of his last days. His face was terribly thin. He wore a thick red woollen cap to keep his head warm, and a large woollen picnic blanket was draped over his depleted arms, body, and legs. Laura told him he looked like a 'Guy' she was wheeling round the streets before bonfire night. By then, the effort of speaking was proving exhausting for her father. His thin croak usually trailed off before he reached the end of any sentence he was trying to convey.

But on this occasion, he appeared determined to express himself and be understood by his daughter. Small, puffy bursts of breath threw out syllables that Laura had to catch and thread together like beads on a string.

'You . . .' he said, and then looked at her as if he expected her to understand the rest of the sentence without him having to speak. When Laura looked back at him, puzzled, Will tried to continue. He stared at her and forced his jaw open to say something else. 'Good . . .' he finally said.

'Me good?' Laura asked.

Will nodded.

'Me good?'

Will stared at her. Laura could see his cheek muscles flexing beneath his skin, trying to open his jaw for another attempt at speech.

'You good . . . doc . . .' he said. Laura's confused expression forced Will to make one final effort. He gripped the arms of his wheelchair and braced himself, as if getting out these words would take all his remaining energy. 'You-gooddoctor . . .!' he spluttered.

Laura repeated what she believed her father had said back to him, and looked at Will for confirmation: that she would make a good doctor. She asked him to confirm that was what he had said. But he could not. His breath had shortened and he was struggling to breathe. He looked back with an intensity she had never seen before. But was it 'yes' or 'no' answer to her question? He couldn't say.

It was the coherent version of her father Laura now brought to mind in the front row of St Mark's. She pictured him smiling at her from within the casket.

'Well?' Laura imagined him asking, 'have you given any thought to my suggestion?'

'Are you suggesting I *shouldn't* feel miserable above all else?' Laura heard herself reply.

'No, no. Of course not. But I don't want the sadness to permanently immobilise you, Laura. I want it to act as a spur in your life, even as we find ourselves at the end of mine.'

'I have given it some thought,' Laura said.

'Good,' she heard her father's voice reply.

'I've been trying to clarify whether you actually said what I thought you did, or whether I was imagining it?'

'What do you think I said?'

'Did you say – because it was difficult to make out since your breathing wasn't very good and you were all over the place towards the end – did you really say I should be a doctor?'

'Is that what you heard?'

'It's what I thought I heard.'

'Did you ask me for clarification at the time?'

'I did.'

'And what did I say?'

'Your breathing became very laboured and you mumbled something I couldn't really understand. Your head looked very precarious on top of your neck. You were so thin.'

'So, what do you think I said by way of clarification?'

'I don't know. I'm making up this entire conversation. Is any of it really true? Did you really say I should become a doctor? Or did I mis-hear you, and all of this is simply me trying to convince myself into believing something I would like to be true?'

'*Would* you like to become a doctor?'

'I haven't given my future much thought, to be honest.'

'Perhaps you should.'

Laura looked at the coffin, wishing more than anything that he *could* still talk to her. But even within her own head her father had fallen silent.

Laura considered it indisputable that since she had been cashiered from the Women's Auxiliary Air Force her life *had* lacked much forward momentum. She had joined the Observation Corps, but more as a way to make some form of contribution to the war effort than an activity with any long-term ambition. For a period, she had thrown herself into spending every last moment with her father, to generate as many memories with him as possible. But with him gone she felt utterly adrift. She didn't know what she wanted from the rest of her life. His final, confusing words to her simply bounced around her mind like a diminishing echo. Her life felt frozen, while everyone else inched forward.

Look at Kate. Kate hasn't wasted any time since losing Jack. Training to be a nurse and building a new life for herself. Perhaps Dad was simply making an innocent association in his head. One daughter a nurse, so could the other be . . . a doctor? Or was he was just rambling . . .?

Laura watched her mother return to her seat. Reverend James stood and deferentially nodded his head at Erica as she walked past, then took up his position behind the lectern.

Laura looked beyond Kate, at Dr Rosen, the locum GP who'd taken over Will's surgery after he became unable to work.

That's what a doctor looks like. I don't look anything like as clever as that.

Laura felt her mother take her hand and squeeze tightly. She glanced at Erica's make-up, done 'for Will's sake', her mother had said. It scarcely masked the deep rings beneath her eyes. Laura could see that Erica sat with her chin set, jaw clenched. She knew her mother would want to bury her father with the utmost dignity.

'No tears, girls.'

Laura rested her free hand on top of Erica's and gave it a gentle squeeze of love and admiration.

Laura tuned back into the service and heard Reverend James make a clunky reference to the Pauline epistle to the Colossians, in which Paul wrote about the apostle, Luke, the physician who had 'medicines for the souls'. Reverend James proceeded to make a tortuous analogy between the apostle and Will's life work, claiming that in healing the physical body Will also healed the spirits of patients troubled by illness. Erica turned her head and whispered softly into Laura's ear.

'Dad would hate this.'

Laura nodded, and looked at the coffin. Its occupant remained silent.

It suddenly hit Laura that her father was soon to disappear into the ground *forever*. Not only for the foreseeable future, but for the dark, terrifyingly unforeseeable future, too. Not just for a bit of it. For the unimaginable *all* of it. And once he was buried and covered up, and the earth patted down flat so as not to look like anyone or anything was buried at all, the business of the world would rush in and fill the empty space where Will once was, and it would be as if he had never existed. Laura felt her throat fill with inconsolable, choking misery, and squeezed her eyes as tightly as she could to prevent a single molecule of water from escaping between their lids.

Steph Farrow sat next to her sixteen-year-old son, Stanley, at the very back of the church, yet still felt conspicuous and self-conscious. It had been just under a week since she had stood at the kitchen sink and watched Stanley run screaming for his life along the far field. Just under a week since she snatched the shotgun from the cupboard in the hall, and burst out of the farmhouse to save him. Just under a week since she had aimed the gun at the German pilot's back and pulled the trigger and watched him flop dead and bloody on top of her son.

23

She couldn't stop thinking about it, not even in church, saying farewell to the man who had delivered her son.

The pilot's face haunted her, even in sleep. She'd woken with a gasp every night since, jolted into consciousness by his eyes boring into her like two tiny blue lamps switched off. There was no escaping him.

It had taken about ten minutes for Steph and Stanley to come to their senses after she fired the lethal shot. Stanley bubbled over with euphoria that his life had been saved. Steph's reaction was the opposite. She began to justify what she had just done. She relived the nightmare over and over again.

'He was trying to kill you,' she told Little Stan, almost as if he hadn't been involved. 'He was beating you. He'd chased you across the field with his pistol, shouting at you that he was going to kill you.'

Stanley didn't understand Steph's need to justify anything.

'You killed a Nazi! You killed one of the bastards!'

In her recollection of the episode, it was always herself, Stanley, and the German pilot. Though their farmhand, Isobel, had been present on the farm at the time, she never featured in Steph's memories of the actual shooting.

Something had begun to bother her. If the pilot had wanted to seriously hurt or kill Stanley, he'd plenty of opportunity. Why hadn't he fired when he'd chased Stanley? Why hadn't he shot him when he had the upper hand on the ground? She'd picked up his revolver and found a full chamber of bullets. The German had the means to kill Stanley six times over, so why was her son still alive?

Little Stan had wanted to telephone the police straight away, and spread news that the terror gripping Great Paxford for the past four days had been brought to an end. Steph's immediate reaction was that she didn't want the authorities involved. Like many working country-folk, Steph had a natural aversion to the police, whose services they almost never required.

'How can we not call them?' asked Stanley. 'He's dead.'

Steph's mind raced, ideas coming thick and fast.

'No one knows he was here. Why don't we just . . . bury him? Somewhere on the farm where no one would ever know. Or take him somewhere more remote and do it there.'

Stanley stared at his mother with disbelief. This was the most exciting event in his life, even more exciting than the war because it was so close to him, and his mother was trying to sweep it under the carpet and pretend it never happened.

'If we don't tell them people will still think he's out there, somewhere, waiting to attack them, or blow something up.'

Stanley's imagination usually reached for the most lurid version of any given scenario. Steph wasn't to be diverted from her preferred course of action.

'Then we could dump the body where it'd be found,' Steph replied. 'That'd put an end to it.'

Stanley was bemused that his mother didn't see the situation as clearly as he did.

'Ma – he's got a bloody great hole in his back! As soon as they found him all the questions would start about who did it?'

'But why would they think of us?' Steph asked.

'I don't know how the police work,' Stanley said. 'But they'd start snooping around, trying to find out who killed him. We'd all be questioned. We'd have to lie and I'm no good at that.'

This was undoubtedly true. Whenever he lied his cheeks and ears glowed bright red, and his voice became strained as his resolve to brazen it out crumbled. Ever since he was little, Stanley (also known as 'Little Stan' to differentiate from his father, Stan) had no choice but to tell the truth at all times, and he became known for his honesty.

'Besides,' he said, 'we've nothing to hide. So why hide or bury him? Why not just tell everyone we got the Nazi bugger? They'd be relieved. You saved everyone, Ma! Why *shouldn't* we say?!'

The church choir and congregation began to tear into 'Abide With Me', its familiar melody and stirring lyric pulling Steph back into the present.

We have nothing to hide. Except I killed a man believing he was killing my son. I panicked. Believing something isn't enough to take a life, is it? Even a Nazi's.

Steph stared at the crucifix suspended above the altar, and tried to sing along with the hymn. After a few moments, she gave up. The words were irretrievable from the fog inside her head. She was back in the field with the shotgun, then telephoning the police, trying her best to sound matter of fact. But when the moment came to say, 'I've killed the German pilot,' instead she said, 'I've *got* the German pilot.' It took a minute and a half for the operator to be clear what Steph was trying to tell her.

Then everything happened very quickly. Catching the missing pilot had been an absolute priority in the area for both police and army. Six officers were at the farm within twenty minutes. Once they had ascertained that the dead man was the missing German airman, they telephoned for an ambulance to have the body removed. The officer in charge then asked Steph, Little Stan and Isobel what had happened, taking the boy's words first.

As Stanley spoke, the officer carefully wrote down his account in a small notebook, nodding along with the narrative, stopping Stanley's flow only for clarification of certain points.

Steph looked up anxiously when she heard Stanley tell the officer that he had been chasing the German, and not the other way around. She assumed her son wanted to appear more heroic in his account, and didn't contradict him.

Then it was Isobel's turn to give her version of events, limited to what she had heard and – due to her limited vision since birth – not seen.

Finally, Steph gave her account.

When they had all finished, the officer seemed happy with their combined explanation. Steph asked if the name of the farm could be kept out of the official report. She wanted their lives to be allowed to continue as if this had never happened. The officer seemed doubtful.

'Difficult, Mrs Farrow,' he said. 'Not often a Luftwaffe pilot drops out of the sky and goes on the rampage. People are naturally curious about the details. They'll want to know where he was found. What he did. What he looked like. Human nature. We can't help ourselves. The papers will want to know all the relevant details.'

'But in the story you give to the papers, can't you just say "farmland" without mentioning which farm?'

The officer looked at her for a few moments, his brow furrowing.

'Lot of credit coming your way for doing this, Mrs Farrow. Lot of credit. Gratitude. Why wouldn't you want people to know?'

'Do you think I'm proud of it?'

'Most would be.'

'Did you look at his face? He was no more than twenty years old.'

'A good Nazi is a dead Nazi. You've done a great service to your country,' he said. Your community'd want to celebrate you, I'm sure.'

'I just want things to go back to how they were.'

The officer looked at her and could see that Steph had been affected by the event. He nodded sympathetically, and said, 'I can't promise, but I'll do what I can.'

'Thank you.'

The following day it seemed that the officer had been true to his word. News of the pilot's death was released. Such was the overall sense of relief, no one seemed interested that the details failed to include specific reference to the land on which the airman had been found – or any mention of the role played by the Farrows in his demise. The statement from the police, as quoted in the local paper, was only that the pilot's body 'had been found on farmland on the outskirts of Great Paxford'.

If some Great Paxfordians *had* been thirsty for more detail, their attention was quickly drawn to the tragic news of Will's death – a man they loved and revered. Within an instant the dead German appeared to be entirely forgotten; except by Steph, Stanley and Isobel. Steph swore Stanley and Isobel to absolute secrecy about the shooting, despite Stanley being frantic to tell everyone how he had struggled in mortal combat with the armed Nazi, before his mother had killed 'the Hun' to save his life.

Steph had wondered if there was to be an investigation into the incident, but the officer thought not.

'A Nazi was trying to kill your son – you killed him. Case closed.'

Case closed. So why do I see his face everywhere? Why can't I sleep? Why do I feel like crying all the time? What do I tell Stan? Case bloody open, day and bloody night.

Teresa sat beside her new husband, Wing Commander Nick Lucas, in the middle of the congregation, her hand resting lightly on his. She was trying to decide what to say to Erica and her daughters at the end of the service. Teresa's only previous experience of funerals had been of three elderly relatives, where both the proceedings and consoling words were pithy. Teresa learned that when an elderly person dies you mourn the loss but celebrate the life that went before it. Though Erica and the Reverend James had done their very best to celebrate Will's life and service to the community, everyone knew that at forty-seven he had died too young.

Teresa knew that Nick had acquired more experience than he could have ever wished of how to respond to tragic death, having to write letters of condolence to parents of young airmen killed in action almost daily. When Teresa had asked him what she should say to Erica on their walk up to church, he suggested she simply say what she felt in the moment.

'If you try and think of the right thing in advance the danger is it will sound rehearsed and rather hollow. You're a highly intelligent, intuitive woman. See how you feel at the time. I guarantee that whatever you say, it will be the right thing.'

'Is that how you write your letters? What you feel at the time?' she asked.

'There's a world of difference. I don't know the bereaved. I'm a figure of authority representing the RAF. And I have too many of these damned letters to write. If I wrote what I felt each time they would be unfit to send. But Erica is your friend. You might not know the right thing to say now, but it will come. Trust me. I've never known you to put a foot wrong in the time we've been together. Not once. It simply isn't in you. You make everyone you encounter feel at ease.'

When the service ended and the villagers shuffled silently out of St Mark's, Teresa walked towards Erica standing beside Will's coffin, and wrapped her arms around her and held her tight.

'I've not known him as long as most here today, Erica. But in the short time I've been in the village I've come to appreciate what a wonderful, wonderful man he was. I can't begin to understand how you're feeling, but if there's anything you or the girls need, come to us. Please.'

Erica whispered, 'Thank you . . .'

'I mean it.'

'I know. Look after Nick,' Erica said softly. 'We never know what's around the corner.'

Teresa stepped back to watch Erica and her girls become encircled by well-wishers waiting to offer their profound condolences. She relocated Nick, who had been watching Teresa from the main entrance.

'How was it?' he asked as she approached.

'Fine, I think,' she replied, thinking Nick looked the most handsome man present in his uniform.

'You're incapable of putting a foot wrong.'

Teresa kissed him on the cheek and felt a sharp pang of guilt as she recalled the moment she had leaned forward and kissed Annie passionately just a week before in hospital. How could she betray her new husband like that? And with one of his closest friends? Having crash-landed a Hurricane she had been delivering to Tabley Wood, Annie had come close to losing her life. Motionless and pale beneath the white bedsheets, Annie had looked so vulnerable and helpless as she lay recovering from surgery.

By any normal measure, I certainly put a foot wrong by doing that. Two feet. I wish Nick didn't think I was perfect. When I visit Annie, it isn't out of duty, as a 'friend'. Life would be so much easier if it was.

Teresa felt Nick thread his arm through hers.

'Let's go home and make love,' he whispered in her ear, with a smile. 'I have an urgent need to re-affirm the life-force!'

Pat and Bob Simms stood in silence in the cemetery grounds that encircled St Mark's, as Joyce, Frances, and Sarah chatted with Erica. Pat felt acutely self-conscious that they were standing within sight of the flat headstone on which she and her lover had hidden notes for one another when he was stationed nearby with his regiment. Bob had discovered their means of exchanging notes via the headstone while Marek had been stationed in Cheshire, and Pat now wondered if he felt its proximity as she did. Her pulse surged for a moment in panic, then subsided to its resting rhythm.

Let Bob fixate on the past. Marek and I are focused on the future. Pat watched Alison Scotlock engaged in an intense conversation with Laura, who was nodding intently. Pat wondered what Alison might be saying to the girl, then remembered Alison's husband George had died just days before the end of the First War, and imagined she might be telling Laura about her own experience of grief and loss, and how all things eventually pass. It's what she believed herself about her thirteen-year marriage to Bob, which had long-since turned sour. Pat glanced at him. Bob was quietly rolling a cigarette.

If you had been killed at Dunkirk, I wonder what I would have felt? At the time, I assumed I wouldn't grieve at all. I hated you intensely, and remember lying in bed hoping you'd be killed. But if it had actually happened, I suppose it's possible I'd have remembered the man you were when we first met, and grieved for him? And by extension, in time, for the life we might have had in place of the life you forced upon us? Grief for time lost. I think that's the only way I could have got through any kind of funeral service for you – focused on the man you used to be, and might have been. Not who you became.

33

Bob was now looking at Erica and the girls.

'I suppose you need to go and say something to Erica and the girls,' he said, clearly wishing to leave.

'Shouldn't you as well? Will was very good to you when you came back from Dunkirk.'

'He performed a service for which I paid him.'

'He made himself available day and night.'

'Uhuh . . . so he could charge me more.'

'Bob, not everyone is obsessed by money.'

'I've yet to meet a doctor who isn't. The man thought we were beneath him, Patricia, and you know it.'

Pat felt a small wave of fury rise within.

'I'm going to offer our condolences,' she said.

'Fine. I'll see you at the house.'

Pat walked away from Bob, towards Erica and her daughters.

Don't look back.

If she had, she would have seen Bob skulking away from St Mark's, a cigarette already between his lips.

As she approached the Campbells, Pat felt less afraid of Bob than she had been for as long as she could remember. Whether it was because he had been unable to physically attack her while they lodged with Joyce Cameron, or whether it was because the contact she now had with Marek gave her greater strength to endure any onslaught from her husband was difficult to say. Marek was a source of inspiration and strength in his own right. Whatever the reason, Pat had recently started to respond to Bob's digs and sporadic outbursts with a grain of disdain mixed into her sense of dread. Standing up to him still left Pat feeling sick to her stomach. Yet the nauseous feeling was worth the look in his eye that she hadn't previously seen: a glimmer of panic that his power over her was no longer as complete as it had been. As she drew level with the Campbell women, Pat cleared her head of all thoughts of Bob, and held Erica in her arms. It reminded her of the last time she had held Erica, in the aftermath of the Spitfire crash that had decimated each of their homes.

'Will was the most remarkable man,' she whispered. 'I always felt blessed to be your immediate neighbours.'

Erica knew she was referring to Will's ability to patch Pat up whenever Bob had struck her, without ever prying.

'He knew what you put up with,' said Erica, only slightly cryptically.

Pat nodded. 'He always respected my privacy. Never asked me what had happened. Never put me in a difficult position.'

'He'd always wait for a patient to take the lead with a matter like that.'

Pat's eyes opened a little wider with surprise. 'There were *others*?'

'Of course, Pat, dear. Many others.'

As Erica said the words Pat instantly felt how naive it was of her to believe that what happened between her and Bob happened to no other woman and their husband.

'It never occurred to me,' she said.

'Will saw it almost every month. He respected the difficult position most of the women were in. He didn't want to add to their burden by prying.'

'I was lucky to have him as my doctor,' Pat said after a moment. 'We all were.'

'As was I to have him as my husband and companion,' said Erica. 'The luckiest woman in the world.'

Chapter 4

O N THE NIGHT following Will's funeral Steph struggled to sleep. The bedroom was dark enough, and with just a light breeze blowing through the farm beyond the window there was little noise to keep her awake. Yet she was unable to settle into that dark, quiet space where consciousness dissolves. Instead, her mind began repeating Stanley's pleas for help and the German pilot's shouts for Stanley to stop crying out. And then the blast from the shotgun that Steph had been holding, which had silenced both young men. And it wasn't only the sounds that repeated in Steph's mind. It was also the images.

After what seemed like hours, and with a long day in the fields ahead of her, Steph gave up. She lay in bed doll-like, staring up at the ceiling. She turned her head to the left and imagined her husband lying in his customary position, his back curled away from her. She stretched out an arm and placed her hand on his pillow and wondered how much longer he would be in training before he got deployed. After a few moments, Steph pulled the pillow over and buried her face in it to see if there was any vestige of Stan's aroma left. Some trace of his sweat perhaps, or the oil he used in his hair. But the pillow only smelled of carbolic soap.

Steph suddenly pictured the dead pilot's face staring up at the sky and felt wretched to her core. She covered her face with her hands and began to silently cry. The surge of despair subsided after a few minutes. Steph lay face down on the mattress with her eyes open, the pillow now tear-damp on her face.

Ten minutes later, still awake, Steph got out of bed, slipped on her dressing gown, and crept downstairs so as not to wake Stanley.

At the bottom of the stairs Steph crossed to the kitchen window behind the sink and looked out. The night's gloom reduced the farmyard to indefinable dark shapes and lumps. But as her eyes grew accustomed Steph began to see beyond the farmyard and into the field. There she could just about pick out the figure of her son fleeing across the far field, and the figure of the German pilot in pursuit. She heard Stanley's screams and the pilot's shouts. And then she heard the shot.

Steph felt herself unsteady on her feet and turned away from the window. She was breathing hard. She crossed to the dresser and opened the left-hand drawer that contained the farm's paperwork. Slipping her hand beneath the documents she allowed her fingers to root around for a few moments until they made contact with a slim, soft leather wallet. She pulled it out and took it over to the kitchen table. She sat and held the wallet in her hands, staring at it, feeling the weight of it as proof that what she could no longer stop thinking about had really happened. As she had already done many times, Steph opened the wallet and saw the German pilot's documentation from the Luftwaffe. She looked at his name. Christophe Hauer. He was twenty years old. There were other details, but the pilot's name and age were all the information Steph could comprehend.

Christophe Hauer. Christophe. Not Christopher. Here he would be Christopher. But in Germany he was Christophe. I prefer it. It's softer.

When the officer who had taken their statements asked if either Steph or Little Stan had found any personal effects on the airman, or in the small camp he had made for himself in the wood beyond the far field, both shook their heads. It was true in Stanley's case. However, after they'd moved Christophe's body into the barn as protection from crows and foxes, Steph had found herself alone with the corpse for a few minutes.

In the silent, still air of the barn, Steph hadn't been able to take her eyes off the lifeless German at her feet.

When the authorities arrive, he'll be taken away. It'll be like this never happened.

Eager to find out *what* she could *while* she could, Steph had knelt beside the dead man and searched the pockets of his flying jacket and trousers. She'd quickly found the wallet she now held at her kitchen table, and slipped it into her trouser pocket.

In addition to the pilot's identification papers, the wallet also contained a little German currency and a photograph of the pilot dressed in his Luftwaffe uniform with two smartly dressed older people, who Steph presumed were Christophe's parents. The trio were photographed in a formal, unsmiling pose, seated side by side at a table inside a photographer's studio. The words on the back of the photograph read, 'München, 1939'. The absence of anyone else in the picture made Steph believe Christophe was an only child.

Like my Little Stan.

She estimated Christophe's mother was around her age, and wondered if she knew that her only child was dead. Or would she just be told he was missing in action? Or would she know nothing at all, and continue to believe he was still alive, fighting for his country? Steph had little idea how the English government relayed news of dead personnel to loved ones, let alone how the Germans handled such news.

Perhaps Nazis don't care what happens to their boys. Perhaps they celebrate the sacrifice for the Fatherland.

Steph couldn't understand how any mother could celebrate the death of their child, Nazi or not. She felt tears once again begin to roll down her cheeks. She cried often since the incident, sometimes without even knowing she was. She could be walking around the farm and catch sight of the far field, and stop and stare at it, as if it had forever changed into something hostile and fearful. The next moment, tears would fall from her face onto her overalls.

I never shouted at him to stop. I never gave him a chance to look up and see the shotgun. I just aimed and pulled the trigger. I panicked. There's no other word for it.

In Steph's mind death was part of the seasonal rhythm of the farm, a state of no return, with no time for sentimentality. With so much work to do, the concept of heaven made little sense to her, except as something reassuring for those who needed it. In her view, the constant renewal of death with life underpinned the natural world. But the incident with the pilot was different. A life had been taken *unnaturally*, before it should have been. And *she*, Steph Farrow, had taken it – another thing that should never have happened in the natural course of things.

His mother will never see or hold him again.

Sitting at the kitchen table, Steph felt the temptation to go up to Stanley's room, to wake him up, and hold him.

He wouldn't understand. He thinks I should be happy about saving his life. I might be if I believed I had saved his life. But was he ever in danger of losing his life? Really?

No one should have a gun and use it the way I did. You shout. You call out. You shouldn't just shoot. Stan wouldn't have just shot. Everything's ruined. Every last thing. I need to speak to Stanley. Stanley would know what to say. What-ever he said would be for the best.

Instead, Steph reached into the right-hand dresser drawer, where she kept a small block of white stationery she used to write letters to her husband Stan while he was away. She sat back down and began to slowly write, feeling intense gratitude towards Teresa for recently teaching her the skill to communicate with Stanley at distance.

She didn't give details about what she had done. She wrote only that she wished Stan was home because something 'had happened' that he would know how to deal with better than she did. She was still writing when the sun began to hover below the horizon. After reading the letter slowly back Steph screwed it up and put it in the grate in the Aga, where it burst into flame and vanished in a plume of smoke.

He's enough to contend with.

Next thing she knew, Steph blinked as the first rays of sunlight slowly inched across her face and pierced her eyes. She remembered that she had barely slept once again. There was nothing she could do about that now. A new day was coming into being, full of things that needed seeing to. Steph rose from the chair, replaced the pilot's wallet in the dresser's left-hand drawer, filled the kettle with water, and put it on the stove to boil. She then shuffled over to the stairs and plodded wearily back up to her bedroom. It felt as if lead weights had been hung around her ankles.

In her bedroom, she hung up her dressing gown and began to get dressed. Work would be a useful distraction from all that had prevented her from being able to sleep.

Throughout the morning, a raw winter wind blew a thick blanket of grey cloud straight off the Atlantic and across the region. Locals were used to such winds, and knew enough to stay indoors as much as possible. Sheltering inside was not an option for Steph and Stanley. The harvest over, the land needed preparing for next year's crop.

Buttoned against the elements, Steph drove their green tractor slowly over the earth of the far field, as Stanley sat beside her looking backwards, ensuring they were keeping the plough – and furrows – in a straight line. Owing to poor drainage the far field was usually the last to be ploughed over. But this year Steph wanted to do it first. Though the police had reassured her otherwise, in the back of Steph's mind the far field felt like the scene of a crime. She wanted to obliterate the scene at the earliest opportunity.

His blood is on this field. Plough it under!

Steph wouldn't stop, even when the weather closed in further, hammering them with icy nails of rain that turned the field into little more than a quagmire. The tractor laboured on, consuming more fuel than Stanley wanted. But there was no going against his mother when she was in this mood.

So focused were they, neither initially saw the saloon car wending its way off the main road towards the farmhouse. Stanley was the first to notice.

'Who's this then?!' he called over the rain.

Steph put the tractor into 'idle' and watched the saloon park outside the farmhouse. In her experience, sleek black cars like that never came unless they were on official business of some kind or other. Since she wasn't expecting anyone from the Ministry, she assumed it was someone about Christophe. A ball of dread rolled slowly around her stomach.

You can't just kill a man – even a German – and get off scot free.

She longed for Stan.

After several moments, the driver of the saloon got out and waved in their direction. He pulled down the brim of his Trilby then lifted up the collar of his overcoat and waited, seemingly assuming the Farrows would naturally come to him.

'Should we go see who he is and what he wants?' asked Stanley, feeling the same excitement as when interviewed by the police about the pilot's death.

Steph didn't answer as she watched the stranger.

'If it's the police again, let him come to us. We're not at their beck and call.'

'But they might have more questions,' said Stanley.

'Then he can wait for us to finish.'

'You don't want to mess him around, Ma.'

'Not messing him around. He's come uninvited. We've work on.'

His mother's resolve made Stanley nervous. It was how she steeled herself for conflict.

Steph put the tractor back into gear and continued to plough.

'Eyes on the back, Stanley.'

Stanley twisted in his seat so his body was facing the tractor's rear and tried to fix his eyes on the field behind. But he kept glancing across the farmyard to the stranger, who started to walk towards them.

'Ma, he's coming!'

'Eyes to the back! Concentrate on what you need to do!'

Steph was unable to disguise the nervousness in her voice. She could feel her heart beating hard.

'He knows we've seen him. We should stop. We're only making trouble for ourselves!'

The man continued his inexorable way towards the tractor, stumbling over furrows, twisting his feet free from sticky mud in his bid to proceed. No matter how coated with mud and run-off his shoes and trousers became, he kept walking towards them. When he was within shouting distance he raised his arm and waved a second time.

'Mrs Farrow! I should like to talk to you! To both of you!'

'He wants to talk to us. We should stop. Ma?'

Steph didn't respond so Stanley reached forward and switched off the ignition, yanking out the key.

45

'We can't just ignore him. It's daft.'

Whatever this stranger represented in relation to the death of the pilot – assuming that was what he was here for – Steph wanted no part of it.

'Mrs Farrow, my name is Philip Shepherd . . .' he said, catching up to the tractor. 'I'm a reporter from the *Liverpool Echo*. I would like to speak with you about what happened here last week.'

'He's a reporter, Ma!' Stanley whispered in her ear. 'A reporter!'

Steph felt a shiver of fear shoot down the length of her spine.

'Mrs Farrow?'

Steph slowly turned in her seat and faced the reporter. He was middle-aged, portly, with an unkempt beard that had spread like topsy across his substantial jowls. His cheeks and nose were red with rosacea from too much beer. His shoes were so covered with mud it was impossible to tell where his feet ended and the earth began, which gave him the appearance of having emerged out of the soil in front of her. His overcoat and trilby were drenched, and clung limply to his stout frame. In appearance, he cut a sorry sight. By contrast, however, his tone was educated and determined.

'My paper would like to run the story about what happened here last week. We know our readers would love to hear all about your magnificent act of heroism, Mrs Farrow, taking on a Nazi and saving your son. What do you say?'

Steph looked at the reporter as the rain continued to fall.

'I told the police I didn't want my identity made public.'

'That's what I heard,' he said. 'But a story like this has a habit of getting out, one way or another. It's an amazing tale, Mrs Farrow. Farmer's wife shoots German pilot to save her son. It's a tale for our times, don't you agree?'

'Do I look like a farmer's wife up here? Or do I look like a farmer?'

'Point taken, Mrs Farrow. Both, of course. I didn't mean to imply—'

'I don't want to be in your paper, Mr Shepherd. I don't want anything more to do with what happened. It's bad enough it did. I want no glorifying of it. I just want me and Stanley to be left alone to get on with running the farm.'

'I understand that, of course, Mrs Farrow,' Shepherd said in the syrupy voice of an old pro used to prising stories out of reluctant members of the public. 'But like I said, we want to run this story, and we have a duty to do so. Think how chuffed your neighbours will be when they find out you were the one who killed him! None of you will ever have to buy a drink in the village pub again.'

Steph looked at Shepherd and couldn't think what to say that would make him turn around and leave. She could see in his eyes that he had come all the way from Liverpool and was damned if he was going to leave empty-handed.

'We're going to run the story, Mrs Farrow. One way or another. Now, it's your story, and this is your opportunity to tell it. In your own words. Far better than me cobbling it together. Come along now. What do you say?'

Shepherd looked at Steph, unblinking, and smiled at the precise moment his expert eye detected her resolve gave way, and moved in for the kill.

'You're clearly an inspiration to your son and husband, Mrs Farrow. But when this gets out, you'll be an inspiration to every woman in the country.'

'I don't want to be an inspiration to every woman in the country. I just want to be left alone.'

'This was a Nazi sent to drop bombs on us, Mrs Farrow. He got what he deserved. You're an ordinary woman, salt of the earth, who did something *extra*ordinary. Your story will help other ordinary people believe that they too might be capable of *extra*ordinary things in the difficult times ahead. Let them hear it from your own lips. It's what the people need to read after a long and terrifying summer. Hitler hasn't gone away, Mrs Farrow. He's rebuilding the Luftwaffe as we stand here getting rained on. He's taken one country after another to the east, and he's still got his eye on us as a thorn in his side. If he takes us he will have a free hand across the world. People are still very fearful of invasion, Mrs Farrow. Your husband—'

Steph bristled. 'What's he got to do with any of this?'

'He enlisted, didn't he, Mrs Farrow? I'm assuming he enlisted, otherwise he would be working the farm with you. Think how proud he'll be to see his mates reading your story in the paper.'

Stanley could scarcely hide his excitement. 'Will there be a picture?'

Shepherd smiled. 'Of course, son. I have a camera in my car.'

'I don't know anyone who's had their photograph in the paper, Ma.'

Shepherd understood the need to maintain pressure. People reluctant to talk to the press usually crumbled only when they realised compliance was unavoidable. He could use the son's excitement to press the mother.

'I have all the details, Mrs Farrow. I can write the story today. Why not make sure we get it right as far as you and your lad are concerned?'

Steph sighed, and suddenly felt cold and wet. The fight drained from her. Perhaps if she were less tired she might have the strength to tell Shepherd to sling his hook. Stan would likely have run this man off the farm. But Stan wasn't here, and she lacked the energy to continue to go toe to toe with someone who clearly understood how to get what he wanted.

'What do I have to do?' she asked wearily.

'Simple,' he said. 'We go inside. Warm up with a nice cup of tea. Then just tell me what happened and leave the rest to me.' Shepherd paused momentarily for effect. 'I give you my absolute word, Mrs Farrow, I'll do you proud.'

Steph looked at him. She felt her life start to tip over onto its side. There was nothing she could do to stop it.

'Have there been others, Mrs Farrow? Other papers? What have they offered you, Mrs Farrow? I was told I would have this account as an exclusive, but I wouldn't put it past the people I have to deal with to sell the same promise to our rivals. What have they offered? Whatever it is, I can match it. For a story like this, we would be prepared to pay. What would you be willing to accept?'

Steph looked at Shepherd and blinked slowly. Great fatigue weighed upon her. All she wanted was for Shepherd to stop talking.

Chapter 5

A s the emotional turbulence of her father's final days caught up with her, Laura became overwhelmed with fatigue. With no previous experience to draw upon, she had no way of knowing how her father's funeral would affect her. She knew the ceremony was designed to propel them along a managed pathway to preserve their dignity. But she was unsure whether she would be able to remain *managed* all the way to the end. She had told herself not to fight the occasion but to try to glide through it as painlessly as possible. Yet Laura had all but collapsed at the sight of her father's casket being lowered into what Reverend James referred to as 'his place of rest'. It didn't look like a place of rest to Laura. It looked like an empty hole in the ground that had been crudely hacked out by gravediggers.

Despite her best efforts, Laura only managed an hour at the wake before it became evident to Erica that the occasion was proving too much for her youngest daughter, and sent her upstairs to rest.

'She's overwhelmed,' Laura overheard Erica telling their guests as she went upstairs. 'They were extremely close.'

Laura lay on her side on her bed with the light off and stared at the wall. The indistinct murmur of visitors downstairs filtered up through the floorboards and under her bedroom door. She curled herself into a tight ball and willed them all to go away.

She wasn't sure how long she lay there when a knock interrupted her mourning.

'Who is it?' she said, turning towards the door

'Someone to see you,' said her mother from the other side.

Laura wiped her face with the heels of her hands and crossed to the door and opened it. Erica stood alone on the landing.

'Tom was on his way to report for duty at Tabley Wood but wanted to stop by and pay his respects, and see how you were. I can ask him to come back another time if you'd prefer.'

Laura thought for a moment. She really wanted to see no one, but if Tom had made the effort to come to the house and enquire after her it would be rude not to show her face and accept his condolences.

Laura came down the stairs a minute after Erica, and found Tom standing in the hall, looking into the front room where various villagers reminisced about her father's medical brilliance. She was struck by Tom's stoic stillness as he waited in his RAF uniform, while others milled around with drinks and sandwiches and all manner of sombre expressions on their faces.

As soon as he heard Laura's footsteps on the stairs Tom turned his head and smiled at her.

'I wasn't sure you'd come down,' he said as she reached the bottom. 'I wouldn't have blamed you. I'm sorry, I can't stay longer.'

'Why don't I walk you to your car?' Laura suggested.

'Not much of a walk.'

'Then we'll just have to go very, very, very, *very* slowly,' said Laura, putting on her coat and opening the front door.

It felt good to escape the house. Tom's RAF car stood at the bottom of the Campbells' front path, a mere fifteen yards away.

'I just wanted to say how extraordinarily sorry I am at your loss, Laura. Your father was – as you've heard many times today no doubt – a wonderful man.'

'Yes,' Laura said impassively. 'Thank you.'

'Did you know I was at the station when he hit Wing Commander Bowers? I saw it all,' Tom said. 'It was all I could do to stop myself cheering.'

'I'm not sure it was very productive,' Laura said.

'Perhaps not,' said Tom. 'But if nothing else, punching a Wing Commander in the mouth on an RAF station to defend the honour of his daughter took a tremendous amount of spunk.'

Laura hadn't thought of it like that.

'Anyhow,' Tom said, 'that's all I came to say.'

'Thank you.'

'That and I wanted to let you know I'm around if you ever need to talk. Or even if you just need taking out of yourself for an hour or two. We could go for a walk, or something like that.'

Laura looked at Tom and nodded. 'Thanks. I'd like that,' she said.

'Excellent,' he said. And then again, 'Excellent.'

Laura stepped forward and kissed him on the lips, softly, pressing hers onto his for a few moments to make the point of how much she liked him. She then stepped back and smiled at him. He looked back and smiled, pleased that she felt for him what he felt for her. Suddenly, he checked his watch.

'Christ – I'm so late!'

'Tell your boss you were saying hello to the daughter of the man who punched his predecessor in the mouth – I'm sure you'll be forgiven,' Laura said.

Tom pulled Laura to him and kissed her. 'I miss you,' he said. 'An extraordinary amount.'

'Good,' she said, and kissed him again. 'Now go to work. Don't you know there's a war on?'

He grinned and walked to his car, got in, started the engine, and roared away.

Laura stood on the front path listening to the drone of Tom's engine fade into silence. She looked up into the cold, dead, starry sky. It was a struggle for her to put mortality into any kind of context, but the finality of her father's absence was beginning to sink in. 'Forever' meant nothing that ever happened with him could ever happen again. No sight nor sound of him. No touch nor smell of him. Her father had been wiped from the earth.

She wondered how she would feel every time she went to church, or cycled past.

Will I stop and visit his grave each time? Will I try, but fall out of the habit, and then possibly forget he is there at all?

'Never . . .' she said out loud, the word forming a fine, cold mist in front of her.

Laura was suddenly aware of a pair of hands resting on her shoulders, and turned to find Erica standing behind her.

'Come inside, my darling. Before you catch your death.'

Laura didn't want to return to the house. She didn't want to have to talk to anyone, and she knew she wouldn't sleep now even if she wanted to. She simply wanted to stand out in the cold, alone.

Everything has changed, and everything will remain changed. My father will remain in the ground for as long as there is ground. There's no going back to before.

Nevertheless, to satisfy Erica, Laura allowed her mother to steer her slowly back towards the house, where she received sympathy and condolences with a fixed, sad smile on her face for the remainder of the evening.

Chapter 6

ARRIVING HOME AFTER Will's funeral, Teresa and Nick went upstairs and made love, then lay in bed for a few minutes, savouring the moments before Nick would have to get up to have a bath and get back into his uniform and return to Tabley Wood.

'How many funerals have you been to since the outbreak of the war?' Teresa asked, looking at him intently.

'One is too many,' he replied, resting his flushed chin against Teresa's right shoulder.

'Of course, but in terms of a number?'

'Must we discuss this now, darling?' he protested. 'It's bad enough I have to attend them, without having to quantify how many.'

Teresa fell silent, not wanting to spoil the mood.

He gave her a soft kiss on her still-hot cheek. Teresa's curiosity wasn't easily silenced.

'Do you get used to them?'

'*Darling . . .*' Despite feeling it, Nick tried to keep any hint of genuine irritation from his voice.

'You hardly talk about them so I have to try and guess the effect they have on you. I want to know if I'm guessing correctly, or if you're constantly thinking what an insensitive cow I am for not appreciating how difficult it is for you.'

'Being sent to boarding school at a young age taught me how to compartmentalise different aspects of my life,' Nick said. 'Especially how I felt about different things. It didn't always pay to wear one's heart on one's sleeve in the company of so many quite merciless boys rather skilled at exploiting weakness in others. As a consequence, I was often accused of being somewhat aloof during my adolescence. I wasn't. But I learned to mask what I really felt. It's never been a more useful ability than now.'

'I'm the same,' said Teresa, obliquely. 'I've always admired people who aren't as buttoned up as I am.'

'Yes,' said Nick. 'But in my current position at Tabley Wood, it's expected. I'm no use to anybody if I walk around teetering on the edge of hysteria.'

'So, in answer to my question?' Teresa persisted.

'I think the more one does of *anything* the less it's likely to take you by surprise. That's how it is when I attend yet another funeral. I don't get used to the fact that I'm attending the burial of yet another young man who should not, ordinarily, be being buried. But I have, I suppose, become familiar with how it plays out, and am prepared for the worst because I've often seen it.'

Nick got out of bed and went to the bathroom. Teresa sank back into the pillow and her own thoughts.

Men are so strange when it comes to talking about what they feel. Almost as if they are suspicious of saying what they mean most of the time. It turns every conversation into a game of cat and mouse. As if they're under interrogation. It's quite tiresome.

Nick eventually returned washed and refreshed. He put on his uniform, kissed Teresa goodbye, and left the house for Tabley Wood. He would know within fifteen minutes of arriving whether or not it was likely to be a busy, intensely stressful night, or one that contained no German raids, and would allow him momentary peace of mind that none of his men would be killed or injured over the next few hours.

Teresa lay in bed, listened to the assured purr of Nick's car disappear into the chilly night, and felt the customary evening solitude start to creep up on her.

In the fantasy of married life Teresa had fabricated to persuade herself that marriage to Nick would be, if not a wholly positive experience, then broadly so, she miscalculated they would spend most of their evenings together. It was a vision of married life she had lifted almost entirely from films and magazines. It was a signal failure on her part not to have factored Nick's job into the equation. Consequently, she had been unable to predict how intensely lonely she would become when he was away. Especially at night. Much of this was the result of having spent *every* night in Alison Scotlock's company for the duration of her stay as Alison's lodger. Alison worked from home, and was always there when Teresa returned from school. They prepared their evening meal together, and ate it together. They washed up afterwards together, and settled together for the duration of the evening until it was time to retire.

Even in the absence of romantic possibility, Teresa had always preferred the company of women to men. Yet she also craved to be seen by society as 'normal', as it brought the anonymity that allowed Teresa to pass without scrutiny. For that, she believed she needed to be attached to a man. In Nick, she had come across the kindest, cleverest and bravest man she had ever known. He provided her with a sense of security she felt unable to achieve any other way.

It wasn't as if the conversation was always scintillating. Especially towards the end, when Alison was trying to encourage me to take Nick seriously as a suitor. That became quite repetitious and irritating. Alison was never good at disguising her intentions, however benign she thought they were. But often, it was just cheering to look across the room and see another human being.

Teresa started to wonder if she should think about getting a dog. She wondered what Nick would think of the idea.

If I present the company of a dog as a means of making me feel less lonely in his absence, I suspect Nick will be for it. But that doesn't mean it's a good idea, simply that I've resigned myself to the fact that I am going to be lonely most days because I've been forced out of teaching, and most nights while the war continues. Which could be, well, who knows how long? It feels a little feeble – is that too harsh a word? Not really. It feels a little feeble to settle for the company of a four-legged substitute for a career and a husband. Nick is wonderful when he's here, but when he's not I'm simply wandering around empty rooms, trying to make time pass.

How do other women manage? I read, then there is the WI, of course, but only one meeting a month, and a committee meeting every week or so. I could go over to Alison at the cottage, or invite her over here. Yet whenever I do that she develops a look in her eye that suggests I'm not taking married life seriously, and am constantly looking to return to the time when we spent our evenings together, like the two spinsters. God, it's only been two months and I don't know how much more of this I can bear.

Through great effort of will, Teresa tried to stop herself thinking any more thoughts, having suddenly become self-conscious that she was turning into one of those people who talked to themselves more than was healthy.

For a few moments, she lay staring at the ceiling trying to induce some form of meditative state, or simply sleep. Any time a conscious thought appeared to be in the process of forming she distracted herself by digging her fingernails deep into the flesh of her leg. After she had done this a few times she became curious to see what her leg looked like with these new indentations. It was not a pretty sight. The marks were deep and red. In one of his more attentive moods, Nick would certainly ask how they had come about. Clearly, this was not a productive solution to the problem.

That lay in admitting what the real problem was.

Teresa's sense of isolation was genuine, but it was only part of the story. The other part was knowing that there was a solution that she dare not think about. And the more she dared not think about it, the more she wanted to.

Teresa got out of bed and crossed to the window. Somewhere in the dark shapes of the night, not in view but behind those forms she could see, lay the cottage hospital, within which lay Annie, recovering from her crash injuries.

I'm here and she's there. It feels as if she is far away because it's dark. But she isn't. Not far at all. A twenty-five-minute ride. Nothing really. Though Nick wouldn't want me to go out of the house at night like that. He worries about all the military transport haring around at the moment, not to mention the odd stray bomb. If I wasn't married to him he wouldn't have any thoughts about what I did at night, and I would have no thoughts about any concerns he might have. So why not – just for the moment – imagine we're not married, and be free?

Ever since she had kissed Annie in the hospital ward Teresa had been trying to keep the question, 'What next?' at bay. The kiss had felt like crossing the Rubicon. From time to time she could feel the soft warmth of Annie's lips on her own. They were yielding, responsive but without seeming eager or greedy. In a word, the kiss had been perfect. For the first in a long time Teresa had felt she was in exactly the right place beside exactly the right person.

Is she thinking the same thing? Annie can't come to me. She can barely move at the moment. She has to wait to see what I'm going to do. So, what am I going to do? What I usually do? Hide? Wasn't the kiss a statement of intent of some kind? Or just a moment of weakness? Or betrayal? Nick— Stop thinking. Stop. Thinking.

But Teresa could not stop thinking. She had grown tired of having to prompt her husband into divulging feelings he kept to himself, like carefully nurtured secrets. Tired of being made to feel that she was prying and intrusive, when all she wanted was the kind of easy, uncomplicated sharing of thought and feeling she found in the company of women.

Teresa experienced a sharp pang of guilt. Nick was Nick. He had never pretended to be anyone else. It was one of his most attractive qualities. He just wasn't *female*, and there came a point when – however much she enjoyed Nick's company – she yearned for female company. More precisely, she yearned for *a* woman. To talk to. To hold. To touch. And be touched *by*. However gentle Nick was, however considerate and intelligent and funny, he could never provide everything Teresa needed. He could never offer her true intimacy.

She had no secrets from Annie. Annie knew everything about Teresa's relationship with Nick. The same could not be said about Nick with regard to Teresa's relationship with Annie. In her imagination, Teresa and Annie would spend time in a variety of ways, and always ended in bed together. Sharing a bed was always the endpoint of her fantasies involving Annie. Not so that she could imagine the sex they would enjoy together, though she did that too, but mostly for the intimacy she imagined they would have, woman to woman, skin on skin.

Annie's response to the kiss on the ward presented the possibility that Teresa need not simply *imagine* herself and Annie spending time together in the future. If she had interpreted Annie's response correctly, and she was sure she had, the door was open to something more concrete than fantasy. Could Teresa walk through it? Is that what Annie was waiting for? Had Annie made all the running she could make, and now needed Teresa to demonstrate her boldness? The kiss was a beginning, but what would be the end?

Stop thinking. For God sake, stop thinking. Just stop. Just stop.

Teresa walked into the bathroom, washed herself, got dressed, went downstairs, put on her coat, opened the front door, pulled her bicycle away from the front wall of the house, blew out her cheeks, and set off into the blackout towards the cottage hospital.

Chapter 7

PAT HAD STAYED at the church far longer than she intended. She hadn't anticipated how much she would enjoy simply being out of Joyce Cameron's house, away from Bob, even if it was at a funeral. Funerals were social events of a kind, after all, and once feelings of sympathy had been delivered, talk had turned with others to the war and village life. When Erica asked Pat to return to her house for Will's wake, Pat had seen no reason to decline. It was Bob's own decision not to accompany her to offer his condolences in person, and his decision alone to return to his work. He was in no position to begrudge Pat spending a couple of hours in the company of her friends at Erica's house.

This was what she told herself after she finally left Erica's, and made her way back to Joyce Cameron's cottage. Joyce had decided to stay a little while longer, sensing an opportunity to play Great Paxford's 'mourner-in-chief' before anyone from the rest of the village could assume the mantle.

As she approached the cottage, Pat expected to hear the familiar, jarring fusillade of Bob's fingers hammering away at his typewriter keys. But there was no sound at all coming through the windows. It was nearly half-past nine in the evening, so Pat supposed Bob must have taken himself to bed. She quietly entered the cottage, and silently removed her hat and coat and placed them beside Bob's on the coat rack. She was so intent on not making any noise that might disturb her husband upstairs that she nearly jumped out of her skin when Bob pulled open the door to the living room and hissed, 'Where *the hell* have you been?!'

Pat was used to being ambushed by Bob, though each time took her by surprise in its own unique way.

'You scared the life out of me!' she cried, catching her breath.

'Answer my question!' he demanded.

'You know where I've been,' she said, trying to sound utterly reasonable in the face of Bob's unreasonable question. 'You saw me walk over to Erica at the church. I then went back to her house, for the wake.'

'You should've told me,' he snarled. 'I've been waiting here for hours. I had to make my own supper.'

Pat looked at Bob piteously. It was at times like this that she felt more hostility towards herself for being married to such a creature than towards Bob.

'I would have thought it was fairly obvious that if I didn't come straight back from church I would've gone back to the Campbell house with everyone else.'

She maintained her tone of matter-of-factness, forcing Bob to choose between backing down in the face of her reasonable manner, or continue to feel slighted by her failure to show him due deference by returning for his permission to go to the wake.

Bob gripped her wrist tightly and pulled her towards him. His face was inches from hers now, and she could smell the familiar smell of beer on his breath, confirming her suspicions that he had been drinking.

'What should have been obvious to you, *Patricia*, is that you don't stay out all night as if you *don't* have a husband waiting for you at home.'

His grip on her wrist tightened and Pat could feel the muscle beneath her skin crushed against the bones of her forearm. She winced with pain but continued to stare at him with defiance.

'I didn't stay out all night. Only for a few hours. You decided not to come over and offer your condolences directly. I assumed you had come back to work and that I was a free agent for the night.'

'As long as you're married to me, you are *never* a free agent,' he said, spittle flying into her face. 'Do you understand?'

'I *understand* that no one will ever speak of you, Bob, as I heard *everyone* at Erica's house speak of Will.'

She could see in his eyes that her words were taking longer to process in his brain than if he hadn't been drinking all evening. His grip on her wrist was like a vice, as each word registered, one after the other.

'What did you say when people asked where I was?' he demanded.

'I said nothing, Bob. Because nobody asked.'

The pain in her wrist was now excruciating. Through bitter experience, Pat knew not to try to pull away. It would trigger a rapid escalation in violence towards her. Instead, she tried to distract herself from the pain by whispering a single word to herself, over and over.

'*Coward. Coward. Coward . . .*'

Bob couldn't hear what Pat was saying, but he could see her lips moving.

'What? What are you saying?'

Pat looked at him with disdain.

'You wouldn't behave like this if Joyce were here,' she said. 'That makes you a coward, Bob.'

She could see his breathing become more laboured as he tried to work himself into a fury against the restraining force of the alcohol coursing around his system.

'But she will be any moment. I could see her making the rounds outside the village hall, saying goodbye, as I left the house.'

Bob glared at his wife for several long moments and then threw her arm back into her face with such force that her hand slammed against her nose. A few seconds later, Pat felt a dull trickle of blood from her left nostril. At that moment they both heard the sound of Joyce's footsteps coming up the garden path towards the front door.

'Sort yourself out, woman,' he snapped. 'Make yourself decent.'

Pat knew this meant she was to make sure that no trace of his aggression towards her should be visible to anyone else.

'Then make a pot of tea. And put some biscuits out.'

Pat nodded passively.

Bob looked at her coldly for several more moments before returning into the front room and slamming the door behind him. Pat slowly wiped the blood that had been accumulating above her upper lip with the back of hand and looked at the red smear.

Bob draws my blood. Marek only ever draws my love.

She straightened herself out, calmed herself, and hurried through to the kitchen just seconds before Joyce came into the gloomy hall.

Chapter 8

IN THE DAYS following Will's funeral, his wife and daughters drifted slowly from room to room, unable to settle in any of them. It was as if in Will's absence Laura, Kate, and Erica didn't know how to pick up the threads of their lives. In the past, when Will might have been away at a medical conference, or visiting his parents in the south of England, he was always expected back. No routines need be disrupted. Even during Will's last days when his presence in the world diminished hour by hour, the timetable of the house was built around him. Now Will was dead and buried the Campbell women struggled to process his permanent absence.

Kate took refuge in the fact she was due to return to Manchester to continue her nursing studies, hoping the day-to-day demands at the hospital would take over her days, much as they had when her own young husband had been killed in training.

For Laura and Erica, the changes to daily life were both small and large.

Eating with Will in the dining room was something Erica tried to maintain until the very end. On the occasions Will was unable to leave his bed, Erica and the girls decamped to his room and ate with him. Now, with Kate returned to Manchester and Laura in and out of the house doing an increasing number of shifts at the Observation Corps, or seeing her beau, Tom, Erica had to get used to eating most of her meals alone. Sometimes she would open her mouth to say something to Will or one of the girls then realised they weren't there. She closed her mouth and continued to eat in silence.

When Laura was at home, she had become used to popping in on her father at irregular times. Either in his surgery when he was still working, or in the sitting room, or latterly, when he was laid up in bed. Now Laura found herself coming downstairs and automatically heading towards her father's surgery to pop in to say hello. Each time she had to stop short of going into the room where she imagined he would be. With the recent deaths of her brother-in-law, Jack, and now her father, maturity came to Laura both fast and hard.

The other new accommodation Laura had to make was the way people in the village reacted when she walked or cycled through on errands or to get to the Observation Post. People she scarcely knew well would nod solemnly at her as they passed, or offer strained smiles within the shadow of the brim of their hats. Some stopped to ask how she was 'bearing up', an expression that left Laura nonplussed until she realised that those asking were only being polite and required the most basic reassurance. Laura quickly understood that all questions about her feelings in the aftermath of her father's death were not required to be answered honestly, but with a formality that belied her true feelings and, where possible, in a mildly comforting tone.

I'm feeling terrible, the worst I've ever felt in my entire life, and I don't expect that to change soon, if ever. But if I said that to people they would be horrified.

Yet Laura had also seen a few people coming towards her cross the road ahead to avoid having to say anything to her, not having the wherewithal to broach her father's death. Initially this angered her. But gradually, she found it suited her, as she had less and less desire to talk about her feelings, regardless of whether they had become sanitised for public consumption.

And all the while her father's last words to her played on a loop, 'You good doctor . . .'

It was while walking with Tom one cold, blustery, mid-November afternoon that Laura finally built up the nerve to mention her father's final words to her. Tom turned to her with an expression of surprise, as if becoming a doctor was the last thing he imagined Laura either could or should pursue.

'Do you think it's a ridiculous suggestion?' she asked, already suspecting his answer.

Tom hesitated for a few moments, collecting his thoughts so that he could say what he meant very clearly, without offending her.

'It's not that I think it's ridiculous. I've simply never heard you express any desire to study medicine.'

'You haven't heard me express my desire to study anything in particular.'

'True,' Tom said, feeling relieved that he appeared to have avoided an accusation of disloyalty. 'But I always imagined people drawn towards that field express an interest relatively early, and pursue it single-mindedly. Certainly, the boys in my last year at school who wanted to study medicine made that intention clear by about fourteen or fifteen.'

'That doesn't mean everyone has to. What happened at your boys' boarding school doesn't have to be a template for everyone else, does it?'

'I didn't say it did,' said Tom, back on the defensive. He was wary about being drawn into an argument, and struck out for firm ground. 'So, does that mean you have given it serious thought?' he asked in an upbeat fashion that he hoped Laura would interpret as him thinking it was a terrific idea.

'Since Dad suggested it, you mean?'

'I imagine you've given it some thought since then. But before that. Off your own bat. Had you ever thought of going into medicine and becoming a doctor independently of anything anyone else may have said to you?'

Laura gave his question a few moments' thought.

'No, if I'm honest. But as I just said, I haven't given a great deal of thought to what I might do. I think the war sort of stopped me going down the "planning" path.'

Tom frowned before he could stop himself. 'I don't really think you can use the war as an excuse.'

'Why not? I would have thought it's the perfect excuse for not being able to seriously think about one's future. We could be invaded tomorrow and be turned into a slave nation, working for the Third Reich.'

Tom smiled. He admired Laura's combative spirit, refusing to be subdued by counter-arguments.

'Given we aren't yet slaves for the Fuhrer, I'm still unsure the war's a reasonable excuse for not thinking about what you might like to do with your life. Especially for girls.'

'A bomb might fall on me tomorrow,' Laura interrupted conclusively. 'An army truck might run me over. Another aeroplane might crash into our house, killing us all. It would be the most awful luck, but it could happen. Anything could.'

Tom took a deep breath, controlling his impatience at what he considered to be Laura's wilful determination to disagree with him.

'Including absolutely nothing,' he said. 'Look, all I'm saying is that in my experience chaps who want to become doctors express some form of vocational spirit beforehand. I suspect that's a requirement, don't you?'

Laura looked into the far distance, over the rolling landscape of Cheshire.

'It may be a requirement of "chaps". But I don't think it should necessarily exclude the rest of us who haven't previously given it a great deal of thought, but who then *do*.'

'But isn't it entirely possible you are only thinking about it because your father suggested it?'

'Meaning what? What are you getting at, Tom?'

'Your father was very ill at the time. Every word he was able to say carried additional weight because of the effort it took to express it. I'm simply asking if you might be thinking more seriously about what he said because of his condition than if he had expressed the same view when he wasn't sick.'

'I have thought of that. I'm not a complete idiot, Tom.'

Tom started to feel boxed in. Whatever he said in relation to Laura's father's final words to her seemed to be inadequate or provocative. While this walk with Laura was a very welcome distraction from work at the station it wasn't the calming, peaceful stroll with 'his girl' that he'd been looking forward to all morning. He glanced at her, and could see she was frustrated. He took a deep breath and decided to try a different tack.

'Perhaps I'm completely wrong. Perhaps you're right. Perhaps chaps and girls take different routes towards deciding what they want to do with their lives. Perhaps it does sometimes take someone else to see something in us to make us think of pursuing a particular course we never previously thought of. That's certainly been true for me recently—'

Laura turned and smiled. Tom felt his heart lift a little.

'That's all I mean,' she said. 'Perhaps my father saw something in me that I haven't seen in myself. After all, I enjoy the sciences. And I've always taken an interest in what he was doing in the surgery.'

Tom nodded. 'Who would be more qualified to see the makings of another doctor in his own daughter than *a doctor*? Perhaps you should speak to Dr Rosen about it. She may have had a similar experience.'

'Because she's female? Not all women are the same, Tom, you must have noticed that much.'

'I didn't say that. I meant, because she's a doctor, and because she's a female one she might have a useful perspective on what we're discussing.'

Laura continued to look at Tom, nodding encouragingly, not wanting to make him feel too self-conscious. She did value his perspective on things. It had been Tom who'd suggested she apply to join the Observation Corps after she was thrown out of the WAAF, and she had never regretted following the advice.

'She might,' Laura said. 'It's not a *completely* stupid idea.'

'Thank you *so* much,' Tom said, grinning.

He pulled Laura to him and kissed her on the lips. She kissed him back twice as hard. She always kissed him back twice as hard. After a moment, she pulled away and looked at him with a puzzled expression.

'What did you mean when you said, "that's certainly been true for me recently"?'

Tom looked confused, as if he had completely forgotten everything he said the moment he said it. Laura re-phrased the question.

'You said, perhaps it takes other people to see something in us to make us think of doing something we hadn't previously thought of doing. You then said, "that's certainly been true for me recently." What did you mean?'

'Just something Wing Commander Lucas said to me a week or so ago. He asked if I'd ever thought of becoming a flyer, because he thought I had the right temperament for it.'

Laura looked at Tom, and suddenly felt a little sick.

'A pilot? You told me you had no desire to fly.'

'That was true a while ago. When we met. A lot has changed since then. Perhaps I have, too.'

Laura looked at him, blinking slowly to try to keep her emotions from running away with her. His being a ground-based RAF driver wasn't the only, or even the main reason she had opened herself to the possibility of becoming Tom's girlfriend. But had he been a pilot when they met that would never have happened. Not after she had lived through Kate's torment over Jack.

'You can't be a pilot,' she said.

'Why not?' asked Tom.

'Because you're a driver.'

'I could *drive* a plane. You'll have to do better than that.'

'All right. Because I forbid it.'

Tom looked at Laura and could see she was deadly serious, however comical her words initially sounded.

'So . . . you can become a doctor because your father suggested it, but I can't become a pilot because my boss suggested it?'

'He only suggested it because he's short of pilots.'

'I don't think that's true. Anyway, who's to say your father only suggested you become a doctor because we have a shortage of male doctors at the moment?'

Laura's eyes started to prick. She blinked hard to force back any tears that threatened to form.

'I don't care, Tom. You are not to become a pilot. Not if you want to continue to step out with me. I expressly forbid it.'

Tom realised that saying anything more would only add fuel to a fire he wanted to extinguish as quickly as possible.

'It was only a passing comment,' he said. 'That's all it was. I do understand how Jack's death affected you.'

He kissed Laura on the cheek, threaded his arm through hers, and pulled her forward gently to resume their walk. She allowed him to lead her on, and they walked in silence for nearly a minute.

In that brief period, Laura understood how deeply her feelings for Tom now ran. She didn't know the precise statistics, but she knew enough about the survival rates of RAF pilots to want Tom to be anything but one of them. That said, she didn't want to push him towards an entrenched position, so she chose to drop the subject in the hope the idea would wither away from neglect.

From Tom's perspective, he had no desire to re-ignite the conversation about Laura becoming a doctor – an idea he didn't wish to encourage as it could take her out of the area and, given the rapid churn of events caused by the war, out of his life.

They continued in silence, arm in arm, each keeping their own counsel, pretending to admire different parts of the windblown, rain swept Cheshire landscape they were slowly passing through.

Chapter 9

WHILE ANNIE HADN'T fully recovered from her injuries, at the start of her most recent visit Teresa learned that the aviator was making great strides. Annie was over the worst of her operation and entering a period of recovery. The medical staff were very attentive and revered Annie as an exotic (an air*woman*!) who had sustained her injuries in service of her country. Teresa had noticed the hospital staff gave Annie little extras on the quiet. Three pillows instead of two. An extra potato for supper. A little more fruit than other patients on the ward. Annie accepted them with small smiles of appreciation.

But she clearly hated lying around in hospital 'like a corpse' – as she described herself – and was working hard to make her way to the lavatory and back without an escort.

'It means I don't have to wait until a nurse or orderly is available. Nor do I have the distraction of someone lurking outside the toilet door,' Annie said. 'Bugger that for a game of soldiers!'

Teresa had been visiting Annie daily, resisting the urge to walk over in the morning so as to give herself something to look forward to as the empty hours passed. It helped give the day some structure. Prior to getting married, teaching had left Teresa with no time to worry about how to fill her day. Every minute was accounted for. Yet since being unceremoniously yanked from her position in the village school to allow the local authority to hand her job to a man, finding a way to shape her waking hours had proved a tremendous challenge.

She read a great deal more than she had previously, and enjoyed it. In the spirit of supporting her local novelist, Teresa had even attempted Bob's novel based on his supposed-exploits during the Dunkirk evacuation, but found it written like a newspaper story – fast-paced, thick with plot but thin on character, lacking in any emotional depth or psychological insight.

Teresa also had time to almost scientifically cleanse her house of all dirt, something that had become a creeping obsession; an outcome Teresa regarded ironically, since her previous disposition was to relegate housework to the very bottom of any list of necessary things to do.

She went for long morning walks into the countryside, where her enjoyment was marred by the knowledge that she would rather be walking with Nick or Annie. Before her marriage, Teresa went out almost daily with Alison and her dog. Now, though walking alone did allow her mind to slip its bridle of domesticity, it nevertheless amplified how estranged she had become from her old self.

It was little wonder Teresa had come to rely on her hospital visits to Annie as much as – if not more than – Annie looked forward to them.

Usually, they would chat as they played a board game, the board resting on Annie's lap as she sat up in bed. Or they chatted as they played cards. Annie was fascinated about Teresa's life with Nick.

'I'm not meaning to pry or pass judgement,' she said. 'I just want to understand what you enjoy about married life? Because for me, if one's preference is for women it makes little sense to marry a man unless it's due to some form of *force majeure* – a pregnancy, or . . .' Annie decided not to finish her sentence.

'Or in desperation?' Teresa was not so coy as her playing partner.

'I know many women opt for marriage as a way of obtaining a certain kind of social acceptability—'

'A shield against the prying eyes of others,' said Teresa.

Teresa's life was lived on the precipice of possible scandal. She had seen at least three friends make just a single mistake, have their sexuality exposed, and fall into the abyss of disgrace. One had tried to take her life as a consequence, so malicious had been the level of humiliation she had been forced to endure for loving another woman. Connie, Teresa's lover before she sought sanctuary in Great

Paxford from possible scandal in Liverpool, planned to start a new, freer life in America, but was lost in the Atlantic when the ship carrying her was torpedoed by a German U-boat. The threat of exposure gave Teresa's life a constant thrum of stress that she had learned to live with, though it took its toll on her. Its level had risen unexpectedly with marriage, as her union with a man of status like Nick elevated the height from which she might potentially fall. It wasn't that Teresa had any cause to distrust Annie *per se*, but fear of betrayal had become a form of self-protection. In her experience, when provoked, folk reverted to self-preservation, whatever the cost to others.

'I'd never have placed you in the category of someone who felt the need to take such a drastic course as *marriage*,' Annie said. 'You always seemed to be brimming with a mixture of self-confidence and a take-me-or-leave-me defiance.'

'Appearances can be deceptive,' said Teresa. 'Also, you have little idea of what I've experienced in the past that's left me with a deep-rooted fear around exposure. I'm assuming you've had little of that.'

Annie shook her head. 'No,' she said. 'None. As a pilot, I operate in a man's world. I get respect for my prowess in the cockpit. Where RAF pilots are only required to master one or two aircraft, we in the WAAF have to fly all sorts. We're valued for what we do. The men I work alongside essentially treat me as an honorary man, and take little interest in my private affairs.'

'But what if one of them should begin signalling romantic intentions?'

'Instant deflection. I tell them I never mix business with pleasure.'

'I don't have the same luxury,' Teresa said. 'As a teacher you find yourself continually vulnerable to questions about your private life – from pupils and parents alike. They all want to know what's going on.'

'That's not fair.'

Teresa shrugged. 'It's part of the job. Children are just fascinated by everything about their teachers. Parents want to be reassured we're a sound influence on their kids. I'd be the same.'

Having spent more time alone in Teresa's company, Annie had started to develop an understanding about where her fears originated.

Though Annie had been sceptical about Teresa's motives for getting married to Nick, she realised Teresa didn't feel as absolute about her sexuality as she did. Teresa apologised neither for the feelings she had for Nick nor for those she admitted having for Annie.

Annie asked Teresa to describe how she managed such conflicting feelings

'It's difficult to explain,' Teresa said. 'I don't see them as "conflicting". My feelings for each of you don't cancel out my feelings for the other. The strength may vary from day to day. They ebb and flow to varying degrees, but both are present at the same time. I suppose it feels sort of fluid. But I never feel as if I'm switching between you.'

'Like a movable feast?' asked Annie. 'Depending on what you fancy from one day to the next.'

Teresa shook her head.

'I can't control it. It's simply as if I carry both feelings with me simultaneously, and each satisfies a different aspect of me.'

At the WI committee meeting later that afternoon in Frances's dining room, Teresa struggled to keep up with the discussion. Like an engine with a faulty clutch, her mind kept slipping between the business at hand and her earlier conversation with Annie at the hospital. The latter was making concentrating on the former almost impossible.

Noah, Frances's soon-to-be adopted son, was living permanently at the house and attending the village school. The boy was the product of a ten-year, secret relationship between Frances's husband, Peter, and his company accountant, Helen, both of whom died in a car accident. In spite of his beginnings, with Noah Frances appeared more content and vibrant than her friends had seen since the time before Peter's death.

Having solemnly iterated the committee's condolences to Erica Campbell for the benefit of the minutes, Frances briskly moved through her analysis of the soup kitchen at St Mark's, and the beds they'd set up in the village hall to serve the trekkers from Liverpool and Crewe seeking safety from nightly bombing before trudging back to work the next day. On average, the project was managing to feed between one hundred and one hundred and thirty men, women and children each night, and the village hall could accommodate almost as many.

'And we shall continue the operation for as long as it's needed, ladies!' said Frances with her old gusto. 'The feared rise in crime from the trekkers has failed to appear and the naysayers have fallen silent in the face of the programme's clear success,' she reported with relish.

Teresa had undertaken more shifts at the soup kitchen than most. With Nick remaining at the station each night until the fate of all his pilots had been established, Teresa had found it increasingly difficult to fill the long evening hours by herself. Pouring soup and cutting bread for grateful strangers offered welcome relief from loneliness. She usually chose shifts with Alison, and watched with pleasure as her former, introverted landlady quietly blossomed under the attention of the trekker, John Smith, who – rather tellingly from Teresa's perspective – also made a point of making it into Great Paxford when Alison was on shift. It made Teresa's heart leap a little with joy to see Alison become the focus of a man who so clearly admired her.

Also, helping at the soup kitchen afforded Teresa an opportunity to interrogate trekkers for the latest news about her home city.

Liverpool had been under heavy bombardment by the Luftwaffe from the moment German High Command shelved its plan to invade Great Britain in favour of neutralising it at arm's length. The explosive assault on its food supply, energy resources, infrastructure and population was relentless. The city's docks were ablaze most nights, and the city itself, a great mouth on the west coast of Britain gulping in valuable resources from the Atlantic, offered itself as a major and easy target for German bombs.

Teresa sometimes felt intense spasms of guilt that she had made her life in the rural community of Great Paxford while her fellow Liverpudlians suffered and died beneath the German blitzkrieg. At the WI meeting, as she contemplated the latest information she'd received about her home city suffering a particularly heavy raid that lasted over ten hours, Teresa suddenly became aware of Frances speaking about yet another new initiative she hoped the members might implement. Teresa re-tuned her internal wireless to Frances's wavelength and turned to face the branch Chair.

'As successful as the soup kitchen has been,' Frances said, 'we must not pat ourselves on the back and merely tread water. Our women are capable of great things, but they must be pushed – just as our menfolk are being pushed beyond what they think possible in north Africa. Lord Beaverbrook has urged the nation in every sphere to achieve maximum capacity and maximum output. When I heard him on the wireless I didn't only hear him speaking to our factory workers making products for the war. I heard him speaking to women like us, and I asked myself, "What else can we do?"

'An answer came to me the next day as I was walking back from my sister's house with Noah. We were passing a field and watched a farmer's wife picking her way across the sodden earth towards her husband and workers with wrapped sandwiches for their lunch. By bringing them their food she ensured they could eat on the land and not lose time by tramping back and forth to the farmhouse. Noah and I watched to see how far she would have to go, and I must admit she went so far that we lost track of her. And it occurred to me that not only was making all those sandwiches using that woman's time that might be better spent on farming, but so was the daily hike backwards and forwards to deliver them.'

Teresa saw Alison watching Frances with a sober eye. When she had been lodging with Alison, Teresa had regularly burst out laughing at Alison's colourful descriptions of some of Frances's more vaunting ambitions for the WI.

'Sometimes I think she genuinely sees us as a battalion of social warriors rather than a group of women who like to meet once a month mostly to have fun and do useful – and sometimes not so useful – things. Lord knows, there is only so much we can do.'

She knew Frances agreed with that in principle, but sometimes allowed ideas to run away with her. At which point 'there's only so much we can do' became 'there's only so much you can do, but with me cracking my whip you'll do so much more than you ever wanted, or dreamt of doing!'

Though they laughed at Frances from time to time, it was always with great affection. Both Teresa and Alison knew the value of her leadership, and that without her the branch would either be closed, or a shadow of what it currently was.

Teresa tried to keep a grip on what Frances was now saying. *Something about a farmer's wife and sandwiches?*

It sounded as if she was proposing the branch should organise some sort of vehicle to be driven from farm to farm at lunchtime, distributing beer and vittles to farm workers, and thereby release all farmers' wives to more productive labour on the land.

Before she could speak up, Sarah said what she was thinking, 'We couldn't possibly obtain enough petrol to make the idea viable, Frances.'

As she generally did where her ideas were concerned, Frances had already second-guessed the most obvious objections, suggesting that instead of using a car or a van, the branch could send its members out on bicycles.

Teresa frowned at the prospect.

'Who's going to organise that, day after day? What if someone falls sick and can't do their round? What happens to the farmers' lunch under those circumstances?

And how many lunches can any woman realistically transport around by bicycle?'

As Frances launched into a rearguard argument of what was to prove an insufficiently supported venture, Teresa's mind once again drifted back to her most recent visit to the cottage hospital. Meanwhile, the meeting moved on to a resolution tabled by Sarah that the WI should go out of its way to ensure the women of Great Paxford had as enjoyable a 1940 Christmas as was possible with so many men away.

'And for the children,' Teresa said, her attention brought back to the dining room by the word Christmas, 'a family time.'

The other committee members turned to her.

'If I was still teaching at school I would use this Christmas to remind my children of the values we're fighting to preserve. The same values, and way of life, Hitler's trying to destroy.'

Alison looked fondly at her former lodger and smiled. *Never stops thinking of the children.*

'Isn't that a bit difficult?' Frances asked. 'It is all rather dark, after all. Dunkirk. The Blitz. Mass bombing. Invasion. I look at Noah racing around pretending to shoot everything and I don't know where to start to talk to him about it all.'

'There are ways of doing it nicely,' Teresa said. 'I'd ask them if they were looking forward to Christmas. And I'd talk to them about how it's going to be very different to previous Christmases, because they won't be able to see some people who matter to them very much. But I would explain it's important to make Christmas as cheery as possible because if we are all miserable and down then the Nazis have started to win. We mustn't let the children think that could be a possibility, as it would start to affect them quite badly.'

Teresa looked around the room. Everyone at the table nodded in agreement.

'There will be some people who will want nothing to do with Christmas at the moment,' said Frances, 'and we need to respect that. I am thinking mainly of our members who may have lost men at Dunkirk or in the RAF.'

'Or relatives in Liverpool,' said Alison.

'How is *your* Liverpool friend?' Sarah enquired.

Alison looked at Sarah sharply. 'Liverpool friend?'

Sarah nodded. 'I've not seen him in the village for a while.'

'He came last week,' Alison said, clearly ruffled to be talking about the friendship which had been developing since they'd first met at Frances's house, when John had brought Noah back to Great Paxford after he had run away from boarding school.

'So, he's all right,' Sarah said. 'That's good.'

'He is,' said Alison, 'but there's a tremendous amount of suffering. Tremendous. The hammering the city takes each night, it's a wonder anyone's still there.'

Everyone around the table fell silent as they thought of all the people killed nightly and horribly during the German raids.

'We can't do more for them than we are doing currently,' said Frances, 'and we don't want to appear more interested in the welfare of outsiders than of our fellow villagers. So, perhaps we can do more to support our own people and what *they* might be going through, by holding a party of some kind in the village hall that all our families – in whatever order they may currently be – could attend?'

'Might a party seem a little too frivolous to some?' asked Sarah.

'Nonsense!' said Frances. 'I can't think of a better way of thumbing our nose at that ghastly little man and his ridiculous little moustache than by British people having fun under the flight path of his horrific bombers!'

It was agreed, almost by royal decree. Frances was as close to someone with royal bearing as the village could offer – and though not actually royal, she could muster imperiousness as well as any with true blue blood. The WI would put on a Christmas party in the village hall for all the families of Great Paxford with the only requirement being that everyone should have fun.

As she cycled slowly home after the meeting, Teresa wondered what to make for supper. She had yet to hear from

Nick about whether he was likely to be home in time, or would be eating at the station. As had become one of many new habits, Teresa would prepare something that could be warmed up at short notice. Nick came home for his evening meal more than he had during the first few weeks of their marriage, when Teresa was finding her feet as a cook. He now generally finished what she put in front of him with accompanying agreeable noises. Teresa's early suspicion that he was putting it on for her self-esteem had ebbed away. She narrowed her focus to food she knew he liked, and cooked those seven dishes for him on rotation; so far, without complaint. In the meantime, she was teaching herself a few other recipes for when Nick grew tired of the predictability of her current menu.

The discussion at the committee meeting about doing what they could for people close to home had given Teresa an idea. She wondered if it wasn't time for Annie to leave hospital and free up her bed for someone else. She sensed the medical staff were unlikely to hasten their favourite patient from the ward, and considered whether *she* might take on the task of seeing Annie through her rehabilitation. It was entirely possible that Annie might prefer to return to the south and recuperate with her family. Teresa had no idea, as she had neither broached the subject of Annie leaving hospital, nor Annie's family situation. Under the right conditions, it might be that Annie would prefer to stay in Cheshire, near her colleagues at Tabley Wood. Staying in Teresa and Nick's house. Looked after by Teresa.

It's just a thought. Nothing more. An idea. A suggestion. After all, I now have the time at my disposal to look after someone as much as the nurses at the hospital. It would be a little project. Company for me, too. Would Nick object? Difficult to say. Annie has known him far longer than he's known me. I don't think he would. In fact, I'm sure he would think it's an excellent idea all round.

Teresa pedalled home with a renewed sense of purpose. She now had two conversations to plan. All in all, she felt the committee meeting had proved very productive.

Chapter 10

Pat and Joyce strolled back from the WI committee meeting debating what to have for lunch, only to find Bob in the kitchen making pilchards, boiled potatoes, and carrots. It would be an understatement to say they were taken by surprise. In Pat and Bob's time as lodgers in her house, Joyce couldn't recall ever actually seeing Bob in her kitchen. As for Pat, the last time she could recall Bob ever preparing food for her was when they lived in Manchester; before they moved to Great Paxford fifteen years ago so Bob could pursue what he called 'the writer's life' of quiet, rural contemplation interspersed with bursts of intense creativity. In their early Manchester days Bob frequently cooked for Pat. His speciality was adventurous dishes designed to show off his skills. The desire to impress Pat waned significantly after they were married, and disappeared completely within ten years.

'What's brought this on?' asked Pat, looking at the bubbling pans on the stove, trying to suppress any tone of incredulity in her voice.

'Can't a man make lunch for his wife and landlady?' Bob replied with a warm smile.

'Please don't call me that, Mr Simms,' said Joyce. 'You know very well I don't see our association in that light at all. You are my very welcome *guests*.'

I don't like this. Something's afoot. Bob never cooks.

'I'm not objecting to you making lunch for me – us – Bob. But you must admit it's unusual.'

'Let's not go overboard, Patricia. It's only pilchards, boiled potatoes, and carrots. I thought it high time to demonstrate a little appreciation for the two women who look after me.'

Pilchards, boiled potatoes, and carrots?

Pat suddenly remembered that the last time she had made that same meal the pilchards had been on the turn and caused Bob terrible food poisoning. He'd wolfed down the fish without noticing they were tainted, and collapsed shortly afterwards. Almost the first words he uttered upon his return from hospital were to accuse Pat of trying to kill him.

There are days I wish I had been trying to kill him – I might have done it with more conviction and finished the job.

Now, as she waited in the front room with Joyce, Pat silently interrogated what kind of 'message' Bob might be trying to send by making the same meal for her.

Assuming he is sending me a message. Of course, he's sending a message! Bob never does anything without a reason. Everything is calculated to bring him some kind of advantage. So why would he decide to do this now? This of

all meals. Pilchards. Potatoes. And carrots. What's he up to?
What has he done? What does Bob want?

In her heart, Pat knew not to trust Bob when he treated her with respect. Even if he seemed to mean it at the time, it seldom lasted – either because something would come along to darken Bob's mood, or because he was simply unable to sustain pleasantness for more than a few days on end. Pat watched as Joyce poured them each a small sherry 'to celebrate the special occasion'. For Joyce, this was clearly an event to savour.

'Who would imagine a writer of Mr Simms's stature would be making *me* luncheon?' she said, in an arch attempt to cast herself as utterly undeserving of a meal as sumptuous as a prosaic plate of pilchards, potatoes, and carrots. 'I shall be dining out on this for years to come.'

Pat knew Joyce was not a stupid woman, and yet she also knew Joyce had read Bob's 'Dunkirk' novel and had genuinely enjoyed it.

'Not because it possesses any great literary merit,' she had confided to Pat. 'But because it's an easy, thrilling read. To be able to turn such a vast, terrible event as the evacuation from Dunkirk into an engrossing thriller is no mean feat, Patricia. No mean feat at all. Great skill is clearly involved. Of the highest order.'

What Joyce described as 'no mean feat' Pat considered to be rather disgusting, considering so many casualties of the evacuation were fresh in the ground or lying at the bottom of the English Channel. But whether Pat liked it or not, Bob *was* an accomplished writer of breathless plot that was almost entirely devoid of credible characters or insight. Bob had struck lucky with his first book – also a semi-fictionalised account of his experience of war: in the trenches of Flanders. What luck he'd had had been short-lived. Bob's attempt to rise to the challenge of surpassing his first novel came to nothing, and Pat found herself stuck with that most wretched of all creatures: a once-published writer of modest and dwindling ability.

Finally, lunch was ready, and Bob invited his wife and Joyce to seat themselves at the table while he fetched in the meal. Pat was on her guard from the off, scrutinising Bob's every gesture for some nuance that would give away his true intent.

Has he decided to kill me, poisoning me as he believed I once tried to poison him? Smell the pilchards before eating them. Taste a little before swallowing. Is he particular about which plate is mine and which is Joyce's? Or does he have to poison us both to make it appear like a terrible accident?

When the time came to eat, Bob looked at the two seated women and smiled.

'*Bon appetit*, ladies,' he said, pronouncing the French with heavy emphasis.

'It looks very appetising, Mr Simms. You've done a splendid job.'

'You haven't eaten it yet, Mrs C. Don't be impressed by appearance alone.'

Pat watched as Bob tucked into his own lunch, made by his own hand. She held back until Joyce had eaten several mouthfuls of hers, swallowed and survived, then slowly cut into various items on her own plate as if they might reveal the small drop of poison she imagined had been cunningly deposited into the middle of a potato, or a pilchard's belly.

'Come along, Patricia,' Bob said playfully. 'You've hardly touched yours.'

Pat looked at Bob, sensing she was being lured into a trap of some kind. Joyce continued to happily munch her way through her plate of food, oblivious to the currents of suspicion and presumed malice that invisibly swirled around her.

'Truth is, Bob, I'm not really all that hungry,' Pat said. 'Frances put out a lovely tea for the committee meeting. I'm still a little full from fruit cake.'

Bob turned to her, his eyes narrowing. 'But I've made this *specially*.'

'I know you have, Bob—' Pat said softly, careful not to sound ungrateful. 'And I greatly appreciate what you've done. Joyce and I were wondering what to make for lunch on the way back, so you can imagine how much of a welcome surprise it was to come in and find you at the stove.'

Bob looked at his wife. 'Well,' he said calmly, 'it's up to you. I can hardly be held responsible for what you may have already eaten this morning.'

He doesn't mind if I don't eat it. Perhaps he has simply made us lunch, with no ulterior motive other than to be pleasant and thank us for doing his bidding day and night.

'If you don't want it now,' Bob continued, 'why don't I put it in the oven for later, and you can have it this evening?'

Wait, wait, wait. One way or another he wants me to eat this. If not now, then tonight.

'Or *you* can have it later, Bob. I know how much you like pilchards.'

Bob leaned towards Joyce for a moment.

'I *did*, Mrs C,' he said conspiratorially. 'Until Pat tried to kill me with a pair last year!'

Joyce's eyes widened like saucers, eager to hear the story that Bob's headline promised.

'Food poisoning!' he said.

'You have to be so careful with fish,' Joyce said.

'I was in hospital for three days. I haven't touched pilchards since. But I woke up this morning and just had a yen for them. As if my fear had suddenly lifted and my old love of them had returned. Funny how the mind works. Perhaps it's very difficult to maintain certain feelings indefinitely. Eventually, the mind gets tired and says, "You know what, old chap, this is taking up too much energy, why not like them again?" Things change, don't they, Mrs C? That's what life is, don't you think – constant change?'

'That is a very wise thing to say, Mr Simms. A very astute observation.'

Not that astute. Fairly obvious.

99

'But you don't have to worry about these pilchards, Mrs C. Fresh off the boat this morning – I checked their eyes. Clear as marbles.'

Bob resumed eating.

'So, will you be all right to have mine later if I didn't feel like them, Bob?' Pat asked, trying once again not to sound suspicious.

'Why not? Better than letting them go to waste. Criminal to allow a fresh pilchard to go to waste, wouldn't you say, Mrs C?'

Joyce nodded. 'Brain food, they say,' she said. 'Good for your writing, no doubt.'

Bob smiled and nodded.

Pat watched him. The smile seemed genuine. Making lunch for them seemed genuine. Bob seemed almost carefree as he finished his own meal, and then carefully collected their plates and took them into the kitchen. Pat expected him to come back, but she soon heard water pouring from the tap as Bob washed up the plates and cutlery.

'What a lovely surprise this was,' Joyce said to Pat. 'I don't think I've ever had a man prepare a meal for me. Douglas never did. Not once.'

'And how many did you make for him?'

'Well, of course, thousands if you include breakfast. Many thousands over the years.'

Pat nodded. 'Perhaps I'll resist jumping over myself with gratitude that Bob's managed a single plate of pilchards since – I can't remember when.'

'Credit where credit's due, Patricia,' Joyce counselled. 'He didn't have to make us lunch at all.'

'True. Good old, Bob. Hurrah for him!'

The trace of irritation in Pat's voice wasn't actually directed at Bob's effort, poisonous or not. It was more a reflection of her frustration at not having been able to work out his underlying reason for making lunch. His writing had never been unduly troubled by subtext, and whenever he tried to behave archly Pat generally saw through it swiftly enough. Good Bob or bad Bob – what Pat saw was generally what Pat got. This lunchtime, however, she couldn't make a judgement about him either way. And without knowing the trigger for Bob's ostensibly pleasant behaviour she was unable to verify if he was being genuine or disingenuous. History had taught her to veer towards the latter. For her own safety, Pat's suspicion that he was up to no good remained.

Did he simply wake up this morning yearning for pilchards? It's possible, I suppose. Up until the day they nearly killed him he always enjoyed them. Or is all this a reflection of how pleased he is at how well his book is doing? He's always more pleasant when he feels appreciated and valued by the wider world. And if it is neither of those, if this is all just a terrible mask of some sort, the façade won't last. It never does. Some thorny thing will slip out. Stay on your guard, Pat. Smile. Nod. Play along. Don't draw attention to yourself. Keep safe. For Marek.

Chapter 11

WHILE STAN WAS away on active service, Steph took up the habit after supper of relaxing in his favourite chair, imagining that its arms were his. After a hard day's labour, she liked nothing more than to sink back into it, allowing its familiar scent of Stan to give the illusion he was close by. She would sit of an evening with a large mug of tea, and watch her son dozing on the old sofa. Steph too would gradually drift into sleep, waking an hour or so later to send Stanley up to bed, following shortly once she had washed up after supper, swept the floors, and cleaned and re-fed the stove.

This evening, however, Steph's mind was too occupied to even begin to drift away, ruminating over the recent visit by the reporter from the *Liverpool Echo*. The interview with Philip Shepherd had progressed in a similar fashion to the interview Steph and Little Stan had undergone with the police. Steph gave the same account as before, and Stanley repeated the little white lie about chasing the German pilot across the field and running him to ground, and not the other way around. When Steph heard Stanley repeat the falsehood she felt less bothered than she had the first time.

What difference if a small adjustment makes him feel better? It doesn't change what happened. Neither of us knows what the German was shouting. Stanley did end up fighting him hand-to-hand, which was brave of him.

Yet the issue continued to niggle away. Stanley's revised account demanded Steph collude with him. For a woman as steadfastly honest as Steph Farrow, it was a source of discomfort. While Steph could be excused for corroborating a slightly inaccurate account to the police in the immediate aftermath of the event, there was less excuse for repeating the deliberate error several days later. The first time could be discounted as a mistake in the heat of the moment. The second, if it ever came out, could seem like calculated misrepresentation.

But how could it be discovered? There were only three of us there, and one is dead. The boy only changed what happened to make himself bigger in the detective's eyes. Lads brag. Pride's a sin not a crime.

As she recalled the event to Shepherd, the dead face of the German pilot kept rising in her mind. Eyes motionless, looking upwards. Mouth locked into a grimace of surprise and pain. Shepherd hadn't been able to tell Steph when the article was likely to appear, only that it would be soon.

'The nation's back's against the wall. Hitler will try and invade us again, most likely. Your story, Mrs Farrow, will give people heart, make them feel that even if we are invaded, we could resist the Nazis on our own soil.'

Steph got out of the armchair and walked over to the dresser and opened the right-hand drawer. She took out the pad and a pen, and sat at the kitchen table to painstakingly write a letter of explanation to her husband about what was likely to appear in print any day now. With the promise from the detective that her details would not be revealed, Steph had hoped that this would all go away, and she wouldn't have to tell any of it to Stan – at least until the war was over. The last thing she wanted was for him to be worrying about her and Stanley when he should be worrying about keeping himself alive. Now, with the publication of her story in the *Echo*, she had no choice but to tell him everything before he either saw it himself in the newspaper, or worse, one of the fellows in his battalion brought it to his attention.

As she sat thinking how to start, she heard a noise from the front parlour. She turned and saw Stanley sitting up on the sofa, fuzzy with sleep.

'You should go to bed, son,' she told him.

'What're you doing?' he asked. 'Who're you writing to?'

'Think it's time I told your dad what happened. Don't want him finding out from anyone else. When the story comes out in the paper someone's bound to see it and tell him. Best it comes from me.'

'What're you going to say?'

'Like I said, what happened.'

Steph knew her son was asking her what she was going to tell his father about the pursuit across the field. He looked at her, knowing he couldn't openly ask her to lie. She looked at him for a few moments, before putting him out of his misery.

'I'm going to tell him you chased the pilot across the field and wrestled him to the ground.'

Stanley nodded in silence.

'Got no choice, have I, Stanley?' Steph said, a touch coldly. 'It's what you told both the police and the newspaper man. Have to keep it up now, don't we?'

Stanley nodded a second time.

'This is what happens when you don't tell the truth, Stanley. You have to keep not telling it.'

'I didn't mean to. When the policeman asked what happened that's how it came out in my head.'

Steph looked at him soberly. There was little point going over this now. *What's done is done*.

'Go to bed, Stanley.'

Stanley nodded, came over to his mother, kissed her forehead, and made his way slowly upstairs.

''Night, Ma . . .' he called from the staircase.

Steph didn't respond. She waited until she heard his bedroom door close before looking down at the empty sheet of paper on the table. The expanse of white paralysed her thinking. She picked up the pen, hoping it would trigger the flow of words. As someone new to expressing herself through the mechanical act of writing, the trigger failed to fire.

How do you tell your husband you've shot a man dead? How do you not make it sound like an adventure story, with a happy ending? How do I tell him it's robbed me of sleep every night since it happened – that I see the lad's face all day, and think about his mother constantly? How do I tell him I pulled the trigger without shouting a warning? And that Stanley ran for his life from the pilot but has told everyone it was the other way around?

Steph got up from the table and made herself another cup of tea and then sat down again and stared at the sheet of paper for over half an hour, trying to find a way to begin a letter she knew she had to write. Eventually, knowing she would be unable to sleep for another night if she didn't at least try, she picked up the pen and increased her grip on it. She took a deep breath, and in her slow, child-like hand, Steph began . . .

Dear Stan.

Hope you are not bored in barracks waiting for mobilisation. This is not a letter I ever thought I'd write to you. But what happened here a week and a half ago was never something I thought could happen. A German plane was shot down during a raid. One of the pilots went missing in the area. There was a manhunt but he wasn't found. Stanley was working by the copse at the bottom of the far field and he saw him camped in the trees. The German saw Stanley and there was a chase. Stanley chased the pilot. And ran

*him to ground. They fought on the field and I thought
the German was going to shoot Stanley. I ran out of
the house with the shotgun—*

Steph stopped writing and slowly read over the words she
had written. The story still seemed alien to her, as if the
events they described belonged to someone else.

This is the hardest thing I've ever done.

She picked up the pen and carefully placed the nib on the
page once more, and continued . . .

*Believing Little Stan was about to be shot I pulled
the trigger. Stanley was scared but unhurt. The pilot
died. I am struggling, Stan. People want to offer me
congratulations but I run from it. The dead man was
young, Stan, you see. Just a few years older than our
boy. I need you here. I need you here . . .*

Steph couldn't think of anything else to add. She signed
her name carefully, folded the page, and put it inside an
envelope.

The next morning, she slipped out before dawn into a
stiff rain to post the letter. She kept the letter dry in her
pocket, ensuring its precious message wasn't diluted or
damaged by water. As she heard the envelope hit the bottom of the post box she prayed for its swift delivery, and
an even swifter reply.

Chapter 12

ALTHOUGH LAURA WAS generally fearless when cornered, she felt considerably less brave offering herself up to the judgement of others. Avoiding public scrutiny in the wake of her ignominious affair with Wing Commander Bowers had been a significant reason behind joining the Observation Corps, where she could hide away for hours at a time, miles from anyone, and still fulfil a deep-rooted commitment to the war effort. However, the possibility that Myra Rosen, a young doctor no more than ten years older than Laura, might prove unable to stifle a sneering smile or a snort of derision at Laura's suggestion was too much for Laura to bear.

Instead, she raised the subject with Brian Bennett during her next shift at the Observation Post. Laura had come to appreciate Brian as a man of advanced years with a well-developed, sanguine eye on the world and the people in it.

Brian was an amateur astronomer who had applied to the Observation Corps in the mistaken belief it would give him access to telescopic equipment he was unable to afford himself. He was quietly scouring the dark skies above them through the post's powerful field binoculars when Laura casually mentioned that since her father's death she had been giving her own future a great deal of thought.

'I'm not surprised,' said Brian, as he continued to peer upwards. 'Death has a way of focusing the mind. If only briefly, before we fall back into old habits and start wasting time again.'

Laura hadn't expected quite such a philosophical response, but was grateful he hadn't lapsed into a series of platitudes about her father's demise. She wondered if Brian's interest in astronomy fuelled his tendency towards cosmic pronouncement, or whether it was the other way around. As she was trying to work out which it would be, Brian lowered the binoculars and looked across at her.

'Your father's death is a tragedy, Laura – for the village and for you personally, of course. But it is also a spur – not for the village, we'll just get on and find a new doctor. We have already, in the shape of Dr Rosen. Observe how quickly the village has mourned and moved on. Because that's what life does. It *moves on*, whether we want it to or not. We have to move with it or wake up one day thirty years hence and wonder why we did nothing with our lives. In that sense, it is a spur for *you*. Take heed.'

'That's precisely it, Mr Bennett. My father never wasted a moment of his life. Even when he was in his armchair smoking his pipe, he would invariably be reading the latest copy of *The Lancet*, or a research paper – to broaden his knowledge to make himself a better doctor for his patients.'

'There you are then,' said Brian, as if Laura had just confirmed everything he'd just said.

'There I am . . . *where*?' asked Laura, not catching Brian's drift.

'By your own analysis of your father's life you clearly understand the importance of using time effectively. My grandmother had a little phrase when I was a child, I've always remembered it. "Brian," she'd say, "waste time and time will waste you." I had no idea what she meant until I was old enough to learn the difference between indolence and relaxation. I recently read Howard Spring's new book, *Fame Is the Spur*, and it occurred to me he'd got the title wrong.'

'Because *time* is the spur!' Laura blurted out, finally coming into alignment with Brian's thinking.

'Precisely!' he confirmed. 'Fame is nothing but a desire for recognition. To achieve self-worth, we must feel the breath of time on our neck, urging us on productively, before it runs out.'

Laura was starting to enjoy this conversation, and barely noticed the evening air had chilled into night.

'So, what have *you* been thinking about your future, young lady?' Brian asked, his mind proving itself sharp and focused.

'Shortly before he died, in what I think were his last intelligible words to me, my father told me that he thought I might have the makings of a doctor.'

'I see,' said Brian.

He looked at Laura for a moment, then raised the binoculars to his eyes and looked directly at her. She was momentarily disconcerted.

'What are you doing, Mr Bennett?' Laura asked.

'Seeking the doctor within!' he declared, lowering the binoculars with a chuckle.

Laura persisted. 'Do *you* think it ridiculous?'

'Why should it be ridiculous?'

'Because becoming a doctor hadn't occurred to me before he mentioned it.'

'I see. Well, at what age did you learn to ride a bicycle?'

'I can't remember exactly. About nine or ten, I suppose.'

'Not earlier?'

'No.'

'Why not – a lot of children do?'

'Didn't want to.'

'And now you ride around like an expert.'

'I don't know about "expert", but I suppose I'm as good as anyone.'

'And what happened aged nine or ten to prompt you to learn?'

'My sister told me I should so we could go riding together.'

'Do you see?' said Brian. 'It took someone else to spark your interest, but once sparked you dived in and ran – or cycled away – with it.'

Laura saw the point Brian was trying to make, then just as instantly recognised its flaw.

'But shouldn't *wanting to become a doctor* come from within? From a sense of vocation?' In effect, she was putting to Brian the same argument Tom had put to her.

'These terms – "a sense of vocation" - what do they really mean? What is *a sense of vocation*, Laura? When does it begin? What doctor or chemist or astronomer can put their hand on their heart and say, "This was the moment I knew beyond all doubt I would become what I am today." Not one. Perhaps, living in your father's impressive shadow had made you secretly believe you were not clever enough to become what he was, closing all thought you might be a doctor too. Yet he could see it in you, even if you wouldn't even look to see it in yourself.'

Laura looked across at Brian Bennett and felt her heart pump with excitement. *What if he's right?!*

'My dear girl,' he continued, 'we must each find our own way through life. At times the path is crystal clear. Other times, it's confusing, or even obscured completely. If, on those occasions, we're lucky enough to find people who can point us in the right direction we shouldn't discard their insight because we feel we should have had it ourselves. We need all the help we can get to make a go of things. You're young. Your head is pulled in all sorts of directions from one minute to the next. You can't think of – or notice – *everything*.'

'You think I should listen to my father's advice?'

'Who knew you better than anyone?'

'My mother and father.'

'And of the two of them? Not who *loves* you more, because we must assume they loved you equally. But who would you say *knows* you best?'

It was a difficult question in one way, and easy in another. Laura didn't want to be disloyal to her mother but she knew that her father understood her better than anyone else did, or probably ever would. Throughout her childhood Laura was routinely known as 'daddy's little girl'.

'My father,' Laura said quietly.

'Well, there you are,' said Brian. 'There you very much *are*.'

Brian returned the binoculars to his eyes and turned his face once more to the stars.

'That doesn't mean you have to become a doctor, of course. That remains your choice. But in your position, I would at least consider your father's words as an invitation to take yourself seriously. Don't forget, when you applied to join the corps you hadn't been an observer before. I was opposed to you joining. But when you fought for it I saw something in you and decided, yes, this girl might have what it takes.'

'Does it take much to stare at the sky, Mr Bennett?'

'No, it doesn't. But it takes a great deal to sit patiently by yourself for hours on end, and then spring into action when the telephone rings, keep calm under pressure, keep the binns steady and in focus, and provide precise, detailed information that could save the lives of airmen when they are scrambled on the information we give Fighter Command. Without us the air-raid warning system can't operate, and interceptions can't be made.'

Laura pulled her collar around her neck against the night air. She could already taste the frost in it.

'What are you looking at?' she asked.

'Right now . . . Polaris,' he said. '*Alpha Ursae Minoris*. Also known as the North Star or Pole Star. The brightest star in the constellation of *Ursa Minor*.'

'You know so much.'

'Some might say that what I know amounts to a mass of useless information.'

'Where did your interest in astronomy come from?' she asked.

He lowered the binoculars and looked at her, and chuckled.

'In all honesty . . . I've no idea.'

'Why do you like it so much?'

'Puts everything into perspective. Makes everything very clear, at least to me.'

'In what way?'

'I look up and take great comfort from the fact that there is no sense to be made of anything really. There's no hidden meaning to any of it. It just *is*. So why worry unduly? Of course, that's easy for me to say because I'm sixty-seven, but I like to think I thought the same when I was half my age. Take what I say with a pinch of salt. My life's on the wane. Yours lies ahead of you. You've no choice but to worry about everything until you find a place in all this. So. Forgetting everyone else, what does Laura Campbell want to do with her life?'

Laura looked at the kindly, lively face regarding her, waiting for her answer. Brian wasn't being nosey or putting pressure on her to commit to anything she didn't wish to commit to. He simply wanted to see if Laura could answer the question.

Laura thought for a moment and then opened her mouth to speak. At that precise moment, the telephone rang from Sector Control, warning of an inbound Luftwaffe raid of up to forty aircraft, half an hour to the east, on the run in to Liverpool. In an instant, all thought of herself evaporated from Laura's mind and she gave herself over to her training. Brian immediately telephoned Tabley Wood and half a dozen other stations in the region with the information of the inbound raid, and within minutes they could hear the distant crackle of local aircraft being fired up for take-off.

Moments later, they heard the elegant hum of Spitfires overhead, and then the louder roar of Hurricanes as they set off to intercept the enemy.

Laura and Brian watched through their binoculars as the aircraft disappeared over the horizon to take up defensive formations high above the altitude of the approaching bombers – from which they would swoop down and wreak havoc.

They waited with bated breath. They knew they had a few minutes before the sky would explode with tracer fire. As Brian had instructed her, Laura used the time to make a final check of the instruments used to calculate the altitude and distance of approaching aircraft. Brian had his binoculars glued to the horizon throughout.

'Battle stations, Laura. Here we go . . .'

The distant drone of the German bombers was carried on the freezing air from twenty miles away.

Laura lifted her own binoculars to the sky and waited for the first pricks of darting tracers to make themselves apparent. The independent focus on her binoculars was set, so she carefully adjusted the main focus. With a tiny movement of her thumb on the focus wheel everything suddenly came into sharp resolution – first the moon, and then, like tiny shooting stars skittering across the dark canopy, tracer fire to and from the approaching German planes.

'Someone's made a mistake!' Laura shouted. 'There's more than forty coming! Lots more!'

Brian lifted the telephone receiver and looked at Laura. 'Estimate?!' he barked.

'Over a hundred! Perhaps more!'

Brian swallowed hard and dialled Sector Command.

'Put your helmet on, *Doctor* Campbell,' he shouted, 'this could get very, very busy!'

Chapter 13

I T WAS 8.24 P.M. WHEN the air-raid warning spilled out across the region. Where once the siren spurred each Great Paxfordian to race for the community shelter at the Barden house, the alarm had become so familiar, and its consequences for those living beneath it so remote, that only the most neurotic and fearful still hurried to safety. The rest either walked at a leisurely pace, or calculated the odds of being struck by a German bomb and stayed at home. It was hot and sweat-inducing enough inside the cellar, so why make themselves even more uncomfortable by unnecessary exertion?

Many cautious types – such as Sarah Collingborne, Alison Scotlock, Pat and Bob Simms, Teresa Lucas – stuck by the early estimate that their greatest chance of survival was by taking the least chance at all times. This meant going to the Barden shelter to sit out each and every raid, because the Barden shelter was by far the best in the village.

Superstitious types – such as Miriam Brinsley, Joyce Cameron, Mrs Talbot – worked a more primitive rationale. For them, going to the Barden shelter during a raid had kept them alive so far, so if they continued going it should keep them alive in future – while this logic was flawed because past safety is no guarantee of future safety, it made sense to them on an intuitive level, and allowed them to feel they were in the hands of a higher power of some sort.

When the air raid sounded the women clearing away that night's soup kitchen looked up for a moment, then continued to clean up at the same pace as before, knowing they would get to the shelter soon enough, and wait with mounting boredom for the all-clear.

Before leaving for the evening shift at the soup kitchen, Teresa had set out a cottage pie for Nick to heat up in the event he came home for supper. She cycled through the village smiling as she reflected on the hospital visit she'd had with Annie that afternoon. They'd played Scrabble for a while, before Teresa gently turned the conversation towards Annie's convalescence.

'I haven't given it any thought, if I'm honest,' Annie replied.

'Don't you think you should?'

'I suppose. I rather hoped I could stay here, and you could keep visiting as often as you have been.'

Teresa smiled. 'Not much fun for me, though is it? Cycling over here every day to play Scrabble with someone who's barely literate.'

'What chance do I have against a schoolteacher?' Annie protested. 'The odds are stacked against me.'

'Ex-schoolteacher,' Teresa reminded her.

'You'll be back in a classroom soon enough. Things will change after the war,' Annie said, with a certainty Teresa had always found immensely appealing. 'Women are capable of everything men are in *every* sphere of life. Do you really think shooting planes out of the sky comes naturally to boys? Flying doesn't come naturally to our *species*. They're not unaffected by what they do. Far from it. But they go up the next day and do it all over again, *because that's their job*. It would be the same for women.'

'You really believe you could do that?'

'Easy to be told I couldn't when I'm not even given the opportunity to try. We're at war. We're all finding out what we're capable of *in extremis*, wouldn't you say?'

Teresa nodded. She had certainly discovered all manner of new things about *herself* since war broke out.

As her shift at the church drew to an end, Teresa imagined what life might be like with Annie at the house. She pictured them taking walks together, and reading together, though Teresa had never seen Annie read. She imagined Annie at the kitchen table, laughing as Teresa struggled to achieve another new recipe for Nick's benefit. Mostly, she saw them sitting with one another at night while Nick was away at Tabley Wood; or sitting as a trio when Nick returned from the station, drinking whisky and sitting in silence. The thought of entering almost any room in the house and finding Annie within excited Teresa greatly. She was still thinking about it when the air-raid siren sounded at 8.24 p.m., and wrenched her from her reverie.

'Off to the shelter?' Alison asked, approaching from the makeshift kitchen.

Teresa turned to her oldest friend in the village and smiled.

'I assume nights like this are when you worry most about Nick. I know he doesn't go up with the rest of the boys, but he must find it excruciatingly stressful waiting to find out who's made it back and who hasn't.'

Teresa nodded, accepting the opportunity to pretend to Alison that she had been thinking about Nick's welfare, and not Annie's.

Not that she wasn't acutely sensitive to Nick's state of mind when he came home after each raid. Teresa took great pride taking care of her husband on those occasions; making sure he ate properly, and didn't drink too much; listening to his feelings about the losses; and holding him tightly when he broke down in her arms. It was simply that for much of the evening she had been distracted about Annie leaving hospital, and where she might go afterwards.

Teresa wanted to deflect Alison away from talking about Nick, as it inevitably led to a conversation about 'married life' in which Alison coaxed Teresa to deliver reassuring nuggets of information that confirmed that getting married to Nick was the best thing that could have happened to her.

'I haven't seen John for a while,' Teresa said. 'I thought he was developing something of a pattern of coming most nights you're here.'

'I don't think that's the case,' Alison said, dismissively. 'I don't think that's possible.'

'My understanding,' said Teresa playfully, 'is that he finds out when you're going to be on shift at the soup kitchen, and makes a point of coming on those nights.'

'Now that is completely untrue. And it's the kind of untruth that could be quite damaging, so I'd rather you kept that kind of gossip to yourself if you don't mind.'

It was dark, but if it was possible to hear another woman blush then Teresa could have sworn she heard Alison do precisely that just then. She smiled. However, the last thing she wanted was to make her old friend uncomfortable.

'I'm only playing with you, Alison. I didn't mean any harm. He's a really lovely fella. I'd be made up for you if he took an interest.'

'Really,' said Alison as tartly as she could muster. 'Take an interest in what?'

'In *you*, of course. You've always been meticulously private, and I respect that, I really do. But this is me you're talking to. What haven't we told one another while I lodged with you? I can't think of anything.'

'I've told you before how easily gossip can get whipped up from dust in the gutter in a small village like this.'

'I'm not trying to make gossip. And I'm certainly not passing any on. It's just an observation I've made whenever John comes into the church.'

'What observation?'

'He comes through the door and immediately looks for you. And when he sees you, he makes a beeline for you. You're not telling me that's not true.'

Alison hesitated, and decided she could allow her guard to slip a little with Teresa.

'I'm not going to tell you that, no. He does seem to do as you say.'

'And you're not telling me you don't enjoy that he does?'

Alison had gone as far in this conversation as she was prepared to go.

'Any friendship that may have been struck between myself and Mr Smith—'

'No, no—' Teresa interrupted, 'I'm not having that "Mr Smith" nonsense. You call him *John* now – I've heard you, so you can't pretend it's still oh-so-formal between you . . .'

Alison sighed. 'Any friendship that may exist between myself and John is purely that – a *friendship*. There is much to admire about him, and it is easy to be in his company. But that's as far as it goes.'

'For the moment.'

'For all time!' Alison declared conclusively. 'Now can we please change the subject?'

They walked on in silence for a few moments, and then Teresa said, 'You are allowed to be happy, Alison. God knows there's little of it around at the moment, so when you stumble across it, no one's going to hold it against you for grabbing some of it.'

Alison didn't speak. Instead, her hand found Teresa's and she squeezed it for a few moments in appreciation before letting it go.

'Is it because he's a coloured?' Teresa asked, unable to let the subject drop.

'Is what because he's a coloured?'

'That you're so worried people might think there's a romantic connection between you?'

'I'm not worried anyone would think that because there is no romantic connection between us.'

'Or might be in the future . . .'

Alison stopped and faced Teresa. There was enough ambient starlight for the younger woman to see the intense expression on her friend's face.

'You grew up in a city with all sorts of people from all over the world living in or passing through it. You're used to that. I'm used to that. But a lot of people here are not. Anyone who doesn't look like them is not merely a stranger, but potentially *strange*. Consequently, to be feared just for being different. People don't like other people who are different.'

'You don't have to tell me that.'

'No, I don't. You may not have seen the way some in the village look at John when he comes in with other coloureds. The fact that their ancestors were torn from Africa and shipped like cattle cuts little ice with the likes of Mrs Talbot. They just see "different". They just see "strange". And it makes them fearful and unpleasant.'

'But not you.'

'I see someone who is simply interesting. I see someone with a different perspective on the world – even on this war. I see someone who makes me smile even when I don't feel like smiling. I want to protect him while he's coming here.'

'Why is it so difficult for people to live and let live, do you think?'

'I think it's human nature to be constantly looking over our shoulder for potential danger. Dangerous animals. Strange-looking people. We live in civilised colonies like towns and villages but that doesn't mean we're as sophisticated as we'd like to think. And of course, quite a lot of people don't want to be sophisticated. They're quite happy living a simple life, with simple pleasures, and simple thoughts. They wish to get on within a small circle of operation, untroubled by anything beyond their own experience.'

'But John—'

'John is very good with people. He has a gift for putting them at their ease. I've seen the look on some people's faces, though. They don't want him to put them at their ease. They just want him to go away. That's why I'm mindful. People can be funny buggers. You have to hold them at arm's length, wear kid gloves.'

By the time they were within five hundred yards of Frances Barden's house the all-clear sounded across their region, and they walked back the way they came arm in arm, wished one another goodnight, and went their separate ways. The hundred or more bombers that Brian and Laura had reported had overlooked them once again, aiming their bombs on Liverpool's morale.

At home, Teresa sat in the dark in her front room, waiting for Nick to return. She looked around and imagined the armchair they had bought for visitors filled with Annie.

Imagine if Annie were here now. What might we be doing? I wouldn't be sitting alone in the dark for one thing.

An image of them upstairs in bed together flashed in and out of Teresa's mind, taking her by surprise. She felt herself blush hard. She placed the fingertips of her left hand to her cheek and felt its heat. She felt ashamed . . . yet thrilled by the glimpse of what might happen with Annie in the house.

Teresa sat back in the armchair and waited for Nick. She wouldn't mention the idea tonight. He would be too tired, and if the raid had gone badly he would want to talk about his men. If it went well, and all his boys returned safely, there was a good chance he would want to go to bed and make love before falling into a deep, revitalising sleep.

Another image of Annie lying in their bed flashed through Teresa's mind. This time, Teresa closed her eyes to keep it in place so she could linger.

The image was of an afternoon. Sunny outside. Annie lay naked under the sheets, looking at Teresa, smiling. Her strawberry blonde hair, customarily tied in a single thick plait when she flew, had been let down, and fanned out from her head onto the pillow, framing her elegant face. Teresa, also naked, slipped into bed beside Annie and held her in her arms. They kissed and lay together, looking at one another. A bright shaft of sunlight suddenly passed over Annie's left eye, causing her to close it. Teresa placed her hand to shield it from the bright beam. Annie craned forward and kissed the inside of Teresa's palm, then lay back down again and opened her eyes.

'My heroine,' Annie said, smiling.

Teresa now opened her eyes and allowed them to slowly acclimatise to the gloom of the unlit front room of her marital home. She looked at the window and sighed loudly. She wondered how long it would be until Nick's return, and how long she could leave it after that to ask him about moving Annie in to live with them.

Chapter 14

Sᴀʀᴀʜ Cᴏʟʟɪɴɢʙᴏʀɴᴇ sᴛᴇᴘᴘᴇᴅ out of the small front door of the squat house near the canal in which she now lived after the diocese had asked her to vacate the Vicarage, and immediately felt the icy wind on her face. A grey, sparkling sheen of frost glazed every surface, making Great Paxford appear like a frozen village in a fairy tale, awaiting the arrival of a prince to kiss a deserving female and bring everything back to life. The war had exerted a similar effect, placing normal life on hold until Hitler's grip on the world could be smashed.

For Sarah, the only man with the power to bring her out of emotional hibernation was not a prince but a vicar. Nor would it require a kiss. A single look from a bus or train window, or even a letter, would be sufficient to instantly shatter the ice that seemed to have enveloped Sarah's spirit since Adam's capture at Dunkirk.

She now walked slowly towards the village centre, feeling the soft crunch of frost beneath her shoes. Her breath billowed from her mouth, and hung in the air in front of her, kept visible by the low temperature of the air. She was on her way to sit in on an early shift at the telephone exchange, with Pat.

In Adam's absence, Sarah had found herself brooding about him, almost to the exclusion of everything else. Even when she spent time with her sister and her adopted little boy, Sarah would spend the greater proportion of it thinking about Adam. She recognised it as a form of constant, internal yearning.

Of course, Sarah did count herself immensely fortunate to have received a telegram informing her that Adam was *missing* after Dunkirk, and not dead. So many women in the area had received the very worst news about their sons, husbands, and brothers. Sarah had been told Adam had been taken prisoner, but not where.

With so many questions about his whereabouts, his state of health and mind, and when she might see him again, swirling around her head from the moment she woke in the morning until the moment she went to bed, Sarah needed to keep herself distracted. Consequently, she decided to volunteer as an operator at the telephone exchange. In addition to keeping herself busy by learning a new skill, she fancied that occasionally listening in to other people's chitchat might prove an easy diversion from her constant internal, revolving monologue about Adam.

Pat was her designated mentor. Having shown Sarah the basics of how to operate the equipment, she was now training Sarah by example, so that by the time Sarah could fly solo she would look and sound as good as any of the more experienced operators. Sarah would watch and listen as Pat took and connected calls, and then gently cross-examine Sarah about what she had seen Pat do, and why.

'I'm not going to pretend this is difficult,' Pat had said at their first training session, 'because it isn't. Not if you've half a brain. But you do need to concentrate, and you need to be precise with your connections. Also, the correct manner is essential, regardless of whether the call is social, a local crisis, or one concerning a national emergency. Don't be alarmed. A national emergency has yet to trouble the exchange – though we've had plenty of calls relating to local crises. That said, you never know what your first call is going to be, so you have to be prepared for all eventualities.'

Sarah had wondered if she would be expected to talk in a certain way.

'No one's expecting you to put on a voice. You should speak with a tone you feel comfortable with. But you need to strike a balance between friendliness and professionalism. People want to hear reassurance on the other end of the line. But they also want to know their call is in good hands, and that you'll do your very best to connect them where they wish to be connected.'

So it had proved. The work wasn't difficult, but close attention to Pat's operation of the switchboard showed that a degree of practice would be required until it became second nature to Sarah.

On this particular morning, Sarah had left the house a little earlier than usual, hoping to enjoy a slow walk during which she cleared her head of all her thoughts about Adam, and be in the right frame of mind upon her arrival at the exchange. This generally took the form of Sarah wondering what Adam's equivalent task might be right now. When she ate breakfast, she imagined Adam eating *his* breakfast, and dreaded to think what it might consist of.

She would chat to him about it, and imagined his wry responses. The same for lunch and supper, and indeed, throughout the day.

This hadn't been a calculated treatment for her loneliness, but had arisen naturally, as she realised he was unlikely to be coming home soon. It enabled Sarah to imagine her husband into her life in some form, and incorporate phantom-Adam into her daily routines.

She arrived at the exchange on time, expecting to find Pat had already opened up with everything ready for their shift together. Only, Pat wasn't there. The exchange was empty. Sarah looked on the desks for a note of explanation, but there was nothing. Sarah closed the door behind her and sat down to wait, turning on the switchboard in readiness. She took a deep breath and savoured the combination of the interior, musty smell of the exchange and its particular kind of almost-silence. Suddenly, the switchboard lit up.

Sarah wasn't yet a qualified operator but she knew enough to take a basic call and re-route it correctly. She looked at the switchboard and saw the call was coming from Joyce

Cameron's house. Sarah knew that Pat and Bob were currently lodging with Joyce, and surmised the call might have something to do with Pat's failure to arrive on time.

Pat was famously punctual. Any delays usually meant something had happened at home. An argument. Or worse. Sarah wondered what state Pat might be in when she arrived.

What do I say, Adam, if she comes in with a bruise on her face?

Sarah imagined Adam sitting opposite, taking his time to think it through, and then advising that she make no reference to the bruise if there is one, but simply offer friendship and – by implication – support.

I should answer it. I'm sure I can do it. Better that I possibly mess it up than not try and deal with it at all.

Sarah removed her hat, then reached forward and placed the headset over her hair and ears, and plugged in the connector.

'Hello,' she said in her best, nicely modulated 'exchange' voice.

'Mrs Collingborne?' said the man's voice at the other end. Sarah immediately recognised it was Pat's husband, Bob.

Sarah hadn't liked the man even before she had discovered that he was verbally and physically violent towards her friend. Being the wife of the vicar hadn't helped, as it meant she was forced to be civil to every one of her husband's congregation, irrespective of what she knew they got up to in the privacy of their own homes.

'Yes, it is, Mr Simms,' she said calmly. 'Is anything the matter? I thought I was doing another shift with Pat this morning.'

'That's why I'm telephoning. Pat's running a little late. She wanted me to telephone ahead. Let you know she's on her way.'

'Very well,' Sarah replied. 'Thank you for letting me know.'

'She didn't want you sitting there not knowing what was happening.'

Sarah didn't want to speak to Bob for any longer than necessary.

'It's very kind of you to call. Now I know she's coming I'll wait. Goodbye, Mr Simms.'

The call ended and Sarah pulled the connector from the switchboard.

When Pat arrived a few minutes later she was bruise-free and all smiles. She apologised for being late – even though it was only by five minutes – and explained that Bob had decided to bring her breakfast in bed that morning. Pat had been surprised to say the least. She actually couldn't recall the last time he had done that – or anything like it. She told Sarah he had made Pat and Joyce lunch a couple of days earlier, but didn't believe it was anything other than a rather strange one-off.

'I was very suspicious, in fact.' Pat knew that Sarah would understand why she said that. There were a select few women in Pat's circle who had a pretty decent idea about Bob's behaviour towards Pat over the years, and Sarah was one of them.

'Why suspicious? Because he never did anything nice for you?'

'Certainly that,' Pat said. 'But also because of the food he prepared. It was the same that gave him terrible food poisoning a while ago.'

'I remember,' Sarah said. 'You told us he accused you of trying to kill him.'

'I couldn't understand what sort of message he was trying to send by making it. I half thought he may have been trying to get his own back in some twisted way. But in the end . . . I think he made it simply because it's one of his favourites, and it's one of the few things he can make well.'

'But why *had* he made you lunch?' Sarah asked.

'He said it was to thank us both for looking after him so well.'

'And he meant it?'

'I can generally tell if he's being sarcastic. He seldom sees a need to disguise his feelings. But I couldn't see any trace of that.'

'And now breakfast in bed this morning?'

'I really don't know,' Pat replied. 'I did ask what it was in aid of. He said he just woke up and wanted to do something nice for me.'

Pat didn't tell Sarah that this particular outbreak of Bob's pleasantness followed close on the heels of being particularly *unpleasant* on the night of Will's funeral.

'It would be about time, wouldn't you say?' Sarah asked, hopefully.

Pat forced a tired, wan smile.

'Or is it just too little too late?' Sarah said, trying to read between the lines.

'I'm not an unpleasant woman, Sarah . . .'

'Of course you're not! On the contrary . . .'

'It's not that making me lunch and bringing me breakfast in bed would be a matter of being "too little too late". More . . . *why* is he doing it? Until I know what's really behind it I can't take him on trust.'

Sarah nodded her agreement. 'How will you find out?'

Pat shrugged. 'I'm not sure. He's after something, I'm sure of it.'

Pat didn't want to talk about Bob anymore. She smiled at Sarah and reminded her of the routine they went through before starting each shift.

Sarah listened carefully, and made some notes in a small notebook she kept in her coat pocket. But she was only half listening to Pat's advice about operating the switchboard. She watched her friend's face, noting to herself that Pat had lost some weight, which revealed more lines around her eyes than she'd noticed before.

Beside the notes about being an effective operator, Sarah made another note in much smaller handwriting.

It read, 'Keep an eye on Pat over next few weeks. Bob's afoot. Tell F.'

Chapter 15

STEPH WAS ALONE in the farmyard tending the chickens when she heard the gate creak on its rusting hinges. In the wake of the incident with the German pilot, she liked spending time with the chickens – their fuss and noise distracted her from dark thoughts. As she cleaned out their run, collected their eggs, and fed and watered them, the inquisitive birds demanded just enough of her attention to block out everything else.

Steph turned towards the gate, expecting to see Stanley and Isobel coming back into the farm after repairing the damage to the fence in the far field, caused by the German pilot climbing over in his pursuit of Stanley. It was only when she brushed the hair from her eyes that Steph realised the man walking determinedly towards her was not Stanley.

'Stan!' Steph cried, dropping the basket of eggs she was holding and running into her husband's arms. 'You got my letter! I was waiting for a reply!'

'This is it. You didn't sound in a good way, so I discharged myself and came straight home.'

'I didn't ask for that. That's not why I wrote.'

'I know. But you knew I'd come.'

Steph nodded. 'I hoped.'

'I can go back if you want,' he said, smiling and kissing her face all over. 'Just say the word, girl.'

Steph gripped his face between her hands and stared intensely into his eyes. 'I need you more than Churchill does.'

'I'm not sure he needs me that much at the moment. Had us spending most of our time doing drills and playing cards.'

Having rushed to join up at the outbreak of war, Stan had found himself rescued from Dunkirk by a small fishing vessel, which managed to dodge a German air attack and bring Stan back to the south coast. He was then kept in storage with his comrades at an army base, while the government and military calculated their next move. It was there that he was able to tell Steph where he had been, and that he was now safe.

In the interregnum between being de-mobbed after the First War and joining back up for the Second War, Stan had forgotten that being a soldier involved vast amounts of doing nothing at all, interspersed with frenzied bursts of taking the most appalling risks with one's life to secure small strips of territory. Word spread it was unlikely British troops would set foot on European soil until the Allies had achieved air superiority, and no one could tell how long that might take. Sitting around for weeks doing endless amounts of square-bashing and kit cleaning wasn't what Stan had expected when he'd joined up. On the farm or on the battlefield, mending a fence post or attacking an enemy position, Stan was at his best when using his hands. Boredom, not Hitler, became Stan's enemy. Surviving Dunkirk had been exhilarating. Enduring the inaction that followed had given him increasingly itchy feet. In a reserved occupation, Stan had been contemplating discharging himself and returning to the farm. Then Steph's letter arrived. It forced his hand.

They kissed for what seemed like a minute.

Steph looked noticeably thinner to Stan. The veins on her hands stood out, suggesting she wasn't eating properly. He could see dark rings beneath her eyes. Her lips, usually full and red, were dry and pale. She looked utterly drained. Stan wrapped her in his arms.

'It's going to be all right . . .' he whispered. 'Trust me.'

'How can it?' she replied in a whisper. 'You can't undo what's done, even if you think you can. And be careful what you say in front of Stanley. He thinks I'm fine.'

'Then he's an idiot. I could see straight away you're not right.'

'He sees what I want him to see – his mam, coping.'

'But you're not.'

'I can't get the pilot's face out of my head. Or that of his mother and father.'

Stan looked at her, puzzled how she could picture the pilot's parents when she'd never set eyes on them.

'He carried a photograph of them in his flight jacket. He was barely older than Stanley.'

'You said. Several times.'

He threaded his arm through hers and began to walk her back towards the farmhouse.

'Let's get you inside. Brass monkeys out here.'

Steph lowered her eyes to the ground as they walked across the yard.

'I didn't have to do it, Stan. I didn't shout out. I never gave him a chance. The look on his face when I rolled him off Little Stan, onto his back—'

'It was an act of war, Steph, what the *kraut* did to Stanley. What you did in response – also an act of war. You think 'cause it happened on the farm it wasn't, but it was. The Germans are bringing the war here with this bombing. This lad fell out of the sky and brought it to ground level, that's all. You said he had a gun . . .'

Steph stopped by the front door and nodded. 'Never used it, though.'

'Didn't want to attract attention with a shot. Everyone would've come running.'

Stan had been preparing what he wanted to say to Steph all the way home – a little speech intended to erase the feelings of guilt that poured out of every line in her letter to him. He thought he'd try to speak less as her husband than a serving soldier who'd seen more death and destruction in war than he ever wanted to recall.

'A soldier would've called out for him to stop in that situation,' she said. 'You would have.'

Stan nodded. This is where he wanted to get her, to this comparison.

'A soldier's trained, Steph. You're not. You're being far, far too hard on yourself. You were a civilian woman faced with extraordinary danger, and you dealt with it the best you could. In my eyes, brilliantly.'

'How can you say that?'

'Stanley's still alive – that's how. And if the *kraut* had finished off Stanley, you think the Nazi bastard wouldn't've come for you and Isobel?'

Steph looked at Stan and suddenly felt nauseous. 'Let's shut up about it for now,' she asked.

'For now,' he agreed. 'But there's still the article in the *Echo* to deal with.'

'I thought of telephoning the newspaper to ask them not to print it.'

'You don't want people to know?'

Steph shook her head. 'The reporter persuaded me. Said it might give people a bit of a boost. But the more I've thought on it, it doesn't seem that way to me. He said people will only think good of us. But some people are strange, Stan. They don't go the way you think.'

'Good 'uns will.'

'But there's not just good people. There's all sorts.'

'Bloody good story, Steph.'

'To everyone but me, maybe. And Stanley. He thinks it'll be wonderful. Thinks people'll see him as a hero.'

'Probably will. What's wrong with that if he was?'

'He's too young to get caught up in all that.'

'Could help bring him out of himself. Grow up a bit.'

Stan looked at his wife's profile. Her mouth was set firmly against the idea, and she looked straight ahead. He knew better than to press her when she was in this mood.

'Let's talk it over later before we telephone anyone.'

'So glad you're back, love,' she said, kissing him on the cheek and squeezing his hand tightly.

'Me too. Can't begin to say how much I've missed you.'

Stan gently guided Steph into the farmhouse and closed the door behind them.

Over supper they pretended to Stanley that all was well. While Steph washed up, Stan asked his son to recount the episode with the German pilot in as much detail as he could recall, which Stanley gleefully did. Once again, the boy adjusted the fact of who had been chasing who across the far field that afternoon. The father praised the son for his courage, and told him how proud he was of him. The son glowed.

Later, in bed, Steph asked Stan if he would re-join his battalion if and when all this fuss about the pilot blew over? He shook his head.

'Made me realise, my place is here.'

Steph kissed him.

'Besides,' he said, 'not sure the army'd be too happy seeing me coming and going as I please, despite being reserved occupation.' He pulled her closer and held her tightly in his arms. 'No, love,' he said. 'I'm back for good.'

Chapter 16

ONCE IT HAD been decided the WI would put on a Christmas party for the children of Great Paxford, Frances asked Noah what kind of party the children might like. She discovered that his least favourite option was one that included girls, while his frontrunners in terms of games were those that involved splitting the boys into two factions and have them fight one another. Clearly, the war had sunk its teeth into Noah's imagination deeper than Frances had thought. Though, given the child had lost both parents and his home as a direct consequence of it, she oughtn't have been surprised.

'Are you sure the other boys would want to play games of that nature?' Frances had asked.

'Yes,' he replied, with an air of certainty Frances found amusing and slightly alarming in equal measure – she admired his conviction but was apprehensive about its future impact on the world when he grew older. Though she was a woman of firm opinion herself, she had often tempered Peter's more dogmatic positions concerning a variety of issues. She could see the same streak of unflinching certainty in Noah, and wasn't sure whether to encourage it to arm him against an unflinchingly competitive society, or soften it with the notion of seeing other people's point of view. For the moment, compromise seemed not to be of much interest to Noah.

'The boys at school will like these games because we play them all the time at playtime.'

Frances wasn't sure if this was true or whether Noah had quickly developed the rather masculine skill of making up facts to suit whatever argument he was advocating. She would ask his teacher.

Talking to Noah more about the kind of Christmas party they might put on, Frances began to feel increasingly out of touch with what children like to do on such occasions. This partly stemmed from her own dislike of mass gatherings of children when she had been a child, and partly from a lack of exposure to children's parties for most of her adult life, on account of not having children of her own to take to them. Until now.

Consequently, she thought it might be a good idea to approach younger members of the WI, on the basis that it wasn't so long ago that they were children too, and could more easily recall what they liked and disliked about parties. Frances lighted upon Laura as a good person to approach. Laura was only seventeen, and had that nice mixture of seriousness coupled with a capacity for enjoying herself when the occasion arose. Frances had also noticed

Laura was very good around children. She thought taking on the responsibility of organising a children's Christmas party would develop Laura's organisational skills, and provide a helpful distraction.

With her father dead, and her boyfriend contemplating becoming a pilot, and Laura herself weighing up the legitimacy of following Will's suggestion that she too might become a doctor, there was a lot of seriousness currently in her life. Putting on a Christmas party for children sounded like the perfect antidote.

'I'm so pleased,' Frances told Laura, beaming. 'It's one thing to have initiatives at the WI. But the real skill lies in finding the right people to implement them.'

'Does it matter that I'm so young?' Laura asked.

'There are some members – no names – who are three times as old as you, and I wouldn't ask them to organise turning the lights off after a meeting. This is not about age but competence. If you're old and wise enough to be in the WAAF you're old and wise enough to do this.'

Laura hesitated for a moment, before replying. 'You do know I was made to leave the WAAF?'

'I do. Most unfairly. Your mother explained it all to me in excruciating detail. The old boys' network at its worst, if you ask me. An officer behaves appallingly by seducing a young girl and they know punishment is due, but they can't bring themselves to punish one of their own or it might be their turn next. So, they punish the girl, and sign off the paperwork. Abysmal cowardice, but that's the way the masculine world works, Laura. According to their rules. Now you know, you can and must be more watchful.'

Laura loved listening to Frances speak like this. Not only because she was so supportive, but she never minced her words. Frances's characterisation of standing up against unfairness sounded like not only the right thing to do, but terrifically exciting. She agreed to take on the party on the spot.

Organising games would be easy enough. Laura could remember enough games that children liked to play from her own attendance at many parties over the years. Musical chairs, pin the tail on the donkey, pass the parcel – the key thing was to keep children entertained in a non-stop blizzard of activity and then, when they were exhausted, feed them with all sorts of nice, sweet things. It was a formula for success that had stood the test of time.

Laura remembered she had attended one party held in a barn, after the parents of the featured child decided to try and be a little bit different to other parents. The occasion had gone very well until the time came to eat.

Several children had over-indulged far too quickly and suffered instant and painful brain freeze, and started to cry. This took no one by surprise and the distressed children were swiftly taken care of. More problematic was a greedy child called Oliver, who wolfed down three portions of jelly and ice cream, and then managed to ingest a single piece of straw from one of the many bales scattered around the barn. It got wedged in the back of his throat, which prompted the child to unceremoniously vomit up his recently consumed party food. Oliver's vomiting immediately triggered the gag reflex in at least eight others, who proceeded to vomit themselves, and the party came to an end. Not one child – including Laura – escaped without being vomited on by at least one other child.

No barns. And perhaps no jelly and ice cream, to be on the safe side. But you have *to have jelly and ice cream. What else? Sandwiches and cake . . .*

Laura had asked Frances to give her a budget to work from. Instead, Frances had told Laura that she would rather Laura plan the party she wanted then come back to Frances – and Alison as branch treasurer – to see if they had the funds and rations to cover the expense. Frances did hint that Laura not think too lavishly, as much of the WI's reserves had been spent setting up and supplying the soup kitchen for trekkers. It was with this in mind that Laura went into Brindsley's butcher's to speak to David, who was now running the business side of the shop while his mum took care of baby Vivian, and his father took care of the heavy lifting, carving, sawing, and serving. It was hard to believe she and David had been at school together just a year before. In such a brief slice of time, Laura had lived through scandal while David had been to sea and back, returning badly scarred. Both were now determined to build new lives for themselves.

'Ham goes a long way at a party,' David said, repeating lines he'd heard his father say dozens of times to customers seeking catering advice. 'Cheap. But not as cheap as luncheon or potted meat, which you can spread as thinly as you want. How many people are you expecting?'

Laura had calculated up to thirty might attend; possibly more if the older children felt supremely bored at home and turned up to kill some time.

'Have you thought about sausages?' David asked, trying to give Laura more options. 'Everyone likes sausages. Children love 'em. And we can make them up specially for the party. You tell us how much meat you can afford and we can add as much bread as you like to make your budget stretch. The children will have no idea. To them, a sausage is a sausage. They're not fussed.'

Laura and David discussed how little meat a sausage required to still be considered – and taste like – a sausage, then calculated how much that amount of meat would cost if each child were to consume two sausages apiece. She then did the same for ham, on the basis of half a slice per sandwich, and three sandwiches apiece. As she made the calculations she glanced momentarily at David, and saw him smiling at her.

'Why are you doing that?' she asked.

'Doing what?'

'Smiling like that. What am I doing wrong?'

'You're not doing anything wrong, as far as I can see. I've just never seen you this serious before. I mean, I've seen you miserable. You know, over the Wing Commander Bowers business—'

'We no longer mention that man.'

'But I've never seen you like *this*. Business-like. Behaving so grown up, I suppose.'

'I want to make a good fist of it.'

'When I told Ma you were coming over to talk numbers for the party she said, "Laura's just the young woman for the job." "Young woman", Ma said. Not "girl".'

Laura could feel herself blush from Miriam's compliment.

'I think Dad's death brought home how quickly time passes. It feels like yesterday when he first told Kate and I he was ill. A few minutes later – so it sometimes seems – he's gone. It's the same for everyone.'

David nodded. 'One minute I'm doing my job below deck. The next I'm in the water trying to swim away from burning oil. The next I'm in hospital with half the skin on my back gone. The next I'm back in Great Paxford, stepping off the bus.'

'I want to do something with my life, David. Before it just drifts away.'

'Doesn't everyone?'

'I see a lot of people just living quietly day to day.'

'Maybe that's their way.'

'One night I was sitting beside Dad at home. He was dozing. It was near the end. I looked at his face and thought, *You haven't wasted a minute*. I thought perhaps that's why he accepted his diagnosis the way he did. Not that he wasn't afraid of dying, because I think he was a little.'

'Blokes on the ship said they weren't afraid of it. I didn't believe them.'

'Dad packed his life. He wanted more time with us, but I think he felt he'd led a fulfilled life. I'd like to feel the same, if possible.'

David had never heard Laura talk this way before. He thought he was the only person his age in the village who considered these things. They were both growing up.

'So . . . what *do* you want to do?' he asked.

Laura hesitated for a moment, as if daring herself to say the next sequence of words, and then said them.

'I've been thinking of becoming a doctor.'

Laura deliberately left off the story about her father suggesting it with his almost last words to her. She scrutinised David's face for his reaction. He was a no-nonsense boy who knew his own mind and held worthwhile opinions he could back up. And he'd known her all her life. She trusted his judgement, perhaps more than Tom's.

David looked at Laura impassively for several seconds, and then nodded.

'I can see that,' he said seriously. 'That makes sense.'

Laura felt her heart skip a beat with gratitude. David had affirmed her. She wanted to kiss him. She didn't. Instead, she placed her hand on his and squeezed it.

'Thank you,' she said. 'That means more to me than you know.'

Walking home from Brindsley's, the meat-related details of the Christmas party resolved, Laura felt the first fragile shoots of optimism for the first time since she had seen her father's coffin lowered into the earth. She made a diversion to St Mark's, pushed open the gate and walked across the soft grass of its cemetery towards her father's resting place. The earth was dark and fresh. The headstone absent, under construction.

She stood in silence, imagining Will lying in perfect repose six feet below. 'Were you serious?' she asked finally. 'Is this something you really believe I could do? That I'd have a genuine aptitude for? Or was it one last, desperate throw of the paternal dice before you left – pushing me towards something, anything, and medicine was the only thing that came to mind?'

A final thought occurred to her that she didn't say out loud out of respect for her father.

Or were you, in your last moments, as the cancer ate into your brain, simply going mad? And your suggestion that I consider medicine merely an expression of your final insanity?

Laura looked at the earth, as if in expectation of some signal that her father had heard her. Instead of a sign from below, it began to slowly rain from above. Cold, wet drops spattered against the back of Laura's neck and trickled down, beneath her collar, causing her to shiver. She found it impossible to grasp that her father would not find some way to claw his way to her and give her his answer; impossible that he would remain in a box in the ground not only for the duration of her life, but for as long as the Earth revolved around the sun.

She waited there for several minutes, and then turned her collar up against the strengthening rain and hurried home.

Chapter 17

TERESA HAD WAITED several days before deciding it was pointless to hope for the perfect time to speak to Nick about bringing Annie to convalesce in the house. The perfect time to speak to him simply didn't exist, for the simple reason that Nick was pre-occupied with the war twenty-four hours a day, now and until either the Luftwaffe had turned Liverpool and Britain's industrial belt to rubble, or the RAF exacted such a price on the German air force that the Blitz stopped. Neither seemed likely to happen any time soon. Nick had explained to Teresa that though the Germans had developed the X-beam to help guide their planes towards their targets, the British had developed RADAR to detect those planes on approach. Consequently, he'd told her, the battle was balanced, intense and brutal for both sides.

'But we can drive them back?' Teresa had asked.

'If we can stay in the fight long enough. Though after their attack on Coventry on 14 November, there's no doubt the Luftwaffe has the upper hand.'

To try to stay worthy of Nick's conversation about his job, Teresa followed the war closely in the newspaper, and on the radio, and was always ready to open a conversation about this or that aspect of the defensive campaign against the Germans. The problem was that Nick was privy to so much more information about it all than she was.

On the evening she had decided to broach the subject of Annie to Nick, she thought to lead up to it by mentioning an article she had read in the *Liverpool Echo* about the poor conditions at the internment camp in Huyton, on the outskirts of Liverpool.

'Don't you think it's fair to say,' she began, 'that if we're going to arrest and detain these poor unfortunates we at least have a responsibility to keep them in reasonable conditions?'

Nick was in no mood to argue, but could see that Teresa wanted a conversation after being in the house all day by herself.

'I suppose it depends what you mean by "reasonable conditions"? What may not be reasonable to you might be perfectly reasonable to someone else under the circumstances of war, where resources are scarcer by the day, and *no one* could be said to be living in the lap of luxury.'

'It's bad enough that these perfectly innocent people have been rounded up like potential spies—'

'How do we know they aren't spies?'

'Of course they're not spies, Nick.'

'We don't know that. Isn't that the issue? We have to scoop them all up because we simply do not know who is or isn't – *or might become* – a spy against us. It's not pretty. It's crude, but every other country is doing exactly the same thing with their foreign nationals. Yes, it's cruel, and yes, it's probably unfair in almost all of the cases. But that's war, darling.'

Teresa hated it when Nick used the phrase 'That's war, darling' to counter her anger against what she perceived to be unnecessary cruelties of conflict.

When Teresa read aloud the daily statistics of the dead and wounded from the London Blitz, tears falling onto the newspaper, Nick said softly, 'I'm afraid that's war, darling. It's twisted and simple. Whoever kills the most people wins. The quicker they kill us the quicker they break our morale, the quicker we surrender. At least, that's their theory. It will be ours too, if we get the chance to mount a concerted attack back.'

She was determined not to allow Nick to mollify her about the camp at Huyton. 'Very well. If you think it's all right for these poor souls – who have done nothing wrong except speak with a different accent—'

'Darling,' Nick countered, hoping to bring what threatened to be an argument to an end before it could really ignite, but Teresa hadn't finished.

'If you think it's all right that they're kept in substandard conditions, do you think it's right for them to be penned in while the Luftwaffe attacks the city night after night? The trekkers are free to leave each evening to seek safety in the countryside, but these people have to take their chances inside a camp they cannot leave. They're sitting targets.'

'But they're not targets at all, Teresa. Not really. Not in as much as the Germans aren't targeting them, but the docks.'

'What if a stray bomb hits the camp?'

'Well, yes, that would be terrible. But—'

'*That's war, darling.*'

Teresa looked at him defiantly as she threw his expression back at him. Nick narrowed his eyes to get a better focus on precisely what might be going on inside his wife's head at that moment. He took a long, deep breath, then let it out slowly.

'This evening one of my boys was hit, Teresa. Not him. The plane. Fuel line was cut. Started a fire—'

'Nick,' Teresa said calmly but firmly, 'it isn't fair to roll out another terrible incident about one of your boys to shout me down.'

Nick looked at her coldly, as if he momentarily hated everything about her. It sent a small chill down her spine.

'His fuel line was cut,' he continued calmly.

Teresa sat back and waited for the story to come. It would be terrible and tragic and she wouldn't be able to pick up where she left off.

'A fire started behind the cockpit. He tried to bail out but the canopy wouldn't slide open. The flames got into the cockpit and we could hear him screaming with terror and pain. I told him to put the plane into a steep dive which might drive the flames back up the plane, away from his position. Which he did. And it worked. Only, he hadn't noticed that his altimeter had also been shot up, so he had no idea of his altitude. His radio went dead almost immediately.'

Teresa looked at Nick and clenched her jaw with frustration. 'As I said, I think it's very unfair the way you tell me these things to shut me up.'

'I thought you wanted to know what I'm thinking about? So that's what I was thinking about when you started on about bloody Huyton. I was trying to weigh up whether it was better that I was able to con him into killing himself by smashing into the ground than to let him burn to death?'

They sat in silence for a few moments.

'You can be quite cruel sometimes,' she said quietly.

'I know,' Nick said. 'I didn't used to be.'

Teresa felt the fight go out of her.

What the Hell. Just ask him. No preamble, he's not in the mood. Frankly, neither am I.

'I've been thinking about Annie,' Teresa said, as matter-of-factly as she could.

'What about her?'

'She's due to be released shortly and is dreading having to return home to continue her convalescence with her family.'

'I understand they're fairly appalling. Which explains her predilection for flying hither and yon as much as she can. What about asking her to come here?'

Teresa looked at him. 'What?'

'To convalesce here,' he said. 'Among friends.'

Teresa looked at Nick for a moment, her brow furrowed as she processed his proposition.

'Unless you think it might be a burden for you? I rather thought you might enjoy some company. What were you thinking about her?'

Teresa felt her heart jump a little for joy.

'On similar lines. Not quite what you were suggesting. I mean, I hadn't arrived at a conclusion like you have,' she lied, 'but on reflection I think I might very well enjoy the company.'

'Annie can be pretty full-on when she gets the wind in her sails. And I've no idea how good a patient she is. But it would only be for a few weeks. If it didn't work out for whatever reason we can revisit the idea and think again.'

Once Nick had said the words out loud Teresa felt a little lightheaded with fear that her own feelings on the matter would be utterly transparent. She pretended to consider the proposition for a few moments.

'Getting Annie back on her feet *would* be a little project for me – for us both, I suppose,' she finally said.

'Well, if you're game, and she is, I think it could be terrific for both of you,' Nick said. 'I'm being a somewhat shitty husband at the moment. You could do with some decent company. And if she's recovering she can't get up to too much mischief!'

Teresa sometimes wished Nick was not the decent, reasonable man he was. Had he been difficult and bad-tempered she would undoubtedly feel less guilt about the way she occasionally thought and behaved.

But if he was not the man he was I would never have married him.

'When might you ask Annie?' he asked.

'I'm going to visit her tomorrow. As usual.'

'Excellent, ask her then,' Nick said, like a Wing Commander agreeing a decisive plan of action. 'If she hesitates, tell her it was my idea.'

'Are you sure?' Teresa asked. 'It won't irritate you having someone else in the house?'

'Annie is like you – bursting with life. I can't have too much of that around me. Tell her she *has* to come and recuperate here. Tell her it's an order, from me!'

Teresa smiled, as Nick would have expected her to, and as she wanted to.

Bringing Annie into the house, into her daily life with her husband, excited and terrified her in equal measure.

Chapter 18

PAT LAY IN bed and watched Bob undress and put on his pyjamas. She tried to gauge his mood. She hoped he'd want to get under the blankets, turn his back to her, and go to sleep – though it hadn't always been that way recently. She had become convinced the success of his novel had an uplifting effect on his libido, which he then inflicted on her. When they had first moved into Joyce's house, Pat had hoped their landlady would be a light sleeper, as this might curb Bob's activities. On the first occasion Bob tried to have sex with Pat in Joyce's cottage, Pat had urgently whispered, 'Joyce might hear!' at the first loud creak of a bedspring, and Bob had reluctantly rolled off, lay in the dark bemoaning Joyce for ten minutes, and fell asleep.

It wasn't to last. They soon discovered Joyce slept like the dead after a significant nightcap, which she poured herself *every* night. When the mood took him, Bob waited until they could hear Joyce snoring heavily through the adjoining wall to her bedroom, and then rolled on top of his wife to exercise his 'conjugal rights'. However, being mindful of waking Joyce with his exertions had forced Bob into becoming a quieter, subtler lover who had to take his time before climaxing. This meant he spent more time looking down at Pat, and she sometimes wondered if he wasn't looking upon her beneath him with some semblance of actual tenderness – as if he were recalling their earlier life together, when they were keenly attracted to one another.

Bob turned off the light and climbed into bed beside Pat. To try and discourage him from doing anything but sleep, Pat had already rolled onto her side, facing away from him, and pretended to be unconscious. If she actually had been unconscious she wouldn't have heard Bob lean over and whisper her name. The fact that she wasn't made it more annoying that Bob didn't seem to care either way. If she had been awake she would have to answer; if she had been asleep, he would almost certainly wake her up to answer.

'I'm tired, Bob,' Pat said, laying on how sleepy she was with a trowel.

'I wondered if you might like to . . . you know . . .'

Pat opened her eyes, on the alert. And puzzled. Bob hadn't asked if she would be interested in having sex for years. He simply imposed himself on and inside her, with almost no consultation.

'I thought if we were quiet . . . you know . . .'

Pat reached out and turned on the small light on the table beside the bed, then turned and looked at her husband. He squinted in the sudden illumination, raising a hand against the light.

Pat looked at him in the gloom, wondering what he was up to. 'What're you doing, Bob?' she asked. 'You never ask me if I want to have sex. You always presume consent.'

'Because we're married.'

'That's not what being married means. You don't even ask if I'm in the mood.'

'Because you never are.'

'Well, I'm not tonight. But why ask? Why are you pretending to be considerate?'

'Why do you think I'm pretending?'

'Because I know you.'

Bob looked at Pat for several moments. 'Perhaps you *knew* me. But perhaps I've changed.'

Pat considered this for a moment. *Bob doesn't change. Don't listen to this. Bob does not change.*

'I'm not only talking about tonight, Bob. I'm talking about breakfast in bed. I'm talking about lunch. Making me tea in the afternoon when I come back from a shift at the exchange. Little compliments about my cooking now, even though I've been making the same food for years in exactly the same way. The remark you made yesterday about my hair.'

'I like your hair.'

'You never comment on my hair.'

Bob looked at Pat in the semi-darkness. 'There are a lot of things I haven't done that I should have. I want to change that.'

Pat's mind raced. In the past, Bob had often adopted a milder tone with her in the days following a particularly nasty outburst. It was standard practice on his part, and what contributed to her view of him as a profound coward. 'Hit me if you have to,' she once told him defiantly, 'but don't be so spineless as to pretend to be sorry afterwards.' This was a different, softer tone to any she had previously heard from him.

Before she had time to respond, he continued. 'I can't expect you to believe me. I know that. But I don't want to carry on the way we have. I see the way other men are with their wives – I used to watch how Doc Campbell was with Erica – and I wished we could have something similar.'

'I think it's called "love", Bob. You killed it, remember, with the back of your hand. Then your open palm. On more than one occasion, your fist.'

Bob looked down and said nothing. Pat imagined his anger must be boiling over, and braced herself for what she thought would be an inevitable onslaught in one form or another. Muted perhaps, because of Joyce next door. But Bob could be just as effective at low volume.

But Bob didn't move. Instead, he lifted his eyes and looked at her. She couldn't be sure in the low light of the bedside lamp but . . .

Are his eyes wet? No. They can't be . . .

'I want to try and find it again, Patricia. I know how badly I've treated you in the past,' he said, his voice almost a whisper.

163

'The past and the near past,' she corrected him softly, not allowing him to consign his dreadful behaviour to ancient history. He nodded, accepting her qualification.

'I can't erase that. I know that. I can't ask you to trust me. I know that too. I have to earn it back.' He hesitated. 'I want to try. That's all I can say to you.'

Pat's eyes were now properly accustomed to the low light in the room. She saw the glint in his eye.

Is that—? Is that a tear?

'What's brought this on, Bob? Why are you doing this now?'

She was careful to eliminate any trace of suspicion from her voice. Not because he appeared to be tearful. Bob had cried crocodile tears in the past, and they counted for nothing soon after. Pat didn't want to sound sceptical because she wanted to draw as much of this – whatever it proved to be – out of Bob as she could while he was willing to speak, if only to protect herself with as much information – or misinformation – as possible.

'It was at the funeral. I was watching Erica crying over Will, and it struck me that if it had been my funeral you'd have had to pretend to cry over me. Or not cry at all. I'm right, aren't I?'

Pat felt her heart thumping softly. She hadn't expected this accurate assessment. She felt a throb of emotion rise in her throat, before forcing it back down.

Don't be fooled. It's a ruse. It's always a ruse with Bob. Always. Because it's always the same Bob underneath. You

164

know this. Don't be taken in. See how far he's prepared to go with this, but do not for one moment be taken in by it.

'Do you want me to lie, Bob?' Pat asked, pushing to see how much honesty he was willing to take. He shook his head.

'I know what you think of me,' he said.

'Have I not earned the right to think it?'

'I'm not the man I used to be, Patricia. I'm not the man you married. I'm a better writer, but not, I think, a better man . . .'

Bob's voice trailed off. Pat had no idea what to do. She had never seen or heard him like this – solemn, repentant.

That's all it is, Pat. An act. He knows you want him to change. He's reeling you in for – you don't know. But that's what he's doing. Do not be fooled by this for a second.

'Would you have gone with the Czech if I had been a better husband to you?'

Is this what this is about? Is he trying to get back at Marek somehow?

'What's he got to do with this?'

'I know you. I drove you towards him. It happened to be him. It could have been anyone.'

Pat couldn't deny the large element of truth in what Bob was saying. She was not unfaithful by nature. If she had been happy with Bob she may have been flattered by Marek's attention when it came, but she would not have encouraged it, or taken it seriously. Within a minute or two she would have made it crystal clear she was a married woman and that would have been that.

And I would never have known the greatest joy, or pleasure, of my life.

Pat looked at Bob facing her somewhat sheepishly on the bed.

Our marital bed. When exactly did it become the deathbed of our marriage? The first time he took me against my will? The hundredth?

'I don't want to tonight, Bob. If that's what this is all about. I'm just too tired.'

'What?'

'If you've got bored of me just lying beneath you counting the seconds until you've finished. If you're trying to have me *participate* in some semblance of love-making . . .'

'Is that what you think?' Bob sounded quietly aghast.

Pat hesitated, but she was too committed to backtrack.

'I can't think what else,' she said blankly. 'I really can't.'

For the second time in their conversation, Pat anticipated an outburst and stiffened her body against an assault she felt was certain to follow. Instead, Bob covered his eyes with his hand, and lowered his head. Then, softly at first, then louder, came the sound of a rising howl of anguish.

'Bob?' she asked quietly. 'Are you crying?'

There was a moment's silence before he managed to speak. 'What must you think of me . . .?' His voice was barely audible.

Pat's mind turned to the Mass Observation reports she had been writing for weeks. All she thought of Bob was described on those pages in exhaustive detail. Even though the brief for Mass Observation report writers was wide open for them to write about any aspect of their lives during the war, she wouldn't know how to write about this.

Pat looked at him. If it had been any other human being in front of her like this, and if she believed the pain they were trying to express was real and not put on to try to trick her, Pat would have held them in a tight, calming embrace. As she had held Erica at Will's funeral. As she had held Frances at Peter's. As she had held Sarah when the news came through of Adam's capture at Dunkirk. As she had held Marek on the one occasion he had broken down in her company – at the thought he might be killed in action and never see Pat again.

'I'm sorry . . .' Bob whispered a little pathetically, unable to look at her. 'Forgive me . . .'

Bob sat with his head down as one, then two tears fell from his cheeks onto the bed linen. Pat stared at him. At the tears now freely flowing down his cheeks and silently dripping onto the bed.

Oh my God. Is this real? Is he really experiencing genuine remorse?

'Forgive me,' Bob repeated. 'Forgive me . . .'

Chapter 19

Laura sat at the dining table waiting for Dr Rosen to finish in surgery. At the Observation Post, Brian hadn't convulsed with laughter or recoiled in horror at the suggestion that Laura might become a doctor; further, David Brindsley had taken the idea seriously. They had come to know Laura well; if she was serious about the idea then they felt convinced she could succeed. This gave Laura succour to continue to contemplate the idea in earnest, but she knew neither man was really qualified to make a judgement. It reminded her of one of her father's most firmly held beliefs: ideas must be tested to destruction – only if they survived did they have merit.

Laura knew she had reached the moment when she had to *properly* test the proposition. There were two people with whom she could do this. The first, and perhaps the most qualified of anyone she knew, was Dr Rosen.

Laura waited until Myra had finished for the day, and listened from the front room as she closed the surgery door. Laura took her opportunity and fully opened the door into the hall and stuck her head out.

'Myra, could I have a word?'

Myra turned to Laura. 'Of course,' she said. 'But I'm somewhat tired. Can it wait until morning?'

'It could, yes,' Laura replied, 'or . . . I could walk you back to your lodgings?'

Myra agreed to talk as they walked. Laura smiled, grabbed her own hat and coat and followed Myra out of the house.

'You don't mind if we walk briskly, do you?' Myra asked. 'Only I've been sitting behind the desk all day and could do with blowing away some cobwebs.'

'Not at all. Dad always took a brisk walk at the end of the day for the same reason. And to smoke his pipe, of course.'

'I'm almost certainly not going to be following his lead on that score,' Myra said with a smile, 'but it was actually his suggestion. He warned me that patients don't just bring their ailments with them into the surgery – but also their lives. He told me to take the time to shake off their concerns at the end of the day or be consumed by problems I can do nothing about. He was right. Also, it's very cold at the moment, so walking at a fair lick will keep us warm.'

Laura found this encouraging. In his last days, it seemed her father was dispensing his reflections to others as well as herself. If Myra took his suggestions seriously, why not she?

'The reason I wanted to speak to you in private, Myra, is because I wanted to ask your opinion.'

'I'm really only qualified to give medical opinion. On everything else I'm pretty hopeless, I'm afraid. For example, I was convinced Germany would never invade Austria and then Czechoslovakia. And equally convinced we would never declare war on Hitler. Wrong on every count.'

'It was a medical opinion of sorts I wanted to ask you about.'

Myra's face frowned as she silently scrolled through the medical conditions a young woman of Laura's age might experience. As she had asked to see Myra in person, away from the house and her mother, Myra swiftly arrived at the most likely issue.

'Do you suspect you might be pregnant?' she asked as matter-of-factly as she could.

Laura's mouth fell open at the suggestion, though Myra took it as amazement at her prowess and continued.

'You needn't worry about me telling your mother. Though that might become necessary as I'm technically her employee. It could be a conflict of interest for me to know something so personal about her daughter that she doesn't. Even if it wasn't strictly a conflict of interest, it will certainly put me in a difficult position. But we can discuss that later. When was your most recent period?'

If Laura's mouth could have opened any wider it would have hit the ground. Instead, it began to emit a strange form of laughter in response to Myra being both colossally wide of the mark about Laura's enquiry and improperly assumptive about her private life.

'I'm *not* pregnant!' Laura finally exclaimed.

'Are you sure? I don't mean to be rude, but you wouldn't be the first young woman to find herself in the family way. Especially now, when all bets are off about the future.'

'I can absolutely guarantee that I am *not* pregnant, Myra.'

'You don't have to beat around the bush with me, Laura. I consider you a friend now, as well as the daughter of my employer. As such I would do whatever I could to help you.'

'I appreciate that, but me falling pregnant would be a biological impossibility.'

Myra thought she understood what Laura meant, but needed absolute clarification. 'So, you and your young man, Tom—'

'Can we *please* change the subject back to what I actually wanted to ask your opinion about?'

Myra had been sure she was right. Her diagnostic powers were certainly formidable, and her ability to read between the lines of what people said against what they meant had grown daily since taking up the post at the surgery.

'Of course. What did you wish to ask me?'

Laura hesitated for a moment and took a deep breath. 'It's about my future.'

Myra kept silent and nodded, listening.

'You know what it takes to become a doctor, Myra,' Laura said.

'I do. A lot of hard work on top of proving wrong a lot of people who think it's not a job for women.'

'I've been giving my future a great deal of thought since my father died.'

'And you thought you might go into medicine?'

They were now at the nub of it. There was no turning back.

'In your expert opinion, is it a ridiculous idea?'

'I know you're clever, but are you good at science?'

'I think I am when I apply myself. At school I didn't always do that. But as I grew older I found science increasingly interesting. But then war broke out, dad became ill . . .'

'Do you want to help people, Laura? Work with the sick? You don't have to answer definitively, but do you think that is something you might become good at?'

'In the way my father did, yes. I don't want to mimic him in any way. But I saw the impact he had on this community, and I saw the pleasure that gave him. If I could achieve a fraction of that same satisfaction I think I would be very rewarded indeed.'

Myra smiled at Laura as they walked side by side in the cold evening air.

'I am so pleased you said that. Because I have come across many young people who talk about becoming doctors because they want to fix people and do good, and all of that. But very few of them understand that to do it effectively, over the length of a career, they must derive a great deal of personal satisfaction from doing it. Because the last thing the medical profession needs are saints or martyrs. Believe me, they are no good to anyone.'

Laura wanted to push Dr Rosen for an unequivocal answer. 'Given your own experience, Myra, do you think I could do it?'

Myra slowed her pace to a stop and looked intensely at the younger woman. 'I'll let you into a little secret, Laura, by way of answering your question.'

Myra paused for dramatic effect, much as she might pause with an anxious patient before telling them their anxiety was misplaced and they could look forward to a long and healthy life.

'*My* father was also a doctor. A damned good one. I know *exactly* where this comes from. Of course, I think you could do it.'

There was only one person remaining for Laura to speak to on the matter. She felt guilty about talking about herself to her mother so soon after they had buried Will, as if the rush to get on with living might feel disrespectful and unseemly. At St Mark's, during the burial service, Laura had overheard people mention 'a period of mourning', but she had no idea how long such a period should last. Nor did she believe her feelings about her father's death could be contained to a prescribed timeframe.

In Laura's mind, she would be mourning the loss of her father for the rest of her life. There would never be a right time to bring anything up about going forward when everything seemed to have come so resolutely to a halt. So, she just came out with it over supper.

'What would you say if I told you I was thinking of trying for medical school?'

The spoon with which Erica was eating was halfway between the bowl and her mouth. She set it down and calmly took another piece of bread from the plate in the centre of the table and looked earnestly at Laura.

'Is this in response to your father telling you he thought you'd make a good doctor?'

Laura couldn't believe her ears. 'He told you that?'

Erica smiled indulgently. 'Darling, your father and I talked about everything.'

'Why didn't you say something?' Laura asked, dumbfounded. 'Those words have been going around my head since he mentioned it. I wasn't sure if he was serious, or speaking in some kind of morphine-induced delirium.'

'He was quite, *quite* serious. The reason I haven't mentioned it was because it was a private conversation between the two of you. And if it was something that had no interest for you I felt I had to give you the opportunity to leave it at that.'

'So how do you feel now you know I *have* been giving it serious thought and believe it's something I really want to do?'

Erica stood up and crossed to the other side of the table where Laura was sitting and crouched beside her daughter. She took Laura's hands in her own and looked at her with great intensity.

'I think it's possibly the greatest testament to your father there could ever be.'

Within seconds tears were welling in Laura's eyes. 'I'm not sure I'd want to be a GP.'

'He didn't care. He saw himself reflected in you in so many ways. But always with what he would call "a unique twist of Laura".'

'I really want you to know that I'm not just wanting to do it because Dad mentioned it.'

'Many people came to their areas of expertise by very circuitous routes. It doesn't matter, as long as the passion to do it has been *truly* ignited.'

'I truly believe it has.'

Erica nodded. 'Horrible as it is to say, but now is a good time to apply, what with so many young men being siphoned off to the war.'

'I don't want to get into medical school through the back door because there aren't enough better-qualified men.'

'I didn't mean that. I meant a lot of medical schools have a traditional bias against taking female students. They won't be able to uphold that.'

Laura nodded. As ever, her mother made sense.

'There's only one issue about it, darling,' Erica continued. 'And I'm afraid it's one we have to take very seriously.'

'What issue?'

'Money. We had some savings put aside in case you and Kate wanted to go to university. But we always calculated that your father would have to continue to work for the duration. Now that he's gone—'

'I'll go somewhere that offers a scholarship!' Laura declared.

It seemed like the perfect solution. And indeed, it would have been the perfect solution in Erica's eyes if only Laura had hitherto demonstrated the academic aptitude of a scholarship girl. Laura's evident natural intelligence always put her near the middle of most of her classes, but she had seemed to lack the drive to be at the very top of them.

Erica wiped her eyes and looked at Laura with great affection.

'There will be tremendous competition for scholarships. I imagine there will be a great many extremely bright girls seeking to capitalise on the situation.'

'Then I'll *compete* with them.'

Laura's tone was a mixture of defiance against any who might dare suggest she lacked either the intelligence or ambition to gain a scholarship to a medical school.

'You'll have to be ferociously single-minded,' said Erica.

'I can be single-minded.'

'You'll have to be ferociously focused on your studies.'

'I can be focused.'

Erica smiled encouragingly, but without complete confidence. Laura wasn't narrow in her approach to life and her schoolwork, but demonstrated an interesting, broad outlook, and enjoyed the company of a large group of friends. Her daughter's attitude to her life had not been business-like, or goal-centred in any way, but had always been more free-form and improvisatory. It was what made her one of the more interesting younger cohort at the WI. It was what had made her susceptible to the dubious charms of Wing Commander Bowers, who had used her so disgracefully; and what enabled Laura to come through that experience stronger, wiser, and with a greater understanding of how some men – and some organisations – can behave towards women. Studying for a scholarship to medical school would require a dedication to her studies and a tunnel-vision to her future that Laura had not previously demonstrated. Erica told her directly. Laura nodded.

'I think for the first time in my life I know what I want to do. Competition or not. I want to make Dad extraordinarily proud of me.'

Erica looked at her daughter and brushed an errant strand of hair from her face.

'Your father was always *extraordinarily* proud of you. So, if you are going to attempt this, don't keep looking over your shoulder for him to spur you on. He's gone, my love. You have to drive *yourself*. There really is no other way. And don't be ashamed by how selfish and self-centred I believe you will need to become in the weeks ahead. Become that to achieve your goal. Only then revert to the wonderful, warm and generous Laura we all love and adore.'

Chapter 20

STEPH SAT AT the kitchen table when Stan telephoned the *Liverpool Echo* to tell them to pull the story about his wife and son struggling with and then killing the German pilot. He asked to speak to the reporter who'd come to the farm on a tip-off from a police source. The reporter, Philip Shepherd, wasn't yet in the office, so Stan was diverted to the duty news editor, who told Stan in an unapologetic voice that it was too late – the story had already been splashed across that morning's front page, and as a consequence the paper was selling like hot-cakes.

'Never seen a run like it, Mr Farrow,' the editor told Stan. 'Not since the evacuation of Dunkirk. Your wife's a remarkable woman.'

'I don't need you to tell me that,' Stan said, irritated by an overfamiliarity. 'Is there nothing you can do? Only, she's changed her mind.'

'Sorry. But whether she likes it or not, she's about to become a local hero. Wouldn't bet against her becoming a national one too. Her story's just what the doctor ordered. Bloody hell, the only way it could be better was if she'd killed Hitler himself.'

When Stan put the receiver back on its hook he turned slowly and looked at Steph.

'Well?' she said.

'We're too late, love. Paper went out this morning.'

Steph's eyes widened with alarm.

'Nothing they can do.'

'How long before everyone round here finds out?'

'I don't know. Maybe they won't. Don't think many read the *Echo* in the village.'

'But who comes *into* the village every night, Stan – trekkers from Liverpool. One of them's bound to bring a copy with them.'

'Well, we can hardly stop them on their way in and take it off them, can we?'

'This is horrible.'

'Is it, love? I mean . . . it *did* happen. The bloke on the telephone called you a hero. Worse things to be called.'

Steph shook her head. 'I'm not.'

'Everyone else seems to think so, so maybe . . . you're wrong.'

'I was there, everyone else wasn't – including you.'

Suddenly, the telephone began to ring, causing them each to jump a little.

'Don't answer it,' Steph instructed, her voice tinged with panic.

'It might be the sub-editor saying there's something they can do after all.'

'What can they do – go into every kitchen in Liverpool and take them all back? Don't answer.'

Stan could see from Steph's expression she was as adamant as she was frightened. He crossed to the table and sat opposite her. He took Steph's hand in his, and held it as they waited for the telephone to stop ringing. Without realising she was doing it, her hand slowly gripped tightly around Stan's. Eventually, the telephone was silent.

'You can't undo it, Steph. You can't go back and unkill the man.'

'More than anything else in the world, I wish to God I could.'

Suddenly, the telephone began to ring again, causing Steph to startle. Stan began to get up but Steph pressed his hand down onto the table, and shook her head.

'It might be important,' he argued.

'More important you leave it.'

Stan slowly sat back down, believing that once Steph's initial panic had subsided she'd be more open to reason about the story coming out. As they waited for the ringing to stop, the door to the farmyard opened and Stanley looked in at them.

'Heard the telephone. Thought something must've happened. Why aren't you answering?'

'Your mam doesn't want to.'

'Why – who is it?'

'We don't know.'

'Makes no sense.'

The telephone stopped ringing.

'The story about the pilot's out today, Stanley,' Steph said.

'In the *Echo*?'

Steph nodded.

'Everyone'll know it was us.'

Steph nodded.

'We'll be famous!' Stanley said, excitedly.

Steph looked reproachfully at her husband and back at her son. 'What did we do, Stanley?'

'What do you mean? You were there. You shot the bugger.'

'What did we *do*, son?' she repeated, unable to suppress the miserable tone in her voice.

'Steph . . .' Stan didn't know why Steph was asking Stanley for an account of what happened. Not only had he clearly repeated it many times, it was about to become a matter of public record. His wife didn't turn her head towards her husband, but continued to stare at their son in the farmhouse doorway.

'What did we do?' Steph repeated a third time, determined to force Stanley to answer her question.

Stanley looked as confused as his father. 'You know what we did. I came upon him, camped in the woods. Chased him across the field, ran him down, fought with him on the ground—'

Stanley's account stopped the moment he saw his mother slowly shake her head. His confusion deepened.

'We both know that's not true. Don't we?'

Stan turned to his wife. 'What do you mean it's not true? What's not true?'

'Stanley didn't chase the pilot across the field. Did you, Stanley?'

Stanley's confusion transformed into fear. 'What's got into you, Ma? Why're you saying all this?'

'You weren't truthful in your account to the police, and then in your account to the reporter. I backed you up because I thought it didn't matter . . .'

'What do you mean?' Stan asked, rising from his chair. Steph now turned to face him.

'Stanley told the police and the reporter that he chased the pilot across the field and brought him down. He didn't. The pilot chased Stanley across the field, and brought Stanley down.'

Stan looked at his son. 'That right?'

Stanley didn't understand why any of this mattered.

'Stanley? Is that right?'

Tears pricked Stanley's eyes, and he nodded.

'Then why say different?'

Stanley looked at his parents helplessly, unable to speak.

'A young lad surrounded by the war day and night,' Steph said. 'What's the better story – that he fled for his life from a German pilot, screaming blue bloody murder for his mammy? Or he bravely chased a Nazi with a gun, and ran him down with his bare hands?'

Tears rolled down the boy's cheeks.

'Why'd you have to say that?' he said to his mother. 'Why'd you have to say it?'

'Because it's the truth, Stanley. And I can't carry on pretending it isn't. I thought it didn't matter to the police. But you said the same to the reporter, and now you're going to have to keep saying it every time you're asked about it. We all are.'

'He changed the story to make himself look better,' Stan said. 'No harm done.'

Steph looked sharply at her husband. 'He *lied*, Stan. There's the harm. I lied too. There's more harm!'

The telephone began to ring for a third time.

'And now *you're* going to have to lie.'

'You backed him up. Like any mother would. And I'll do the same, like any father. The bones of what happened doesn't change. They make you even more heroic. You stopped a Nazi who was chasing your son. An English woman defended her son against a Nazi pilot. That's what the story is. That's all they'll care about.'

'I don't care about other people. I care about *us*. All you bloody men talking up the glory, so lads like Stanley don't know whether they're coming or going.'

The telephone stopped ringing.

'But Steph, love,' Stan pleaded, 'it makes no difference!'

'It makes a difference to *me*! That's why I changed my mind about all this coming out. We're going to have to go in front of the village and carry on lying, over and over – because people will want to hear it from the horse's mouth.

183

And in the great scheme of things it mightn't matter if Stanley was chasing the pilot or the other way around. But it matters to me because we've lied to talk it up, and we'll carry on because we have to, for the lad's sake. Over and over. You'll never have to buy a pint again, Stan. Nor you, Stanley, when you're old enough. Stanley the hero! So much better than Stanley the terrified lad, shitting himself.

'And me? The "courageous hero farmer's wife"? I shot and killed a boy, Stan! Without warning him. In uniform, maybe. But a lad, nonetheless. Don't think this isn't going to follow us, because it is. It's going to hang over us because the truth will out. Isn't that why we brought him up the way we did, to tell the truth and have nothing to fear? Or don't we believe that anymore, Stan? Now it suits us not to?'

The three of them looked at one another, as the telephone started to ring for a fourth time, the sound increasingly urgent and unbearable.

Stan could no longer stand it and crossed to the device, tore it out of the wall, and dashed it against the floor. Steph wasn't finished.

'If they find out we lied about one part of the story who's to say they won't start thinking we lied about all of it.'

'How will they find out?' Stanley asked quietly. 'You said yourself, Ma – the German was the only other one there, and he's dead.'

Steph looked at her son and felt her eyes fill with tears.

'You should've let me bury him in the wood and say no more about it. You should've let me bury it and let everything stay the same.'

Stan crossed to his wife and took her face in his large, rough hands, and tilted it upwards so that she had nowhere else to look than into his eyes.

'This is what the war does,' he said. 'It buggers everything up. Makes people behave out of themselves. There's no shame in it.' He turned to his son standing behind him. 'There's no shame in it, son. It carries us all along, one way or another.'

'I shouldn't've shot him, Stan,' Steph said. 'He wasn't trying to kill Stanley. He was just trying to stop him screaming out. His hands weren't around his throat but over his mouth. To stop the boy from drawing attention.'

'Enough!' Stan barked loudly, trying to keep his breathing under control as adrenaline started to course through him. 'You never say that to anyone, *ever*.'

Stan realised he had to take control of the situation. This is why Steph had written to him.

'We say the same story with every telling, whoever's asking. No one suspects anything different. We say the same thing over and over until everyone's sick of hearing it and stop asking. Because we can't go back.'

'Pa!' Stanley said. 'Ma!'

Steph and Stan looked over at their son, whose attention had been taken by something outside. They crossed to the window and saw a sleek black Daimler slowly making its way along the small road towards the farmhouse. Steph threaded her arm through Stan's and gripped onto him tightly.

'Who is it, Pa?'

'Doesn't matter who it is. We say the same story with every telling. Isn't that right, Steph?'

Steph watched the black car approach with deep foreboding.

'That's right, Stan,' she said quietly, with heavy resignation. 'Over and over and over . . .'

Chapter 21

ANNIE WAS SITTING up in her hospital bed, her eyebrows raised in mock-indignation at Teresa.

'An *order*? Nick is in no position to give me orders. He's RAF, I'm ATA. He has no authority over me.'

Teresa smiled at the thought of Nick even trying to exert any kind of authority over Annie.

'It's an expression of how much he'd like you to complete your rehabilitation with us.'

Annie's expression turned suddenly serious. 'Us?'

'Friends,' Teresa said firmly.

'At your suggestion.'

Teresa shook her head. 'It was Nick's idea,' she said.

This was the truth but not the entire truth. The more she considered it afterwards the happier she became that Nick had pipped her to the post – no suspicion would be attached to Teresa for inviting Annie to live with them during her final rehabilitation.

'You don't think me coming to live with you and Nick represents a risk?' asked Annie.

Teresa looked at Annie calmly and shook her head. 'I don't see why it should.'

'Don't be naive, Teresa – it doesn't suit you. Given the way we feel about one another ... I mean, must I spell it out?'

Since she had kissed Annie as she lay in bed in hospital, Teresa had never attempted to repeat it, and had reproached herself for giving in to her impulse. She was certain she could be Annie's friend and nothing more. It really was the best for all involved.

'I thought it would be good for both of us. You would have a comfortable setting in which to recuperate, and I would have company. There are days, Annie, when I don't speak to another soul from the moment Nick leaves for Tabley Wood at daybreak, to his return in the early hours.'

'You knew what you were getting into before you married.'

'I'm not asking for sympathy. When Nick's at home it's wonderful. But it's not always easy to fill time when it's just you. I hadn't anticipated losing my job, and finding myself the domestic equivalent of being confined to barracks.'

'Millions of women live the same way. The vast majority.'

'It's simply not something I ever anticipated for myself.'

'You just said it was wonderful when Nick was home.'

'It is. We get on very well. I imagine that as marriages go ours is wonderful. We like each other immensely—'

'Well, you are streets ahead of most married couples I know. My parents loathe each other with a perverse form of passion – you'd never leave a loaded shotgun in the house for fear of what might happen.'

Teresa wanted to end this conversation about her own marriage, and redirect it back to the matter in hand.

'We're both very fond of you, Annie. We want to help you get better as soon as possible. You and I barely know one another. I thought it could be an opportunity to properly remedy that. Become close friends.'

Annie looked at Teresa for several moments, trying to gauge her real intention. 'Close friends?' She made the words sound like a joke. 'Two weeks ago, you kissed me in this very bed. Or have you forgotten?'

'Of course not. But—'

'You visit me nearly every day—'

'Because I enjoy *your company*.' Teresa felt a need to get a grip on the conversation. 'I couldn't betray Nick's trust,' she said firmly. 'I suspect you feel the same.'

Annie smiled for the first time in the conversation. 'Don't be too certain about that. I've been told on more than one occasion that my moral compass is distinctly erratic.'

'And how do you respond to the people who say that about you?'

'I tell them they're wrong. I have a very highly developed sense of morality. If "problems" *do* arise it's because that's overruled by my passions.'

Teresa looked hard at Annie. 'If you came to stay with us, *nothing* . . . untoward . . . would happen. I simply can't allow it.'

'You sound like a schoolteacher.'

'I sound like *a wife*.'

'But you'd be tempted.' Annie looked at Teresa and smiled. 'I know I would be.'

Teresa hesitated for two seconds. 'It's the only way it could work,' she said.

Though Teresa could be as *tempted* as the next woman to imagine something illicit and secret, she wasn't prepared to jeopardise the respectability she had sacrificed so much for. In the cold light of day – and Teresa had many cold days, and much cold light in which to consider her situation – she realised that Annie could only come on fixed, and mutually understood terms of *friendship*.

'I think we could become the most wonderful friends if you came to stay,' Teresa said, underlining the point once more. 'But of course, you may have other plans.'

Annie did not. Once she knew she would soon be leaving hospital Annie thought she would take a guest room above a pub near Tabley Wood – a popular watering hole for pilots at the base. She thought it would do her good to be near other aviators. She subsequently realised that if she were to be told by her surgeon she could never fly again, a distinct possibility, it would in fact be agony to be in such proximity to active flyers. The only alternative to the pub was to go back to her parents' home in Surrey, but the prospect of recuperating amid their ongoing and deeply entrenched acrimony left her in a state of dread.

Annie accepted Teresa's invitation on the terms offered. The calculation hadn't taken long to make. In addition to being attracted to Teresa, she liked her enormously. Sexual gratification could be found elsewhere, if a girl knew where to look, which Annie did.

Teresa left the hospital immensely pleased with the arrangements, but the closer Annie's arrival came, the more enthusiastic Nick was about having his old friend stay at the house while the more nervous Teresa became. Nick relished setting up the front room as a makeshift bedroom for her, moving furniture so it could be converted from a living room into a bedroom within minutes, and vice versa.

Watching him merrily prepare for Annie's arrival filled Teresa with a sense of foreboding.

Why did I ask her? Why hadn't I sat on the stupid idea until I'd come to my senses? If only I hadn't felt so damned isolated stuck out here. If only I still had my job. If only, if only, if only. If only I was someone else entirely.

It wasn't that Teresa didn't trust Annie or herself to keep to their agreement. It was the fear – no, the conviction – that Nick might eventually notice something passing between the two women that he couldn't quite explain; a look, a gesture made unconsciously that nevertheless belied a strength of feeling that didn't quite tally with his understanding of their relationship.

I can be as vigilant as I like, but how can I guard against things I'm unaware of? It's impossible.

On the day of Annie's arrival, Teresa was unable to relax. She tried to sit in every chair in the house, but found none allowed her to become calm. Finally, Teresa found herself standing helplessly in the front room, waiting for Nick to fetch Annie from the hospital, hands clasped in front of her to stop them trembling. She tried reassuring herself she had nothing to fear, that she and Annie would behave as agreed, and that Nick would be, in turn, too busy and too exhausted to notice any small slips that might occur.

It will be all right. It has to be . . .

Chapter 22

I wonder what you'll make of this, dear reader, because try as I might, I can't make head nor tail of it. I've now been writing to you, whoever you are, for several months, so you should have a vivid impression of my marriage by now. And of my husband, admittedly as I see him (I have tried to be truthful). You know almost everything about me, because I've held nothing back. What would be the point? The purpose of these reports is to provide an honest portrait of life during wartime. I recognise that being honest about the way I perceive my marriage may not be the same as being accurate about it. And I suppose the point of this is that you get my perspective, my story, and that is always going to be biased in favour of the scribe.

But I am asking you to make a judgement now, so it is important you feel able to do that. I have written previously about my affair – no – I no longer wish to call it that. An 'affair' reduces what it is to a sideshow, something taking place in the shadows to add a little spice to life but never directly threatening the main event. My relationship with the Czech soldier is no longer a sideshow. It is the most important relationship in my life now and in the future. We recently met and re-confirmed our commitment to be together if we each survive the war. That is possible if the Nazis don't kill him, and if my husband – in a rage against whatever perceived slight so moves him – doesn't manage to finish me off. If we are both still standing at the end of all this I shall leave my husband. I said it to my love, and I say the same to you. It is our stated aim. My husband knows nothing of this. He knows – as I have previously written – that I have had an 'affair' but assumes he has managed to stop it by intercepting any correspondence I might receive from my soldier. He hasn't.

This is what I want your view on. My husband has started to be pleasant towards me with what you might call 'small acts of kindness'. Things he has never done before, or so long ago I cannot recall them. He has made me lunch. He has made me breakfast in bed. He has started to speak to me in a calm, solicitous voice, and no longer seems to bark at me. Sometimes I glance up and find him looking at me, and he smiles warmly, like he used to when we first met. This morning he even brought me some winter flowers he had picked from the banks of the local canal. Instead of me constantly bringing him endless cups of tea to keep him going while he works, he has started to bring me tea in the morning and in the evening. He washes up the dishes after supper – something he has never done at any time during our marriage. He has even tried to 'make love' to me. Before, it never felt like love at all. It was a physical act of pleasure for him only. I hated it. Now, he is showing signs of consideration. I still view it as violation. The fear hasn't gone away — it is important for you to understand this. I still fear him, because previous experience tells me this is a game of some kind, and that it will build to a horrible climax and we will return to how things were before. Why do I think this? Because this is what has always happened. Through bitter experience I have grown to believe he is incapable of change.

But. Dear reader. But. What if he is?

Is it possible for a man like this to change? My history with him says not. Yet, we change physically, so why not psychologically, over time? I have changed upon meeting my soldier. Is it not possible the discovery and apparent ending of that relationship has changed my husband in some way? Now he firmly believes he has me to himself once more, could he have realised how close he was to losing something he valued? I'm not even talking about 'love'. I mean the things I do for him. He'd miss them terribly if I were not here. Has he made a calculation that to keep me he must treat me better? If not with real respect, then at least the pretence of it? Or else eventually lose me to another man.

Or am I reading too much into the situation? Being ludicrously optimistic because my mind leaps upon any small reduction in the perpetual war of attrition he has been waging against me. Interpreting his behaviour in a way I want to see, not because that is how it is.

What would you advise, dear Mass Observation reader, in your room piled high with manuscripts from women like me? To take him on trust? Or trust nothing?

Or does it matter either way, if my soldier and I are waiting to be together? It matters because I have to live with whichever configuration it is. If he is being genuine then shouldn't I be genuine back – even if it doesn't materially affect what I plan to do once the war ends? And if this is a ruse to have me lower my guard, then shouldn't I be extra-vigilant, and play a game of my own out of self-protection?

You cannot see how he is towards me, so I am telling you his change in behaviour has all the appearance of being genuine. Perhaps this is the case. Let us say it is. He has been this way before and I have seen it crumble away at the first sign of stress. His book is selling well at the moment, and he is feeling confident and loved by readers once again. What happens when that inevitably subsides? When the tide of publishing drags the accolades and royalties back out to sea. Will he revert?

I have been thinking about broaching this matter with him. Asking him what has brought about this change? I have grown so used to thinking inwardly about everything. I am well aware of my own capacity to convince myself that a situation is one way when I have simply been too close, too affected by it to see its details clearly. Perhaps it is better to ask him directly, and gauge his answer. If he is now being genuine in his care towards me then he would understand my suspicion. If he is not, am I naive to believe he would reveal his true purpose? Wouldn't he continue to play this part of loving husband in which he seems to have cast himself? Or will he step out of this character and be his true self once more?

This will surprise you, but I suspect I would prefer the third possibility. I do not have the energy to begin to try and like him once more. I cannot 'love' him again – I am certain. When he is at me constantly I know where we stand. It brings my hatred of him to the boil and that sustains my defiance, which keeps me going.

What do you think, my dear, patient reader? Does a leopard ever change his spots, or can it only cover them temporarily? Can such a man as my husband ever truly change for the good? What should I do? Try and give him the benefit of the doubt? What, I wonder if you were sitting here with me, would you advise?

Chapter 23

THOUGH THE BLACK saloon approaching the farm-house had looked like an official vehicle of some kind, causing a spike of dread to rise in the Farrows, it was in fact the car of a young, ambitious BBC radio producer who had read about Steph and Stanley's 'triumph' over the German pilot in the *Liverpool Echo* at breakfast that morning. Eager for a scoop in his own medium, he had set out immediately for Great Paxford to try to record an interview with Mrs Farrow and her son that would be broadcast on the wireless at the earliest opportunity. In the producer's view, it would be 'a story of immense interest to our listeners'. The producer wished to get to the Farrows before any of the newsreel competitors, as he knew that the first outlet to secure an interview would receive the most honest emotional account, uncontaminated by rehearsal and repetition. After the producer had explained himself, Steph was initially reluctant, but he told the Farrows that once Steph and Stanley had completed an interview with him she could legitimately tell anyone else who came calling that she'd said all she wanted to say on the matter. It seemed unarguable to Steph. She would tell the lie once more, and never again.

'Besides,' he told her, 'radio is neither as intrusive nor as exposing as the newsreels. No camera means you have no need to be self-conscious about how you come across. On the radio, you simply relax as far as you can and talk into the microphone in the same voice and volume you would to talk to a friend, and say what you want to say. The nation would be fascinated to hear yours and Stanley's story, Mrs Farrow. In your *own* words, not some hack reporter's.'

Watched by Stan in the corner of the kitchen, Steph and Stanley gave their account of the event, and then answered the producer's questions about how it had left them feeling. Stanley's answers were predictably full of derring-do and excitement and bravado, as he told the producer that he felt proud of what they'd done. He interpreted the behaviour of the German as 'like a madman', and was glad he and his mother had been able to stop him before he turned his madness on others.

Stan could see the producer was more interested in Steph's account of the shooting, and of how it had left her. Steph was far more measured and far less gung-ho than her son. Stan could see she was struggling to contain her sense of guilt at having shot the pilot, and tried to encourage her across the room by gently nodding along with her account. She said that the event itself passed in the blink of an eye, or so it seemed. But the consequences, she had started to realise, would remain for a long time; perhaps for the rest of her life.

'Why do you say that, Mrs Farrow?' the producer asked.

'If I was a soldier it might not,' she replied. 'But I'm just a farmer's wife. I look after my animals. Tend the land. I'm not meant for anything else.'

'But in a way,' persisted the producer, 'do you not feel you were serving your country?'

'I was saving my son,' she said. 'Others can see it how they like. There's nothing I can do to stop them. Everyone's full of invasion talk. I saw my son fighting for his life and did what any mother would've done.'

'Most mothers don't know how to handle a shotgun, Mrs Farrow,' the producer said, with a hint of amusement in his voice.

'Then they'd do what they had to do. I just did what I had to do to save Stanley. I didn't think much about it at the time. Like I said. It all happened so fast.'

The producer was about to bring the interview to a close when Steph gestured that she had one more thing to say.

'Is there anything you'd like to add, Mrs Farrow?' he said.

'Only . . . I'm not proud of what I did. I'm pleased I saved my boy, of course. The pilot was a German, but that's not what I saw when he was lying on the ground. I saw a young boy, little older than mine, put in a plane to drop bombs on us, told it was the right thing to do. I imagine his mother and father waiting on news of him.'

The producer, Stanley, and Stan looked at Steph as her eyes welled up.

'Think you've got enough,' said Stan gently, bringing the interview to a close.

The producer leaned forward and turned off the recorder.

'Not as straightforward as you thought, is it?' said Steph, wiping her eyes.

'On the contrary, Mrs Farrow. I imagined this event might have a profound effect on you all. I think it's wonderful that you've managed to convey that to our listeners. We want to communicate the complexity of what happened – that there's no simple response to it one way or the other. War – and this was an act of war that you and your son were engaged in – is a complex, messy experience. We all know that. Hearing how it affected you will help prevent people imagining winning this is going to be easy, and not a very hard road indeed.'

When the BBC producer had packed away his recording machine and microphone he thanked Steph and Stanley for their co-operation and gave them a final piece of advice.

'Don't let this event take over. I've seen that with people I interview. Traumatic events dominating their entire lives. At the right time, put it behind you.'

The Farrows watched the producer's car disappear the way it had come. Steph let out a long sigh, and felt drained.

'I need some air,' she said. 'I might go for a walk.'

'I'll come with,' said Stan.

'No. I've some things to pick up from the village. I could use the time to myself. Stanley – why don't you show your dad what we've done to the farm while he's been away?'

'How bad is it?' said Stan, smiling, ruffling his son's hair.

'Everything's better – you'll see,' said Stanley.

'Better? Right then – I'll go back to the battalion if you don't need me.'

Steph looked sharply at Stan. 'It's the army that doesn't need you. I couldn't stand you leaving again.'

On her way into the village, Steph reflected on the interview she'd just given. Even the act of talking into the microphone had subtly altered the way she'd spoken, making her more careful about the choice of words she used, and her tone. What had first been an account of what had taken place that afternoon was inevitably becoming 'the story' of what had happened, and Steph had been all too conscious of how she was telling it. The producer had asked her to address the microphone as if she were speaking to a close friend, so the account would sound intimate and immediate. But he also told her to hold nothing back. If she stumbled during the telling that would be fine; he would edit out any mistakes when he returned to the office.

I don't want to tell it again. If people want to know they can read the paper, or listen to the wireless. The BBC man was right. It happened, there's nothing I can do about that. As terrible as it is, there's nothing I can do. An act of war. That's right. What else was it but that? He wouldn't have been on our land but for the war. Wouldn't have attacked Stanley. I wouldn't have . . .

Steph closed her eyes for a moment and forced herself to leave the sentence unfinished.

Let God sort out the whys and wherefores. That's His job, not mine.

Walking along the road lined by high trees on either side, Steph felt herself becoming calmer, and tuned in to the surrounding environment by way of distracting herself. The wind rushing through bare branches. Crows calling to one another in the high wind. It was good to get away from the farm for even an hour.

Everything will be better now Stan's back.

Steph entered the High Street and saw Mrs Talbot and two friends standing outside the newsagent's, talking animatedly amongst themselves, looking at a newspaper one of them was holding. Steph averted her gaze so as not to catch theirs, but it was too late. Mrs Talbot had seen Steph, and nudged her two friends to pay attention. As Steph drew closer one of the women held aloft the newspaper. It was a copy of that morning's *Liverpool Echo*, and the page was open on the interview Steph had given to the reporter, Philip Shepherd. Steph had no idea what to do, so she continued to walk towards them. As she drew closer to the three women, Mrs Talbot began to applaud her. Almost instantly, the other two women followed suit.

'Please, don't,' said Steph as she walked past.

'You deserve it,' Mrs Talbot called out. 'He could've killed anyone one of us. Or more than one. You stopped him going on a rampage, Mrs Farrow! Bravo! Mrs Farrow! Bravo!'

As they clapped, heads appeared in shop doorways along the High Street, wanting to know what the noise was for. Steph hurried past with her head down, and went into Brindsley's. The butcher's was full of women queuing for that week's ration. All eyes turned on Steph.

'Here she is!' said Bryn as soon as he saw Steph, his large face beaming. 'Great Paxford's very own Nazi hunter!'

On cue, the women in the shop broke into a round of applause for Steph, each channelling the great sense of relief they had experienced when they learned the German pilot was no longer at large. None could have imagined for a moment that it would be one of their own who brought their terror to an end.

'Thank you!' one called out.

'Our hero!' called another.

'All the army, police, and Home Guard looking and it takes one brave woman to do the job!' said a third.

Steph stood transfixed, trapped in their applause, wanting none of it. She turned to Bryn and blurted, 'I'll come back later,' then stepped back out of the doorway and hurried home. She took the back route, avoiding streets, houses and roads, crossing fields and footpaths where she was unlikely to encounter anything but wildlife. Finally, she ran up to the farmhouse and went inside, shook off her coat, changed into her overalls and went back out and into the chicken coop. As the hens clucked softly around her feet, Steph stood rooted to the spot looking at the door, breathing heavily, like a fox in a hole waiting for the hunt to pass.

Chapter 24

THERE WAS SNOW in the air on the day of Laura's meticulously well-planned Christmas party. Not a blizzard, but enough to send parents and children hurrying towards the warmth and shelter of the village hall. There, Laura and the women of the WI waited to greet them after working from sunrise to bedeck the hall with as much Christmas spirit as their combined skills could muster. The sight befalling all visitors was certainly one for sore, wind-lashed eyes. The walls and ceiling dripped with colourful bunting in Christmassy red and green, and table after table groaned with pies and cakes and buns and jugs of squash, all miraculously made out of rations, aided by a little added WI hustling of local suppliers to give a bit on the side for a unique occasion. The hall smelled – and looked – delicious. A local four-piece band was tuning up in the corner beside the centrepiece of the entire event: the largest Christmas tree Steph had Stan and Stanley carry back from a local copse. It was two feet short of the ceiling and glittered with stars and reindeer made from twigs and pieces of wood that had been glued together and painted in bright, eye-catching colours.

The children stared around the hall in amazement at the transformation the women had wrought, and their parents put their hands to their mouths and tried not to cry with joy at the wonderful effort that in the darkest time provided them all with some cheer.

Laura and her team greeted everyone with broad smiles, and the promise of an afternoon of unmitigated fun followed by a dance for the young and 'not so young'. She had persuaded Myra Rosen to come, and had even managed to get Erica out of the house for the first time since Will's funeral.

Laura had been thorough in her preparation. She had drawn up a list of everyone in the village and had hand-written – and hand-delivered – invites to everyone. A week after delivering the invites, Laura returned to each home to ascertain how many would be attending so the WI could organise itself into sub-groups for food, decorations, Christmas tree, games, and dance. In all, forty-three families said they would be coming. It was more than Laura had anticipated, and the prospect of having to keep so many children entertained and fed left her momentarily paralysed with terror, remembering Teresa once telling her that there was nothing quite as horrifying as a room full of bored children. There were so many constituencies to satisfy. Laura had initially consulted her mother – a woman who had spent quite some time trying to keep her own children entertained over the years.

'Just keep them busy,' Erica had advised airily.

'What if some of them don't want to "be kept busy"? What if some of them just want to sit at the side and watch?'

'Then let them.'

Laura didn't find this satisfactory.

What if all the children decided to sit at the side and not take part in the fun and games? The party would come grinding to a halt.

Laura wanted each child to enjoy themselves enormously, and return home at the end of the afternoon with their parents bubbling over with excitement about the time they'd had at an event that would give them a warm glow for weeks afterwards. If the war continued, this might be the only bit of cheer they had.

Teresa arrived with Annie in her wheelchair, 'for an afternoon out'. While Teresa and Laura kept the children busy and entertained, Annie sat in a corner with a glass of squash and watched with admiration and amusement as Teresa cajoled and marshalled the children to do her every bidding, without ever once raising her voice. Periodically, girls and boys would approach Annie and stand a little way off and stare at her in the wheelchair. Annie initially found this disconcerting, but eventually realised they were simply inquisitive, and asked them if they had ever seen someone in a wheelchair before. When they shook their heads, as they invariably did, Annie asked if they wanted to know why she was in a wheelchair? And when they nodded their heads, as they invariably did, Annie told them the story of the fateful night she had been forced to make a crash-landing in heavy rain at Tabley Wood – sparing no detail except the gruesome nature of her injuries, which she skilfully elided over. Within seconds, the children's mouths dropped open in mute awe, as they realised Annie was not only a 'girl pilot', but *a girl pilot who flew Hurricanes and Spitfires*. The girls listened with deep awe to hear of their own doing something that they had only previously believed men could do. For nearly all of them, Annie was suddenly the most impressive person they had ever met. When her tale was over, Annie, enjoying the effect her storytelling had wrought, gently sent the children back to the throng with the following words. 'You didn't know women could fly planes, did you?' The children shook their heads. 'Well, now you know they can crash them too!' The children laughed, and returned to their friends to tell them all about Annie, and what a wonderful story they had missed by gorging themselves on jelly and cake.

While the adults looked on with grown-up drinks and bided their time for the dance later, the party games flowed seamlessly from one into the next, with Laura making sure that what small prizes were awarded were dispersed equitably. Overly competitive boys were reined in so that their determination to win everything at all cost didn't come at the expense of other children's enjoyment. There was one nosebleed through over-excitement during a game, causing a small girl named Molly to crash into a large boy named Hugh, face-first. There were two grazed knees when children playing a game of chase stumbled and slid along the parquet flooring longer than their skin could take.

Despite the presence of Erica and Myra, Laura dealt admirably with these minor injuries.

'The first thing you have to do with an injured child,' her father had once told her, 'is to stop them crying. Only then can they begin to tell you where it hurts, and how much.'

Laura had followed Will's advice and found it worked like a dream.

The children acquitted themselves with admirable restraint when it came to the food. Despite the abundance, they seemed to have an innate comprehension of how much they could personally eat before they overdid it and threw it all up. However, all attempts at moderation went out of the window when it came to ice cream.

'Watch this . . .' Teresa whispered to Laura as the children began to make in-roads into the scoops of ice cream in their bowls. 'Watch the boys.'

'What do you mean?' whispered Laura.

While the girls took small sips at ice cream on their spoons, in less than a minute one boy after another succumbed to the mind-numbing pain between the eyes that the too-rapid ingestion of ice-cold food induced. One by one they dropped their spoons and clasped palms to their foreheads and screwed up their eyes in temporary – though nonetheless real – pain, and emitted low moans of torment.

'However much you tell them to go slowly,' Teresa whispered to Laura as they watched the boys' parents mock-scold their offspring for failing to learn from the past, 'they can't! They have no self-restraint whatsoever. The girls, however, have learned from experience. It always makes me smile.'

Once the food had been eaten, and the ice-cream casualties tended to and reassured, it was time for all the children to eagerly sit before Teresa – as they had done daily when she had been their teacher – and listen to a story. While Teresa was an excellent reader, what marked her out from other teachers was her unique ability to make up a story on the spot, from an assortment of components she encouraged the children to call out. From fragments of character and incident, Teresa was able to weave magnificent tales that held the children's attention from start to finish, wrapping up with a moral flourish that left them in no doubt how life would be better with just a little application, and consideration for others.

Annie listened as attentive as any of the children as Teresa took suggestions that she tell a story about a girl who wanted to be a pilot but no one would let her, so she built her own aeroplane out of things she found around the house, in a nearby wood, and various things washed up on a nearby beach, and taught herself to fly. Teresa incorporated Annie's recent crash, and turned it into a discreet parable about success coming through failure, and the importance of never giving up nor letting a setback stop you from later success.

'Grit, children,' Teresa said softly to her rapt audience of shiny eyes, 'grit is the most important attribute. The ability to get up and try again. And again. And again. That's what's going to get us all through this war, mark my words.' And each child did mark them.

By the end of the story, the young heroine was airborne once more, and flew higher than ever in her new plane, high above the clouds, where she saw other girls in their own makeshift aircraft, performing the most amazing acrobatics in perfect formation.

As Teresa brought her story to its conclusion, Laura was ushering Brian Bennett into the hall for what she hoped would be the *pièce de résistance* of the children's afternoon. Brian had brought a large canvas bag with him, and waited patiently, if a little nervously, at the back of the hall, and watched the children and parents alike give Teresa a rousing round of applause as she ended her tale. Annie had tears in her eyes.

'Whatever that woman was doing,' Brian whispered to Laura, 'I don't think I can follow it.'

'You will not only follow it, Mr Bennett,' assured Laura with quiet certainty, 'you will beat it hands down.'

Brian didn't look so sure as Laura rose to gather the children for the finale of their afternoon. It was dark and cold outside. Laura asked them to put on their coats and gloves and line up by the front door. Some thought it was time to go home, and when they were told it wasn't they became very excited and jumped up and down.

Laura and Teresa eventually calmed the children, and Laura asked Brian to come and join them, and show the children the content of his canvas bag. Despite being tired, the children's eyes widened in expectation as Brian untied the bag's fastenings and pulled out his beloved telescope. The children were mesmerised.

'Now,' said Brian, 'we all know when Father Christmas is at his most busy, don't we?'

Every small hand shot up. Brian surveyed the bright, eager faces and picked Noah to give the answer.

'Christmas Eve!' Noah declared.

'That's right. But what very few people know is that in the weeks before Christmas Eve, Father Christmas and his reindeer start to practise flying across the sky. After all, it's nearly a year since they were last out, and they have to cover such great distances, so quickly, that they have to get back up to speed and sharpen their navigational skills in the days before Christmas Eve to make sure they can give all the children their presents.'

Brian looked from face to face, each was focused on him intently, as if they were being given top-secret information they had to memorise. 'Very few people know about this. But . . . I do.' He dropped his voice to a whisper. 'Do you know how?'

The children shook their heads in silent wonderment.

'Because . . . *I've seen him*,' Brian tapped his telescope gently, 'with this.'

As one, the children's eyes widened even more. Some gasped.

'And today . . . *you* are going to see him, too.'

This time the children let out a collective gasp. Laura looked across at their parents and grinned. She knew Brian would enthral the children, as he had always kept her entertained during their long shifts together at the Observation Post. Here he was, coming up trumps, and bringing the children's party to a wonderful conclusion.

Brian led the children out of the village hall like the Pied Piper. The snowy sky from earlier had blown through, leaving a pin-sharp clear night sky. The children watched as Brian swiftly set up the instrument on its tripod, then pointed it at the bright moon. All the parents had come out to watch, as eager as their children to find out what Brian was about to do.

'How do you know where to look?' asked Noah.

'Now that, is a very good question, young man,' replied Brian. 'Over the years, I've discovered that Father Christmas likes to practise for Christmas Eve by going around and round the moon. I've tried to work out why, and I think it's because it's not too far away, and it's bright, so he can always see where he's going and will always end up where he started without ever needing a map.'

The adults grinned. The children nodded with utter certainty. To them, Brian's explanation not only made perfect sense, it was the *only* possible explanation.

'That's why – if you look hard enough in the weeks before Christmas – you'll see what almost no other human beings on Earth get to see. Father Christmas and his sleigh going around and round the moon. But of course, you won't see him as you would if he was standing in front of you now. The moon is close to the Earth compared to the sun and the stars. But it's still a long way away. Even with a telescope, you can only see Father Christmas as a tiny, tiny dot passing across the moon's face. You have to look very hard. Be very patient. But eventually, all your hard work will be rewarded.'

Brian looked at the children who stared back at him as if they had just been told the most magical thing imaginable. Not one of them felt the cold, despite standing still in an almost sub-zero temperature.

'Now,' he said, 'who would like to try first?'

Adult or child, every hand shot up.

And so, one by one, each child put an eye to the telescope's eyepiece, and looked as hard as they could possibly look to see if they could make out the tiny, tiny dot passing across the face of the moon that Brian had encouraged them to seek out. And one by one, every single child claimed that they *had* seen Father Christmas driving his sleigh across the moon in practice for Christmas Eve!

'That was the most brilliant thing I have ever seen,' Annie whispered to Teresa.

Teresa agreed. 'I've taught children for years. But what you just did . . . what *is* it you just did, Mr Bennett?'

Brian smiled. 'I didn't do anything. The children did it all, up here,' he said, tapping the side of his head. 'Think about it,' Brian said with a sly smile. 'Who wants to be the kid who *didn't* see Father Christmas fly across the face of the moon when all your friends *did*?'

As parents ushered their children back into the hall, the band struck up their version of 'Over the Rainbow' and for one night the people of Great Paxford sank back into an almost forgotten pre-war mood of singing and dancing and sharing time and space with loved ones, friends and neighbours.

The only person unable to leave the war outside the hall for the evening was Sarah Collingborne, who had received her first letter from Adam that morning via the Red Cross since his capture at Dunkirk. It was short but very, very sweet, informing Sarah that he was well considering, and keeping his spirits up as he counted the minutes and hours until they would be reunited. He asked Sarah to tell his congregation that he was thinking of them too, and wished he could be there with them as they endured the war.

Sarah hadn't shown the letter to anyone – not even to her sister, Frances. Savouring every stroke of Adam's pen, she wanted to keep the feelings it generated to herself for as long as she felt it reasonable to do so.

As she sat along the wall of the hall and watched the village let its hair down, and sipped at a glass of beer, Sarah knew everyone present would be overjoyed to hear that their vicar was alive and well, albeit under German lock and key.

Yet for the moment, he was *her* husband, and his words were exclusively, exquisitely *hers*.

Chapter 25

Knowing how to be a perfect houseguest *and* a good patient meant Annie settled quickly into Teresa and Nick's domestic routine. As a patient, Annie never complained about her injuries or the privations they enforced, and embraced all the advice Teresa had been given by the hospital to help Annie towards completing her recovery. Now, as a guest, Annie expressed endless gratitude for Teresa and Nick's hospitality. Despite having limited capacity to move around, she offered to help out wherever she was able, and by the end of Annie's first week it felt to Teresa and Nick that the house was indeed a livelier, more interesting place as a *ménage a trois* than when it had been just the two of them. Not that the house *wasn't* lively and interesting with just her and Nick, but, as Teresa explained to Alison while they waited in line at Brindsley's to place their Christmas orders, Annie had 'a particular gift for bringing out the best in people'.

'She's very good company. She's very inquisitive about what I might be doing, and why. And always has something interesting to say about it.'

Teresa explained that Annie made sure she never got in Teresa's way.

'She's able to help prepare meals by sitting at the kitchen table in her wheelchair, and showed me some French skills she'd picked up from her time at boarding school. I've been able to make food that's at least on a par with what Nick can find at the canteen at Tabley Wood. Which means he comes home more often for dinner, and we spend more time together than before.'

Teresa told Alison that Annie had also proved invaluable when Nick returned from the station late one night, following a raid. Previously, when it had only been Teresa and Nick, Teresa did her very best to stay up to talk to him about the night's events. She often found it a struggle. Not because she didn't care about what had happened, but because she often found it difficult to get past Nick's suspicion that she was only asking from a sense of obligation, not because she was genuinely interested in what had happened.

In reality, while Teresa was concerned about Nick's wellbeing in relation to his work, she did struggle with the repetitious nature of the reports he'd bring home. She simply lacked sufficient understanding to see each of them as subtly distinct to another.

As a fellow pilot, however, Annie had a direct connection to operational activity, shared many friends at Tabley Wood, and would question Nick at length about what had happened that night. They would then pore over details and silently raise a glass to pilot friends who hadn't returned.

While Teresa could make a decent fist of going through the motions of that, she couldn't bring the same authenticity.

Also, being from the same world, Annie could joke with Nick about things at work in a way Teresa never could; offering him a valuable opportunity to let off steam. Nick and Annie shared a similar black humour about flying and flyers, and Annie knew just how far she could push him. Teresa was never sure.

Teresa had worried that Annie would watch her carry out her domestic responsibilities with a certain degree of disparagement, but this hadn't been the case at all. Having been shipped off to boarding school by parents who employed servants to wash and clean up after them, Annie was deeply impressed by Teresa's diligence and attention to detail when it came to the upkeep of the house. She had initially believed this was an attempt to please Nick. But Teresa put her right on that score.

'My mother would kill me if she came here and saw a speck of dust. It's been drummed into me from birth.'

Attraction was a constant energy between them. Yet Teresa found herself able to pull back before anything untoward happened. They had agreed nothing of a sexual nature could happen, and each had behaved accordingly, diverting their energies into developing their friendship. They each wanted to see if they could become genuine friends, and not merely exist 'on friendly terms' due to their mutual association with Nick.

'Are you all right?' Annie would ask a minute or two later.

'Yes,' Teresa would reply. 'You?'

Annie would nod, and normality would be restored.

They spent long evenings discussing their respective backgrounds, and previous lives: Teresa, growing up in urban Liverpool where being attracted to other women was a social curse; Annie, growing up in rural Sussex with fields and horses, and then at school in Dorset, where having discreet relationships with other girls passed without comment.

Where Teresa's family life had been close and loving, Annie's had been drained of parental love, her childhood enveloped in a cloud of bitterness between her mother and father, prompting Annie to become emotionally self-reliant at an early age.

The conscious suppression of their mutual attraction was additionally aided by the fact that Annie was still recovering from serious injuries, and required a great deal of looking after. The sense that it would be entirely inappropriate for anything beyond a form of medical care hung over them. Annie would tire easily, requesting Teresa read to her from whichever book she had on the go when she could no longer keep her own eyes upon the page. Teresa was happy to oblige, as it reminded her of her happiest times at school, when she would animatedly read to her rapt class.

If there was shopping to be done, Annie would ask Teresa to push her into the village in her wheelchair.

Taken together, Teresa estimated that Annie's presence in the house nearly doubled her workload, which left her too tired to think errant thoughts. In truth, she always loved to be kept busy, and she loved the company she had been missing since becoming married. Furthermore, she could discern Annie's recovery by the day, and felt a genuine friendship developing between them. It all left her with a re-discovered sense of accomplishment she had lost when forced out of her post at the village school.

I can do this. I can be in control of myself. I can see temptation for the destructive force it is, and turn a different face to it. I can be a good friend to Annie and a good wife to Nick. The two don't have to be irreconcilable.

Over supper one evening, Teresa looked up at Annie and said, 'I like this friendship lark, don't you?'

Annie laughed and nodded. 'Very much.'

Teresa lifted her glass of wine in a mock-toast. 'To friendship,' she solemnly declared.

Annie followed suit. 'To friendship. Long may it last. In all its forms.'

Teresa smiled broadly and watched Annie continue to eat. Behind her smile she wondered what Annie had meant by 'in all its forms'. She resisted the temptation to ask for clarification, preferring to let sleeping dogs lie. She silently patted herself on the back for the way everything had worked out between them, and by association, with Nick.

It is possible to be around someone one is attracted to without acting on those feelings. I'm not a slave to my emotions, or my libido. I can simply be 'a friend', and nothing more.

Teresa ate on, feeling for perhaps the first time in a long, long while that she had everything under control.

Chapter 26

WHENEVER BOB PREVIOUSLY expressed a desire to improve his behaviour towards Pat, she applied a single measure of his apparent sincerity: how long would it last?

Invariably, the answer was 'not very long at all'. His resolve almost always broke within a few days or weeks when a new slight struck him, or anxieties bubbled up from within. A rejection letter from a publishing house or newspaper always darkened his mood. A sudden attack of writer's block condemned him to hours of self-destructive recrimination. An attack of insecurity about the quality of his work, or the lack of respect he received from Pat triggered an outburst towards his wife.

When it happened – whatever *it* happened to be – Bob's capacity to maintain his conviction that he wanted to treat Pat better crumbled, and his dormant resentment would flare up once more. As a consequence, Pat was as mistrustful of his declarations of reform as the wife of a career alcoholic.

Yet, Pat had never seen Bob break down and actually cry real tears of apparent remorse before, and she wondered if this act represented a deeper, more meaningful feeling. Could it mean this outbreak of repentance would last longer than previously? Or even, *for good*? It was almost certainly too much to hope for.

Rather than wait for time to reveal that Bob would be unable to sustain his new state of kindness towards her, she decided to take control of the situation and confront Bob head on about what had taken place in their bedroom. She chose her moment carefully, while Joyce was out visiting a friend. With her absent, there would be no reason for Bob to hold back. Pat wouldn't enjoy the experience, but it would at least give her greater clarity on where she currently stood.

Pat came into the front room after washing up from supper, and found Bob sitting in the armchair reading through a sheaf of property listings from a local estate agent. It came as quite a shock to her. They both knew they couldn't remain living with Joyce indefinitely, but Bob hadn't yet raised the question of where they would next move to, and Pat had casually assumed they might stay for the duration of the war. Bob appeared to have other plans.

Pat glanced at the papers, concerned he might be thinking of moving away from Great Paxford. She seated herself opposite Bob and softly cleared her throat.

'Property details?' she asked.

Bob nodded. 'We can't live here much longer. I certainly don't want to, and I can't imagine you feel comfortable playing second fiddle in another woman's house.'

'I appreciate we can't live here indefinitely. But I really don't want to leave Great Paxford. My friends are here. My life is here. My job at the exchange. The WI.'

Bob's face gave nothing away.

'If the book continues to sell at its current rate – and the publisher seems to believe it will – we could afford a smarter house. Detached. Possibly even with some land.'

'But those houses tend to be away from the village,' Pat said, trying to mute the tone of protest from her voice. 'Well away.'

'Well, yes, of course,' Bob replied. 'That's the nature of things. We'd be exchanging more space for proximity to Great Paxford. But we might find ourselves closer to *another* village. Or a city, even. Think about that, Pat. Going back to the city!'

'Which city – Manchester? You're not thinking of Liverpool because there's hardly anything left.'

Bob considered the idea for a moment, his eyes widening at the prospect.

'Or *London*. I've always told myself I wouldn't return to London unless I was a success *on London's terms*. Now we could.'

'Don't you think it would be perverse to be the only people moving *into* London during the Blitz.'

The instant the sentence left her mouth Pat felt a pang of regret. Under normal circumstances, Bob would take it as a rebuke at worst, a mockery of his pretension at best. Yet Bob's face didn't darken. His eyes didn't narrow into their customary slits through which he looked daggers at her.

'It would be unusual,' he said, smiling. 'However, there might be some logic to moving back now – or when the worst of the bombing is over. The place will be a terrible mess. Property prices will have plummeted. We could pick up a real steal.'

Pat wondered if the idea he'd just aired amounted to a form of war profiteering, or was simply shrewd thinking? Either way, she decided not to pick him up on it.

'We don't know anyone in London anymore,' she said calmly.

She was aware that she was trying to properly argue against moving to London, while also trying to provoke Bob to see if his patience would snap.

'We could make friends easily enough,' he replied. 'London has a thriving literary scene. I'm sure we would be welcomed. My success would almost guarantee it. We might even find ourselves somewhat celebrated. Think about that, Patricia. The literary salons of London!'

Pat thought about it for less than a second and failed to muster the slightest enthusiasm. On the occasions she had visited London in the past, it had always felt like a vast, incomprehensible network of streets and towns smashed together with the sole intention of making any visitor dizzy and lost, with no way of working out how to escape. The volume of people and traffic scared her, and the accents left her wondering what anyone was saying half the time. And then there was the pall of smog that hung over the place, stinging the eyes and throats of any who dared venture out in it. Pat felt it would be easy to disappear without trace in London, never to be seen – or remarked upon – again.

'I don't want to live in London. As I said, all my friends are here. My job at the exchange. The WI.'

'You can make new friends. Find a new little job if you really want one. Join a different WI. It is a national organisation, after all.'

Pat was aware that the conversation was in danger of straying away from the course she had intended and tried to rein it back.

'Wherever we go, Bob, I would need to know where we stand.'

Bob looked at her, cocking his head slightly to the right, as if trying to better understand her words by looking at them from a different angle.

'What do you mean – "where we stand"?'

'More specifically, where I stand in relation to you.'

Bob's brow furrowed further. 'I still don't understand what you mean.'

Pat couldn't tell if he was being deliberately obtuse or genuine in his incomprehension.

'The other night, Bob. When you . . . fell out of sorts in bed . . . and said all that about being sorry for the way you've treated me . . . what brought it on?'

Bob considered Pat for a moment. 'Are you doubting my sincerity?'

A shiver ran the length of Pat's spine. Bob had a genius for getting to the subtext of her questions, and she suddenly couldn't tell if his temper had just been knocked off its previously even keel.

'I'm not doubting it, Bob. I'm simply curious as to what brought it on, that's all.'

Bob might say anything in the moment that he either believed or wanted to believe, or wanted Pat to believe; but if Pat couldn't trust him to speak truthfully it made no difference. Only by his actions would she know the truth.

'Did you mean what you said about the way you've been treating me over the years? Were your tears genuine?'

Bob looked at her for a few seconds, then nodded.

'They were,' he said quietly. 'I don't want to continue the way we have been,' he said. 'It's no way for either of us to live. We fell into a rut—'

'No, no—' said Pat, interrupting. '*You* fell into a rut and pulled me down with you. Every time I tried to climb back out you pulled me down again. And then you started to dig, making the rut deeper and deeper over the years, until it was impossible to even *see* over the side, let alone climb out of. I'm sorry, Bob, but I can't have you characterising things as having been some kind of joint enterprise.'

Pat took a deep breath, knowing that under any other circumstances this would be an intolerable provocation. More than anything, he hated being forced to take responsibility for his bad behaviour. She braced herself for an onslaught.

'You're right,' he said, his voice not rising an iota. 'That has to end.'

'For how long?' Pat asked. 'You've never managed to stop before. There have been weeks here and there—'

Bob nodded. 'You know how it is, Patricia. I can only say what I feel. I can only say what I hope you will believe . . .'

'Why now, though? What has brought this change of heart?'

Bob looked at her, maintaining eye contact for what seemed like minutes.

'Marek,' he said, simply.

The sound of her lover's name coming from Bob's lips stunned Pat into silence.

He's never spoken his name before. Marek has only ever been referred to as 'the Czech' or 'the Czech bastard', spat out like a bitter pill Bob refused to swallow.

'Marek?' Pat said, hesitantly.

'I tried to understand your attraction to him, and came to the simple conclusion that you must consider him a better man than I.'

Pat struggled to stop herself bursting into laughter at Bob's observation.

'Once I realised that, I realised I could no longer blame you for your behaviour where he – and I – were concerned. I then realised that if I had any hope of keeping you, I had to change. Only time will prove if I have,' he said, his words echoing her own thoughts.

Pat looked at him. Bob held out the sheaf of papers from the estate agent.

'Why don't you have a look through these while I get back to work? Mark any that might be of interest and we can discuss them later.'

Pat looked at the sheaves of paper and felt intensely confused. Instinctively, she reached out and took the papers.

'Thank you,' she said.

'I know you probably think I could drag you some-where you don't want to go, but I really couldn't,' Bob said. 'And wouldn't want to. I want you to be happy, Pat. To make a fresh start. Don't you want that?'

Pat nodded.

'If that meant a little sacrifice in the form of giving up your job at the exchange, or not being as active in the WI, wouldn't it be worth it?'

Pat looked at Bob for several moments and then, want-ing to seem encouraging, nodded a second time.

'Perhaps,' she said, trying to sound both open to the idea and non-committal in the same sentence.

Pat left the front room and closed the door behind her. She stood in the hall holding the paperwork Bob had just given her, not knowing what to think of Bob's explanation for his resolve to change.

But if . . . if . . . if . . . if Bob can change?

It was a question she was convinced she knew the answer to. And yet she was hearing words and a tone from Bob she had never heard from him before.

What do I feel about all this?

'I have no idea,' Pat whispered, to the empty hall.

You can't trust him.

'I know,' she whispered. 'But what choice do I have?'

Chapter 27

THE DAY AFTER Laura's successful Christmas party, the temperature of the air around Great Paxford suddenly plunged close to zero, and a harsh north-easterly wind blasted flurries of early snow around roofs and gutters, and across the village's de-marked roads like swirling clouds of white smoke. Laura and Tom had been caught outside when the weather turned, walking beside the canal. Laura was halfway through detailing the extent of what lay ahead if she hoped to gain a scholarship to medical school when he took her arm and stopped her. Finally facing a silent Laura, Tom calmly told her his news.

'I've put myself forward for bomber-pilot training,' he said, as matter-of-factly as he could, as if to downplay the significance of the news he had been waiting to say all afternoon.

Laura was unsure whether she had heard correctly, or if the wind had played tricks on her hearing.

'You've done what?' she said.

'I mentioned I was thinking about flying a couple of weeks ago,' he said, trying to sound nonchalant.

'I didn't think you were serious,' Laura replied, struggling to stay calm. 'Besides, I told you what I felt about it at the time.'

'Yes. I know. You did. You were very clear. I know it's dangerous, but . . .'

Laura's position was that she had seen her sister go through the wringer when her young husband, Jack, had perished during flight training. She couldn't bear the possibility of going through anything similar.

'Why have you pursued it,' she asked, 'when you knew I was against the idea? I mean, you know that one of the reasons I chose to go with you is precisely because you *didn't* fly.'

'And there was I thinking it was because of my irresistible charm and good looks.'

'That helped, of course. But what I mean is,' Laura said, struggling to make her position clear, 'I would never have opened myself to the possibility of stepping out with you – of even considering your world-class charm and good looks if you were a flyer. I'm sorry, Tom, I just wouldn't have. I've never made any bones about that. Why have you pursued this?'

'Things change,' Tom said quietly. 'The war is changing all the time,' he continued, believing that the more he spoke the more likely it was that he would win Laura to his position. 'We have no choice but to change with it. You were in the WAAF. You got thrown out—'

'Grossly unfairly,' Laura added.

'My point being that you're now in the Observation Corps – something you would never have seen yourself doing a year ago. So now, to cripple the supply of new planes to the Luftwaffe, the RAF will have to ruthlessly bomb Germany's industrial heartland. Where single-pilot fighters were needed to win the Battle of Britain, huge bombers are needed to pound Germany into submission, just as they're trying to pound us. Each bomber will require a *team* comprised of pilots, gunners and bombardiers. A year ago, we never would have thought this would be necessary. A year ago, we never imagined Hitler would send hundreds of planes over Britain at night to drop bombs on civilians. I want to fly in the defence of my country, Laura. If it turns out that it can't be as a pilot, then it can be as another aircrew member. I want to do my bit.'

Tom's final sentence was delivered with such earnest passion that Laura sensed further argument would be futile. She had seen countless young men of the village succumb to the same desire. The more she heard it the more Laura realised war dominated their psychology as an experience against which they were drawn to test themselves, as their own fathers had during the Great War. At least, that was the theory before they found themselves facing enemy fire. According to her father, a medic at Ypres, once men found themselves up to their necks in blood and gore they spent much of their waking life praying to simply survive, all sense of 'greater glory' blasted away.

'You've already made up your mind. I respect that,' Laura said. 'My father tried to join up again when war was declared. In fact, it was his army medical that discovered his cancer.'

'It hasn't been easy to find the right time to tell you, given how strongly I know you feel about this. And how excited you were after the Christmas party, and about becoming a doctor.'

'*Trying* to become a doctor.' Laura looked solemnly at Tom. 'Wouldn't you sooner fly a Spitfire?'

Tom shook his head. 'According to those in the know, bombs are going to win this thing. Besides, I took the test for fighter pilots on the QT and my reactions weren't quite fast enough. But they might do for large bombers. And as I said, if I fail the test to *fly* the buggers I'm pretty certain I could make aircrew.'

Laura digested this information, and Tom's determination, in silence.

'Well, look at us,' she finally said. 'While I'm trying to get into medical school you'll be trying to get into the cockpit of an RAF bomber. All I can say is I hope I succeed and you fail.'

She smiled, trying to make light of what was in fact her most fervent hope.

'Before, when you declared that I mustn't become a pilot or we could no longer see one another, I couldn't tell whether you were over-reacting in the heat of the moment, or were serious.'

'I was entirely serious, Tom,' Laura said, entirely seriously. 'A hundred per cent. I do understand why you want this, and that there is nothing I can do to dissuade you. It would be pointless anyway. Your determination is reflected in the fact you went ahead without discussing it with me first. My opinion was clearly not a significant factor in your decision.'

'Now wait—' Tom tried to interject and halt Laura mid-flow, before the conversation ran away from him. He was too late. Laura was already bowling towards her conclusion with unstoppable momentum.

'I do understand why you did that, Tom. I don't hold it against you in any way. In your shoes, I expect I would have done the same.'

'Thanks,' he said drily, hoping the matter had found its way to a conclusion.

'But it doesn't alter my conviction that I cannot have a relationship with a flyer.'

Tom stood rooted to the spot. A coot raced across the surface of the canal and sank into the water a hundred yards ahead.

'What?' he said.

'I saw it almost destroy my sister, and I'm not as strong as she is.'

'I disagree. You got through the business with—'

Laura couldn't allow him to finish his sentence.

'Are you seriously trying to compare enduring a stupid affair with having to survive your death?'

Tom looked at Laura, not knowing what to reply. Eventually he said quietly, 'I'm rather hoping not to be killed, actually.'

'But that's not in your hands, is it? While not being involved with someone to whom that could happen *is* in mine. I can't do it. I can't and I won't.'

She couldn't stop tears from welling in her eyes but she was loath to be controlled by them.

Laura felt a thick lump in her throat. She recognised it from the church at her father's burial as the sensation that foreshadowed loss. It was this that told Laura her relationship with Tom was now over.

The tears came, by the canal and later that evening at home, when Laura sat in the armchair beside the fire as Erica dozed in Will's armchair. Looking at the small framed photograph of Kate and Jack on the mantelpiece, Laura's sister beaming with pride beside her new husband in his pressed RAF uniform, Laura knew she had made the only decision possible. Despite how much pain she was feeling at the prospect of losing Tom as her chap, it was better this than living with the uncertainty of his survival from one day to the next, and then – God forbid – with the utter devastation that might come if the very worst should happen to him.

I won't go down that path. I won't get involved with anyone until the war is over.

'Good luck, Tom,' she whispered, focusing on Jack's handsome young face. 'God's speed, my dearest boy . . .'

Chapter 28

FOLLOWING THE INCIDENT at Brindsley's, Steph refused to set foot outside the farm. She sent Stan and Stanley into the village for any provisions they might need, and they found themselves receiving smatterings of applause and admiring looks as they strolled along the High Street. Stan was nonplussed by it, but Stanley enjoyed the attention, and the accolade he heard on more than one occasion that he was 'a hero'.

It was while Stan and Stanley were off in the village that Steph heard footsteps approaching behind her one afternoon while hanging out sheets to dry in the yard. For a moment she froze, expecting to hear the fruity tones of another reporter from another newspaper, come to find a new angle on her story. Instead, it was Sarah Collingborne's voice she heard.

'Steph?'

Steph turned and found herself facing both Sarah and Frances, wrapped up in winter overcoats, gloves, and hats.

They smiled a little too brightly as Steph turned, as if to signal extreme good intent.

'How are you, Steph?' asked Frances.

Generally, Steph would have taken Frances's query as an inconsequential opening to a perfectly ordinary exchange. But she could tell from their faces that the two sisters had not come for an amiable chat over a cup of tea. Frances *really* wanted to know how Steph was. Steph recalled Sarah had been in Brindsley's when the applause had started.

'Been better,' Steph said, smiling bravely.

Frances could see from the dark circles beneath Steph's eyes that her friend clearly hadn't been sleeping well.

'We've come to talk to you about what happened,' Sarah said. 'I think people have read the article in the *Echo*, and heard the interview on the BBC, and assume everything is hunky-dory. But I didn't believe that was the case when I saw you dash out of Brindsley's.'

Steph had neither prepared for nor wanted this conversation, and to some extent felt ambushed into it.

'I didn't ask to be interviewed either time,' she said. 'They came and persuaded me it would be for the best. I didn't imagine people reading the newspaper, or listening to the wireless. I was just glad to get it over with and thought that might be the end of it. When Stan came home we even tried to get the article stopped. Stan telephoned the *Echo*, but they said it was too late.'

Frances nodded. 'Of course. From their perspective, they had the most marvellous story. They weren't going to let that go. I expect they sold a lot more copies that day, because of you.'

'No idea. Stan thought so.'

'It *is* a remarkable story, Steph,' said Frances. 'Truly remarkable. I know you won't thank me for saying this, but everyone in the village is extraordinarily proud of you.'

'Well, they shouldn't be,' said Steph dolefully.

'You forget how terrified everyone was in the days leading up to it.'

'Perhaps,' said Steph, unwilling to soften her harsh view of her actions. 'But it would have been better if it had ended almost any way other than how it did.'

'The only way it could have ended worse,' said Sarah, 'is if Stanley or yourself had been killed instead of the pilot.'

'May we come in?' Frances asked. 'We have a proposition we would like to put to you.'

Steph ushered the two women inside the farmhouse and put the kettle on the stove.

The proposition Sarah and Frances had come to put to Steph concerned her new status in the village. Frances presented it matter-of-factly.

'While the village considers you a hero for your action against the German pilot, saving your son from a potentially lethal attack, and possibly saving future casualties too, you don't see yourself the same way, and want nothing more than for normal life to resume as quickly as possible. Is that about right?'

Steph nodded agreement.

'The two positions are fundamentally incompatible,' Frances continued. 'The village has a strong desire to express its appreciation, Steph, irrespective of whether you want it to. They are responding to an incredible story which you just happen to be a part of – so they are responding to you in the same way. Merely telling everyone you want to forget all about what happened won't make them be able to leave you to get on with life and put it behind you.'

Steph knew that Frances understood better than she did how large groups of people behaved. Sarah took up the baton from her sister.

'If the desire to celebrate you goes unexpressed it will continue to bubble under the surface. People will watch you from a distance, and talk about you behind your back. Not unpleasant things from their perspective but if you shy away from it they won't feel able to be as open with you as they were before it happened. And it will simply continue because they won't have been able to express their feelings about it all.'

'Like a blister that's bubbling up,' Steph offered. 'Needs pricking.'

Frances looked at Sarah for agreement, and Sarah nodded.

'Let them express their goodwill towards you, Steph, and this will settle down much, much quicker than if you don't. I promise you.'

'How?'

'We propose that you allow the WI to make a special presentation to you at our next meeting, allowing the women to express their admiration and gratitude for what you did.'

'You might think about offering a small question and answer session at the end of it,' added Frances. 'To allow their curiosity to become completely sated.'

Steph looked at the two women for a few moments. She felt the same sadness rise that she'd felt almost every waking hour since the moment she pulled the trigger of the farm's shotgun and ended the pilot's life.

'But I don't want their admiration,' she said. 'Or gratitude.'

Sarah nodded. 'But you *saying* that won't make it go away. Let them get it out of their system in one evening. Talk about what happened a little – as much as you want. Then tell everyone that you just want to get on with life on the farm. After all that, the ladies will be very protective towards your desire for everything to return to normal.'

'More or less,' added Frances a little unhelpfully.

'What do you mean, "more or less"?' asked Steph.

'You can't turn back the clock completely. You will always be known as the woman who killed a Nazi pilot who was about to kill her son. But that's as far as it will go.'

'I'm not sure he was,' Steph said.

'You're not sure who was what, Steph?'

'About to kill Stanley.'

'He had a gun, didn't he? I'm sure I read that he had a revolver of some kind.'

'He did.'

'Well, then.'

'Before I ran out of the farmhouse he had ample chance to shoot Stanley. Didn't fire once.'

'But Stanley said he thought he was going to shoot him.'

'But he didn't though, did he? He could've, but he didn't. What does that make me, eh?'

The two sisters regarded Steph in silence, and glanced at one another, hoping her sibling would be able to answer her question.

Eventually, Frances said, 'In the heat of a potentially terrible moment you acted out of maternal instinct. Every single member of the WI will understand that, Steph. Every single one will think, *There but for the grace of God go I.*'

Stan thought Steph was unwise to agree to Sarah and Frances's proposal. He couldn't see how talking publicly about something Steph never wanted to speak of again would do anything but make it more likely the whole business would roll on. Steph wasn't sure he was right.

'If I satisfy their interest there's nothing left for people to be interested about. We can all just get on with it.'

On the night of the WI meeting, Steph got ready as usual, applying a little less make-up than was her custom, so as not to appear as if she was going to enjoy being the centre of attention. Frances had offered to send the car to collect her and take Steph to the village hall, but Steph declined.

'What's she thinking?' she said to Stan. 'I want to show I'm no different to how I was. How can I do that if I arrive in a fancy car driven by a bloody chauffeur?!'

Stan laughed, and agreed. 'I'll walk you, if you want.'

'When've I needed you to walk me to WI meetings? I've got legs, Stan. I'll make my own way. Give me time to think about what I'm going to say.'

Frances had suggested Steph arrive at the hall twenty minutes after the monthly meeting started, to give her time to set the scene. Steph turned down this suggestion too, on the grounds that she didn't want anything to be different to any other meeting. She didn't want to set herself apart from the other women in any way.

'The sooner they see I'm no different the sooner everything goes back to how it was.'

As Steph entered Great Paxford proper, she saw other women up ahead, walking towards the village hall. She didn't speed up to join them, but kept pace behind, happy to be unseen. It didn't last long.

'Steph!'

Steph turned and saw Erica walking towards her with Alison. Even with these two women, who she knew well and considered friends, Steph felt a surge of anxiety about how they would treat her.

'We heard you on the wireless,' said Erica. 'You were wonderful. Very calm. Very thoughtful answers. At no point did you give the impression that you felt anything but sadness for what happened. Is that how you really felt?'

Steph nodded. 'Still do.'

'Has it changed you in any way?' Alison asked.

Steph turned to look at Alison. It was the first time anyone had asked her that.

'Yes,' she said. 'I think it has.'

'I couldn't imagine it not,' said Alison. 'Not only because you went through a true life and death experience. But what happened with the pilot . . . I mean . . . well . . . things happen in life that you can't reverse, don't they? There's no returning to the moment before. I felt it when my George was killed in 1918. It was as if a door had been closed between us and no matter how hard I tried to turn the handle I couldn't go back and find him. It was the first time in my life that had happened to me. Horrible.'

'That's exactly how I feel at the moment. Will must still be reachable because he always has been. But I have no way of reaching him, and have to come to terms with the fact that I never will.'

Alison smiled with empathy and gently touched Erica's forearm in support.

'Fortunately for you, Steph, with Stan and Stanley you don't have to go forward *alone*. You can deal with it together.'

Steph felt Erica thread her arm through hers, Alison on the other side did the same, and the three women walked towards the hall.

'Can I sit with you?' Steph asked.

'Of course,' said Alison.

'I mean, between you?'

'Of course. Make yourself comfortable. Everyone's so looking forward to seeing you,' Erica said. 'They all heard what happened in Brindsley's, and they want to show that you have nothing to fear from them. There's some curiosity about what happened, but for the most part I think everyone simply wants to welcome you back, and help you get through what we all understand must be a difficult time.'

The evening went better than Steph could ever have expected. When she entered the hall, the women stood up to give her a round of applause – Steph later discovered that Erica and Alison had been tasked by Frances to gently ambush her on the way to the meeting, and slow her down long enough for the members to get into the hall and prepare for her arrival. Steph had expected some form of greeting, and took the applause with good grace, before sitting between Erica and Alison on the front row. She stood to sing 'Jerusalem' with the rest of the members, and caught several pairs of eyes looking at her, the women smiling with kindness when their eyes met hers. She then sat and listened to the evening's agenda, and when Sarah came to 'any other business' Steph was invited to the front to answer questions about her recent ordeal.

She had never spoken in front of so many people before, and though the women were all friendly, she wasn't quite sure what they expected or wanted from her that evening. She decided to take the bull by the horns as she stood before the members.

'I would like to make one thing clear,' Steph said at the beginning of what she considered would be an ordeal, trying not to be intimidated by rows and rows of faces looking directly at her. 'I don't want to talk about the event itself. About what happened. The death, I mean. It's been written about in the *Echo* and elsewhere, and I talked about it a bit in the interview I did with the BBC. I don't want to talk about it again. I find it too difficult.'

The rapt faces facing her nodded and turned to one another and softly murmured agreement with Steph's discretion.

'But I will answer any questions about what happened before and after. If there are no questions about that, that will be fine too.'

The moment Steph stopped speaking about thirty hands shot up, and for the next hour she fielded questions about how they had come upon the German pilot, what caused him to attack Stanley, what did the pilot look and sound like, how did she feel once she realised the pilot was dead?

Steph answered as best she could. Some questions about her feelings were more difficult to answer than others. But she tried, and found that as she talked she started to feel everyone's warmth towards her as an almost physical effect. It melted the icy dread she had endured as she walked to the hall earlier that evening. She was among friends, and they wanted only the best for her.

Chapter 29

No one in the village could have imagined a year earlier that they would be facing the prospect of spending Christmas in an air-raid shelter. Though an unofficial postponement of bombing had been agreed by both sides from Christmas Eve to the twenty-seventh, after Chamberlain's humiliation at Munich there was no great faith the Germans would stick to the agreement. Many hung decorations inside their shelters and squeezed in small Christmas trees to take the rough edge off where they expected to spend some time over the festive period.

Frances had worked hard alongside her household to decorate the shelter in the cellar to a high specification, so that those taking refuge might feasibly forget they were cowering for their lives for the hours they were below stairs. Some thought it more than likely Hitler would take Christmas Day as the perfect opportunity to strike England with its guard down. It was a measure of how quickly the war had degraded any sense the German High Command had any lingering decency or compassion. Frances was determined that even if the Germans bombed Great Paxford all through Christmas Day there would still be somewhere they could all spend Christmas together.

For her, the annual event was a cornerstone of British life, and to turn away from what it represented meant to lose something of themselves. She was loath to do that when the country was being pounded nightly, and when thousands had been consigned to early graves and hundreds of thousands had been left homeless. Everything had changed and yet Frances wanted to hold onto the idea that the very best of British life was battered and bloody, but essentially the same.

'They'd do it,' he told Frances and Claire, the housemaid, over supper one night. 'They'll win by any means. You only have to look at what they've done already. What difference does it make to them? Catch us napping on Christmas night after lunch – perfect opportunity. That's why I'm spending Christmas Day in my uniform – ready to be called out.'

On Christmas Day, no church bells rang out, leaving the congregation to gather at St Mark's in an eerie silence. Reverend James delivered a humdrum service about the need for unity and steadfastness, finished with a hope that the world would come to its senses and end the war sooner rather than later.

'Adam would have come up with something far more interesting to say than this stream of cliché,' Frances whispered to Sarah, by way of commentary. Sarah smiled nodded, and imagined the interesting, moving and stirring sermon Adam would almost certainly be giving to his fellow prisoners of war at that very moment, somewhere in Germany.

Following the service, the villagers chatted happily outside the church. With the siren blessedly silent, they wished one another 'Happy Christmas' and then walked slowly home through freezing winds to warm up, exchange gifts with their family, and get ready for lunch. Petrol rationing prevented people from travelling far to lunch with relatives, so most hunkered in their own homes, and hoped that cards conveying seasonal wishes would make do in their absence.

Due to the increasing shortage of consumer goods, a national campaign by the government had discouraged spending money on presents, and the population was instead asked to buy war bonds. But the impulse to give gifts was not so easily subdued, and people made presents of practical items. The women of Great Paxford's WI produced an impressive array of scarves and gloves made from wool of colours no soldier or seaman would be permitted to wear. Fathers carved toys out of wood for their children, while less fortunate children received gifts donated from around the Commonwealth, and charities.

Christmas lunch was a feast, where culinary ingenuity would be at the heart of the menu. Meat was expensive, and the ration allocation for a family of four was unlikely to cover the cost of even a small chicken. This was less of an issue in a rural community like Great Paxford than in Manchester, or Liverpool, Birmingham, or London.

While basic rations were saved to make the Christmas table as full as possible, some villagers slaughtered hand-reared chickens for their Christmas lunch; while others ventured into fields around the village in the run-up to Christmas day to pot rabbits and – if landowners and game-keepers failed to stop them – grouse and pheasant.

Tea and sugar rations were increased during the week before Christmas, but very little fruit was imported, and nuts were expensive. Alcohol was less available, so people resorted to distilling their own concoctions of variable quality in sheds and cellars on the QT. In the preceding month, the WI put on demonstrations to help their members make provisions stretch, and taught how they could improvise cakes and puddings without dried fruit and marzipan.

While the war had imposed all these food privations, it had also ignited a spirit of coming together in the village to support one another, and make sure no one struggled to provide for their family over Christmas. Some members of the village even sought to share what they had with any trekkers who wandered into Great Paxford over the holiday period, and a lucky few were given a rabbit or a brace of woodpigeon to take home for a Christmas lunch for their families.

Christmas lunch at the Farrows' was a muted affair. Stanley and Stan had spent the preceding week taking as much game as they could off the land, keeping what they needed and selling the rest to Brindsley's. Customarily an opportunity for kicking off their work boots, letting their hair down, and drinking a little too much, this year's Christmas was haunted by the ghost of the German pilot. Or so it felt to Steph, whose mood set the tone for everyone else. She sat at the table watching her husband and son tear through plates of rabbit and potatoes, wondering what kind of meal the Hauer family would be having. She tried to imagine Stanley's chair empty at her Christmas lunch and it immediately brought a large lump to her throat.

Stan kept an eye on Steph to make sure she was coping. She had returned from her evening at the WI in good spirits. Contrary to his own belief that she shouldn't have spoken to the meeting about what had happened, it actually seemed to have been helpful. But while it had done the trick in keeping the village's interest at bay, it hadn't had the same effect on Steph's own conscience, and her spirits seemed to have flagged by the following morning. Stan didn't know what to say or do.

'Nothing you can say,' Steph told him. 'Just have to live with it.'

'But how can I help you do that?' Stan asked, nonplussed. 'One minute you seem back to your old self, the next you've gone right back down.'

'You can start by not asking how I'm feeling all the bloody time.'

That's how things stood during the Farrow Christmas lunch – Steph trapped in guilt; Stan unable to stop wishing he could do more to release his wife from what seemed to him to be a prison of her own making. Stanley barely noticed any of it, locked in imagining what it would be like to wear the uniform of an English soldier, and carry a rifle, and use it against an enemy who always had the same face in his mind's eye – that of Christophe Hauer.

No presents were exchanged, and nothing was said during the meal.

At the Campbell house, Christmas lunch had the potential to be just as sombre as at the Farrows', but for the determination of Kate, Laura, and Dr Rosen to make it a celebration of Will for themselves, yes, but chiefly for Erica. As the various dishes came and went, each of the young women took it in turns to tell their favourite stories about Will. Some simply praised him to the skies for being a wonderful father and husband and mentor, while others affectionately mocked one or other of his idiosyncrasies – the fact that he liked to keep his pipe in his mouth long after its tobacco had been consumed so as to chew thoughtfully on the mouthpiece; or the way he used to fold over corners of pages of *The Lancet* or other scientific publications he read so as to be able to return to the favoured article at a later date; or the fact that he used a secret rating system for malingering patients, based on how long they could remain in the consulting room before Will felt able to gently prise them out of the surgery.

'I was amazed to discover that he categorised the entire village by a scale of *minutes per appointment*,' Myra told the others. 'He knew which patients were fine with five minutes of his time, and which didn't feel satisfied unless they'd had ten or fifteen.'

Erica nodded. 'He always said the five-minute crowd subsidised the fifteen-minute crowd,' she said, 'believing ten minutes was a good average to aim for.'

Eventually, the conversation about Will dropped, as his absence suddenly struck Kate and she stopped speaking mid-sentence and started to cry. Once she had recovered, Dr Rosen revealed that owing to her Jewish faith this was the first Christmas lunch she had ever experienced. The Campbells were curious about how she found it.

'I like it very much,' Myra said. 'Though I have to admit I was expecting more mention of Jesus.'

'We leave him at church,' said Laura.

'Did you see Tom?' asked Erica.

Laura nodded. 'We said hello.'

'How did you feel?'

'He made his decision for himself, which I respect. I made mine for myself, which he respects. I think. I have a lot of work ahead of me, so . . .'

Laura trailed off, glancing at Kate, who knew Laura had broken off with Tom because of what she saw her go through with Jack.

'What do Jewish people usually do at Christmas, Myra?' Kate asked, changing the subject.

'Nothing much,' Myra replied. 'We have plenty of religious festivals to celebrate, sprinkled throughout the year, so we don't exactly feel left out.'

After lunch, Laura went up to her bedroom to study, while Kate, Erica, and Myra retired to the parlour to listen to the King's speech on the wireless. They dozed through the first part, finding his thin, carefully modulated voice a little soporific. They only perked up when the King altered his tone from the general to the specific, and tried to be both reassuring and rousing about the war.

'. . . I am confident that victory is assured,' the King said, 'not only by the prowess of the Armed Forces of my Empire and of those of my Allies, but also by the devotion of the Civil Defence Forces and the tenacity and industry of my people. These are now enduring, where they live and labour, the perils as well as the hardships of war. The staunchness of the men of the Merchant and Fishing Fleets has added lustre to the ancient traditions of the sea. The resistance of my people has won the admiration of other friendly Powers. The relations of my Government with that of the United States of America could not be more cordial, and I learn, with the utmost satisfaction, of the ever-increasing volume of munitions of war which is arriving from that country. It is good to know in these fateful times how widely shared are the ideals of ordered freedom, of justice and security . . .'

Kate and Myra silently noticed Erica looking longingly at Will's armchair. Almost as soon as the broadcast was over, Erica excused herself and ran upstairs to her room, closed the door behind her, lay on the bed, and began to sob so loudly the others could hear.

Kate and Laura – following the same instinct – went and stood outside their parents' bedroom, wondering what they should do. Was it better to go in and try to console their mother, or leave her to her grief?

After a few minutes, Erica stopped crying and the girls heard no further sound from within. Prompted by her sister, Laura carefully opened the door and looked inside. There, she saw their mother curled up asleep on the bed, holding the pillow from Will's side of the bed tightly against her slight frame. She looked at Erica and could see that her face was still wet from crying so hard. Laura recalled a saying her father had once told her. 'We're born alone and we die alone.'

At that moment Laura realised that we have no choice but to also grieve alone.

The gales of laughter filling the dining room at Teresa's house were not *entirely* directed at her first attempt at Christmas lunch with all the trimmings, but it probably accounted for seventy per cent of it. The remaining thirty per cent was due to the copious amount of wine Teresa, Nick and Annie had consumed while they waited for what seemed like an age for Teresa to cook the turkey.

Knowing how tortuous was the route by which Nick had acquired the bird, involving at least two connecting RAF flights from Norfolk, Teresa had been determined to make sure she didn't ruin it by overcooking. Consequently, she undercooked it by at least two hours, so Christmas lunch inexorably slid into Christmas dinner. Not that Nick or Annie seemed to mind. With the threat of air raids lifted for three days, Nick welcomed the opportunity to subside with relief into relaxed good cheer with his two favourite women, and soon found himself sinking without trace in a heated but well-lubricated debate with Annie about whether females could make competent fighter pilots.

'It's never going to happen, so why don't we talk about something that might?' he said, smiling broadly, blinking slowly.

'It's never going to happen *unless* we talk about it!' said Annie, aggrieved. She turned to Teresa for support. 'You agree, don't you?'

Teresa hadn't given the subject a moment's thought, and felt immediately conflicted. While she didn't want to contradict Nick in his area of expertise, she couldn't think of a reason why women shouldn't be fighter pilots if they could match the prowess of male counterparts.

'Wouldn't women lack the necessary killer instinct . . .?' she asked tentatively.

'Utter nonsense . . .' Annie muttered. 'The RAF doesn't recruit killers, it recruits future pilots *who can be trained to kill in combat*. So why not train women too?'

259

'Well,' said Teresa, 'if it's simply a question of *training*—'

'It isn't *simply* a question of training, darling . . .' said Nick, trying not to sound patronising, and failing appallingly.

'Is it because we lack the requisite stamina for the job? Is that what you're going to trot out next?' asked Annie, jumping in before Nick could dominate the conversation. 'Because I can tell you as a veteran flyer of planes from one end of the country to the other, in all weathers, *without a parachute* . . . that's complete nonsense. As is the idea a trained woman can't pull the trigger in exactly the same way a trained man can. Do you think I would hate a German pilot up my backside trying to kill me any less than a chap would?'

The conversation rolled on as Teresa excused herself to check on the turkey. Standing in the kitchen prodding the finally browning carcass, she looked back towards the dining room and smiled at the sound of the sozzled argument filling the house. She found Nick's attempts to be more forward-thinking very endearing, even as he usually faltered and retreated into an innate, good-natured conservatism Teresa knew had been bred into him. She equally loved the unapologetic way Annie relentlessly tackled this streak of Nick's, as if her life's work was to push and push until he threw up his hands, the scales fell from his eyes, and he suddenly agreed with everything Annie believed was true.

But most of all, Teresa stood smiling at the success she had self-evidently made of inviting Annie to stay at the house to recuperate. She couldn't deny that there had been several moments when the atmosphere between them threatened to shift from friendship to the temptation to something more. They had each recognised those moments, and they had only happened while Nick was at Tabley Wood. But when Teresa re-established the tone of self-restraint Annie had, like the perfect house guest, followed her host's lead by going into her room, while Teresa invariably found an excuse to leave the house to allow the atmosphere to cool. As the kitchen started to fill with the smell of a successfully cooked Christmas turkey, Teresa felt content.

Lust is a sin. But I've proved I can resist it. You've made it to Christmas a happily married woman, Miss Teresa Fenchurch. Who would ever have thought that would happen?

The predominant sound rising from the Christmas lunch table at Joyce Cameron's house was the clink and scrape of Joyce's silver cutlery against her bone china, as Joyce, Pat and Bob silently munched their way through thick slices of turkey that Bob had secured as a 'thank you' to Joyce for taking them in so generously. Both Bob and Joyce were thoroughly enjoying the meal Bob had asked Pat to prepare as her part of their appreciation for all Joyce had done for them.

'This meat, Patricia,' said Joyce, 'um, um, um . . . delicious. Quite, quite delicious. Moist! I've been cooking turkey for years, my dear. Literally decades, and I can't get moisture like this. You must tell me how. You absolutely must! I put a bird in the oven and whatever I do it comes out as dry as a bone.'

Pat glanced across the table at Bob, who smiled at her, pleased that his wife's cooking was being so enthusiastically appreciated.

'Pat has some secrets I'm sure she'll take to the grave,' Bob said. 'Don't you, Pat?'

Pat looked at Bob for a moment, testing his words for ambiguity, finding none.

'One or two,' she said, non-committally, smiling shyly.

'Promise me one thing,' Joyce asked, wiping her small mouth delicately on her napkin, 'I shall be your first guest in your new house.'

'Of course,' said Pat, 'we wouldn't dream of asking anyone before you. Not only that, you must feel free to drop by any time you choose, and treat it like a second home. After all you've done for us, it's the very least we could do.'

Bob nodded. 'Absolutely.' He sounded entirely sincere.

Tears welled in Joyce's eyes. 'That's so kind of you both. Since you told me that you have found somewhere and will be leaving, I've had moments of distinct panic at being left alone here. Knowing you are nearby, and that I can pop in for a cup of tea and a piece of your delicious cake, Patricia – and you must feel the same, of course – it makes all the difference. Truly.'

'It isn't exactly "nearby", Mrs Cameron. The new house is six miles away,' Pat said. The distance from everyone she knew made Pat nervous, and she had yet to tell anyone but Joyce about the planned move.

'Six miles I shall gladly walk to visit you both,' said Joyce. 'Or cycle, or catch a bus. Is it on a bus route?'

'I think so,' said Pat, none too sure but not wanting to disappoint Joyce.

Bob wrapped his fingers around his glass and slowly got to his feet, the ligaments in his damaged left knee audibly creaking as he reached his full height. The two women looked up at him and momentarily wondered if Bob had to excuse himself from the table for a moment, before realising he was going to propose a toast.

'I should like to propose a toast to you, Mrs Cameron. For everything you've done for Pat and me. You're a remarkable woman with a generous heart. I know some in the village are scared of you from time to time—'

'Only because I seemingly put the fear of God into some of the dafter ones . . .' Joyce said, nonplussed.

'Well, hand on heart you've been nothing but wonderful to us,' Bob continued. 'The absolute embodiment of Christian charity. You are a magical woman, Mrs Cameron. And something quite magical has taken place in your house between me and Pat. I'll leave it at that. Enough said.'

Bob looked across the table at Pat, who was listening attentively, and now smiled.

'Quite magical. We shall be very sorry to leave, but leave we must before we overstay our welcome.' Bob charged his glass towards Joyce. 'To you. The second favourite woman in my life.'

Bob looked at Joyce, then glanced across at Pat to reinforce that he meant she was the first most important woman in his life. Pat dutifully charged her glass to Joyce, who was beaming from ear to ear. 'Hear, hear,' Pat said quietly, and took a slug of wine.

'For my part,' said Joyce, 'I shall treasure the memory of your time here for the rest of my days. It has been my pleasure to have hosted such a wonderful couple as you both. And to get a glimpse at the inner workings of a famous writer! Though I am forced to confess . . . I shan't be sorry to see the back of your rather loud typewriter, Mr Simms!'

'Yes . . .' said Bob. 'Sorry about that.'

'Not at all. Tool of your trade. But now it's my turn to make a toast.'

Joyce stood as Bob sat. She raised her wine glass and looked studiously at the Simmses seated before her.

'To new friendship. May you enjoy the same degree of happiness in your new home as you did in your old.'

Pat looked across at Bob. His eyes met hers for a moment and then appeared to dip with shame. His face flushed red.

He's changed. I never would have believed it's possible, but . . . he's changed. Look at his cheeks. You can't fake that. Not even Bob at his worst could put that on.

Pat felt an unfamiliar spasm of sympathy for her husband as he suffered in silence for the domestic crimes of their past.

The question is . . . can I?

On Christmas night, the temperature dropped quickly as darkness fell on Great Paxford. The looming black silhouette of the church stood guard on top of the hill. Owing to the suspension of hostilities, the blackout was not enforced, and children looked out of well-lit windows, reminding themselves what their own streets looked like under streetlight. Slowly but surely, a hard frost froze fast over every exposed surface, locking the village into a brief, silvery, silent night.

As they looked out of their windows, wise heads reminded themselves that these unthreatened moments were nothing more than a mirage of peace, and would pass as swiftly as Christmas itself.

Chapter 30

IF THE VILLAGERS of Great Paxford had been determined to celebrate Christmas partly in defiance of Hitler's determination to break their morale, there was little appetite to do the same on New Year's Eve. With no allied troops on the European mainland except those captured at Dunkirk, and the resumption of nightly bombing on 27 December, there seemed little to look forward to in the coming year except more of the same, or far worse. In the Lucas household, Teresa, Nick, and Annie shared a solemn sherry at the stroke of midnight, sang 'Auld Lang Syne' as a sad lament for friends and colleagues lost over the preceding year, and retired for the night.

Nick dropped off almost immediately, leaving Teresa lying on her back, listening to Annie's slow movements downstairs. It was during such moments, caught between a sleeping Nick beside her and an audible Annie elsewhere in the house, that Teresa most felt like an actor lingering in the wings to play the part of a happy housewife, while being all-too aware of a longing to be her true self in a world that didn't feel like a theatre. Though she felt in control of herself, she nevertheless wondered what Annie was doing down there, and whether Annie was thinking about her?

To quash these thoughts Teresa turned onto her side and looked at Nick. She reached out and gently lay her hand on his chest, feeling his warmth. He was without question handsome, funny, extremely intelligent, compassionate and immeasurably brave. She forced herself to look at her husband as she whispered his virtues over and over, until her eyes grew tired, her lids closed, and she too eventually fell unconscious.

At breakfast, Nick asked if Teresa would take a walk with him. When she asked if she should prepare Annie's wheelchair so that she could come too, Nick shook his head.

'Just the two of us, if you don't mind.'

To Teresa's ear, Nick spoke as if he was inviting a subordinate into his office for a quiet reprimand, and her heart began to race.

'Have I done something to upset you?' she asked.

Have you seen something? Overheard something? Does Annie keep a diary that you've caught a glimpse of?

Nick took a bite of toast and shook his head.

'Of course not. And even if you had – and I can't for the life of me think what that might be – I'd hardly ask you to go for a walk to discuss it. Whatever made you think I thought you'd done anything wrong?'

'It was just the way you said "will you take a walk with me". It sounded like something you might say to a trainee pilot who wasn't going to make the grade.'

'I simply want to talk to you alone.' He lowered his voice. '*Without Annie.*'

For the remainder of breakfast, Teresa wondered if Annie had irritated Nick in some way, causing him to want to discuss getting her out of the house. She couldn't think of one. Annie's date of departure was not something they had ever discussed in concrete terms. Her invitation to stay for the duration of her recuperation was left open-ended. Annie would leave whenever Annie felt ready.

Outside, the air was bitingly cold, exacerbated by a stiff wind that had been blowing since Christmas Day. A few crows and a couple of seagulls were managing to cruise the currents of the slate-grey sky, but for the most part wildlife around Great Paxford had decided that sheltering from the weather was the best option.

'I don't want you to be alarmed,' Nick said in an opening sentence that achieved nothing but instantly alarming Teresa, 'but I've decided to fly again.'

Teresa wasn't sure what Nick meant. Since they'd been married she had become used to RAF words and phrases that were unique to the service, excluding any not privy to their lingo.

'I'm not sure I understand what you mean,' she said.

'For as long as we've known one another I've been ground-based, running the station. But I need to get back in the air.'

'Why do you need to?' she asked. 'Surely, you're needed more on the ground, directing operations, looking after your boys. Running the station, as you say.'

'I need to stay sharp.'

'Surely, knowing how to fly isn't something that fades after a few months out of the cockpit?' she said.

He hesitated. 'I need to stay fighting sharp.'

They walked in silence as the words sank in.

'Fighting sharp . . .?' Teresa repeated, as if she had entirely forgotten that Nick wasn't merely the Wing Commander at Tabley Wood, wasn't merely a pilot, but was at heart a *fighter* pilot.

'The skills required to fight up there need refreshing and updating to meet the changing tactics and technology of the Germans. Strategy and tactics are evolving constantly to deal with the ever-changing threat, and as we learn more about the most effective means of combat. For example, and this is strictly *entre nous*, we learned a great deal from the formations the Luftwaffe flew during the summer. They were devastatingly effective. But once we had adopted something similar we discovered similar advantages. Theatre is always changing. Pilots have to change with it. I'm no different.'

'But you're the Wing Commander . . .' Teresa said, trying to keep her voice level and devoid of the rising sense of panic she was now experiencing.

Nick nodded, as if to give the impression that he was carefully weighing up Teresa's words in the spirit of discussion, and not landing her with a fait accompli.

'Even if I was *entirely* ground-based,' he said, 'I would still need to maintain my fighting edge. By flying.' He looked away from her, casting his eyes across the frozen field to their right. 'On ops.'

Teresa understood that beneath Nick's smart uniform and urbane demeanour, her husband was a man trained to kill other men. But because his work was based on the ground this was information she stored in the very back of her mind. Suddenly, she had to pull it forward and process what Nick was telling her.

'Nick, look at me.'

He turned his face to her, his expression defensive, knowing this was likely to be a hard sell.

'I am expected to keep up my flying hours.'

'But on operations?'

'You can do all the training in the world. But there is only one real way to stay sharp in aerial combat, and that's by taking part. The adrenaline, the sharpness you get from the real thing can't be replicated in training.' He took Teresa's hand in his. 'Darling—'

Teresa pulled her hand away and stepped back from him.

'I know the survival statistics, remember?'

'Teresa, this is what I do.'

'No – what you do is be a Wing Commander. On the ground. For how long are you going back?'

'Darling—'

'I know, I know – this is what you *do* . . . you *said* . . .'

'The RAF is short of fighter pilots. The freshest are the wettest behind the ears and consequently the easiest to pick off. If it wasn't for the Polish boys we would never have survived the summer. We need every drop of experience we can throw up there to stem the flow of bombers coming across. Force Göring into a re-think. It won't be often, I promise. But if we're short-handed I cannot remain behind my desk.'

Teresa didn't know what to say. His decision had clearly been made. He was simply tying up the formalities.

'If it helps, I don't think it will be for long. We're constantly pounding their factories now, eroding their manufacturing base. Eventually, they simply won't be able to produce aircraft at a sufficient rate.'

They walked back to the house in silence. Teresa felt a whirl of anxiety swirling in her stomach. She brought to mind the lifeless body of the dead pilot in the cockpit of the Spitfire that had crashed into the Campbells' house. For all his skill and experience as a pilot, in that moment it felt all too easy for Nick to meet the same fate. All it took was a single bullet piercing his engine, or his skin.

I can't lose another person to this war. I couldn't bear it.

Teresa decided she wanted to spend a little time by herself for a while, and left Nick to make his way back alone.

'Don't be too long,' he said. 'You'll catch your death if you're out in this for any length of time.'

Careful to make sure she wasn't seen, Teresa made her way to the old wood where she used to walk with Alison and her dog, Boris.

The wind increased in strength. Teresa pulled her coat more tightly around her shoulders and pulled her hat even harder onto her head, hurrying through the trees, aiming for a specific destination.

She finally arrived at a small, almost private clearing she used to visit in the months after the death of her lover, Connie, lost at sea when the liner carrying her to a new life in America was torpedoed by a German U-boat.

Teresa stood in the middle of the clearing, and looked around. Almost nothing had changed. There was the same fallen trunk she used to sit on for hours at a time. She sat down and the memories of Connie's loss caused her chest to ache and her eyes to flood.

'Why did you go?' she said quietly. 'All this now, none of it need have happened if you'd stayed . . . '

Teresa sat listening to the wind whip through the overhead branches and across her face.

'I can't go through that again with Nick. If anything happened to him . . . I believe it would actually kill me.'

Teresa looked upwards, through a gap in the trees to the turbulent sky above, and immediately pictured a Hurricane spiralling earthwards, trailing a black spume of smoke. The average life expectancy of a Spitfire pilot during the Battle of Britain was just four weeks. Five hundred and forty-four were lost altogether. Teresa understood that Nick's chance of surviving the war was slim at best.

'*Why can't I have someone?!*' she shouted at the heavens. '*Why can't I just have one person who loves me?! Why must you always take them away?!*'

She stared at the patch of sky until her vision was too blurred by her own tears to see anything clearly. It started to rain. Teresa wiped her eyes on the back of her coat sleeve and suddenly felt colder than she had ever felt in her life.

Chapter 31

My dear reader, I owe you an apology. When I began to submit my Mass Observation reports I fully intended to make a regular commitment, and send reports at frequent intervals. Writing them only made sense if they offered a continuous insight into my life as I see it. If I was to participate then I wanted to do so properly, and not merely submit a few reports and then run out of steam. I wanted to present a portrait of my life, for as long as I was able. To that end, I have been remiss in recent weeks as I haven't submitted a report since before Christmas. That isn't to say nothing has happened during that period, because things are happening at a rate of knots.

As I say, the reason for the delay between this submission and my previous one some weeks back is not because my life has been inconsequential during this period. Quite the opposite. In fact, I had two significant pieces of news I wish to tell you about.

We are to leave our lodgings and move into a new home. This had to happen eventually, but because we had a very efficient financial arrangement with our current landlady (supported for the most part, by her charitable feelings towards us after we lost our house) I fully expected my husband to exploit the situation for as long as he could. Even as it increasingly irritated him to remain living under the auspices of a woman who annoyed him no end. But that has changed, and I believe it's part of the overall change in him that I've witnessed over the last weeks. I can't deny that the desire to move back into a home of our own has been fanned by the receipt of some insurance money from the destruction of our previous house, in conjunction with some healthy royalties my husband has recently received. This income hasn't left us wealthy by any stretch of imagination, but it has put us in the position to make some significant choices.

If I am completely honest, I didn't expect his desire to move out to last beyond finding out how much he would have to pay for a new property. I was wrong. The new house is wonderful. It has a large kitchen, and a dedicated study on the first floor in which my husband can work without drowning the rest of the house in the sound of hammering typewriter keys. It also has a small garden which I will turn into an allotment in which to grow fruit and vegetables. There is a utility room with a double sink, which will make clothes and linen washing so much easier and more efficient. My husband is very pleased with it. He says it is befitting for a man of his status. I know that sounds very self-aggrandising. However, I don't object because he was always at his worst towards me when he felt least secure in himself. When he feels as if he has status in the world, and is respected, I am the direct beneficiary. If he now sees himself as a man of some standing I hope he won't want to return to the man he was. As much as I've hated him for the way he treated me, I've always known that deep down he despised himself for behaving that way. Let him be a man of status if it makes him happy and therefore bearable to live with. The only drawback to the house is that it's located several miles from the village where I have all my friends and work. But I can cycle to and fro, I suppose.

You are probably wondering how I feel about moving to a new house. In a word, 'nervous'. It does feel like the start of a new chapter in our lives. We shall have to wait and see about that. It affords us space to keep out of each other's way, which was always a problem in the old place, leaving me feeling we were prisoners in the same cell.

Which brings me to my second piece of news, and additionally explains why I haven't submitted a report for a while.

I have received a letter from my lover!

It came via my secret channel – the friend I asked to receive his letters and pass them on to me without my husband finding them. The letter was wonderful. He could offer me no details about where he was being posted, or for how long. Only that he was departing the following day. His words were full of love, and plans for our future together. What I loved most was his refusal to question or qualify that we would have a life together. He writes as if it is a certainty. As if there is no question he will survive this war and come for me. I have no reason to doubt it. After all, this is a man who survived the invasion of Czechoslovakia, fought his way across Europe, and held off the German army with his comrades until they could be rescued. As he told me once, 'I appear to be quite difficult to kill.' I can live off the elation I get when I receive one of his letters for weeks afterwards. I re-read his words over and over until I no longer need to read them at all, because I've learned them by heart.

There you have it. My current position. Making the best of a bad lot for the moment, as we all must do.

That's all for now. He's calling for more tea. Thank you, as always, for reading.

Chapter 32

THERE IS A reason why harmless gossip is the lifeblood of village life. A small population of people living in close proximity cannot avoid one another's business because it's all but impossible to keep out of it. Conversations are overheard. Assignations witnessed. Changes in fortune – up or down – are noted. Secrets are hard to keep. Information leaks out and immediately converted into conversational currency. Members of the community relentlessly measure themselves against the status quo to ensure their position remains secure.

The comments about Steph Farrow that surfaced in the New Year were the opposite of 'harmless gossip'. No one knew where they originated, though Gwen Talbot was among the first to pass them on to whoever she encountered, with the faux-innocence so beloved of those who beseech everyone else not to shoot the messenger. When pressed to say who told her, Mrs Talbot was at pains to forget.

'I can't entirely remember. But they had it on very good authority.'

The gossip concerned Steph's role in the death of the German pilot, and questioned the Farrows' account in the newspaper and on radio. It seemed to cast doubt on the fact that Steph was the Farrow who fired the fatal shot, with one version claiming that it was actually Stanley – with Steph claiming responsibility to avoid her son getting into any trouble from the fact that he had shot the pilot at point blank range when he had his hands in the air. This then swiftly mushroomed as Great Paxford's own version of Chinese whispers took a firm grip. Various versions of precisely how Stanley had shot the German at point blank range spewed forth.

In one, young Stanley was out shooting rabbits and came upon the mortally injured pilot in undergrowth, and shot him point blank in panic.

In another, Stanley came upon the German pilot as he was hanging from a tree by his parachute straps on the Farrows' farm, and Stanley shot him in cold blood where he hung. Why, asked some, could Stanley not have fled the scene without firing, and fetched the authorities to deal with the German? No one knew. In another version, Stanley bludgeoned the German pilot to death with the butt of his shotgun for reasons unknown, and then shot the corpse to make it look as if he'd been attacked.

This gossip ran like effluent through Great Paxford's gutter. If its producers hoped to bring trouble from the authorities to Stanley's feet they were clearly ignorant of the fact that the boy could have shot any number of defenceless German pilots in the face and he would have been released a hero.

It was more likely the rumours were generated to throw a shadow across Stanley's courage.

All versions justified Steph taking the blame for killing the pilot to save her son from the disgrace of being labelled a cowardly murderer. Indeed, many of those repeating the gossip did it *in praise of* Steph's maternal self-sacrifice, and categorically stated they would have done the same.

Once it seemed the gossip that originally maligned Steph had transmuted into yet more admiration for her, another titbit of gossip slipped out – by complete coincidence, via Gwen Talbot. It was also passed on to Mrs Talbot via a well-informed source, purporting to reveal that the Farrow family had somehow benefited economically from the incident. The source couldn't pinpoint by how much, or from who, but nevertheless again had it on 'good authority' that the money had been paid as a form of reward for having shot and killed the German pilot.

Sarah Collingborne had, by chance, been among the first to learn of this via Claire, who had heard it via Miriam at Brindsley's, who had been told it by . . . Gwen Talbot.

Unlike everyone else who simply absorbed the information without questioning any of it, Sarah decided to take issue. She cycled over to the Farrow farm to speak to Steph. When she arrived, she found Steph repairing old coops in the chicken house with Isobel. Sarah asked if either of them were aware of what was being circulated around the village in connection with the death of the German pilot. Neither Steph nor Isobel had the foggiest idea what Sarah was talking about.

'All I noticed is people stopped looking at me after I spoke at the WI. But after New Year, quite a few started looking at me again.'

'You've not heard the gossip, or rumours?'

'Rumours?' said Steph.

Isobel looked up. 'Is this about who shot the pilot? Because I've heard some of those.'

Steph looked from Isobel to Sarah, wondering what they were talking about. Sarah proceeded to tell Steph what she'd heard. The more she spoke, the more Steph shook her head.

'Everything you've just told me is wrong. Stanley didn't shoot the pilot. I did. I wish to God I hadn't but there's nothing I can do about that now. All the stories about Stanley – I don't understand the point of them. We told the truth. Why would people choose to believe a lie?'

'There could be any number of reasons,' Sarah said.

'Such as?'

'Well, to begin with, there's always a small number of people who've decided – for whatever reason – never to believe anything they're told, and prefer to believe an alternative version.'

'Why would people do that?' asked Isobel.

'I don't honestly know. Then there are others who are more malicious.'

'But why go to those lengths? We didn't lie.'

'If you want my honest opinion . . . jealousy.'

Steph's brow furrowed. 'Jealous? Of what? My sleepless nights. Fine. They can have them.'

'Of the attention you've received. The way you've been celebrated as a hero.'

'I never asked for it. Never wanted it.'

Sarah nodded, with an air of resignation. 'If there's one thing I've learned as a vicar's wife . . . there is nowt so queer as folk.'

'Do you know who's saying all this?' asked Isobel.

'I have my suspicions, but it's not for me to speculate.'

Steph looked at Sarah. 'Gwen Talbot, by any chance?'

Sarah looked at Steph, and in her determination not to give anything away, managed to give away that she believed Steph had guessed entirely correctly.

Half an hour later Steph was rapping hard on Gwen Talbot's front door. She ignored the rain that had soaked her from the farm, and stared at the door with a face like thunder. A dog began barking on the other side. Sarah had sensed Steph might be spurred into some form of action by bringing the gossip to Steph's attention, but hadn't anticipated action would happen immediately. She had offered to mediate, but Steph had turned her down on the grounds that she had always fought her own battles, and wasn't about to stop now. She felt deeply offended that anyone could suggest her family was profiting from the German pilot's death.

Steph's mind had been racing all the way across from the farm, churning over everything she was going to say to Gwen Talbot; each iteration gaining in ferocity, her anger like a small tornado inside her head, gathering speed and fury.

Finally, the door opened and Steph found herself face to face with Gwen Talbot. Gwen looked momentarily shocked as she registered who was facing her.

'Something I can do for you, Steph?' said Gwen, trying to sound as if Steph's presence on her doorstep was neither unusual nor unexpected.

Steph looked at Gwen, smaller and thinner in her housecoat than she appeared at WI meetings or on the High Street, where she usually saw her in coat and hat.

'Sorry to bother you, Gwen, but I've been told there's gossip about me going around the village.'

Gwen Talbot looked blankly at Steph. 'Is that so?'

'You keep your ear to the ground, so I thought if anyone knows about it, it'd be you.' Steph looked hard at Gwen, daring her to disagree. 'About me and my lad and the German?' Steph said.

'I've heard bits and pieces, here and there . . .' she said, unwilling to commit herself further.

Steph recalled how the police officer had gently questioned her about the shooting when he came to the farm. Not jumping right in, but holding off, letting her get comfortable, and then pressing her harder and harder for every last detail.

'About who shot him? The pilot.'

Gwen shrugged. 'Something like that.'

Steph nodded, taking her time, letting Gwen see that she wasn't going to be rushed or chased away until she'd got what she came for.

'And apparently . . . about a reward we were supposed to have got for what happened?'

Gwen Talbot shifted uneasily from one foot to the next.

'Is it true?' Gwen asked.

Steph couldn't believe her ears. 'How could you think it's true, Gwen? Even if there was a reward offered, how could you imagine I'd take blood money like that?'

Gwen Talbot looked at Steph for a few moments. 'Some would. Money is money, Steph. You could say you deserve it.'

'Whatever you read in the paper, or heard on the wireless, that's the truth of it. Whoever's spreading different stories is not only a bloody idiot, they're a bloody liar. Next time you see whoever told you this, tell them from me they'd best stop or I won't be responsible for the consequences.'

Gwen bridled. 'Is that a threat?'

Steph looked at Gwen calmly and nodded slowly.

'Anyone doubts me would do well to remember what I've done to protect my son. I won't have him dragged through the mud for the entertainment of tattlers with nothing better to do than spread manure. There's a bloody war on. We should be sticking together not chopping ourselves up, doing Hitler's work.'

Gwen Talbot looked at Steph and sheepishly nodded.

'Tell whoever's spreading this muck to stop. From *now*.'

Steph walked away from the Talbot house knowing Gwen was watching her from the front door; knowing Gwen knew that she knew it was almost certainly Gwen who was the source of the gossip, spreading it as malevolently as she could: because Gwen Talbot seemed constantly on the lookout for any disparity between what she and her family had and what others had.

The rain had eased. As Steph walked along the wet road she opened her arms to allow the stiff wind to dry out her coat. By the time she arrived back at the farm it was bone dry.

When Steph entered the farmhouse, she was met by an ashen-faced Stan, sitting at the kitchen table opposite Stanley, looking sheepish. They had been waiting for her. They watched as Steph hung up her coat and took off her boots, before joining them at the kitchen table.

'What's all this?' she asked matter-of-factly, looking from one to the other, sensing tension between them. 'What's happened?'

Stanley looked to his dad for guidance.

'Don't look at me,' Stan said quietly. 'You're a man now, apparently.'

Steph looked at Stanley. 'Tell me what?' she asked.

Stanley looked at his mother and cleared his throat. Then swallowed hard, and took a deep breath.

'I've signed up,' he said. And then, as if his mother might not know what 'signing up' meant, added, 'For the army.'

Steph looked at her son for what felt like an age. She felt her eyes blink once, twice, three times. Stanley looked at her.

'Steph?' said Stan.

'Mam?' said Stanley, concerned.

For a fragment of a moment the face of the dead German pilot superimposed itself in her mind over Stanley's, before disappearing.

She heard Stan's chair scrape backwards as he stood up with concern.

She saw her husband's mouth open and close as he motioned towards her.

But suddenly, the supporting strength in her legs vanished, and Steph felt them buckle beneath her.

The sight of Stanley staring at her was the last thing Steph saw before she fell to the ground and blacked out.

Chapter 33

'E<small>RICA?</small>'

Erica snapped open her eyes at the sound of her name and looked around the large table in Frances Barden's dining room that was currently hosting a WI committee meeting. She had fallen asleep in the middle of the meeting, albeit momentarily.

After taking apologies for absentees the meeting moved briskly through basic admin to discussing the success of Laura's Christmas party in the village hall.

Frances could barely contain her delight at how well it had gone.

'I have received so many notes and warm words thanking us for putting on the event, with many expressing the hope it could be staged again this year – if possible in perpetuity. I don't see why not. Any objections?'

The women around the table shook their heads.

'Then let's propose to make it an annual event, and send Laura a letter of thanks for her initiative and hard work from the committee, with some flowers. It's a shame she isn't here today to hear how impressed we all are.'

It was at that point the other committee members turned instinctively towards Erica as Laura's mother, expecting to see her beaming with pride; only to see that she appeared to have nodded off.

'I usually have to chaunter on for at least twenty minutes before someone drops off,' Frances whispered, good-naturedly. 'Either I'm growing more boring, or—'

Joyce coughed diplomatically, and softly said, 'Erica?' causing Erica's eyes to re-open.

'I am so sorry!' Erica said. 'I've really no idea what came over me.'

'How well have you been sleeping since Will's funeral?' asked Alison.

It surprised none present to learn that Will's death would have had a profound effect on Erica's sleeping pattern – either due to grief keeping her awake, or because her role as Will's chief carer in the months before his death had left her sleep-deprived, and she was now overwhelmed by exhaustion. However, neither of these were the sole cause of her current bout of narcolepsy.

'This is Laura's fault.'

'How so?' asked Pat.

'Before he died, Will encouraged Laura to consider becoming a doctor.'

'Oh, what an excellent idea!' said Frances. 'I was once told I would make an excellent doctor.'

'Yes, but this isn't about *you*, Frances,' chided her younger sister gently. 'You were saying, Erica?'

'Well . . . Laura took him at his word and considered the idea very seriously, and decided she would like to try for medical school. We can only afford it if she gains a scholarship, so she's been working her socks off morning, noon, and night with revision. I've been providing the poor girl with meals, but also tea and sandwiches, biscuits and whatever's necessary around the clock to keep her energy levels up. I'm also sitting with her in her room for hours on end, testing her, and helping her get to grips with Chemistry – which can be a beast of a subject.'

'Having a pharmacist for a mother must help?' asked Joyce.

'I had a natural aptitude. I don't think Laura's inherited it. She has far more flair for Biology and Physics. It's not an insurmountable task, but it does require a great deal of time and energy – for both of us.'

'Do you think she'll get it – the scholarship?' Frances asked.

'It won't be for the want of trying. And she's certainly taking it very seriously. But even if her Chemistry was better, I honestly feel she's left it too late to put on enough of a spurt. One can't blag the sciences. That said . . . the lesson will be a good one if she doesn't get it.'

As soon as she finished the sentence Erica yawned. The other women around the table suddenly felt the urge to follow suit, and covered their mouths with their hands to stifle their own yawns.

'It will make her more realistic – either about her aptitude for medicine, or how much work it will take.'

'But aren't you tempted to stop her wasting her time, if you consider that to be the case,' asked Teresa. 'From my own experience, you want a child to try their best at everything they do. But that has to be weighed against the likelihood of them eventually succeeding or failing. Learning how to fail and try again is, of course, a valuable lesson all children should learn. But that's a markedly different proposition to *knowingly* watch a child set themselves up for an inevitable and tremendous disappointment.'

'I'm afraid it's complicated by the fact it was her father's suggestion. Because it's so inextricably bound up with Will, I fear there's no stopping her running herself into the ground in pursuit of something she may well be ultimately unable to achieve. But . . . I'll be there every step of the way. And to help her back on her feet when the time comes.'

'Just as you were over that ghastly business with the Wing Commander Bowers,' said Joyce.

'Indeed,' said Erica, not wishing to re-open that can of worms. 'What with that, the war, and Will . . . the poor girl's been blown off-course over the past twelve months.'

The meeting continued through tea and cake, as they discussed the rota for their trekker initiatives, and the specific issue of some women pulling their weight more than others.

'For example,' said Sarah, 'you, Alison undertake far more shifts than anyone else.'

Alison smiled modestly. 'But I really don't mind. Since Teresa moved out I've missed the company.'

'And you've met some *very* nice people . . .' Teresa said, smiling.

'Yes. I've found Liverpudlians tend to be very nice people,' said Alison.

'Any in particular you'd like to tell us about? I won't include any names in the minutes,' Teresa said, arching her eyebrows mischievously.

'If you're alluding to Mr Smith, he's been very helpful.'

The other women looked at Alison in silence for a few moments, and then burst out laughing. Alison watched them sternly for a few moments.

'Honest to God, what is the matter with you? He's brought a lot of people to us – that's what I meant. That's *all* I meant.'

Frances was the first to control herself and nodded in agreement with Alison's explanation.

'He has, he has. Lots of people. Though almost exclusively when you're on shift.'

'Can we move on?' asked Alison, eager to push the meeting beyond her personal life.

'Of course. The point I was trying to make is that we need to balance out the rota so that everyone does their fair share. However much you may not mind doing as many shifts as you do, Alison—'

'John doesn't mind you doing as many as you do . . .' chipped in Teresa, unable to let the opportunity for further teasing pass entirely.

'Teresa!' Alison's voice clearly indicated she had had enough.

Teresa looked chastened. 'Sorry.'

'It's the old story,' Frances continued. 'People assume that those who undertake more than their share of work do so because they like it.'

'But I do,' Alison said.

'Yes, but then they think they don't have to do anything. And that carries over to the next activity. Do you see?'

'You're incentivising others to do less,' said Sarah. 'It's not what the WI is about.'

Alison agreed to rein in her shifts while Frances would nudge slackers to do their bit. Eventually, the meeting arrived at 'any other business' at the end of the agenda. Pat raised her hand and everyone turned to her and waited to hear what she had to say.

'You all should be the first to know. I'm having to resign as Branch Secretary for a few months while Bob and I move into our new house.'

Sarah was keen to know about the house. 'Is it in a village?'

'Not really. It's about a mile outside Buwardsley. In the countryside to give Bob the peace he needs to work.'

'Lot of noisy animals in the countryside, Pat,' said Alison with a smile.

'But not much army traffic. Or livestock. It's at the edge of a wood, so he can take walks and cogitate.'

'It sounds positively pastoral,' said Frances. 'Perhaps we should all move there!'

Pat smiled.

'Won't you miss Great Paxford?' asked Frances.

'I'm sure I shall to begin with. But the surrounding area is beautiful, and I can always get the bus in when I want. Or cycle.'

'And shopping?' asked Sarah. 'You can't just pop down to the High Street.'

Pat smiled patiently at her concern. 'Bob's suggested we plan for a weekly shop on the bus, and develop the garden for most of the veg we'll need.'

'Will you cycle to the WI and telephone exchange?' asked Erica.

'I don't see why not? Though I might have to consider giving up my job at the exchange. We'll have to see,' Pat replied.

'You can't not come to the WI,' said Erica. 'You'll need it even more.'

'I'll get used to cycling more, I'm sure. And when the war's over we'll run a small car of some kind.'

Miriam, Joyce, Teresa, and Alison listened with a completely open mind, as they were the only ones who were oblivious to Bob's ill-treatment of Pat. However, Frances, Sarah, and Erica exchanged concerned glances with one another as they processed the details. For it seemed that not only was the new house designed to enlarge Bob's living and working area, with a bespoke study and spacious living room, it also seemed intended to consign Pat around the clock to a large kitchen and utility/laundry room, with a garden in which she would grow fruit and vegetables for Bob's table.

After the meeting came to its natural conclusion Pat waited until Miriam, Joyce, Teresa, and Alison had left before approaching the others, who were talking quietly among themselves while glancing at Pat with a concerned air.

'I know what you're thinking, ladies,' she said softly, grabbing the bull by the horns.

'Can you blame us?' said Frances.

'All I can tell you is that Bob has – something's changed in him. Whether it's the success of his book, or coming back from covering Dunkirk and realising life's too short to carry on behaving the way he has. But he's different.'

Sarah touched Pat's arm affectionately. 'We simply want the best for you.'

'The three of you have been the greatest friends I could ever wish for. But this move will be good for us. I've really come to believe it.'

They watched Pat leave to catch up and walk home with Joyce. They stood in silence for a few moments.

'Will once had a patient,' Erica began, 'a woman who came to him on and off over the years with cuts and bruises. A broken rib once. Broken collarbone. He knew what was going on. He tried to get her to talk to him about it, but she always covered up. One nonsensical excuse after another, for ten years until they eventually moved away. I remember asking him about it. He felt helpless. He'd seen it in other patients. He could treat the injuries but never the cause. The cause remained locked within the minds of the men who treated their wives like that.'

'But . . . that wasn't during war time,' said Frances. 'So perhaps Bob's experience at Dunkirk really has had a profound effect on him.'

'It's possible,' said Sarah. 'I so want it to be true.'

Erica desperately wanted to tell the Barden sisters about Pat's relationship with Marek so that she wasn't the only one besides Pat who carried the secret knowledge of Pat's affair, and would be able to discuss it openly. But she resisted the urge.

Frances walked Erica and Sarah to the front door, agreeing to keep an eye on Pat.

Frances reviewed the efforts she had gone to previously to help Pat. She had persuaded an old friend to invite Bob into the Press Corps to cover the BEF withdrawal from France. Her stated aim was to get Bob out of the way; her secret hope had been for him to be killed by a German bullet. Admittedly, German shrapnel in his leg had caused him to slow down, but her preference had been to rid Pat of Bob not to merely enable her to outrun him if and when the need arose.

Can men like Bob change? I mean, really change, not simply put on a show of it?

Frances didn't know. And as a woman happily married to a man with a long-standing double life that she knew nothing about until his death, she felt obliged to withhold judgement.

Chapter 34

Erica arrived back from the WI committee meeting to find Dr Rosen and Laura preparing to leave for the Farrow farm. Since Stan telephoned Frances on his wife's behalf to apologise for her absence at the committee meeting, Steph's condition had deteriorated so fast that Stan telephoned the surgery to ask Dr Rosen to make a house call as soon as possible. Myra had asked Laura to accompany her on the basis that she knew the Farrows well.

'Is she all right?' asked Erica, watching her daughter and Myra putting on their coats.

'When I asked the husband to describe what was wrong all he could say was "she's not good". Laura told me she collapsed a few months back, trying to bring in the harvest single-handed.'

Erica nodded. 'Will suspected she had strained her heart through overwork, and prescribed plenty of rest.'

'Well . . . it's possible the rest put her back on her feet momentarily, while missing some underlying condition.'

Erica was immediately annoyed by Myra's comment. 'Are you suggesting Will *missed* something more serious?'

From Erica's tone, Myra knew to tread very carefully indeed.

'I'm not suggesting that – of course not. I mean, he wasn't in the best of health, so it's possible that he might have – not that anyone could blame him.'

'I'm so glad you think so!' said Erica, her face flushing with rising anger. 'But just to be clear, if Will thought for a moment that his health might in any way compromise his diagnostic ability he would have stopped working.'

Laura thought this was an opportune time to step in. 'I'm sure Myra isn't criticising him in any way.'

'Not for a moment,' Myra said. 'There are many conditions that only become apparent by making themselves known after several recurrences. Until a pattern becomes established they can easily be regarded as one-offs.'

Erica looked at Myra for a moment. 'We shouldn't forget what she's recently been through with the German pilot episode,' she said.

Myra's eyes widened. 'That was her?' she said, intensely surprised.

'How could you not know that?' asked Erica in disbelief. 'Everyone within thirty miles knows that.'

'Everyone in the county,' said Laura.

'My work rarely leaves me time for anything else, let alone gossip,' replied Myra.

'It isn't gossip, Myra,' Erica called after them as they departed for the Farrow farm. 'It's the biggest *news* in Great Paxford for years!'

As she and Laura cycled towards the Farrow farm, Myra surmised it may be possible that the shock of being caught up in a life and death situation with the German pilot could have had a similar psychological effect on Steph as soldiers suffering from shell-shock in the Great War.

'I'm not equating the two, of course,' said Myra. 'But participating in a life and death struggle is far removed from what Mrs Farrow could normally expect to experience.'

Laura weighed up the notion. 'Steph's a very strong woman,' she said. '*Very* strong.'

'Physical or mental strength seems to be irrelevant,' Myra said, pedalling hard up a small hill. 'Anyway, it's a good opportunity for you to see how we approach diagnosis. The first thing we have to do is clear the mind of all preconceptions we might have about what may or may not be likely. We then take note of the presenting ailment and previous medical history. And all the while, we listen to the patient and their nearest and dearest. We listen to what is *not* said. We listen to our *intuition* when it pipes up. And finally . . . we simply *listen*.'

They cycled on through the grey afternoon, along roads lined with hedgerows that winter had drained most of the colour from.

As she pedalled, Laura rehearsed Myra's list for diagnosis over and over in her head, but she felt so drained from long hours of revision that by the time they arrived at the Farrow farm the only word Laura could remember was 'listen'.

The front door of the farmhouse was opened by an ashen-faced Stanley, who quickly ushered Dr Rosen and Laura upstairs to his parents' bedroom, where Steph lay asleep in bed. Stan sat on a chair beside her, watching over his wife and holding her hand. When Myra and Laura appeared in the doorway he got to his feet and ushered them in.

'Thanks for coming so quick,' he said in a low voice, trying not to wake Steph.

'Not at all,' Dr Rosen said, matching Stan's reduced volume. 'How has she been since you telephoned? Any change?'

'Much the same. Asleep. Breathing shallow, like.'

Dr Rosen nodded and placed her bag on Stan's chair, opened it up, and took out her stethoscope.

'Does she know I'm coming?'

Stan shook her head.

'Would you mind gently waking her for me – less of a shock?'

Stan nodded and rested a hand on Steph's shoulder and rubbed it gently. After a moment, Steph's eyes fluttered open, and blinked slowly, registering where she was and who was looking at her.

'Doctor's here to see you, love,' Stan said softly.

'Doctor . . .?'

'Your husband is quite concerned about you, Mrs Farrow,' said Myra, taking control of the situation. 'He wanted me to come and see you and see how you are.'

Laura stood just inside the doorway next to Stanley, observing how Dr Rosen dealt with the patient and her family. She then glanced at Stanley beside her. His expression was decidedly anxious.

'I'm sure it's nothing to worry about,' Laura whispered.

Stanley glanced at her and returned his full attention to his mother in bed. Laura decided to say nothing more. Together, they watched as Dr Rosen began her examination, listening to Steph's heart and lungs with her stethoscope while taking her pulse.

'How have you been since the business with the German, Mrs Farrow?'

Laura noted how effortlessly Myra had already imbibed, processed, and was now utilising the information she'd passed on during the ride over.

'Tired most of the time,' said Steph. 'Don't sleep well at all.'

'Always used to sleep like a log, doctor,' said Stan. 'Since I got back it's been like sleeping next to someone trying to fight their way out of a coffin. Before I got home she wasn't even going to bed most nights, isn't that right, son?'

Stanley nodded. 'Just sat in the chair by the fire, or kitchen table.'

Steph peered at her son through the room's low-lit gloom.

'According to your notes, Mrs Farrow, you apparently suffered a collapse last summer.'

Steph nodded. 'Some bastard farmer poached our labour, leaving us completely short-handed for the harvest. If it hadn't been for the WI we'd 've lost the farm.'

'And how has that affected you? In terms of your health?'

'Hasn't.'

'You're quite sure?'

'No reason to lie. Not to my doctor.'

Myra felt a warm glow in her chest at the sound of the words 'not to my doctor'. For the first time she felt regarded as part of the community.

'To be clear, Mrs Farrow,' Myra continued, 'the incident with the German pilot has not left you unscathed. I don't mean physically. I mean . . . inside your head.'

Myra knew she had to tread carefully when trying to ascertain the extent of a psychological issue. The understanding of how the mind processed trauma was a relatively new discipline that many practising doctors failed either to understand or appreciate. The very idea that unseen debilitating forces could be at work inside one's head was downright terrifying to most ordinary people, as they were customarily associated with words like 'mad' and 'lunatic'.

Though she hated to admit it, as she hated to admit any form of weakness, Steph knew she was in trouble.

'I'd say it's left its mark,' Steph said, still trying to play her situation down.

Laura felt Stanley lean a little closer to her.

'I did this,' he whispered to her.

Laura looked round at the lad. 'I don't see how you can blame yourself, Stanley. I read your account of what happened in the *Echo*. As you said, he came out of nowhere.'

Stanley shook his head. 'Not that. That knocked her for six. But *this*. The collapse. That was me. Telling her I've signed up.'

Laura looked at Stanley, confused. 'Signed up?'

Stanley nodded. 'She went down soon as I told her.'

Laura hesitated for a moment, unsure what to do with this information. She suddenly recalled Myra telling her about listening to the patient's nearest and dearest.

'Dr Rosen?' Laura said quietly. 'May I have a word?'

Myra looked across at Laura and could see her indicating that she meant 'in private', outside the room. Myra took out her stethoscope and made her excuses to Steph and Stan, and followed Laura out of the bedroom and onto the landing.

'What is it?' Myra asked Laura.

'Stanley just told me that Steph – Mrs Farrow – collapsed immediately after he told her he'd signed up for the army yesterday.'

Myra looked at Laura for several moments.

'What do you think's the matter with her?'

'She's clearly exhausted. Suffering from the trauma of what happened with the pilot. All could have made a contribution. But chiefly, I'm concerned about her heart. Well, there's a rare condition called right-ventricular strain, which results in a deformity of the muscle of the right ventricle. I can't be certain, but she needs to be examined at the hospital.'

'Stanley thinks he's responsible,' Laura said.

'There's an irregularity in the heartbeat. If it *is* what I suspect, it's unlikely to have been caused by a single event. Young Stanley's announcement may have been a contributory factor – who can say. But it's very unlikely to have been entirely responsible. In fact,' said Myra ominously, 'it may have brought it to light *just in time*.'

'Just in time?' Laura repeated.

Myra nodded. 'Left untreated, the condition could eventually kill her.'

Chapter 35

Teresa and Annie ate supper in silence. Nick's supper was on a plate in the oven. After a few moments Annie looked up at Teresa, who was merely picking at her food.

'Why don't you turn on the wireless and see if there's some music we could listen to?'

Teresa looked across the table and shook her head.

'I'm not in the mood to listen to music. Besides,' she said, 'I want to be able to hear the telephone if it rings.'

'Of *course*, you'd be able to hear it.'

'I want to be sure.'

Teresa continued to pick as Annie finished her supper, placed her cutlery on the plate, reached into her pocket to bring out a packet of cigarettes, and lit one. She took a long drag and watched Teresa.

'This is your own fault,' she said.

'What is?' asked Teresa, trying hard to conceal her irritation with Annie's desire to chat.

'Insisting Nick telephone before he goes up. You're on tenterhooks all night in case he does. And then you'll be a nervous wreck until he telephones to say he's returned safely. Either way you're a quivering mess. It would be far better to stay in the dark and deal with things when or if they happen.'

'I'm not a "quivering mess",' said Teresa, setting down her knife and fork.

'I can see you quivering from here. Metaphorically speaking.'

'The arrangement with Nick isn't designed to eradicate all my nerves – that would be impossible. What it allows me to do is *control* them. Until Nick telephones, my anxiety stays at a certain level. *If* he telephones it will rise to another level. But if the arrangement wasn't in place at all, my anxiety would be at its uppermost all night, because that's how human nature works.'

'*My* human nature doesn't,' said Annie, her mouth betraying the hint of a smile. 'My human nature takes each moment as it comes.'

Teresa laid her knife and fork neatly on her plate and looked coolly at Annie.

'Well, do pass on my congratulations to *your* human nature. It's clearly far more sophisticated than mine.'

'It knows,' said Annie, enjoying the feat of distracting Teresa out of her anxiety for a few moments.

'I wouldn't look so smug, Annie. All it means is you have ice in your veins. It's not the most endearing quality.'

'Perhaps not. But a damned good one for a pilot. You'll be relieved to know Nick has it too. Not here, with you, of course. But the moment he sets foot on the airfield you can hear the tiny creak of ice crystals forming. All else forgotten but the job in hand.'

'You make him sound like an assassin.'

'Aren't they all? Me too, if they'd let me.'

After supper, Teresa hooked her arm through Annie's and helped her to the front room, and slowly eased her onto the sofa. Teresa picked up the newspaper and tried to focus on the mass of print in her hands, as Annie continued to smoke. Each time she tried to concentrate on an article, her eyes lifted over the page and settled on the black Bakelite telephone on the side cabinet.

Do I want it to ring or stay silent? If it rings I could at least prepare myself.

'If we put on some music it will distract you,' Annie offered. 'The newspaper won't do the trick. Trust me – I've tried on many, many occasions. Trying to read while anxious is like trying to sit still on an anthill. Music is the only thing that provides a complete distraction. It floods the senses. That and alcohol.'

'I'm not in the mood for music,' Teresa said, curtly.

'Goodie – a drink then! Come on, Mrs Lucas. You like a drink. All Catholics like a drink. *Especially* the lapsed ones.'

'I'll fix you one if it'll shut you up!' Teresa said, grinning.

'Terrific. But I'll only have one if you have one with me. You should. It'll calm your nerves.' Annie paused for a moment and stopped play-acting. 'Seriously. It *will* help.'

Teresa let out a long-suffering sigh, stood up, crossed to the small drinks cabinet at the back of the room, and poured them each a drink.

'Sherry – how tasteful. You couldn't slip some whisky in that?'

'I could but I'm not going to.'

Teresa handed Annie the sherry glass, sat back in her seat and took a sip, looking directly ahead, waiting for the telephone to either ring or remain silent.

'He's an exceptional pilot, Teresa,' said Annie, calmly. '*Exceptional.*'

'So everyone tells me. He told me himself. But what if he gets caught out trying to help one of his new boys? What then?'

Annie didn't have an answer. She agreed that going to the aid of a relative novice pilot might be Nick's Achilles heel. He wouldn't be able to resist, and in so doing, would put himself at far greater risk than if he were flying solo.

'He feels the death of every pilot in the squadron on a deeply personal level,' said Teresa. 'They're like sons to him.'

Annie looked at Teresa, nodded in agreement, held out her hand and beckoned her over.

'Come here,' she said quietly. 'Sit with me.'

Teresa looked at Annie and felt a pang of electricity shoot through her.

'What are you doing?' she asked.

'What any friend would do. Offering comfort to her friend at a difficult time.'

Teresa looked at Annie's hand, as if it might contain an invisible grenade.

'It's only my hand,' said Annie, as if reading Teresa's mind.

Annie's hand took hold of Teresa's, and held it lightly as she gently pulled Teresa to sit beside her on the sofa. Through her thin cotton dress Teresa felt the warmth of Annie's leg against hers.

'A trouble shared is a trouble halved,' said Annie, gently.

The two women sat this way for five minutes, each thinking about Nick. Annie's hand felt warm in Teresa's, and though Teresa felt she should probably take her hand away, she felt comforted by it and continued to hold it.

'I've recently had nightmares about Nick being shot down,' Teresa eventually confessed. 'Trapped in his cockpit, surrounded by flames, screaming out my name.'

'It's perfectly natural, I suppose,' said Annie. 'But I remember you telling me about looking at the Spitfire that crashed into the doctor's house. Seeing the dead pilot inside. You don't think that's informing your dreams at the moment?'

'It's possible. I did think about that terrible scene a great deal afterwards.'

'So, it could have become embedded in your brain over time,' Annie suggested. 'Imprinted, and now resurrected to generate the most terrible nightmares.'

Teresa conceded this might be true, but also that the visions she was experiencing at night were not so beyond the bounds of what might happen to Nick.

'No. No, I can't say they aren't,' Teresa admitted.

Annie slowly extended her free arm and curled it around Teresa's shoulder for greater reassurance, and gently stroked her arm. Teresa instinctively rested her head on Annie's shoulder, her eyes glittering with tears.

The two women sat like this for endless minutes, sharing their worry for Nick. Teresa now felt the warmth of Annie's whole body against her own, as well as the rise and fall of her chest. Neither felt the need to say anything more, and the longer the silence continued the more it seemed to seal them within this moment.

In Teresa's mind, the objects in the room took on an intense presence, as if they too were no longer the humdrum furnishings of humdrum married life, but had a particular resonance for this particular moment. Even the quality of the air, which Teresa could neither see nor smell, took on a richer texture, accentuating the colours emanating from everything around her. The one smell that was apparent to her, seductively so, was Annie's scent. Not a perfume, because Annie rarely wore it, and certainly not in the house with Teresa and Nick. It was Annie's natural scent – clean, slightly soapy, mingled with her natural aroma. Teresa closed her eyes and let it envelop her, barely noticing Annie's hand around her shoulder now slowly, almost imperceptibly move from Teresa's arm to the hair on the back of her head, which it began to slowly, almost tenderly stroke. Warmth suffused Teresa and she turned to Annie for comfort.

'Your marriage vows never promised that you'd rescind the company of women,' Annie said. 'Never promised that you'd rescind your true nature. In terms of "the laws of marriage" you could only be "unfaithful" by sleeping with another man. In which case, this isn't an act of infidelity, but rather, an act of fidelity to your true self. But in terms of Nick . . . by acting on these feelings you are in fact helping to preserve your marriage rather than see it collapse under unbearable pressure.'

In the heat of the moment, her body flushed with adrenaline and lust, Teresa believed Annie's argument made some sense.

Preparing Annie's bed in silence and then carefully undressing one another and relishing the sight of each other's nakedness. Teresa and Annie made love in the young pilot's bed in the front parlour. When it was over, neither sat up in shame or anger that they had succumbed. Each knew these intimate moments with other women came few and far between in their lives. However they arose, they were to be treasured with every fibre of one's being for as long as they lasted. Consequences – momentarily at least – be damned as they held each other.

Annie was the first to eventually speak.

'I'm sorry,' she whispered, gently kissing Teresa's neck.

'You have nothing to apologise for. It takes two to tango.'

'I don't think I've ever seen two women doing the tango.'

'Well, there's a first time for everything.'

They snuggled closer in each other's arms.

'He hasn't telephoned,' said Teresa.

'Then you have nothing to worry about.'

It was at that moment they heard the sound of an approaching car. Its relevance didn't immediately register with Annie, but the moment Teresa jumped off the bed, ran to the window, and peeped through the blackout curtains, she understood.

'It's him!' Teresa hissed.

'How can you tell in the dark?'

'I recognise the sound of the engine. Oh my God, Annie – shit!'

Annie's experience with emergency situations effortlessly kicked in. She was able to make a rapid appraisal of the situation and reach a swift conclusion.

'Go to bed!' Annie ordered.

'What?' Teresa was clearly panicking and looked at Annie's ruffled bed on the sofa, unable to think clearly.

'Not this one. You're already undressed so stop running around like an idiot, take your clothes, and go upstairs *now*! Get into *your* bed, and stay there! Now!'

Teresa looked at Annie for a few seconds, swallowed hard, nodded, grabbed her clothes and dashed from the room. Annie heard the last of her footsteps pound up the stairs just as Nick opened the front door and came in. The time it took him to take off his cap and coat gave both Annie and Teresa long enough to pull up the blankets and sheets of their respective beds, and go limp like rag dolls in an affectation of fitful sleep.

Nick silently looked in on the front room. He saw Annie was fast asleep and slowly closed the door.

Nick stood in the hall and looked at the kitchen, deciding whether or not to tackle whatever it was that Teresa will have cooked for him to have upon his return from the station. He decided against, and wearily began to ascend the same staircase that just seconds earlier Teresa had thundered up as fast as she could go.

He's coming! What about supper? He must have eaten at the mess. Close your eyes and get your breathing under control . . .

Teresa could feel her heart thumping loudly in her chest, like an animal banging against the bars of its cage. She was convinced Nick would hear it on the staircase.

As he neared the top of the stairs, Nick caught sight of something on the floor, illuminated by a pale shaft of moonlight from the landing window. An item of clothing. A single stocking. He bent slowly and picked it up, recognising it as one of his wife's. He frowned for a moment, as Teresa was usually so fastidious about tidiness.

Stay calm, stay calm, stay calm . . . deep breaths, don't give him any reason to do anything except come to bed and go to sleep.

Teresa lay with her back to the door with her eyes closed, and listened as Nick washed and brushed his teeth before coming into the bedroom, undressing, and joining her in bed.

Teresa felt Nick slip under the sheets and gently wrap his arms around her and pull in close. He affectionately kissed the back of her neck, with no expectation of anything more.

'You didn't call,' Teresa asked sleepily, perfectly acting the role of wife-roused-from-slumber-by-husband-just-returned-from-work.

'Didn't need to. A wonderfully dull night. Luftwaffe grounded. Praise be to thick cloud over northern Europe . . .'

As Nick drifted into sleep, Teresa lay wondering about Annie downstairs. The glow of sexual satisfaction had not been entirely snuffed out by Nick's return, its embers still warming her as the first flickers of guilt began to make their presence felt in the pit of Teresa's stomach.

'By the way,' Nick said sleepily, momentarily rising back into consciousness. 'You dropped a stocking on the stairs . . .'

Teresa felt her heart jump at the mention of what could only be described as her first slip-up. She waited a moment until she was sure she had control of her voice before replying.

'Did I?' she said, trying to drain her tone of all care, as if she had barely registered Nick's observation.

'Not like you, darling . . .' he mumbled, before falling back into unconsciousness, his warm breath softly billowing across her cheek.

Teresa lay in the dark, now with a man's arms wrapped around her.

Not like me. What is like me? When was the last time I was like me? I'm losing all sense of who that is.

After a few minutes Teresa felt constrained by Nick's loving embrace. She tried to slowly free herself without waking him. She was unable to do so, and lay resigned to spending the night in Nick's arms. Her nightdress felt clammy against her skin.

In little more than a year, Teresa had fled her hometown for the anonymity of Great Paxford, lost her lover, Connie, to a German torpedo as she crossed the Atlantic, got married in panic, had the job she adored taken from her, and was now lying in fear of her life with Nick imploding after sleeping with a young female pilot.

Without setting a foot on enemy soil, the war was nevertheless taking a heavy toll on her.

Chapter 36

'Bᴏʙ?'

Pat was trying to get her husband's attention. It was their final breakfast in Joyce's house before they were moving into their own, later that day. Bob was reading the morning paper, engrossed in the latest news of the war. He didn't appear to have heard Pat call his name.

'Bob?'

He heard his name the second time, and looked up at his wife without any hint of the irritation that would have characterised his face at innumerable breakfasts in the past.

'The Australians have captured forty-five thousand Italian troops at Bardia,' he said. 'Forty-five thousand! Can you imagine that?'

'Bardia?'

'Eastern Libya. Next stop, Tobruk.'

'Is that good?'

'It's a start. If nothing else it shows the Allies can be a force to be reckoned with. Albeit against the Italians. Nevertheless, gives us a foothold in North Africa.'

Pat decided she could read the newspaper for herself later.

'Bob, I know it's none of my business. I only ask because we appear to have met the asking price of the new house without having to go to the bank. I've been wondering if we were now in a position of relative comfort?'

She watched as Bob reached out for his teacup and carefully tipped a mouthful of tea past his lips, swallowed it back, and looked steadily at Pat.

'I would say so. Relatively, yes.'

'From the book?'

'From the book, and the advance for the next one.'

'I see . . .' said Pat. 'But we're not so comfortable that you no longer have to work?'

'No. But we are sufficiently comfortable that you no longer need to work at the telephone exchange.'

'I know we've touched on this briefly when we first talked about moving. You know how much I like my time at the exchange. It gets me out, allows me to meet my friends, gives me something to do that makes me feel useful.'

'You don't imagine there will be plenty to do in the new house to keep you occupied?'

Pat hesitated for a few moments. Coming from 'Old Bob' she would have considered such a question a trap.

For, if she were to say no, she didn't think there would be enough to do to keep her entirely occupied in the new house, Old Bob would have taken it as a sign of ingratitude; and would have displayed his displeasure accordingly.

If she were to say, yes, of course there would be enough to do in the new house to keep her fully occupied, Pat will have talked herself out of her job at the exchange. She decided to hedge her bets and observe Bob's response.

'I'm sure there will be plenty to do in the new house, but perhaps we can wait and see if it's likely to take up *all* my time before I give up the exchange.'

'It's considerably larger than our old house,' said Bob calmly.

'I know,' Pat replied. 'I was only telling the women on the committee the other day.'

'A lot more to keep clean. Not to be underestimated.'

'I'm not underestimating it, Bob. Not for a moment. But until we're in and I have a clear idea about what's involved, it's impossible to make a decision, don't you think?'

'Possibly,' said Bob, taking another mouthful of tea. 'Though I see it as akin to the Forth bridge.'

'The Forth bridge?' asked Pat, not understanding what he meant. 'In what way?'

'It takes so long to paint that by the time it's finished the painters are ready to start again.'

Pat looked at Bob for any hint of amusement or malice on his face, but saw neither.

I know he thinks it will probably take me a long time to clean it, but he doesn't know how efficient I can be. I can't recall him ever cleaning anything. He isn't the best judge.

I'm sure I can manage to keep the house clean and *make time to undertake shifts at the exchange.*

'Once everything's had a thorough clean it should be relatively easy to keep the house in good order.'

'I hope so,' he said. 'I'm expecting a lot of distinguished visitors. Don't want to let the side down.'

Pat wasn't sure she had heard right. 'Did you say, *distinguished visitors*?'

Bob nodded.

'Who exactly do you mean?'

'Once we have a place of our own again I hope to take my place within the literary world of the north-west. I'm already being asked to give readings and talks.'

'Are you? I didn't know that.'

Bob smiled with pride. 'I think, first off, I'll host a soiree, and invite local literary notables. Make a bit of a splash and see what the ripples bring. This is all coming together at just the right time. I never thought I'd say it, but the Spitfire that destroyed our old house did us a huge favour.'

'In what way?'

For Pat, the Spitfire crash that had destroyed both her home and the Campbells' had been nothing short of a disaster.

'It compelled us to audit our life,' Bob said.

Pat wasn't entirely sure what he meant. She had seen Bob reflect upon his life over the past few months, deciding that he wanted to reset his relationship with her.

At that moment, Joyce returned from the kitchen with a fresh bowl of golden, shining scrambled eggs, and a large plate of toast.

'More eggs for you. And there's a little bit more black pudding should you want it,' Joyce declared.

'Can't thank you enough, Mrs C,' said Bob.

'I want to send you off on a high note, with the fondest memories of your time here.'

Joyce sat at the table and took Bob's left hand in her right hand and Pat's right hand in her left, and looked earnestly from one to the other.

'Words cannot express how much I have enjoyed having you here these past few months. Well, Mr Simms, perhaps *your* words could express it, but mine are sadly lacking. I have always found winter the most miserable season. But sharing the cold, dark, and damp nights with the two of you has helped me through it no end. Playing cards. Talking *literature*. Listening to the wireless together. I have grown used to your company, and it will take me a long while to acclimatise to its absence.'

Joyce stood where she had been sitting and raised her teacup in the form of a toast to Pat and Bob.

'My dear Mr and Mrs Simms,' she said extravagantly, 'to your future in your new home, and all the success and happiness it will bring!'

Pat felt moved at the sight of Joyce Cameron toasting her. Bob stood next and raised his own teacup to Joyce.

'To you, Mrs C. A woman of rare generosity and intellect.'

Pat turned to Joyce and wrapped her arms around the older woman's small frame, and buried her face in her sweet-smelling hair.

'I can't thank you enough, Joyce. Without you . . .'

Pat's voice trailed off.

Without you standing between Bob and I, he would almost certainly have resumed his old ways. But your daily presence acted like a buffer between us, a reason for Bob to proceed with caution where I was concerned, giving him a long enough pause in the way he conducted unholy matrimony against me to reflect, and make a significant change.

'Thank you, Joyce. I'll never forget your kindness. Never.'

Joyce hugged Pat back with a degree of force that implied just how much she was going to miss their company.

'Good luck, my dear,' Joyce said. 'The fearful, interminable typing aside, you are very lucky to have such a man as your husband to buy you such a lovely new home in which to embark on your new life together.'

Pat stood back from Joyce and looked at her face, each line and wrinkle co-opted into the broad smile across it, while her eyes shone with swelling tears of sadness at their departure.

'I know,' said Pat. 'I'm very lucky indeed.'

She glanced at Bob, who was standing behind Joyce. He smiled at Pat with no side or malice.

For my own sanity, and for the sake of our future for as long as we are together, I must try and forgive this new Bob for what he's done to me in the past, and embrace the New Pat I can become as a consequence. At least until Marek returns. Or fails to. Forgive. Forgive. What choice do I have?

Chapter 37

THE DAY AFTER Laura sat the exam for a scholarship to medical school, Erica woke before sunrise, as was her custom following Will's death. It was as if she now had a surfeit of energy that her body tried to expend by waking her increasingly early, giving her enough hours before bed to burn off what she needed before sleep would come once more.

Following a swift tidy up around the house, the first glow of sunlight in the windows prompted Erica to put the kettle on, then lay the table for breakfast. Erica then poured herself a steaming cup of coffee, and took it into the front room to drink slowly in Will's chair, and reflect on the day ahead.

With Will gone and Myra running the surgery, one day had become almost indistinguishable from the next. A couple of hours in the pharmacy making up prescriptions. Some WI business to attend to. Some shopping. Read the newspaper. Prepare meals. Listen to the news on the wireless.

Now Laura had sat the scholarship exam and required no more help with revision, Erica's days were more difficult to fill. Now they could only wait for the exam result. A sense of hiatus consumed Erica. Caught between Will's death and Laura's future – whatever that proved to be – Erica frequently found herself looking out of the front window at nothing in particular, for minutes on end. If leaves were blown across the road into hedgerows, she would watch them. If clouds were sailing across the sky, she would watch them. Or crows in the trees opposite. Or a cat creeping across a field, stalking a vole. Or a car or van or lorry rattling past. Erica had turned from a participant in life to an observer of it.

As she watched the world go by Erica's mind was nevertheless turning over various ways she would help Laura deal with the ultimate disappointment of not achieving the scholarship she had so determinedly set her heart on just two months before. To say Laura had left it late to go for the scholarship was an understatement. Yet Erica had been determined to help her do her utmost, so she could at least tell herself she had given it her very best shot *in the time allowing*.

Erica had settled on fashioning a version of support and encouragement that Will would have offered had he been alive. And while Erica might have been tempted to tell Laura 'there's always next time', she knew Will would have omitted just such a prompt, refusing to put any more pressure on his daughter to embark on a repeat attempt to conquer what may well simply be – for her – an insurmountable mountain. Finding the right phrasing was key. It wasn't made easier by the fact that Laura had become fixated on achieving the scholarship, and had, in Erica's watchful eyes, set herself up for a crushing disappointment.

But perhaps she needs a truly crushing disappointment to blast her out of Will's shadow, and forge her own path? Currently, it really does feel as if she's become stuck on his final words to her. Once she understands that fate and destiny mean nothing unless underpinned by adequate preparation and sustainable ambition she will have a more realistic outlook.

Erica sipped her coffee and, not for the first time where her youngest daughter was concerned, prayed everything would come good in the end – however that might be.

Laura too, had woken early that morning, but resisted the temptation to get out of bed, or even move an inch from the position in which she found herself when she opened her eyes. She was lying on her back, looking up at the ceiling. Her legs were outstretched under the sheet and blanket, her arms lying folded across her chest on top of the bedcover. She looked across at the piles of books she had worked through over and over during the last eight weeks and a single thought entered her head.

It's over.

She looked down the length of her body shape, and reminded herself of the alabaster effigy of Sir Hugh Calveley, which lay in the centre of the chancel of St Mark's. Aside from the fact that Sir Hugh had been an English knight and commander who participated in the Hundred Years' War, Laura knew little else about him, except the local suspicion that his actual body wasn't inside the actual tomb.

Contemplating her recent effort to gain a scholarship, Laura felt like the alabaster version of herself, lying on top of her bed. To all intents and purposes Laura felt sure that she *looked* like Laura Campbell, and would pass as Laura Campbell to all who knew her. Nevertheless, Laura felt somewhat hollow inside, a pale representation of herself who might prove too insubstantial to convince her examiners that she could one day become a doctor. She wondered if that's how she came across in her examination answers too. Suddenly, she was overwhelmed by the knowledge that she hadn't worked hard enough; hadn't learned enough knowledge; and hadn't managed to properly tackle the paper.

It hadn't been for the want of trying. A swift roll of her eyes around the room revealed the full, fevered extent of her revision.

Papers and cards covered with equations and symbols, immutable laws and theorems, facts and figures, names and dates of discoveries and discoverers, were affixed to every readable surface.

Small stacks of information had been inscribed on small cards, to test Laura's recall as if she had been a 'memory act' at the old Chester Music Hall before it was converted into a cinema, eighteen years earlier.

Laura had thrown everything into cramming her brain with enough knowledge to achieve the result she had come to regard as the only possible path her life could take.

But it hasn't been enough.

Laura tried to clear her head and focused on being still as alabaster. She stared at the ceiling and listened to herself breathe.

Laura turned her head to her bedside table, and the small stack of letters from well-wishers she had received in the weeks leading up to exam day. After looking at them for a moment, Laura reached across and picked them up to torture herself one last time before she threw them away. There were four. The handwriting on the first was her mother's. She unfolded the page and re-read what Erica had written to her.

My darling Laura,

What you have set out to achieve in such a short space of time is remarkable. I don't think I have ever seen anyone work as hard as you have over the past months. You deserve every success. All you can do now is your very best. We are both immensely proud of you.

Mum xx

Only her mother could speak for her father after his death and truly speak for each of them. Laura felt her eyes well up, as they had each time she had read the note. She sniffed back her tears and unfolded the second letter, written in a more masculine hand.

Dear Laura,

Flight training is going well, though I have had my setbacks. I desperately wanted to be a pilot but they now think I might make a better navigator. I suppose it's down to all the driving around Cheshire I've been doing with the Wing Commanders! I think you will remember that I seemed to know my way around the place pretty well. I seem to be more adept than some of the other chaps at finding my way around a map, and getting from A to B by the most fuel-efficient route.

I've always understood and respected why you were unable to continue to see someone in the RAF who wanted to be a pilot. I was always aware how deeply affected you were by Jack's death. I hoped it wouldn't come between us, but wasn't surprised when it eventually did.

Though I was deeply sad to let you go, I knew why you felt you had no choice. Who knows, perhaps when this is all over and we find ourselves still single, we might yet meet again, and see where we are?

You have always been the best girl, and I very much doubt I will find a better one. I felt the same even as I watched Bowers giving you the run-around. The way you dealt with your treatment by the RAF and the WAAF is a testament to your spirit and determination to not be cowed by other people's judgement. Your reports from the Observation Corps are apparently the best the region receives. Always precise, accurate, and crystal clear. Who knows what the future will bring?

In the meantime, we are each compelled to pursue our own course.

I know how much this scholarship means to you, and how damned hard you have been working for it. Your father would be so, so proud. You can do it, Laura. I have every faith in you. The very best of luck.

Tom.

Laura re-read Tom's letter several times, and felt a sharp pain of regret that she had stepped away from a relationship with such a kind and wonderful young man. During long days of revision she had missed him terribly. She lingered over his sentiment about possibly meeting up when the war was over, and in that moment tried to imagine what that might be like. She couldn't see that far ahead.

She pulled out the third letter and opened it.

Laura,

Though we've only known each other for a few months I have come to understand what a clever and compassionate young woman you are. I know many young doctors who lack the qualities you have in spades, so do not entertain for one moment the thought that you could not, albeit with a tremendous amount of application, join their ranks. For you to rise out of the misery of your father's last days in this manner has been quietly inspiring. Don't allow anything to stand in your way. Medicine needs more women like you, so seize your chance. You have worked extraordinarily hard over the last couple of months and deserve every success. The very best of luck with your forthcoming examinations.

Best wishes, Myra Rosen.

Laura smiled.

Typical Myra. Direct, unsentimental, and practical. It's what makes her words have so much meaning. No pretence.

Having her endorsement had meant a great deal to Laura both at the outset of her attempts to work out whether or not she should follow her father's advice, and now, when she was poised to see if she would come good on her determination to do so.

Laura carefully folded Myra's letter, and turned her attention to the final letter in the pile – a stiff white card, with a message in the sophisticated hand of Francis Barden.

My dear Laura,

What a truly excellent young woman you are. The only enduring tragedy of your life is that your father is not here to see how much you have grown into yourself. You have been through so much for one so young, but unlike many others, you have learned from your mistakes, and in so doing, put them behind you.

I am writing on behalf of myself and the WI of Great Paxford in wishing you the very best success in your forthcoming examinations. You are an exemplary young member of our branch, and of the Observation Corps. You succeed in everything you do, and I see no reason why your determination to attend medical college on a scholarship should be any different.

When you enter the exam hall remember that you do not enter alone. At one shoulder will sit the spirit of your father, guiding you as you make your way through the papers. At the other shoulder will be all the women from the branch giving you their support, willing you to do brilliantly well. Which we're sure you will.

I know we have all marvelled at how much you know and what a genuinely clever young woman you are. You are destined for great things! Good luck, my dear.

All love, Frances Barden and all at the Women's Institute of Great Paxford.

Laura was only aware of the tears streaming down her face when they slid off her cheeks onto the card. She had felt overwhelmed by all the support she was holding, and the sense that her father had been with her in the exam hall, giving her the courage to overcome her nerves.

But it's not enough. It's not enough. I know it. And soon everyone else will too. And then what will I do?

Chapter 38

Having given birth to her son at the farm, and having been born on one herself, Steph had never set foot inside a hospital before. She now found herself lying on her back in a ward, intermittently looking at the ceiling and the other patients around her. The nurses and doctors attended them all like telepathic servants, bringing them what they needed without ever having to be asked.

The feeling of being helpless in an unfamiliar environment was overwhelming. At home, she could get out of bed when she wanted, and use the toilet as she pleased. In hospital, if she needed to go she was told to alert a nurse, who would then either escort her out of the ward, or make provision for her to use a bedpan. Steph felt trapped in her tightly made bed like a child in a cot who couldn't be trusted with her own arms and hands. She hated the feeling, and struggled slowly to force her arms out from beneath the sheets and rest them on top. She was a woman of the soil. Her hands were her most vital asset and needed to be available to her at all times.

The last forty-eight hours remained something of a blur. Steph recalled returning to the farm after making it abundantly clear to Gwen Talbot that she should keep her mouth shut about her son and the German pilot, feeling satisfied that she had managed to frighten Great Paxford's most malignant gossip into silence.

She recalled walking up the road to the farm, going inside, seeing Stan and Stanley sitting at the kitchen table looking tense, and then her son declaring that he'd signed up to join the war.

Then nothing at all until waking up in bed several hours later to find herself dozily looking into Stan's face, with that of Dr Rosen peering at her over her husband's shoulder. The doctor had listened to Steph's heart and asked Steph and Stan some questions about her general well-being. She then telephoned the cottage hospital to send an ambulance to come and collect her. Steph had tried to protest, claiming that she wasn't ill but tired, and taken by surprise by her son's announcement.

'If it's something serious we need to know,' Stan said.

'But it isn't, Stan,' Steph replied, trying to calm him down and persuade him not to allow her to be taken away. 'I just need a good night's sleep.'

'Last time I looked you weren't a doctor,' he said. 'You're going, whether you like it or not.'

Stan had accompanied her in the ambulance, and made sure she was settled into the ward, never letting her out of his sight. Steph looked at him as the nurses flitted around, bringing her a small jug of water and a glass. She wanted him to stop worrying on her behalf, but quickly realised it was impossible. They were told the doctor was on his way, and would arrive within the hour. The sense of urgency washed over Steph.

Not so, Stan, who tracked every movement of medical staff in and out of the ward. The hospital was an alien environment for him too, with every movement maintaining his state of alert.

While they waited for the arrival of the heart doctor, Steph and Stan discussed Stanley's announcement that he had signed up for the army.

'Whenever a truck or convoy went past, or the RAF flew overhead, he'd always watch. Wanting to be part of it. I could tell. Like he was drawn towards it.'

'It's the same with all the lads his age. You saw it in the regiment. They were the ones doing all the talking about how much they were looking forward to taking on the Germans, until some of the old boys like me told them to put a sock in it.'

'What do we do, Stan? He can't go.'

Stan looked at his wife, knowing this moment was due.

'How can we stop him? How can we stop any of 'em? It's their time.'

'To get killed?'

'To prove himself. To his mates and the country.'

'Don't give me that "for the country" bollocks.'

'Most of them feel it. Why not ours?'

Steph looked at Stan and felt her heart flutter. 'This is my fault,' she said.

'How is it possibly your fault, you daft cow?' Stan asked softly. 'Don't be bloody stupid.'

'I should've turned down the interviews for the paper and the wireless. It's gone to his head. Thinks he's a hero. He's not. I saw him, remember. Running across the field for his life.'

'I think you've got him wrong, love,' Stan replied. 'I saw the look on his face the morning the BBC man came up the road. I think this is because of that. He was ashamed when you told me who chased who across the field. I'd never seen that look on his face before. Stuck with me. I think this is his way of dealing with it. Putting right what he feels about himself.'

'Then it's my fault for telling you the truth,' Steph said, 'making him feel that way. I should've said nothing.'

'But like you said,' Stan pressed his point. 'Truth will out. And it's best it does, one way or another.'

'Even if it means I've sent our son to war? To be killed? What if he's killed, Stan? What if he's killed?'

'If the shame wasn't already inside him nothing you could have said would've made a difference. He may not show it but he felt it. And now he's doing something about it.'

The conversation was an echo of a similar conversation Stanley was having with Isobel at the farmhouse, as Isobel tried to reassure Stanley that he wasn't responsible for his mother's collapse. Her success was limited, but she persisted.

'You saw what she was like at harvest,' she said. 'Laid up for days because she'd worked herself into the ground. She wasn't good *then*.'

'But she got better,' Stanley protested. 'She came back to work.'

'But perhaps it weakened her. Left her vulnerable for another episode of some kind.'

'The doc said her heart might be wrong.'

'Whatever's wrong,' Isobel said, as reassuringly as possible, 'the hospital will sort it out. It's not your fault.'

When the specialist finally arrived, he asked Stan to wait outside the ward while he gave Steph a thorough examination. Once again, Steph tried to protest against the fuss that was being made of her. The doctor had encountered the reaction from many who lived on the land. They generally disliked any external intervention in their lives.

He reassured Steph he would make sure she wasn't kept in hospital any longer than necessary, concluded his examination, and left the ward to speak with Stan. Steph watched him leave.

I was taken by surprise by Stanley's announcement, that's all. Not the first mother who's had a wobble when her son's said the same as Stanley said to me. Won't be the last.

She lay her head back on the pillow and closed her eyes against images of Stanley fighting in a battle against the Germans that appeared to her one after the other like in a slideshow. Stanley behind a wall, shooting his rifle. Stanley running for cover from artillery attack. Stanley in a trench looking scared. Stanley lying slumped over a wall, dead with half his face blown away. Steph screwed her eyes as tightly as she could.

I had to shoot the pilot so Stanley could live. So he has to live, otherwise the pilot died for nothing.

The moment the doctor came out of the ward Stan jumped up from the chair he'd been sitting on for the past twenty minutes, and approached.

'How is she?' he said, before the doctor had a chance to speak.

'I'm afraid Dr Rosen was correct in her diagnosis, Mr Farrow. Your wife is showing every sign of right ventricular strain.'

Stan looked at the medic. From the doctor's expression Stan wasn't encouraged. But he had no real idea what 'right ventricular strain' meant or entailed for the future. Dr Rosen had explained it to him at the farm, but as soon as Stan heard her say she wanted to get Steph to hospital at the earliest opportunity he had barely registered much else.

'It's a strain?' Stan asked. 'Like a muscle strain?'

'Well,' said the doctor patiently, 'the heart is, of course, a muscle. But it's rather unique and doesn't repair itself in the way other muscles do. In fact . . .' continued the doctor, choosing his words as carefully as he could, '. . . if damaged, it doesn't have the capacity for regeneration that other muscles do.'

Stan tried to digest the information he was now being spoon-fed. 'Her heart's damaged?'

The doctor nodded. 'I'm afraid so. The right ventricle sends de-oxygenated blood to the lungs for it to be re-oxygenated and re-distributed around the body. If the ventricle becomes damaged, its capacity to pump blood to the lungs diminishes, leaving the patient at risk. Your wife's right ventricle is showing definite signs of damage, Mr Farrow.'

'Is that why she fainted?' asked Stan, trying to piece together what he was now being told with what had recently happened.

'The notes sent by your doctor indicated she fainted after being told that her son had joined up. A not uncommon experience in my recent experience. A shock like that can have an immediate effect on the nervous system, and cause blood pressure to suddenly drop. Fainting is the result. So no, Mr Farrow, she didn't faint because of the ventricular strain. However, what your doctor picked up when she examined your wife at home, and what I can confirm to you now, is that the right ventricle of your wife's heart has sustained some damage. When we perform an X-ray procedure I am confident it will confirm this.'

'Damaged by what?' asked Stan.

'Well,' said the doctor, weighing up how to present this to Stan, 'often there is a problem with the lungs caused by illness. That can certainly have an impact – though I see no evidence in your wife's case. Other than that, it seems likely your wife suffered from a heart attack at some point in her life. And this damaged her heart. I gather she collapsed just a few months ago, during the harvest.'

Stan nodded. 'We'd lost our labour. She was determined to bring it in almost single-handed. She said she passed out with exhaustion.'

'That may be her recollection of the event. But I wouldn't be surprised if she actually suffered a heart attack. Again, it isn't uncommon within the farming community, putting themselves under great strain in pressured circumstances. I've seen it many times.'

'When isn't it pressured?' Stan asked. 'Landlords putting rents up. Labour scarce. Ministry on your back telling you to chop and change every other bloody week. All the while making sure to get the crop in before the weather ruins it.'

'I'm sure,' said the doctor, not unsympathetically. 'Of course, the stress she will have suffered after the shooting incident wouldn't have helped. Blood pressure rises and falls in response to our moods. Her heart was placed under enormous strain once again.'

Stan looked at him with his open, rugged face. His temperament for any situation, however difficult, was always to lean towards the practical. If something is bad then something has to be done to make it at least better, if not good.

'What do we have to do then?' he asked.

'Your wife needs complete bed rest. I would like her to remain in hospital for a few more days to absolutely confirm what I suspect.'

'And then she can return to the farm?'

The doctor hesitated for a moment. 'But not to farm work.'

Stan's brow furrowed. 'For how long?'

'For how long? For *good*, Mr Farrow. Your wife's heart has been left in a highly vulnerable condition. She can carefully undertake domestic chores – cooking, cleaning, and such forth. But such is the damage to her heart that any more serious physical strain brought on by manual labour could result in another attack. And that could, I am afraid to say, be extremely serious.' The doctor paused for effect. '*Extremely.*'

'But . . . she's a farmer to her bones,' said Stan.

'Not any longer, Mr Farrow. From this moment on she is a farmer's *wife* who needs to be handled very carefully indeed.'

Stan stood still for several minutes after the doctor left him in the corridor to attend to another patient, his mind racing, searching for something to blame for what had befallen his family, and his wife.

Was it himself? His own vainglory for setting aside his reserved occupation status and needlessly joining up? Leaving Steph and Stan and Isobel to bring in the harvest without him?

Was it the German pilot who had chased their son, forcing Steph to shoot him dead, and live with the consequences, both psychological and physical?

Was it Stanley – declaring that he'd joined up, knowing the effect it might have on his mother who was utterly determined that he would never go to battle?

Or was it some innate weakness in the structure of Steph's heart that had taken all these years to come to terrible fruition, and threaten her life?

Or was it all of these reasons taken together?

Or others that neither he nor the doctor could fathom?

Stan returned to the ward and sat beside his wife, who lay asleep. He wanted to scoop her out from under the bedclothes and hold her in his arms. He wanted to protect her so that her heart could simply tick over at its least strenuous rate forever. But even lifting her gently out of bed would wake her, and Steph needed to rest above all else. Instead, he took her hand in his and held it very gently indeed.

'Steph . . .' he whispered, 'what're we going to do?'

Steph didn't wake.

Stan watched her chest rise and fall in a steady rhythm. His fingers felt Steph's pulse on the underside of her wrist, her permanently damaged heart valiantly beating, beating, beating against the clock.

Chapter 39

THE DAYS FOLLOWING her night with Annie had been agony for Teresa. While she was convinced Nick would never imagine she might be attracted to women, or that Annie – who Teresa believed Nick knew to be a lesbian – would be attracted to his own wife, Teresa nevertheless assumed her sexual betrayal must be radiating from her like a beacon.

This had kicked in the instant Teresa woke the very next day, and opened her eyes to see Nick in a deep sleep beside her. Within seconds, Teresa felt a gut-churning mix of guilt and disappointment for falling short of her ambition with regard to Annie's sojourn at the house. While they had weathered moments of intimacy and suggestion that arose from the usual course of daily interaction, it seemed to Teresa that her resolve had crumbled at the first true moment of serious emotional weakness brought on by intense worry over Nick going back into the cockpit. That the crisis had been momentarily resolved by sex was no excuse in the moral universe that Teresa wished to inhabit. Furthermore, the longer she thought about it the more convinced Teresa became that she may have used her anxiety about Nick to justify sleeping with Annie, given that she had fantasised about being with Annie for months.

Would I do the same tonight if Nick is away from the house? And tomorrow? Now I've proven I have no willpower precisely when the situation requires it . . .

Lying on the pillow beside him, Teresa felt intense pity towards Nick. Intentionally or not, Teresa hated that she was now effectively playing him for a fool. Such were her feelings of love and admiration towards him, Nick was the very last person she would ever wish to force into such a role.

I am responsible for my actions, and through them I have made him foolish, whether he knows it or not. If it ever came out – and it absolutely must not under any circumstances – people would ask, how could he not have realised? How could he have allowed Annie into the house? What kind of deluded idiot doesn't realise what's taking place under his own nose? He doesn't deserve this. And yet I've put him in that position because I lack the very moral fibre that he demonstrates every hour of every day.

For a brief moment, Teresa was tempted to confess.

And wreck three lives?

She had been told by nuns and priests since childhood that 'confession cleanses the soul'. It didn't take her long to realise that the axiom also put those in authority in a position of great advantage over children who had been primed since infancy to hand themselves in for the slightest misdemeanour.

Telling the truth because it should be told is more beneficial than lying continuously. But confession too often gets us off the hook without considering the feelings of everyone who might suffer the consequences. Whatever happens here, I must consider the consequences. If I confess to Nick what's happened, our marriage will end. That would leave us both miserable. It would also shatter Nick's longstanding friendship with Annie.

Annie and I were drawn to one another because that's our nature. She told me that when we first met she went out of her way not to come into contact with me, to avoid any romantic feelings between us.

It's a mess, certainly, and we could have, should have done more to avoid it. But . . . until you become embroiled in things it's easy to assume avoiding it will be straightforward. We should be able to exercise judgement and step around danger. But we don't. Or can't.

We're not animals, and yet—.

I'm going round and round.

Focus on the situation as it now stands. Focus on what you must do. Focus on taking action going forward, not on how you arrived at this point. Focus on how to stop this spiralling out of control. Focus on Nick, because he's what's important now. Because protecting Nick protects me.

This was the argument that stiffened Teresa's resolve to remove Annie from the house.

The day after Teresa settled on this course of action, Annie appeared in the kitchen doorway and asked, 'What are we going to do?'

Teresa looked calmly at Annie and took her time to respond. Say the wrong thing, and the situation could blow up in her face quite horribly.

'What do you think we should do?' she asked, determined to assess the lay of the land before she committed herself.

'I don't want to pretend it didn't happen,' Annie replied. 'I don't want to deny there are feelings between us. That would be cowardly.'

Teresa nodded. 'I agree,' she said. 'So what *do* you want?'

Annie looked at Teresa and smiled.

'Now that particular dam has burst, and in such a wonderful way, I would like to continue in the same vein, but while being exceptionally cautious about Nick.'

'In other words,' said Teresa, determined to clarify Annie's position, 'some kind of *affair* behind his back?'

Annie bridled at the insinuation.

'Saying "behind his back" sounds terrible. But if we were to have an affair we would each want to protect Nick from it, wouldn't we?'

'Of course,' said Teresa. 'It goes without saying. *If* we were to have an affair of some kind.'

The smile disappeared from Annie's face. 'That *isn't* what you want?'

'I'm afraid not, Annie,' Teresa said, unable to completely mask the disappointment in her voice. 'I realise it could mean the end of the friendship that's evolved between us. But I simply cannot take the risk of Nick finding out. And because we are both very close to Nick, the only way of making sure that can never happen is to stop everything between us now.'

'If I didn't know him you might continue?' Annie asked.

'But you do.'

'But if I didn't?'

'This very situation has come about precisely because you know him so well. Which is why it must end, Annie. Before it's too late.'

'Too late?'

'Before we slip up, or aren't as careful or as clever as we think we are, and Nick discovers . . . us.'

'But he won't,' Annie insisted.

'You don't know that.'

'Why would he?'

'I can't live with the possibility he might. I can't live being terrified of him walking through the front door one evening having been told something that someone's seen. Or . . . or entering a room to question me about something he's heard, or noticed. I can't live like that. As much as I have feelings for you . . . I can't do it to him.' Teresa stared at Annie, silently imploring her not to make this any more difficult than it was proving to be. 'It must end, Annie,' she said in a soft, quiet voice. '*Completely.*'

Aside from her intelligence and beauty, the quality that attracted Teresa to Annie was her determination to live by her own compass. Now she feared it, horrified at the prospect of the very quality that drew Teresa towards Annie might be the same one to cause the young pilot to wreck her marriage.

The one piece of leverage Teresa felt she had over Annie was her friendship with Nick. Her own family something of a wasteland, Annie looked upon Nick as an older brother whom she adored. Teresa was counting on Annie not wanting to see Nick hurt by any of this. The situation boiled down to a simple equation. Either Annie could accept Teresa's declaration that there would be no more relations between them and keep her relationship with Nick and with Teresa (as a friend only); or she could create a great deal of trouble now, and lose both relationships.

She looked at Annie and wondered what she thought. She didn't have long to wait. Annie smiled ruefully.

'When Nick came back I saw how fast you shot upstairs and knew you were unlikely to lie with me again. At least,' she said more in hope than expectation, 'not in the house.'

'Not *anywhere*,' said Teresa. 'Waiting for Nick to come upstairs my heart was thumping so hard I thought it would break a rib. I've never been so scared in my life.'

'What have I told you about a life lived in fear?' Annie said.

Teresa, older and a little wiser than when she first met Annie, was prepared for this.

'I'm not afraid of being unmasked. Or of losing my current status – though I shan't lie and pretend that losing the two people I most care about in the world wouldn't affect me terribly, because it would.'

'That needn't happen if we were careful,' Annie said, trying one last time to test Teresa's willpower.

'Isn't the nature of temptation to incrementally lead us away from what's *careful* towards what's *risky*?' Teresa asked. Which is when people get caught.

'I don't want to lose your friendship, Annie,' Teresa continued, 'for a fleeting moment of pleasure. I don't want to lose Nick. And I don't want to see the wonderful relationship you two have get smashed to pieces. He loves you dearly. Sometimes I listen to him talk about you and find myself hoping he talks about me to other people in as glowing terms.'

Annie nodded. 'He does. I can assure you of that.'

Teresa felt a burst of love towards her husband in that moment. It helped propel her argument forward. 'We need to protect him, don't you agree? You know better than I how potentially catastrophic it could be if his mind were to be distracted on a sortie by the discovery that you and I were having an affair.'

After what seemed like an age, Annie finally nodded.

'You're adorable, Teresa, don't get me wrong. Extremely. But you're too nervy. I don't want to be with someone who needs constant affirmation that they're doing the right thing, or that everything will be all right. I can't guarantee either of those. And I can't make up for your insecurity. I want to be with someone at ease with themselves enough to look me square in the face when we kiss, not with one eye glancing over their shoulder for who might come through the door and see.'

Teresa knew that this was Annie's way of conceding defeat, and went along with it for her sake.

'You need to find someone more confident in themselves,' she said.

'I suspect I need girls who only like girls. I thought you were like several women I've met, in lavender marriages. Lesbians, but pretending otherwise.'

'I'm not pretending otherwise. There was a time I thought I might be. But not now. I love him.'

'I can see that. I always saw the social advantage you gained from being married to Nick. But I've come to realise that you really do love him.'

A week later, Annie passed her medical and moved out of the Lucas house to head south for her re-orientation back into the ATA. She had kissed Nick and Teresa goodbye, and made them promise to look after one another.

That night, Teresa was relieved beyond measure to be making supper for two and not three. The air felt fresher in every room of the house, and she realised how close she had brought them all to catastrophe. She felt tremendous relief that she no longer needed to strategize and apply tactical awareness to the basic task of living in her own home.

I've no one to blame but myself. But saying that, there are so many forms of love. Each one, when it strikes, is like being consumed by a fever. I consider myself extremely fortunate. I still have a life. It isn't Annie's, but I could never live like her because I'm not made like her. I sometimes wish I was, but now I have to make peace with the life I have.

After supper that same evening, Nick returned to Tabley Wood. He telephoned the house at 8.16 p.m. to tell Teresa that he was going up with the squadron to intercept a German raid. Teresa sat rigid with terror for three hours and twelve minutes until the telephone rang again, and Nick's voice reassured her that he was intact and coming home. In bed, they made love in the dark. For Teresa, it may not have been the thrilling, exquisite pleasure that Annie had been able to generate, but it was nevertheless sweet and soothing, and sent them to sleep in each other's arms.

Two weeks later Teresa missed her period. She put it down to the stress over Annie heaped on top of the extreme anxiety she felt when Nick went up to fight.

A week after missing her period, Teresa experienced her first bout of morning sickness, mistakenly ascribing it to a piece of fish eaten for breakfast that had been left overnight on a plate on the side.

Two days after that, Teresa knew beyond all doubt that she was pregnant.

Teacher. Grieving lover. Wife. Ex-teacher. Mother-to-be.

In the space of eighteen months the war had accelerated her life beyond all measure.

Unable to entirely wash the taste of bile from her mouth, and still feeling nauseous, Teresa looked at her reflection in the bathroom mirror. She could barely recognise herself.

Chapter 40

WHILE THE SERIOUSNESS of Steph's heart condition was swiftly confirmed by the hospital, she had yet to be told the full extent of the effect it would have on her life. She had been labouring under the impression that she had been confined to a hospital bed to regain her strength under medical supervision, prior to being released back to the farm, in reasonable nick. Stan had asked the hospital to keep Steph for a few more days than they needed her to be there, to allow him time to make the arrangements needed for her homecoming.

The physical arrangements were straightforward enough. With Stanley and Isobel's assistance, Stan undertook an inspection of the farmhouse and farmyard to see where improvements could be made to make Steph's life easier.

Inside the house, Stan put a handrail along the wall of the staircase to ease Steph's ascent and descent. He also fitted a light in the middle of the ceiling above the staircase, allowing Steph to always see her footing.

In the bedroom, Stan had been advised by Dr Rosen that raising the height of their bed and placing a high-backed chair with arms nearby would make a useful transition to Steph when standing up in the morning, and could assist with her getting dressed.

In the kitchen, Stanley sanded down sticky drawer runners so that Steph wouldn't have to struggle to open old, warped compartments. Stan lowered racks and hooks so that items stored or hanging from them were within easier reach than before, preventing Steph from over-exerting herself by having to reach up, or stand on a chair. Stan went through all their cupboards with Isobel, and moved regularly used ingredients items lower down, within easy reach without strain.

'She'll have a right go at me for mucking around with all this,' he said to Isobel, smiling. 'But if it takes the smallest amount of strain off her it's worthwhile.'

In the parlour, Stan rearranged the furniture to make it easier for Steph to walk around, and placed two chairs in strategic places in case Steph ever felt short of breath and needed to suddenly sit.

He cleaned out all the fireplaces and had Stanley clean the chimneys so the house could be properly heated and ventilated. The doctor had told him this would help keep Steph warm, which was important for her circulation, and her breathing free of any smoke inhalation, which would place more strain on her heart.

In the farmyard, Stan lowered the washing line and repaired the decrepit fencing so Steph could lean against it, without fear of falling through.

He replaced the steps leading up to the henhouse, to avoid Steph slipping or falling through the old, cracked steps. Stanley affixed a leather to the end of a pole to make cleaning the outside of the windows easier for her.

As she helped Stan and Stanley with all this work, Isobel started to wonder if Stan had told Steph about the preparations he was making for her homecoming.

'Not yet,' he said, hammering the final tread onto the chicken-house steps.

'Don't you think you should?' Isobel gently chided. 'You could get away with it with me with my eyes, but hers are as sharp as a hawk's. She'll spot in an instant that you're making a home for . . . well . . . an invalid.'

Stan's eyes momentarily flashed with anger. 'That's not what it is, Isobel. It's just smoothing off the place for her.'

'But that's what she'll see if you don't tell her. Why haven't you told her? Why hasn't her doctor?'

'I asked him not to.'

'Why?'

'Because she's in a bad way.'

'How bad?'

He looked at Isobel for a few moments, then looked away, his eyes travelling across the field to the woodland beyond.

'This condition,' he started, 'she's going to have to live with this condition for the rest of her life. Her heart's damaged. It's not like other parts of your body. It can't heal itself. I've had mates scarred for life on their skin. That grows back – different, but more or less the same – and you can get on with it. But this is on the inside, and it doesn't repair.'

Isobel looked at him and gently took his hand in hers.

'You've got to warn her. It's her right. She's a strong woman, Stan.'

'Not anymore.'

'I don't believe that. Perhaps not physically, but mentally . . . she will be. You know it.'

As he lay alone in his bed that night, Stan reflected on his conversation with Isobel. It wasn't Steph's strength he was worried about when it came to telling her the serious-ness of her condition, but his own. He wasn't convinced he could break the news to her without breaking down in front of her, and she didn't deserve that. Isobel had sug-gested asking the doctor to do it, since it was part of his job. Or Dr Rosen, someone Steph knew a little better. Stan had dismissed the idea.

'When she knows what it is she'll want it to come from me,' he said. 'No one else.'

Lying in the dark, the new items of their small bed-room picked out by the dim glow of moonlight, Stan told himself to bite the bullet, go to the hospital tomorrow, and tell Steph the full extent of her condition. He'd ask the doctor to accompany him tomorrow, to answer any medical questions she might have. But *he* would tell her.

Before that, there was something he had to attend to – with Stanley.

Steph was the first patient to wake up on the ward the following day. Of farming stock by birth, her body clock was calibrated to the rise and fall of daylight. It didn't matter if the curtains were open or closed, when the sun began to spray more light into her corner of the world, Steph began to wake.

She lay in bed and looked around at the mounds of people beneath sheets and blankets around her, lying prone in their incapacities, waiting for the miracle of God or medicine to release them from their pains and ailments.

She hadn't been awake more than half a minute before a wave of insurmountable sadness came over her as she remembered Stanley had joined up. She felt a cold fury towards the recruiting sergeant.

He must have seen he was a boy. Legal age means nothing if he's not fit for battle. And he isn't. Never will be. It's not that he's not ready. He's not right for it. Some boys are and some aren't. He'll be an easy—

Steph couldn't finish the sentence. The images of Stanley in full battledress, trapped somewhere crying out for her flashed across her mind's eye once more. However she imagined him, her son never looked like a real soldier. Like a man. Like a fighter, able to defend himself, and take another life if he had to. She had seen him only ever run from a fight.

They could see what he was, so how could they take his signature? Stupid, stupid child. Stupid, stupid. Criminal, that's what it is.

She felt a grinding emptiness in her gut, and felt her heart start to race and her breath shorten. She closed her eyes and slowly counted to sixty, as the doctor had told her to whenever she had to try to bring down her heart rate. Some part of her felt she had already lost her son, that he had already crossed into that place beyond a mother's power to pull her child back to safety and security.

Steph was coming to the end of her breakfast when Stan came onto the ward, flanked by the doctor. Though it was the beginning of the day, each looked ominously serious. When they saw her watching them approach they each switched on a smile. When they arrived at her bed, the doctor pulled the curtain round to give them privacy. Stan kissed Steph and sat on her left, while the doctor stood on the right.

'Good night, love?' Stan asked, stroking a strand of hair back from her forehead.

'Aside from one woman's cough,' Steph said, lowering her voice and pointedly looking towards the ward beyond the curtain. 'Be better once I'm out of here.'

'That can be today, Mrs Farrow,' the doctor said.

Steph smiled. 'Wonderful,' she said.

The doctor glanced at Stan, giving him his cue to speak. Stan swallowed, readying himself for the moment that had kept him up all night. He looked at Steph. She looked back with a slightly quizzical expression, unsure why he was taking as long as he was.

'You'll see some changes when you get back, love,' Stan said.

'Changes?'

'Around the house. And farmyard. Some are repairs, but others are small things I've done to make it easier for you.'

Steph's brow furrowed. 'Easier?'

Stan took a deep breath and glanced at the doctor, who nodded calmly, giving Stan the reassurance to press on.

'You're not well, Steph,' he said.

'I know I've had a bit of a turn . . .'

'It's more than that. Your heart's not right.'

Steph searched Stan's face for a greater understanding of what he was trying to say.

'And it won't ever be what it was,' he said.

Steph looked at Stan and tried to make sense of what he'd just told her. The doctor considered this was the time for him to provide some medical qualification on Stan's announcement.

'It's quite possible you suffered a heart attack during the harvest, Mrs Farrow. We can't be sure. Whenever it happened, the muscle tissue on one side of your heart is damaged and it can't be repaired. The damage is permanent, I'm afraid, and that leaves you in a more vulnerable position than before.'

'How vulnerable?'

Steph looked directly at Stan when she asked the question. Stan took another in a series of deep breaths. He had anticipated this being difficult, but not as difficult as it was proving.

'Stan. Tell me straight. No secrets. None of that nonsense.'

Stan nodded. 'From now on you have to be careful. Any strain could risk another episode.'

'When you say any strain, what do you mean?'

Again, the doctor stepped in to underpin Stan's words with some authority.

'It means you will be limited to light work around the house. But no farm work.'

'What?'

'I'm sorry, Mrs Farrow. Your husband is right. You simply must cut out of your daily routine anything that could risk another attack.'

'But we're farmers. I'm needed on the farm all year round.'

'Steph, what you need is to be well. The rest we can work out.'

'What about the chickens?'

'What about them?' said Stan.

'That's farm work, isn't it? Can I throw a bit of seed around? Hold a bucket of scraps for them? Collect *eggs*?' Her tone was less sarcastic than bewildered.

The doctor nodded. 'As long as it isn't strenuous. That's the benchmark. How much strain will any given activity place on you? Will it leave you short of breath? Will it raise your heart rate?'

'It's not about what may or may not seem strenuous at any given time, Mrs Farrow. What your husband's talking about when he mentions the changes he's made around the farm is a *permanent alteration* to the way you live. Your heart will not get any better. In fact, over time it will slowly get worse because that's the natural way of things. But by adhering to my advice, by eliminating as much risk from strain as you can from your life, you *can* slow down the rate of degeneration.'

Steph looked hard at the doctor, treating his words as she would a foul-tasting medicine he was forcing her to swallow for her own good. She could scarcely believe what she was hearing.

'I'm home now, Steph,' Stan said, softly, trying to coat the terrible news with a warming verbal balm. 'I can do all the heavy stuff. Don't get me wrong – you've done brilliant. But we just have to adapt, don't we? Your health, love, that's the most important thing from this point on.'

Steph turned from Stan back to the doctor, desperately seeking more information – more clarification about how her life was about to change.

'But I don't have to lie in bed all the time? Or sit in a chair by a window like an old biddy, just staring over land I can't even walk across after heavy rain?'

The doctor smiled, and shook his head.

'Not at all. Complete inactivity would be just as detrimental. We want you to lead an active life, Mrs Farrow. That will keep your heart as strong as it can be. It's about finding the balance, and making permanent changes to the way you approach things. So, for example, yes, by all means you can feed your chickens. But before picking up a bucket of feed, or scraps, give it a moment of thought. Is it too full? Is it too heavy? Are you taking even a slight risk? Perhaps ask someone to hold the bucket for you. Minimising the risk of overstraining yourself, that's the question you should keep in your mind until it becomes second nature – which I'm sure it will.'

Steph's eyes glittered with tears.

'Doc,' said Stan in a quiet voice, careful not to be overheard elsewhere on the ward. 'What about . . . *relations*?'

'Stanley!' Steph said, mortified, and wiping her eyes.

The doctor had fielded the question before. Many older couples didn't raise it, but couples in their late 30s, like Stan and Steph, tended to want to know, and usually found a way to ask.

'Actually, it's a perfectly reasonable question, Mr Farrow. There may need to be some . . . adjustment. As a rule, whenever your wife struggles for breath she should stop what she's doing and allow things to return to normal. But take things nice and slow and that side of things should be fine.'

Stan held Steph's hand and gripped it tightly.

'Simply avoid stress, Mrs Farrow.'

363

Steph looked at the doctor and nodded, her eyes slowly moistening as the extent of her condition – and how her life would have to adapt around it – slowly sank in. One thought kept ringing in her ears. A question, to which there was no suitable answer:

How can I avoid stress with Stanley joining up?

On the slow walk back to the farm, Stan carried the overnight bag Steph had taken to the hospital on her behalf. After a week's stay, and leaving with her life turned upside down, Steph was quiet. She watched Stan's feet to her left, sure he was walking more slowly than usual.

'I'm not sure I can keep this up,' she said.

'Keep what up?' he replied.

'You're walking slower than we normally walk.'

'You heard the doc. Avoid stress.'

'But I've never been stressed walking at our normal pace. I never get out of breath doing that, do I? Because I'm *used* to it.'

'I'm just being careful,' Stan said, trying not to sound defensive.

They walked on in silence for a few more moments, and then Stan suddenly scooped Steph in his arms.

'What the bloody hell do you think you're doing?!' she cried.

'Not taking any chances!' he said, grinning.

'You're going to carry me a mile and a half back to the farm, are you?'

'Why not? I've carried men with a full pack further, under fire. You're nothing compared to that.'

Steph looked at Stan's face as he continued home with his wife held firmly in his arms. His pale blue eyes. Weathered skin stretched taut over his cheekbones. Fine, wispy hair, blowing in the cold wind that seemed to simply cycle endlessly through the region at this time of year. She loved him with an incalculable intensity. After a few hundred yards she said, 'Put me down, Stan.'

He didn't, and merely stepped up his pace.

'Stan, I mean it. We have to talk about the farm.'

'What about it?'

'How can we work it if I'm out of action and Stanley's gone. It's a two-man farm at least. Put me down!'

Stan stopped and set his wife back on her feet as carefully as if she had been a Ming vase.

'Nothing to talk about,' he said. 'I've sorted it.'

Steph searched his eyes for more explanation. She seemed to alight upon the answer within seconds.

'Isobel? Stan, she does what she can, and she's taken on a lot more than either of us ever thought she'd be able to when she first came, but there's no way she can take over my duties—'

'Not Isobel.'

'Then who?'

Stan looked at Steph and kissed her tenderly on the lips.

'Ever since the doctor told me how bad you were I've been worried sick.'

'I'm not surprised. With me off the land the farm's going to be—'

'Not about the farm,' he interrupted. 'About *you*. All right, a bit about the farm, but mostly about what happens to you if Stanley went off to fight. I know how much you worried about me when I was gone, but I can handle myself . . .'

The lump in Steph's throat prevented her from speaking.

'Stanley's not going,' Stan said.

Steph stared at him as the wind swirled around them, blowing dry brown leaves across the path. Breaks in the churning cloud revealed patches of metallic blue, shot through with beams of bright winter sunlight.

'Not going?' she said, unsure she had heard correctly.

Stan shook his head.

'He's bloody desperate to go, Stan,' she said. 'Every time a plane flew over or a regiment marched past, it's all I could do to stop him leaping over the bloody gate!'

'I told him if the war didn't kill him, it might kill you.'

'But . . . that's blackmail.'

Stan shook his head.

'I said it's his choice to make, but he had to understand the *real* choices. In the real world, not the world of make-believe in his head, where Jerry is lining up to be shot like tin cans on a fence, and you'll be fine come what may. Real choices with real consequences. I said the war doesn't need him, there's hundreds just like him the war'll chew up just the same. But this farm, and his mam . . . *does* need him. With you the way you are, I need him. I told him I hadn't spoken to you about it. I told him I'd respect his decision if he felt he had to go. So would you. I told him he's in a vital reserved occupation – feeding the nation and feeding the troops. Nothing more important than that. Nothing. No one would blink an eye if he stayed. No training can save you from the bullet with your name on. But it takes real aptitude to pull food out of the ground year after year after year for folk who need it. Real skill and real craft. All the things you need to know to do that. That's aptitude the country needs more than another skinny bloody Tommy on the parade ground, dreaming of killing Germans.'

'What did he say?' Steph asked. Her heart felt as if it was about to burst with euphoria.

'He thought about it. Looked out the window. Gave it some more thought. You know. Then he dropped his head and said he wouldn't go.'

'No, I mean *how* did he say it?'

'He said you saved his life from the pilot, so he owes you.'

'I don't see it like that.'

'I know. But *he* does. That's how he sees it. He stood there and thought about it, worked it all out. He said he could go and get himself killed, and you keel over from a broken heart, and we lose the farm. Or, he could stay and you keep each other going, and we keep the farm.'

'He said all that?' Steph said, scarcely believing her ears.

'He did,' said Stan. 'I could tell it was hard for him. I could see in his face how much he was giving up. All the lads his age going off, and him wanting to join them. Be a real hero. Like David Brindsley, and all the RAF boys in the Black Horse.'

'He said all that by himself?'

Stan nodded. 'That's how I knew our Stanley has become a man.'

Steph threw her arms around Stan, buried her face in his neck, and held on to him for nearly a minute.

'Love you, Stan Farrow,' she eventually whispered.

'You too, love,' he whispered back.

Steph felt all the dread that had collected inside her on the ward drain from her now. The hours she had lain awake imagining a seemingly infinite variety of ways Stanley could die horribly in battle suddenly counted for nothing. All concern for the state of her heart, for the restricted life she would now have to lead, fell from her mind.

He's going to stay. He's going to be safe. He's going to be safe!

The words went around and round inside her head, and seemed to lift her off the ground.

They walked in silence the rest of the way home. Steph looked around at the landscape that had made her the woman she was, one season at a time. Steph kept glancing up at her husband and smiling to herself, her anxiety about her heart fading with each step now that her son was staying with them.

'Mind,' said Stan. 'I'm not having you argue with any of the changes we've made when we get back,' he said. 'Not one word. They're staying, and you're using them, and that's all there is to it.'

Steph looked at him with mock-seriousness. 'Wouldn't dream of arguing, Stan Farrow.'

'You'd better not.'

As the they approached the farmhouse Steph heard the same cry she had heard on the fateful afternoon, moments before she had rushed out to save her son from the German pilot. Only today it wasn't infused with terror but joy.

'Ma!'

She turned to her left and saw Stanley sprinting across the same field he had fled across to escape the gaining German. Stanley's face wasn't now contorted in abject fear, but split by the widest grin.

'Ma!'

Steph stood and smiled as her son rushed up to her and threw his arms around her, almost knocking her off her feet.

She threw her arms around him, and mother and son clung to one another for an age.

'Thank you,' she whispered. 'Thank you, thank you, thank you . . .'

Chapter 41

AFTER A LONG and thankfully uneventful night at the Observation Post, Laura helped Brian clean and pack away their instruments ready for the next shift, later in the day. They had kept each other awake by lively conversation, but their energy for chat was sinking as fast as the sun was rising. Having been awake since 10 p.m. the previous night, both were dog-tired and eager to get back to their respective homes, and beds. They were all but silent as they climbed down the short ladder onto the road.

'See you soon,' said Brian with a weary wave of his hand. 'Pleasure, as always.'

'See you soon,' Laura replied, waving back with a tired smile. 'Likewise.'

Laura enjoyed Brian's friendship, and the verbal short-hand they had developed over many hours sky-watching for the first sign of approaching bombers.

Brian cycled off at low speed. Laura watched him disappear around the corner and expressed a long, leisurely yawn. After staying awake and alert all night, Laura's mind was now pleasantly fuzzy. Having found it difficult to adjust at first, she had come to appreciate the particular light and sounds of dawn, as the world woke around her. The air was still and subdued. The foxes had gone to ground, replaced by the first enterprising birds of the day, out to catch the first available food.

The walk home was quiet. Laura fastened onto the sound of her own footsteps, as if she were following someone else. Her thoughts turned superficially to the various concerns that occupied her. The ongoing feelings of grief and sorrow over her father's death. The empty space she felt from Tom's absence. Her concern over how her mother was coping without Will. The scholarship exam. She was too tired to give any of these much focus, preferring to wander along in the direction of home and allow her mind to do the same. The road from the Observation Post led into the centre of the village. As she walked along the row of houses Laura saw someone approaching in the distance on a bicycle. The cyclist drew closer and Laura realised it was Spencer, delivering his first round of post of the day. He cycled past and called out, 'Just been to yours! Letter for you!'

By the time Laura had registered what he'd said, Spencer was already a hundred yards up the road. Laura nevertheless called back, 'What kind of letter?' But Spencer was no longer within range, and continued to pedal until he disappeared from view.

Laura was only expecting one letter – her scholarship exam result, accompanied by a pleasantly worded missive of regret, informing her in the nicest way possible that she hadn't been awarded a place at the university's medical school.

She hadn't been expecting the letter to arrive on any particular day, and this morning was as good – or bad – as any. Yet it still took her by surprise. She continued to walk home, slowing her pace. Why rush to receive bad news? Whenever she arrived, it would be there to greet her. Better to gather herself for disappointment, and the outpouring of solace from her mother.

Turning the corner to cross in front of St Mark's, Laura was surprised to see her mother walking quickly towards her with a letter in her hand. Erica knew what time Laura finished her shift at the Observation Post, and knew the route home she would take.

'Have you come to intercept me?' Laura asked.

Erica took a moment to catch her breath. Her brow was damp with sweat. Evidently, she had been running to meet her daughter.

'I'm sorry,' she said. 'The letter from the university came this morning.'

'I know,' said Laura. 'Spencer passed me on his bike and told me a letter had come for me. And since that's the only letter I've been expecting—'

'I had an idea,' interrupted Erica, 'and if you'd rather not then you must say, and we'll go home and open it there.'

Laura was momentarily puzzled. 'What idea?' she asked.

Erica's breath was now under control and she looked at her daughter solemnly for a few moments.

'To a very real extent this journey over the past few months was instigated by your father. I thought it might be easier for you to open the letter with him.'

Laura didn't quite understand, but suddenly realised her mother meant beside her father's grave in the cemetery at St Mark's.

'I think it's a lovely idea,' she said finally.

Erica smiled. 'I'm so pleased.'

Erica held out her hand and took Laura's and gently led her towards the church. Once inside the graveyard, the two women swiftly made their way to Will's grave, and took a moment to compose themselves.

'We are here, darling. I've brought Laura. The letter from the medical school came this morning and we thought we would like to open it with you.'

Erica then slowly offered Laura the envelope from the university's medical faculty.

Laura stared at the envelope for several moments. Her mouth became suddenly dry, and her palms instantly clammy.

Laura took the envelope and looked at her mother.

'This is it then,' she said.

Erica nodded. 'Whatever it says, Laura, your father and I could not be any prouder of you. If isn't the news you were hoping for, there will be many other opportunities for you to pursue. You are a very resilient young woman—'

Laura couldn't wait for her mother to finish her well-rehearsed speech to help her daughter cope with the disappointing news she was anticipating, and tore open the envelope.

As soon as Laura read the first line her eyes started to well up. As she read on, her hand covered her mouth in an attempt to keep her emotions in check.

'I'm so sorry, my darling girl,' said Erica, stepping forward to wrap her arms around her daughter. Before she could get to Laura, Laura lifted her eyes from the letter and looked at her mother.

'I got it,' she said, in a voice so disbelieving that it made her reread the letter in case she had made a terrible mistake. She hadn't.

'What?' Erica's voice had been prepared for intense disappointment, not this.

'I got the scholarship!'

Erica blinked for a moment, and then rushed to Laura and threw her arms around her.

'Let me see!' she demanded.

Laura gave her the letter and Erica quickly scanned it.

'You've got it!' she exclaimed, struggling to comprehend the full import of the news.

Erica hugged Laura so tightly with delight that Laura struggled to breathe. But she didn't mind. After nearly a minute they stepped apart, each with tears down their cheeks.

'Do you want to tell him, or shall I?' Erica asked.

'I'd like to,' said Laura.

'Of course,' Erica said.

Laura slowly knelt beside Will's grave, the wet dew on the grass gently soaking her knees. She barely noticed. Laura lowered her face to the fresh brown soil until her lips were just an inch or two away from its surface.

'I got it, Dad,' she whispered. 'I got the scholarship. I'm going to be a doctor.'

Chapter 42

O<small>N THE DAY</small> Pat and Bob moved into their new house, six miles from Great Paxford, Frances and her sister, Sarah, had gone over to Joyce's house to see them off and to wish their old friend well.

Pat had seemed happy to be leaving, while Bob appeared relaxed, courteous, and even friendly towards two women who he had previously held at arm's length. Bob historically regarded with suspicion anyone with whom he had to compete for Pat's attention; and anyone who he suspected of having rather more insight into the way he had treated his wife than he would have liked.

Consumed by curiosity, Frances and Sarah had wanted to pay a visit to Pat's new home at the earliest opportunity, keen to see if it lived up to Pat's description, or whether it conformed to their expectation of what Bob would pay for.

For nearly three weeks after the move no one heard from Pat. She cancelled her shifts at the telephone exchange, and hadn't attended the most recent WI meeting. There was another village closer to Pat's new house than Great Paxford, so it was little surprise that she hadn't come into the village for groceries.

Frances and Sarah planned to take a bus to within half a mile of Pat's new house, but on the day Sarah had received a second letter from her husband, Adam. Her delight scotched all plans of doing anything other than spending the next few days trying to parse every drop of meaning from each line he had penned, and to write back once more. Her joy at finally hearing from Adam was shared by her sister, and the two women set to work de-coding the letter like a pair of cryptographers at Bletchley Park. From what they could glean, Adam was in good health despite a minor illness earlier in the Autumn. In addition, several of his 'chaps' had discussed trying to make an escape from the camp, but Adam had discouraged them until the Spring, when the weather would improve and their chances of surviving off the land as they made their way towards neutral or allied territory would significantly increase.

'They're so lucky to have Adam with them,' said Frances. 'Adding a measure of reality and sanity to their endeavours.'

'He understands the urge to escape well enough,' said Sarah, 'but knows it needs to be balanced with patient planning. There really is little point breaking out only to be shot in the attempt, get captured immediately or die from exposure shortly afterwards.'

She was immensely relieved to receive the very strong impression that conditions were tolerable, the Germans were treating them with a modicum of decency, and that Adam had decided to bide his time for the next few months.

'Who knows,' said Frances, 'if the officers of the *Wehrmacht* came to their senses and mounted a coup, the war could be over at almost any time.'

Another week passed while Sarah penned and re-drafted and re-drafted a letter back to Adam via the Red Cross, with a food parcel. Her letter was also cryptically incongruous, yet contained enough clues for Adam's knowing eye to discern that his wife was telling him to do nothing stupid to jeopardise either his health or life until the war's end.

So it was nearly four weeks after Pat's departure from the village that Frances and Sarah, and now also Alison – keen to see how her old friend was settling in – set out to make an impromptu visit to Pat in her new home. The bus ride out of Great Paxford was unremarkable, and they alighted at the designated stop in the middle of nowhere. Hedge-rows and fields stretched as far as the eye could see, without interruption by any human habitation that wasn't a farm building. Ever prepared, Frances had brought along a map, which they followed assiduously.

Neither Sarah nor Alison quarrelled with Frances's directions. Each knew from experience she was likely to be fastidiously correct, having worked over the route for hours the night before. And if Frances *had* by some peculiarity got it wrong, and was leading them wildly off course, she wouldn't believe it until proof was staring her in the face in the form of an open cave, a gushing water-fall or a precipice greeting them where Pat's new house should have been.

But Frances hadn't got it wrong, and after a mile of brisk walking she lifted her head from the map and announced that Pat's new house should be – no, *would* be – just around the next corner.

And there it was.

From the outside, it perfectly matched Pat's description, except that it seemed much bigger than she had described. Where Pat and Bob's old house had been joined at the hip to the Campbell house, their new property stood alone, beside a young wood recently established by the Forestry Commission.

It was very solid-looking, built of the earthy red-clay brick that was so characteristic of the area, with a dark roof covered with slates mined from the quarries of North Wales. There were two chimneys, and thick, milky wood-smoke pumped into the air from one.

'They're at home then,' Alison observed. 'At least we haven't wasted our time.'

They approached the house and took in more of its features. The front door was acid yellow, beautifully inlaid with stained glass, and framed by a tall, thickly spiked Pyracantha bush. The path leading up to the scarlet doorstep was made up of chequered tiles, with a neatly manicured square of lawn on either side, and rose bushes beneath each of the bay windows. As they approached the clattering sound of Bob's typewriter emanated from within.

'Another book?' Alison asked in response to the noisy typing. 'I read his last one. Awful. God help us.'

'It's a very handsome property,' said Frances. 'A lot for Pat to take care of.'

'Regardless of what you think of it, Alison, Bob must be doing *very* well,' said Sarah.

Frances pulled the front door bell, hearing it chime inside the house. They each fixed a smile on their face and waited for Pat to open the door.

But Pat didn't open the door.

Frances looked puzzled, glanced at the other two, and pulled the bell a second time. Again, they heard it ring inside the house.

'Have you noticed,' said Sarah, 'Bob's typing doesn't stop when we ring the bell.'

'Try one more time,' said Alison. 'Third time lucky.'

Frances pulled the bell a third time. Again, it rang within the house. Again, Bob's typing didn't stop. And again, Pat failed to appear at the door.

'His nibs is clearly not going to be disturbed,' said Frances. 'Perhaps she's in the garden?'

They went to the left-hand side of the property and stood on tiptoes to see over the fence into the garden.

There was no sign of Pat. They did the same at the right-hand side, with the same result.

'She must be out,' Sarah said. 'Why don't we try and get Bob's attention to see if he knows when Pat might return? If it isn't too long we could wait.'

'I rang the bell three times. He ignored it. What would you have me do? Holler through the letterbox?'

'If it's beneath your dignity, Frances, it isn't beneath mine,' said Sarah.

'Or mine,' said Alison. 'Rather that than waste the entire journey.'

Sarah and Alison knelt before the letterbox and called out for Bob, while Frances – after her sister gesticulated that it should be her contribution – pulled the bell once again.

As loud as they hollered, and as hard as Frances pulled, the hammering from Bob's typewriter was incessant.

Frances was the first to give up and stepped back and looked up at the house. The sun had been out when they had first walked up, causing the house to look grand and statuesque. But now, with the sun obscured by tufts of thickening cloud, it took on a darker, more morose character, exuding not a little foreboding. Frances half-expected to see a sign somewhere, declaring 'Trespassers will be prosecuted'.

Sarah and Alison got to their feet and stepped back.

'It wouldn't surprise me if Bob wasn't a little deaf, having to listen to that racket all his working life,' Frances ventured.

'All this way for nothing,' said Alison, flatly.

'Not for nothing,' Frances declared, determined not to be beaten by circumstance. 'I'll leave a note.'

Frances opened her handbag and took out a small brown notebook and pen she carried with her at all times in the event a brilliant idea for a WI initiative came to her suddenly.

'What will you say?' asked Sarah.

'I'm going to say that we came out to see her, hoping she would enjoy the surprise, and that we were disappointed to find her out. And to remind her about the WI meeting tonight, and that everyone would simply love to see her.'

By now, Frances was coming to the end of the note.

'Will you say that despite ringing the bell three times, and screaming like banshees through the letterbox, Bob failed to answer the door?' Alison asked.

'I shan't say that – it would look snarky, and we don't need to look snarky. If he's in full flow then he has every right not to answer the door. I am the same with unexpected visitors and unexpected telephone calls. I don't ask people to come by unannounced, or to telephone, so why must I drop everything and give them my attention?'

'Your views on unwarranted intrusion are well established, Frances,' said Sarah impatiently. The air was starting to chill and if they had decided to leave she wanted to be on her way before it started to rain.

'I'm going to conclude by asking Pat to telephone me so we can arrange another time to come and visit, and ask her when she's likely to be back in the saddle vis-à-vis the branch . . .'

Frances signed her name at the bottom of the page.

'There! Note complete!'

Frances read it back to herself, then tore the small sheet of paper out of the notebook and folded it in half. She then wrote 'FAO Dearest Pat' on one side, and popped it through the letterbox.

The three of them stood for a moment and looked at the house, top to bottom, each hoping they might suddenly catch a glimpse of Pat in one of the windows, responding to the sound of the letterbox snapping shut. But Pat didn't appear. No one did. They vainly looked back along the road to see if Pat might be returning from an errand they had supposed she might have been on. But she didn't.

Frances decided there was little more they could do, and began walking back the way they'd come. Sarah and Alison looked at the house for a few moments longer, trying to size it up.

'Looks like a great deal of work to keep clean,' said Alison.

Sarah nodded. 'It does, doesn't it. A large garden too – no doubt for Pat to keep in order while Great Paxford's own Dickens hammers out his genius.'

Sarah sighed with considerable disappointment at not having been able to see her old friend, then slowly turned and ambled with Alison towards her sister already making her way back to the bus stop along the road.

Throughout her friends' attempt to see her, Pat had sat on a chair in the master bedroom she shared with Bob.

When Frances, Alison, and Sarah had knocked on the front door and called through the letterbox, every fibre in Pat's body was prepared to propel her out of the bedroom, along the upstairs landing, down the stairs, and across the hall to the front door. Though Pat's flesh had been willing to make the dash, her mind dared not give the instruction to get up and run, lest it trigger Bob to burst from his office across the landing and knock Pat to the floor before she reached the stairs. She momentarily considered screaming for help, but couldn't guarantee her friends would hear. And if nothing came from screaming, Bob would punish her severely for the attempt.

And so, instead of running to her friends, Pat had sat in the chair in silence, hoping they would leave quickly before their presence provoked Bob, who never liked to be disturbed while he worked unless it was with fresh supplies of food and drink.

Pat sat with her chin almost resting on her chest, eyes closed against the mind-piercing rattle of Bob's fingers crashing against typewriter keys in his new office, pounding out a synopsis for a new book. Her head throbbed painfully around her left eye socket, where Bob had punched her four days ago, after discovering her writing a Mass Observation report.

Unused to the acoustics of the new house, Pat's customary caution had been disengaged, and she simply hadn't heard Bob leave his new study, and enter their new bedroom, where Pat had been writing on the bed. By the time she realised Bob was in the room it was too late to hide her work and pretend to be doing something else.

And of course, too late to stop Bob snatching up and reading what she had been writing.

After a few moments, Pat had attempted to launch herself at her husband and grab the pages from his hand, desperate to prevent him from reading what she had written about her continued devotion to Marek and her tolerance of Bob for as long as his good behaviour was sustained.

The combination of these two had provoked Bob's initial punch, sending Pat reeling backwards across the corner of their new bed and crashing into her new dressing table.

Pat had sat stunned on the floor, her head swimming, in no position to defend herself against a man who had once vowed to honour and cherish her.

By the time Bob had finished reading what Pat had written she knew his red mist of old would now descend like a thick curtain over whatever passed for his decency, and a beating would begin.

By the time Bob had finished with her, Pat's face was swollen and bloody, and she was sure two ribs – one either side – were either severely bruised or cracked. In addition, two fingers of her writing hand were left in agony – possibly fractured – after Bob stamped on them in a final flourish of intense spite against her writing.

Long after Frances, Sarah and Alison had returned to Pat's beloved Great Paxford, Pat continued to sit in her bedroom, immobile, cowed, listening to her own blood softly thud-thud through the blood vessels around her head and heart.

With eyes closed she was at least able to transport herself back to the fields where she and Marek used to lie in each other's arms, gazing up at the sky, with no thought of Bob in her head. These had been moments she cherished, like vital sustenance, to keep her soul alive. They helped her conjure Marek's voice, and his distinct, earthy aroma within the private recess of her innermost mind, and felt reassured that everything might yet be all right. Whatever Bob did to her physically or mentally, she and Marek had embarked on an act of faith under the canal bridge during that wet, windy night after the WI meeting, and that would continue until they were reunited.

Pat thought of Marek now, putting his life in danger hundreds of miles away, standing up to Fascism. She felt emboldened by his courage. She lifted her head and looked at the closed bedroom door before her.

It's not locked. The only thing keeping me here is my fear of him. That's all he needs. And I sit here and wait for his instruction like the pathetic servant he would wish me to be.

Pat thought of her friends knocking at the front door earlier. She imagined them returning to Great Paxford to excitedly get ready for the WI meeting that evening, just as she normally would on the first Thursday of each month. In the pit of her stomach she felt a sense of yearning for life beyond her new house bubble to the surface.

If Marek is prepared to put his own survival in peril to protect our way of life, how can I sit here and just give in to Bob? Didn't Marek once say that this *was my war? Then I should fight it. Live as best I can.*

She blinked slowly, her resolve forming.

I'm going to go to the meeting.

Pat slowly got to her feet, feeling the fatigue in her knees from sitting for so long in one position while she waited for Bob to give her permission to move. She carefully shuffled to the door and grasped the handle, turning it slowly. She pulled the door open and looked out onto the empty landing. The sound of Bob's typing continued to fill the house from top to bottom.

Tentatively, Pat stretched out her left leg and stepped onto the landing. The rug shifted slightly under her weight as she found her footing, sliding ever so slightly on top of the old floorboard beneath, which suddenly creaked loudly.

The sound of typing stopped behind Bob's office door.

Pat froze as she considered stepping back into the bedroom and closing the door, hoping Bob would think he had misheard, or put the creak down to an old eave in an old house groaning against the wind outside.

But just as she withdrew her foot to retreat into the bedroom, the door of Bob's office slowly opened, and Bob stood there looking at Pat from across the landing.

They stood looking at one another for several moments, each trying to decide what their next move would be.

It allowed Pat time to remind herself that it didn't always pay to cower before her husband when he was angry. Occasionally, if he was tired or simply not in the mood, a sudden burst of anguished fury could be enough to put Bob on the back foot and send him stomping off into his office, or to the Black Horse pub.

Pat didn't feel she had the strength for anger at this precise moment. She felt weak, exhausted, and in severe pain. Her whole body was telling her to go back into the bedroom and sit down behind the closed door. She opened her mouth to speak, but Bob pipped her to it.

'Did I say you could leave the room?' he coldly asked.

Pat knew of old this was a trick question, with no answer that would allow her to avoid some form of reprimand, and punishment.

'It's WI night, Bob,' was all she could say.

'So?'

'I want to go to the meeting,' she said, without sounding like she was asking permission even though they both knew she was. Bob gave it barely a second's worth of thought.

'No.'

'But you said when we moved I would still be able to go to the WI,' she said.

'That was before, when I thought you had changed.'

She looked at him, blinking slowly through blurred vision in one eye.

'I want to go to the WI. I want to see my friends. I have *friends*, Bob. They miss me. And I miss them.'

'You don't need friends. You only need me. Now get back in the bedroom until I say you can come out.'

Pat didn't move. She felt her chest slowly inflate and then deflate, the expansion and contraction of her rib cage sending jabbing spasms of pain around her chest.

'Did you hear me?' he said sharply. 'Get back in that room!'

'I'm going downstairs to get ready,' she said, and stepped out onto the landing proper.

It was all the trigger Bob needed. He shot from his office doorway towards Pat to drive her back into the bedroom.

Ordinarily, he might have expected Pat to flinch and step backwards of her own accord as he advanced, but as he approached the top of the staircase he saw Pat bracing herself against the doorjamb, preparing to make a stand. It didn't matter to him which method he had to use to get his way, as long as he got it. He'd tried nice, and for what?

At close quarters Bob reached out to grab Pat's arm. He failed to register that she was mustering every last drop of energy she had to repel him as forcefully as she was able.

If I have to go down again it won't be with a whimper . . .

'I am going to the WI!'

Pat screamed into Bob's face as loudly as she could, trying to give him pause. Her own face was twisted in fear and fury.

In the same moment, Pat closed her eyes tightly, turned her head away from Bob and lashed out at him with her right arm to repel his advance.

Her hand crashed clumsily against his shoulder, suddenly arresting his forward momentum, causing his bad leg to buckle slightly.

His left foot slipped forward and the rug came free of its moorings, sliding forward on the floorboards.

In less than a second, Bob found himself falling backwards on to the top tread of the staircase. He desperately reached out to grab anything he could to arrest his fall. His hands flailed uselessly. He bounced off the top tread with another cry of pain, then continued over it and down. Crying out angrily, Bob ricocheted off each tread until he landed head-first at the very bottom of the stairs. He reached the bottom with a crack that filled the house.

Silence. Complete and utter silence.

After a few moments, Pat slowly opened her eyes and looked out upon an upstairs landing that had no Bob in view. She looked at the floor and saw the rug, bunched up violently at one end by her feet, where it had come to rest. Pat's attention then slowly turned towards the staircase.

She crept forward, and looked down.

Bob lay on his back at the bottom of the stairs, his arms and legs bent at awkward angles. To Pat, he looked like a puppet whose strings had been suddenly cut. She waited for Bob to move, and reveal the ruse he was clearly planning to spring on her.

But he remained still.

From her vantage point at the top of the stairs Pat couldn't see if Bob was breathing. She took a deep breath of her own and began to slowly descend. When she had reached the mid-point of the staircase she stopped. He still hadn't moved, but was he breathing? She tried to focus on his chest.

'Bob?'

Silence.

'Bob?'

Silence.

Pat crept all the way to the last stair just above where Bob lay, and looked down at him. His eyes and mouth were open, but there was no movement.

'Bob?' Her voice was querulous.

At that moment, Bob's eyes slowly swivelled in their sockets and looked at Pat, holding her uncertainly in their gaze.

Pat was momentarily startled and instinctively took a step back up the staircase. Bob made no other effort in her direction.

'Bob, can you speak?'

Silence.

'Are you hurt?'

Silence.

Pat regained her nerve and slowly crept back to her position, and looked down upon the man who had been the scourge of her life for so many years. For all the scorn and contempt he had heaped upon her with his words, fists and open palms, at this moment it was he who was helpless.

Pat suddenly thought she must telephone for an ambulance. With a swiftness that surprised her, it was almost immediately answered with another thought.

What if I don't?

Pat sat on the step above Bob and looked down at him. He continued to look up at her. His mouth slowly opened as if in preparation to say something. His chest was barely moving, his breathing was increasingly shallow. Pat then saw a dark pool of blood gathering beneath his head, oozing from his left ear.

'Whatever you think of me, Bob,' she whispered with the utmost solemnity, 'I never meant *this*. I never meant to push you down the stairs, only to push you *away* from me. You must have slipped on the rug . . .'

Pat stopped talking. It seemed perfectly clear what had happened and no further explanation was necessary. She continued to look at Bob's face, her eyes meeting his. His eyes moving less and less. Pat could see the life-force ebbing out of her husband in a steady, red trickle.

Is he looking at me? Is he imploring me to call an ambulance? I should. I should. And then what? They come and take him away and make him better? And then—

At that moment, Bob simply stopped breathing. His eyes ceased all movement, and came to rest looking straight up, over Pat's left shoulder, toward the ceiling.

It took several moments for Pat to realise he was finally gone.

It took three more hours for Pat to realise she was finally free.

The moment struck her as she set out towards Great Paxford in the late afternoon. Living several miles from the village and being less quick than usual because of back pain, Pat left in good time to arrive at the WI before it started, not at the very last minute as was customary under Bob's jealous eye.

She had taken the time to do her hair and make-up exactly how she wanted, ensuring her foundation covered any lingering trace of bruising on her face.

She had instinctively called out 'Goodbye, Bob,' as she closed the front door – as if they were a perfectly normal, loving couple, and this was any other WI day.

I'll call the police after I return from the meeting. I'll enter the house and be stunned to find him dead at the bottom of the stairs, the victim of a tragic household accident.

As she approached the village, Pat realised she no longer had to account to anyone. Not to Bob, and not to the police over Bob's death. Everyone knew Bob had been unsteady on his feet following his injury at Dunkirk. They had seen him hobbling around the village on his stick often enough. All the women knew about the WI rug upon which Bob had slipped on the upstairs landing, because they'd all been there when it had been presented to Pat.

I'm free . . .

She had only pushed him away in self-defence – the rest had been entirely out of her hands; a fatal combination of rug, Bob's instability, and a proximal staircase.

Pat checked her watch as she walked past St Mark's, and sped up.

She looked up at the great tower and crossed herself. As she passed in front of the cemetery she instinctively looked towards the oldest headstone, where she and Marek had left messages of love for one another. She then glanced across at the remains of her old house next door to what was left of the Campbells'. The downed Spitfire from the fateful afternoon when Marek had been transported out of the area with the Czech contingent had been removed, but the ruined houses had been left untouched.

They'll be demolished after the war, I suppose. Replaced with something better.

Pat could scarcely imagine that she and Bob had lived out their terrible drama in such small spaces.

As Pat turned the corner onto the High Street she heard the introductory bars of 'Jerusalem' rising from the village hall. She nodded at the men standing outside the Black Horse, supping their pints, humming along to the music from the hall.

'Get a clip on, Mrs Simms! They've started,' said one as Pat passed, causing her to break into as much of a trot as she could manage as the women launched into the first verse.

'*And did those feet, in ancient time, walk upon England's mountain green? And was the Holy lamb of God, on England's pleasant pastures seen?*'

Pat reached the hall and slipped in just in time to join in with the second verse, standing behind her comrades at the back of the hall. No one noticed her lift her head and sing.

'*And did the countenance divine, shine forth upon our clouded hills? And was Jerusalem builded here, among these dark satanic mills?*'

A dark, satanic mill. That's what my life was like with Bob. He couldn't change. I was horribly mistaken . . .

'*Bring me my bow of burning gold! Bring me my arrows of desire! Bring me my spear, oh clouds unfold! Bring me my chariot of fire!*'

Tears suddenly welled in Pat's eyes as she sang, and spilled uncontrollably down her cheeks.

A vast weight seemed to rise from her shoulders, and they pushed back and her spine straightened. This pushed her head back and allowed Pat to sing with greater passion, ignoring the lingering pain in her ribs from Bob's final assault.

She sang loudly, with crystal clarity, hitting every note with perfect pitch.

'*I will not cease from mental fight, nor shall my sword sleep in my hand, till we have built Jerusalem, in England's green and pleasant land.*'

The anthem drew to a close. The women quietly smiled and nodded to one another in recognition of a good rendition.

Just as Frances was about to give the signal for them all to sit, the local air-raid siren began to wail outside, causing everyone in the hall to laugh ironically at the Luftwaffe's unerring timing.

Without fuss, the women gathered their hats and coats and put them on as they had done many times before. Pat hadn't even had time to take hers off.

As she filed out with the others, she felt a hand gently alight on her shoulder, and turned to find Frances smiling at her.

'I'm so glad you could make it, Pat, dear!'

Pat wiped any lingering tears from her eyes as they walked into the cold night air.

'So am I,' she replied, smiling thinly.

'We came to the house this afternoon but you weren't in. We thought Bob might come to the door but he was clearly busy.'

'A new book,' Pat said. 'Once he has the bit between his teeth nothing can distract him.'

'We've missed you,' said Frances, softly. 'Welcome back.'

Pat smiled and nodded. 'Thank you. You must come and visit again, and see the house.'

'We shall,' Frances said. 'We'd like that very much.'

'I'll make a spread, and we'll have a proper house-warming.'

Frances smiled warmly and moved ahead to lead the group to the communal shelter in the cellar of her own house.

Pat kept pace with the women hurrying along, all chatting quietly.

As she took her seat in the shelter, Pat raised her eyes to the ceiling and wondered what might happen in the next hour, the next day, the next week, month, and year. The only thing she knew for certain was that whatever happened, it would now happen without Bob.

No more beatings. No more put-downs. No more fear and dread.

She pictured Bob's face at the bottom of the staircase, still, looking upwards, silent. After a few moments Bob's death mask was slowly replaced in her mind's eye by

Marek's handsome, smiling face, his ice blue eyes radiating love and kindness towards her, prompting Pat to wait for him.

She nodded to herself, then looked round at the other people in the shelter, many smiling at her as she caught their eye.

Poor Bob, they'll say. What a terrible accident. And it's true. A terrible, terrible accident . . .

A low rumble began overhead, presaging the imminent passage of a Luftwaffe squadron of bombers over the area. Everyone fell silent and looked up at the low ceiling of the cellar, as if they could see straight through it, through the two floors of the Barden house, through the roof, and up into the night sky.

'Do your worst . . .' Pat whispered to the planes above. 'I've survived Bob, I'm damn well going to survive you.'

Pat lowered her eyes, bowed her head, crossed herself, and offered a silent prayer to God to forgive Bob Simms for everything he had done to her, and to keep Marek safe until the end of the war.

Dear Readers,

As many of you know, these characters first came to life on television in a drama called *Home Fires*. When the opportunity came to continue their stories in book form I had no idea how they might survive the migration from one medium to another. Ultimately, the only judgement about the success of that which counts is yours. It has been immensely gratifying to learn how seamlessly so many of you have felt the world of Great Paxford has made the journey from screen to page. Your encouragement and support throughout has been immensely important to me, as has your patience as I have written and worked with the hugely talented team at Bonnier.

This second book finds the characters picking their way through as the war begins to set in for the long haul. Under the Luftwaffe bombing run towards the western ports and the cities that support them, the people of Great Paxford are not mere bystanders, watching from afar. With the nightly arrival of 'trekkers' from the bombed cities of Liverpool and Crewe, and their proximity to the RAF station Tabley Wood, the inhabitants of the village feel the war inching inexorably closer to their own front doorsteps.

Gone is the idea that war with Germany would only last a few months. Gone is the idea that Hitler could be swiftly brought to his senses, or that the Nazis could be easily and quickly defeated. The Battle of Britain may have been won by the autumn of 1940, thanks to the superhuman skill and bravery of Fighter Command and its assorted pilots from the UK, the Commonwealth, Poland, Czechoslovakia, the US and France, but any sense that Britain is immune from invasion has been shattered. It has become a daily dread from top to bottom of British life.

The realisation that our characters' lives are being turned on their head is the main theme running through this second book, the war begins to send the citizens of Great Paxford into a tailspin – some more than others. As ever, the stories are less concerned with what's taking place in the war beyond the village perimeter than its consequence on those who live within the village boundary. Does the war change absolutely everything? Or does it allow for the possibility of what passed for 'normal' life before war broke out? As the rules of engagement are established on the battlefield, how have they changed in civilian life as war rages overhead, and on the European continent?

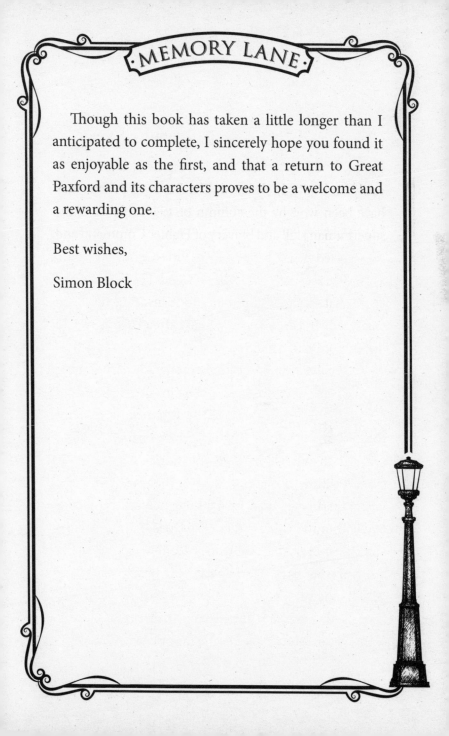

· MEMORY LANE ·

Though this book has taken a little longer than I anticipated to complete, I sincerely hope you found it as enjoyable as the first, and that a return to Great Paxford and its characters proves to be a welcome and a rewarding one.

Best wishes,

Simon Block

Wartime Christmas Cake

During World War II, many ingredients were rationed and difficult to find. This twist on a Christmas classic contains no eggs and no alcohol, and is iced with mock 'marzipan' – but still tastes delicious!

You will need:

For the cake:
- 4oz margarine, lard or cooking fat
- 10oz plain or whole-wheat flour
- 4oz sugar
- 6oz raisins, sultanas, prunes, currants and/or dates – whatever you can find!
- 1 tsp ground mixed spice
- 1 tsp ground ginger and/or 1 tsp ground cinnamon
- 1 tsp bicarbonate of soda
- 200ml milk (or, alternatively, 100ml milk, topped up with 100ml water)
- 2 tbsp black treacle or golden syrup
- 2 tbsp cold tea
- 1 tsp almond essence

For the 'marzipan' icing:
- 2oz margarine
- 2 tbsp water
- 3½oz plain flour
- 4oz sugar
- 2–3 tbsp of almond essence
- Fruit jam, any flavour of your choice

Method:

1. Pre-heat the oven to 160°C/140°C fan/gas mark 3, and grease a large 7in cake tin.

2. In a bowl, rub the margarine/fat into the flour.

3. Add the sugar, mixed spice and ginger to the mix, and stir together. Then mix in the dried fruit.

4. In a separate bowl or jug, dissolve the bicarbonate of soda in the milk.

5. Add the treacle and tea to the main bowl, followed by the milk and soda. Finally mix in the almond essence, then beat everything together thoroughly.

6. Spoon the mixture into the tin, then bake in the oven for 2–2½ hours, until the top is firm. Cover with foil one hour in if the top looks likely to burn.

7. While the cake cools, make the 'marzipan'.

8. Soften the margarine in the water, then stir in the sugar and almond essence.

9. Sieve in the flour slowly, stirring all the while.

10. Turn out the mixture onto a floured surface and knead until smooth, then roll out and cut into a 7in circle.

11. Spread the top of the cooled cake with jam, then cover with marzipan.

12. Enjoy!

Tales from Memory Lane

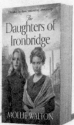

Discover new stories from the best saga authors

Available now